Captured by Mr. Wild

Elle Nicoll

Rose Hope Publishing

Contents

To everyone who has felt lost some days

May you be happy, wild and free

Chapter One

Blake

10 Years Earlier

"Prepare to meet your maker, Anderson!"

A laugh follows the high-pitched squeal as I'm hit in the face with an armful of water.

"You're going to regret that, Daisy!" I yell back as I swim toward my friend, a maniacal grin spreading over my soaked face.

"Only if you can catch me!" she calls over her shoulder as she pushes her arms out and swims back in the direction of the jetty.

I watch the light catching her blonde hair, frozen to the spot for a fraction of a second as the sight steals my breath. But it's enough to allow her to get a head start that has her climbing up the wooden ladder and running down the wooden jetty and onto the grass.

"Truce! Truce!" she surrenders, holding her hands up in front of her, her blue eyes bright and glowing as I catch up and stride toward her.

I see them widen in the moment before I grab her around the waist and haul her over my shoulder, carrying her across the grass toward the campfire where our friends are.

"Blake Anderson! Put me down right now!" She hammers on my back with her small hands as her legs flail around, narrowly missing my crotch.

"Hey! Watch the goods!" I chuckle as I land a playful slap across her wet bikini-clad butt. The temptation to keep my hand there a moment longer hits me like a slap in the face, but I shake it off.

She's your friend, Blake. Don't be a creep.

I deposit her on the ground, and she grins at me as our friend, Kayla, hands her a towel.

"We were beginning to think we would have to eat without you guys," she scolds as Daisy drops to sit next to her.

"Yeah, man. It'll be getting cold," my mate, Travis, says as he hands me a takeout bag.

"Aww, double cheeseburger." I let out a moan and roll my eyes, then reach over and give Travis a fist-bump. "You know me so well." I grin as I take a bite.

"Animal." Daisy laughs as sauce drips down my chin.

I turn to her and wink as I take another huge bite.

"You know it's good though, right?" I say after I swallow.

She opens her takeout bag and holds up an identical burger to the one I'm eating.

"Oh, yeah." She grins, wrapping her lips around it, and I watch as she licks them and lets out a soft moan.

Fuck.

I clear my throat as I cast my eyes to the fire and try to ignore the heat that's threatening to ignite in my pants.

"How's your aunt's latest brew going?" Kayla asks Daisy.

Daisy hands her burger to Kayla and reaches behind her into her backpack, pulling out a glass bottle with a stopper in the neck.

"One way to find out." She grins, waving the bottle in the air.

"You star!" Kayla shrieks, bouncing up and down.

"Oh, God," Travis moans. "If that's as strong as the last one, I think I'm going to pass." He laughs as he shakes his head.

"Won't she realize it's missing?" Kayla asks as Daisy pulls the stopper out and takes a sip. She screws her face up, then laughs, her cheeks glowing under the light of the fire.

"I think she knows. But as long as we're not stupid, she turns a blind eye. Besides, she's not home tonight." Daisy wipes her mouth with the back of her hand as she passes the bottle to Kayla and takes her burger back.

"Your Aunt's so cool." Kayla smiles as she holds the bottle to her lips and tips her head back. "Wow! That is so good!" She laughs as she hands the bottle over to me. "Try it, Blake. It's even better than the last one. What did she put in that one, Daisy?"

I take the glass bottle from her and hold it up, looking at the clear liquid inside.

"Elderflowers," Daisy says as she goes back to devouring her burger.

Daisy's aunt is well known locally as being a bit of a live wire. She makes her own gin, which is ready every summer—just as Daisy arrives for her visit. She lives here, on the lake in Hope Cove, less than two hours' drive from Los Angeles. She's always in her garden growing plants and herbs, some I've never even heard of before. Rumor has it she has some popular *medicinal* home remedies she sells. I always suspected those old person tea mornings were a front for something. Why would anyone want to sit around drinking that and making polite small talk otherwise?

I tip my head back and take a swig from the bottle. The burn hits my throat, stealing the air from my lungs.

"Christ!" I laugh, choking back a cough as my eyes water. "I think it's meant to be mixed, Daisy."

"Nah! Ruins the fun. Gin for the win, Blake." Her eyes light up as she takes the bottle from me and glugs down two giant mouthfuls.

"Slow down." Travis laughs and shakes his head when Daisy offers the bottle to him.

"More for us then." She grins at Kayla, who giggles back.

I catch Travis' eye over the top of the fire, and he rolls his eyes at me, the corners of his lips pulling into a smile as he glances back at the girls.

I know what he's thinking. We've been friends our entire lives. We can read each other with just a glance.

I lift my chin at him and give him a reassuring smile.

They'll be fine.

He arches an eyebrow back at me as Daisy takes another swig from the bottle. I shake my head with a chuckle, scrunching up the empty burger wrappers and shoving them into my bag, being careful not to scrape them against the camera inside, which my granddad gave me. Then I lean over and pluck the bottle from Daisy's hand before she can take another mouthful.

"Blake!" she cries. "Don't be a spoilsport!"

Her eyes have already taken on that glassy quality that comes with hard liquor as she reaches toward me, missing the bottle as I hold it above my head. Her hand lands against my bare chest instead.

"I think you've had enough, Miss Matthews." I tut.

"Please." She sticks out her bottom lip and looks up at me with big eyes.

"No." I smile handing the bottle to Travis, who expertly steals it away, out of sight.

She lets out a frustrated sigh before her eyes light up again. "Let's play truth or dare!"

"Yay!" Kayla claps her hands together, the gin taking its effect on her too, as she sways slightly where she's sitting.

"Oh, God," Travis groans.

"Aww, come on." Daisy takes her hand back from my chest and sits up straight. "It's my last night here. I fly home to England tomorrow."

"Boo," Kayla says sadly.

Daisy reaches over and hugs her. "I know. Big, fat, stinky boo. I hate leaving you guys."

Kayla's arms tighten around her. "You'll be back for the next school break though, right?"

"Aren't I always?" Daisy sighs, lifting her head and looking out over the lake at the sun setting over the treetops in the surrounding forest.

"Why don't you just tell your mom and dad that you want to move here permanently?" Kayla whines.

"They'd never listen." Daisy's shoulders drop as she sighs again. "But, hey! You've got me for tonight!." She breaks into a grin as she glances between me and Travis. "So, who's first?"

Travis lets out a low chuckle and averts his eyes, but it's too late. Daisy rounds her attention on him like a missile on its target.

"Travis..." she draws out his name slowly. "Truth or dare?"

He shakes his head and lets out a sigh, as though he'd rather play anything else. "Truth."

"Boring!" Kayla snorts. "You always say truth."

"Fine." He blows out a breath. "Dare, then."

Daisy lets out an excited squeal as she rubs her hands together.

"Okay, it's got to be good, Oh..." She chews on her lip as she thinks. "I know!" She looks up, grinning, her eyes glittering, the same way they did when she produced the bottle of homebrew. "Your dare is to kiss Kayla!"

"What?" Travis and Kayla both say, glancing at each other.

"You heard me. And you said dare, Travis. So you have to do it!" Daisy grins as Travis and Kayla continue staring at each other.

He runs his hand around the back of his neck. "I don't think—"

"No... that's not..." Kayla cuts in, fiddling with the towel which fell off Daisy's shoulders earlier. "It's a silly dare, Daisy. Think of another."

"Nope." Daisy grins, then waves a finger between the two of them. "Come on! You're like, eighteen. It's not like you haven't kissed anyone before." She rolls her eyes. "You don't have to use tongues."

Travis clears his throat in the silence which follows. Daisy sits patiently, not at all bothered by how uncomfortable her two friends are obviously feeling.

"Daisy," I lean over and whisper in her ear, "think of another dare."

"Shh, Blake," she whispers back out the side of her mouth, placing a finger up to my lips as she keeps her eyes glued on Kayla and Travis.

I sit and watch as my best friend leans over and places his hand on Kayla's cheek. Her eyes never leave his as he leans forward and presses the gentlest of kisses to her lips.

Nice, man. Who knew he could be so smooth?

Travis sits back quickly, and Kayla's cheeks glow as Daisy takes her finger away from my mouth. She turns to me and raises a brow, a smug smile on her face. I narrow my eyes at her, a smile spreading across my face.

Well played, Daisy.

The kiss marks the start and end of the game, and we spend the rest of the sunset sitting and chatting around the campfire before it's the only light left.

"I can't believe it's your last night. I hate goodbyes," Kayla says as she pulls Daisy into a hug.

"Me too," Daisy says, embracing her. She breaks away and gives Travis a hug before smiling at them both. "Thank you for the best summer."

"We'll miss you, Daisy." Kayla smiles before turning and heading up the driveway, back toward town with Travis.

"I'll miss you too," Daisy calls after them. "Make sure you walk her right to the door, Travis."

"I always do," he calls back, lifting his hand in a wave as Kayla blows a kiss.

Then they're gone.

"The end of another summer in Hope Cove." Daisy sighs as she lies back against the grass and stares up at the night sky.

It's cooler now that the sun has set, so she's put her jean shorts and sweatshirt on. It's too big for her and falls off one shoulder.

She looks adorable.

I fight the sudden urge to wrap her in my arms and protect her forever. It creeps up on me, making my heart pound in my chest.

"Yep." I lie back next to her, stretching my hands up behind my head in an attempt to relax.

"Last one before you start college."

I frown, shuffling my back to get comfy. "True."

She turns onto her side, leaning on one elbow. Her large blue eyes gaze at me, still glassy from the gin.

"Do you ever wish you could stay in a moment, Blake?"

"What do you mean?" My eyes drop to her lips as I swallow.

She looks at me, like she's searching my face for the answer to a question which has only just occurred to her.

"I mean. Stay here, forever." She lets out a sigh as she looks at me. "I love coming to stay with my aunt during the holidays. I love this place!" She looks out over the water, the moon shining off its calm surface.

"It's pretty cool, I guess." I shrug.

"You don't know how lucky you are, Blake. I'm miles away from nature back in England. And it's nothing like this." She looks around again before bringing her eyes back to me. "The sound of the water, the sea air, the forest, swimming in the lake!" Her eyes light up. "It's paradise."

She leans closer to me and I can smell the gin, sweet on her breath.

She pauses, and then slowly lowers her lips to mine.

Time freezes for a moment as my heart battles with my head.

My head wins.

"Daisy." I place a hand on her shoulder and gently push her back as I sit up.

"I'm sorry... I..." Her eyes are wide and her hand flies to her mouth.

"No, it's okay—" I reach out to her, but she stands up, pushing dirt over the last dying embers of the fire with her foot.

"It's the homebrew." She laughs suddenly and looks away. "Phew! You were right. It must have been stronger this time."

I blow out a deep breath as I stand. "Daisy, I—"

"Let's not mention it again, Blake," she cuts me off. "Walk with me awhile before you go home?"

I look at her, wishing I could take away the look of rejection on her face.

"Sure." I smile, walking around the lake's edge with her, aware that every second is one second closer to saying goodbye again. Until her next visit, anyway.

We walk for almost an hour. Daisy's back to her usual cheery self—telling me stories about her school back home, and what it's like living in London. By the sounds of it, she doesn't live in the nicest part. No wonder she thinks Hope Cove is paradise.

"Thanks, Blake." She turns to me as we reach the bottom of her aunt's porch steps.

"Don't mention it. I always walk you home," I joke. We've already been 'home' all evening, just hanging out by the lake.

"I mean, thanks for everything." She looks at me, twisting her hands in front of her, a subtle blush colouring her cheeks. Her eyes seem clearer now. The walk probably sobered her up.

I lift my chin. "Like I said. Don't mention it."

"I'll see you at Christmas, then?" She flashes me a grin that lights up her entire face. Something about the way she looks, so light and carefree, makes me pull my camera out of my bag and capture a quick picture of her.

"Ho, Ho, Ho," I answer with a smirk as the flash goes off.

Daisy's mouth drops open as she squints. "Hey! What did you do that for?"

I shrug my shoulders, giving her a half smile. "Just because, I don't know, you look happy."

For a second, I wonder if she's going to give me an earful, but this is Daisy—cheerful, positive, insanely perky, Daisy.

Instead, she throws her arms wide and tips her head back and gazes up at the stars, a giggle escaping from her lips.

"Look at that sky, Blake! How could I be anything but happy?"

I let out a low chuckle, and she brings her gaze back to rest on my face, letting out a small sigh.

"Bye, Blake."

"Bye, Daisy," I reply, waiting for her to open the front door before I turn to leave.

"See you when the big guy in the red suit comes!" she calls with another giggle as she goes inside and closes the door.

I smile to myself as I walk down the driveway. It's only a few months, no time at all, really. I put my camera away and then shove my hands into my jean pockets, whistling out Jingle Bells as I make my way home.

But the guy in red never came.

The reaper in the dark robe came for her aunt that winter instead.

The Daisy I knew never came back.

Chapter Two

Daisy

Present Day

"THANK YOU FOR FLYING Atlantic Airways," the cheerful flight attendant says in a singsong voice as I deplane.

I give her the best smile I can manage as I adjust my bag strap on my shoulder and head up the jetway toward the terminal.

It's been ten years since I flew into LAX airport. In some ways, it's changed. But in others, it's still the same. People are still rushing around, barely looking at their fellow passengers as they race to get to the head of the immigration line. It suits me, though. Being invisible is the best possible thing I can be right now.

I sigh as the line moves along slowly until I'm almost at the front. The guy in front of me mutters something under his breath about not having all day as he stares at a lady standing at the nearest immigration desk. I peer round him to get a better look. She's elderly and seems sweet, looking about the same age my aunt would be now if she were still here. My heart squeezes at the thought.

I watch as she chats to the immigration officer, and he tips his head back and laughs. He hands her back her passport, and she reaches into her handbag and produces a shiny foil-wrapped candy, placing it on the desk as she waves bye to him.

The impatient man gets called to another desk and then the officer with the candy looks up and catches my eye.

"Over here, miss." He raises his hand and beckons me over.

"Thank you." I hand him my passport, and he opens it to the photo page as he looks up.

"New hair?" He raises a brow.

I run my hand around the back of my head self-consciously. "I fancied a change."

He nods before motioning to the fingerprint scanner. I place my hand on the glass and find myself staring at the bright pink candy by his computer monitor as he processes me and stamps my passport. It looks so out of place here, surrounded by gray. It's like a wildflower growing in the middle of a concrete path.

Exposed.

Alone.

"Have a pleasant stay." He smiles as he hands back my passport.

I head over to the baggage carousel and wait for my case, wondering whether this trip was a good idea. It seemed like it when I booked my last-minute ticket—when I had no other choice.

I wrap my arms around myself and watch the bags go round. Mine will probably be last, knowing my luck.

"You look like you could do with a little sugar pick me up."

I turn to find the sweet old lady from the immigration line standing next to me. Her eyes are twinkling as she holds out a bag of bright pink candies.

"No, really, I'm fine." I shake my head. "Thank you, though."

"Take one anyway. You may want it later." She smiles as she takes one out of the bag and presses it into my palm.

Despite myself, I smile. "Thanks." I nod and then take a breath. "I'm Dai—I mean, I'm Dee."

She grins. "Nice to meet you, Dee. I'm Vera."

"Are you over here for a holiday" I ask politely when I realize she's still looking at me.

"Yes." Her face lights up. "I'm here to visit my granddaughter. She runs her own business." Vera beams at me, her voice full of pride.

12

"That sounds wonderful." I smile back before glancing back to the baggage carousel. I can see my bag coming around and step forward to grab it before it passes. As I drag it off, the handle snaps.

"What?" My shoulders sag as I dump my old, battered suitcase on the floor in front of me.

A gentle hand pats my forearm. "Never mind, love. It's easily fixed."

"Thank you," I whisper and then look up into the kind eyes of Vera as my chest tightens. "My aunt bought it for me, for all my visits. That was before she... before she..." I take a deep breath. "I'm here to sort her house out. It's been rented out for a long time. But my parents want to sell it now."

I don't know why I'm telling her all this—a woman I've just met. But she's so kind. She has the sort of eyes you know hold a thousand stories and link to a huge heart. I can't stop the words falling from my lips.

"I'm really nervous about going there again. Now, she's not there anymore."

Vera looks at me, her eyes taking on a warmth and understanding.

"It's tough, love. But remember, things are just things. The real memories stay with you forever. In here." She pats a hand against her chest.

I swear I could wrap my arms around this sweet lady and collapse in a heap on the floor right now from all her kindness.

She smiles at me and then turns to the carousel, taking a step closer and leaning forward.

"Is that one yours?" I follow her gaze to a shiny silver case.

"That's the one."

I step around her and lift it off, placing it on the floor and pulling up the extendable handle for her.

"Oh, you are a gem. Thank you." She places her hand on top of mine.

"It's no problem." I look down and a frown crosses my face as I notice the dry skin around her knuckles—red fissures running between them where it's cracked.

"Oh." She pulls her hand away as she follows my gaze. "It's the dry air on the plane. Wreaks havoc on my skin. I don't know how those flight attendants stay looking so young and fresh. I feel like a dried-up prune after one flight." She chuckles.

"Here, I've got something you can try." I reach into my bag and pull out a small silver tin. "It's a hand balm. Its chief ingredient is cocoa butter, so it's very moisturising. But it's also got lavender and calendula in, so it's soothing as well."

I hand Vera the tin and she unscrews the lid and lifts it to her nose.

"It smells wonderful." She dabs some across the backs of her hands and rubs it in. "Thank you, Dee." She holds the tin out to me.

"No, you can keep it. I've got more."

Vera nods with gratitude and then looks at the daisy sticker on top of the tin before slipping it inside her handbag.

"That's so kind of you. You've made an old woman's day."

"So, where are you staying?" I ask as we begin the walk toward customs.

"Hope Cove. That's where my granddaughter's business is. I'm staying with her at her house. Right on the beach it is, lucky thing." Vera lets out a wistful sigh as we walk out into the main terminal, toward the exit. "How about you, love? Where's this house that holds so many fond memories of yours?"

I swallow as I look back at her. My mind transports back to my aunt's house when I was seventeen years old.

Bring those chamomile flowers in, Daisy. And those elderflowers. We're going to try a new recipe.

"It's, um, it's actually in Hope Cove," I say, forcing myself back into the present.

"Well, isn't that handy? You can share my cab! My granddaughter insisted on booking one." She rolls her eyes and continues before I have the chance to tell her that's kind, but unnecessary.

"I told her, I may be old, but I'm not incapable of getting my own cab at the airport." She tuts good-naturedly. "She wanted to come herself, but she's a staff member down at work. She works so hard." Vera sighs to herself. "You young women. Conquering the world, you are. Just remember to look after yourselves along the way."

She stops and points at a man who's waving in our direction.

"Oh, good. There's John. I'm glad they sent him this time." She lowers her voice as if sharing a secret with me. "The last driver I got liked to sing along to the radio." She frowns. "He had a voice only his mother could love."

I open my mouth to take my chance to decline her offer of a lift again, but she strides off ahead.

"Come on, love," she calls, turning around to smile at me. "We'll drop you off first."

I wrap my hands around my mug and inhale the scent from the fresh chamomile flower tea I'm nursing. It was one of the first things I did after Vera dropped me off here—dump my bag in the hallway and head straight out to the garden to pick the flowers, so I could steep them, just the way my aunt used to when I stayed here.

She loved her garden.

One requirement we gave to letting out the house was that the tenants allowed for a gardener to visit weekly. I'm so glad

Mum and Dad gave in when I pushed for it. This was my aunt's sanctuary. Her oasis.

And for as long as I can make it last, now it's mine.

I gaze around at the flower beds and raised planters, spilling over with flowering bushes in a rainbow of colors. Butterflies and bees buzz around in the warm summer air from plant to plant, investigating the legacy she left behind in the earth.

I take a sip of my tea and smile as warmth spreads through my chest. I already feel calmer, my shoulders less tense, just by being back here again.

The sound of a dog barking in the distance draws my attention out across the small lake at the bottom of the garden. I used to love sitting just here, on these weathered porch steps, staring out across the water. It's close enough to see the deer and fox, which would come and drink from the water's edge over there at dusk. There used to be an old, empty house there, but it looks as though someone has bought it in the decade since I was last here. Now there's a smart honey-colored house occupying the spot. I guess a lot has changed since my last visit.

My back clicks as I stand up and stretch. I really should get an early night. The flight from London has wiped me out.

I turn and look up at the house. It looks the same as it always did. Faded white boards, old drafty windows my aunt would always have opened wide so that the breeze could blow through, bringing in the scent from her beloved flower and herb beds.

There are so many happy memories within these walls.

I wrap one arm around myself as I lift my mug to my lips with the other. I didn't have to come. The realtor could have easily aired the property out since the last tenants left, and arranged for a fresh coat of paint and tidy up, ready to sell. Only I couldn't allow myself to not come back.

Just once more.

And given what happened back home, my parents were more than happy about it. It's for the best, they said. It will be good for me, they think.

I forgot what anything good feels like, a long time ago.

Chapter Three

Blake

"HEY, MAN. HOW'S SHE doing?" Travis slaps me on the back as I lift my labrador, Betsy, up onto the examination table.

"She's great, Trav. You know my girl, always a champ." I lower my face to Betsy's nose and give her a rub behind her ears. Her big, dark brown eyes light up and she pants as her tail swings around in an exaggerated wag.

"Well, she's certainly in fine health," Travis says as he checks her over and makes some notes on her file. "Just the regular flea dose today, then?"

"And some of those shiny coat supplements we got last time. You like those, don't you, girl?" I direct to Betsy, who whines and then lets out an excited bark.

Travis laughs. "You spoil her, dude. She's a young dog, she doesn't need those."

"Ignore him, Betsy." I round my eyes on Travis in horror as I press my hands over her ears. "Only the best for my girl, man. Okay?"

Travis shakes his head with a chuckle as he grabs a bottle of the pills and places them on the table. "It's your money to burn, man."

"Only the best for my girl, Trav," I repeat as I swipe them up.

"What are you doing with yourself for the next few weeks then, now that filming's finished?" He looks at me with interest.

"Me and Betsy are going to have some nice quiet time, aren't we, girl? Plenty of fresh air and hikes." I draw in a deep breath, recalling how clear the early morning air is up in the forest. How it re-fuels me like nothing else.

"Mr. Wild is going back into the wild. Why doesn't that surprise me?" Travis grins.

"Hey, man. I didn't make up the nickname. The group did that."

He barks out a laugh. "Come on! You love it! The idea that there's a group of women out there running an online fan group since they saw the show?" He shakes his head like he can't believe it.

Ever since a TV production company approached me and asked if they could film some of the outdoor survival weekends I run, it's been a constant source of amusement to my mates.

"What can I say? They've got impeccable taste." I flex my biceps and press a kiss to each one. "You have met my friends, Des and Troy, haven't you, Trav?"

He rolls his eyes and lets out a sigh.

"That's right. *Destroy!*" I grin.

"That joke wasn't funny the first time you said it, so it sure as shit isn't funny now."

I turn toward the sound of Kayla's voice as she pokes her head around the door and sticks her tongue out at me.

"Hey, it's one of my finest jokes. That one always gets a laugh from the ladies." I flex a bicep at her as if to stress my point.

"Trav, your next patient is here." She ignores me and smiles sweetly at my best friend, whose eyes sparkle—*fucking sparkle*—in response.

"Oh, God," I groan. "Come on, Betsy. Let's get out of here before their married romantic crap suffocates us." I press a kiss to her head as I lift her down to the floor.

"Nice to see you, Blake." Kayla smirks, leaning down to fuss Betsy as we pass her in the doorway.

"Later, lovebird losers," I call out with a chuckle as I raise a hand in send-off.

The door closes behind me to the sound of Kayla tutting. I smile. She knows I'm only joking. Seeing two of my best friends so happy is incredible, even if I have to witness them eye fucking each other whenever we're together.

As we head outside, a cat runs across the street in front of us and Betsy looks up at me.

"Look, I know you want to, but you can't chase the cats around here. Save it for the squirrels in the forest, okay?"

She lets out a low grumble as we walk back toward my truck.

My phone beeps as we reach the truck, so I pull it out of my back pocket.

Cindy: Herbies tonight?

I sniff and rub my hand across my jaw. That text means one thing. Despite our recent conversation, Cindy's still up for an after-hours fuck later.

I open the door and whistle to Betsy, who jumps straight in the truck and sits on the front seat, waiting for me to join her. I tap out a reply and hit send before heading around to the driver's side and sliding in.

"Come on, girl. Let's go home."

After I've fixed us both some lunch—turkey sandwich for me; just turkey for Betsy—the two of us kick back on the enormous sofas I've set up on the rear porch. Apart from out in the forest, miles away from anyone, this is my favorite place. I got the house at a steal as it was so run-down. But it was nothing some elbow grease and sweat couldn't sort out.

I gaze out over the lake. It's quiet here, just my house, and the one on the other side of the water, set back, away from the town and main residential streets. It's peaceful. Not as peaceful as when

Betsy and I take ourselves off into the surrounding forest for a couple of days at a time, camping, but damn close.

"This is the life, eh, Betsy?"

I reach down to where she's laid her head in my lap and stroke her ears. She lets out a contented sigh and gazes out over the water with me. I love when it's just the two of us. It's been so busy lately. Things got kind of mad when the outdoor survival training company I run attracted the attention of a TV studio. They wanted to make a series showing real people being pushed to their limits in the great outdoors. It was fun. After all, it's what I live for—pushing people out of their comfort zones to help them discover their own strengths. It's incredible what people are capable of when they have the faith in themselves. People think it's all about roughing it and surviving the elements, but it's much more of an inner journey.

Movement on the opposite bank catches my eye and I look over just in time to see someone dive off the jetty into the lake, disappearing under the water, barely leaving a ripple.

"Looks like Daisy's aunt's house has a new tenant," I say to Betsy, whose ears prick up as she watches the surface of the lake.

Daisy.

Even after all this time, I still wonder how she is, what she's doing. We all stayed in touch on social media for a few years after her aunt died. But then one day, it all stopped with no explanation. She deleted her accounts and disappeared completely.

Gone.

Betsy sits up suddenly, her eyes trained on the water as a dark-haired head breaks the surface and swims effortlessly across the center of the lake.

I sit forward and drain what's left of my bottle of water.

"Come on, girl. Let's go be neighborly and introduce ourselves."

We get into my truck and drive the short distance round to the house across the lake.

"Stay, Betsy," I instruct, leaving her sitting on the grass next to the truck until I've met our new neighbour. I know not everyone likes dogs, although how they couldn't fucking baffles me.

I throw a grin back at Betsy over my shoulder, and her eyes light up as she watches me wander over to the jetty.

I raise a hand in a wave to the person swimming toward me.

"How's it going? I'm Blake. Your neighbor," I call, motioning over to my house on the other side of the water.

The person—a woman—whips her head around, looking at my place, and then back in my direction, before swimming over.

I push my hands into the pockets of my cargo pants as I wait for her to reach the jetty. She climbs up the small wooden ladder and I avert my gaze politely, but not before I see a glimpse of a black bikini and a pair of long, shapely legs being wrapped in a towel.

"Hi, Blake." Her voice comes out breathy from her swim.

"Hi, it's nice to meet—"

I raise my eyes to hers and am caught under an intense blue gaze, which steals the words from my mouth. My eyes rake over her face. It's different—older. And her long blonde hair is now short and dark.

But I would know those eyes anywhere.

"Daisy?" I break out into a wide grin. "Fuck me! What the hell?" I take a step forward and wrap my arms around her, breathing in the freshwater scent clinging to her skin.

She makes no attempt to hug me back.

I pull back and fist my hands in my hair as she stares at me. "God, you..." I look over her face again, and then back into her eyes. "You're different, but it's still you! I can't believe this. What are you doing here?"

She pulls the towel tighter around herself and gives me a small smile.

"It's good to see you, Blake. You're looking well."

I feel my forehead crease as I look at her. She's different somehow. I mean the hair, obviously. But something else too, which I can't put my finger on. I probably shouldn't have hugged her. Maybe she didn't recognise me and it freaked her out, thinking some random guy was trying to grab her when she's barely dressed.

Her eyes scan up and down my body, and—hell, I'm a man—I pull my shoulders back and place my hands on my hips, grinning at her as her eyes return to my face.

"Checking out what you've been missing all these years, huh?"

She narrows her eyes at me, and then the corners of her lips curl into a smile.

"I see your jokes haven't improved." She raises an eyebrow at me as I clutch my chest in pretend hurt.

"Daisy, your words wound me."

She winces for a split second. It passes over her face like a ripple on the water, and then it's gone.

"I prefer to be called Dee now."

"Sure." I hold out my hand for her to shake. "Nice to meet you... Dee." She takes it and I wrap her tiny hand in mine. "So, is this some kind of role-play thing you're into now?" I wink.

There's no way the Daisy I know would want to be called anything else. This is the girl who made daisy chains while we lay around under the summer sun, dreaming of the future and what we saw ourselves doing.

Something to do with the great outdoors or photography for me, and something that benefitted animals for her.

She pulls her hand back as though I've burned her. "No. It's who I am now."

I look into her bright blue eyes and nod slowly. "Okay. Dee it is."

Her shoulders relax, and she lowers the towel and wraps it around her waist. I can't help my eyes dropping to her full, round breasts.

Fuck. I do not remember seventeen-year-old Daisy having those.

"My parents want to sell the house," she explains as she slips her feet into a pair of sandals and walks up the jetty next to me. "I'm here to tidy it up."

My eyes cast up and over the white weatherboards of her aunt's house. Sure, it could maybe do with some fresh paintwork, but it's actually in great shape.

She sees me looking and I must have a disbelieving frown on my face as she adds, "There're things inside that need doing too."

"Right." I nod as we walk across the grass toward my truck.

She freezes as her eyes land on Betsy, who's watching us both with interest. I look between the two of them. Dais—Dee's face pales and her eyes widen.

"You have a dog?"

"Not just any dog. The greatest dog ever to exist, aren't you, girl?" I give Betsy a hand signal and she barks excitedly on command, her tail wagging furiously. But her butt stays glued firmly to the ground, awaiting permission to come greet us. "You still like dogs, right?"

"Oh, my God." She drops to the ground and smiles the first genuine smile I've seen, lighting up her entire face.

And just like that, Daisy is back.

I give Betsy the signal and she races over to us and straight into Daisy, almost knocking her over as she licks her face and whines in excitement. Daisy laughs and wraps her arms around her, stroking her in long, fluid movements down her back. Betsy laps up the attention as her tail beats me around the legs.

"I think you've got a fan." I laugh as Daisy falls back on the floor and Betsy jumps on top of her.

"Come on, girl. That's enough." I chuckle and clap my hands. Betsy abandons her playful assault and sits down next to me, her eyes bright and eager.

I hold out a hand to Daisy, and she takes it. The towel has completely unwrapped now and is in a heap on the floor. After helping Daisy up, I bend down to retrieve it and fight my hardest not to let my eyes rake over her body as I stand up. Judging by the pink blush on her cheeks as I hand it back to her, I would say I failed.

"I still can't believe you're back here." I grin at her. "Wait until I tell Kayla and Trav. You know they're married now. You must have seen..." I trail off.

What can I say?

You must have seen it on social media before you ghosted us all?

"I know." She gives me an uncomfortable smile. "I knew about that. But I guess there's a lot I missed."

I look back at her face and the way her eyes pull down as she gives me a sad smile.

Just like that, she's Dee again. A woman I barely know.

"Hey!" My voice lifts as an idea hits me. "I'm having dinner with Kayla and Trav at the diner in town later. Come with me! They'll want to see you."

Daisy shuffles her feet and fiddles with the towel, which she's wrapped firmly around herself again.

"Oh, I don't know. I only got in yesterday, and I'm still pretty jet-lagged, and—"

"Pick you up at six, then?" I grin as I head back to my truck and whistle to Betsy to get in.

"Blake... I..." she calls after me, but I'm already turning the truck around.

I stick my arm out the window and give her a wave as we drive away.

Chapter Four

Daisy

THIS IS A STUPID idea.

I curse myself as I pull on my dress and slip my feet into my sandals. Why did I let Blake talk me into meeting him, Kayla, and Travis tonight? The idea of seeing my old friends both excites and terrifies me. It's been three years since we last spoke online, and a hell of a lot longer since we all saw one another face to face. I suppose I had to expect it, though. Hope Cove's hardly big. I couldn't fly under the radar for long, no matter how much I wish that were the case.

I mean, I would love to see them. Of course I would.

My shoulders sag as I look in the mirror and pull at the front of my dress, so it isn't showing too much cleavage. It's just... a lot has changed. I'm not the girl they thought I was.

I'm not who I thought I was.

And then there's Blake.

Fuck, there's Blake.

I blow out a breath as I picture seeing him again for the first time earlier. Seventeen-year-old Blake Anderson was bad enough. But fully grown man Blake Anderson...

My God.

He's certainly changed, all right. Gone is any lingering awkwardness from being a teenager with limbs too long for his body, and in its place is... a man. A great big hulk of a man—all muscles, tattoos, and those same intense green eyes and cheeky grin. Blake

Anderson certainly took puberty and stuck his middle fingers up at it—after grabbing all the testosterone it had to offer.

I look back in the mirror and frown at myself as I drag my hands through my short, dark hair. It doesn't suit me. The colour is too dark, too intense. It drains me and makes my skin look gray.

It matches the inside now; I guess.

The sound of a vehicle approaching the house makes me suck in a breath. I look out the window and recognise Blake's shiny black truck. I head downstairs and double check I've locked the front door before running over to the truck and climbing in before he can get out.

He's wearing black jeans and a green shirt that matches his eyes, the fabric of the sleeves straining over his biceps.

"Hey, gorgeous." He gives me an easy grin as his eyes drop over my black, floaty dress. "You know a quarter of the population of Hope Cove is over the age of sixty? You'll give them all a heart attack looking like that."

I drop my head. "I'll go change... I'll just be a minute." I reach for the truck handle before Blake's large, muscular hand stops me.

"Hey, I'm joking. You look great." His brows knit together as he releases my arm and sits back in his seat.

I avoid his confused gaze and stare out through the windscreen instead, my arm tingling where his skin just touched mine.

After a second, he clears his throat. "You ready for the best food you've ever had in your life?"

I look back at him. His face is lit up like a kid in a sweet shop who's just been told to get whatever they want.

Despite my earlier reluctance at coming out tonight, I smile.

"Sure. Show me what you've got."

"So then Blake turns to the camera and gives it this smoldering look, and says, *let's get dirty*!" Kayla slaps the tabletop as she erupts into hysterical giggles. "Oh, my God. You have to watch it!" She wipes the tears from her eyes.

I look over at her on the other side of the window booth the four of us are sitting at in the local diner as she creases up with laughter.

"Honestly, it is TV gold! We should play a drinking game based on how many times he tries to pull a sexy face for the camera. He's even got an online fan club. They've nicknamed him Mr. Wild. I mean, they must be blind! Either that or they've got him mixed up with his brother." Kayla continues to laugh.

"Hey! What's wrong with my face?" Blake pipes up.

I turn to look at him just as he throws Kayla what I imagine is his 'let's get dirty' face. She shrieks with laughter again, obviously immune. Yet I can't help my eyes lingering on him a fraction too long, admiring his firm jaw, covered in a short, dark beard.

"How is your brother?" I ask.

His face returns to an easy grin as he looks at me. "Jay's good. He's married now. Him and his wife, Holly, are expecting another baby."

"Really?" I picture his older brother. He always seemed so busy living in LA and working as an actor that I never heard of him even having a serious girlfriend before. But then, I've avoided reading the magazines I've seen with him on in England. They just reminded me too much of Blake, and Hope Cove, and my aunt.

All things from the past.

"Yeah. Holly must be mad, putting up with him." Blake sniggers, but his eyes light up and I know he's joking. He and Jay are close.

They're polar opposites, look-wise. Jay is all dirty blond hair and American jock handsome. While Blake is dark-haired and rugged. The kind of guy who looks like he could wrestle a bear in his sleep. *Single-handedly.*

"Thinking about it. She's English, too. Must be a thing you Brit girls have in common." He winks at me as our burgers arrive.

"I still can't believe you have your own show. That's amazing." I smile, feeling myself relax slightly. It may have been years since the four of us were last together, but sitting here now, I could almost believe it was yesterday.

Almost.

"And I can't believe you ordered a vegan burger!" Blake's mouth drops open as he eyes the food on my plate with what I can only describe as complete bewilderment. "Don't tell me you also joined a convent and started braiding your armpit hair while you've been gone?"

"Ouch!" His face pinches as I'm pretty sure Kayla kicks him underneath the table.

"Don't be a douche, Blake." She rolls her eyes. "Not everyone is a caveman like you, with a lack of social skills." She turns to me, her lips twitching at the corners. "As you'll see, Dee, not much has changed around here. You haven't missed anything."

I smile, relieved she called me Dee. She seems the most accepting of me coming back out of the blue. But that's always been Kayla—happy to go with the flow, and sense when there are some things a person wants to share... and some things they don't.

"Tell me more about the show." I take a bite of my burger and watch Blake lift his to his lips. It looks tiny in his huge hands.

He tilts his head to the side, taking a bite and swallowing before he answers. "It was a six-part series. I had a group of guys and girls, all with their own unique reasons for wanting to push themselves, and I took them out and taught them how to survive in the wild."

"Remember the guy who brought his stuffed lion toy?" Travis chuckles.

I expect Blake to laugh. He's always joking around, but I'm surprised when he takes his time to think before he answers.

"We all need something soft to cuddle up to at night, man. I've got Betsy. Ray needed something too. We had a great chat about it, actually. That lion represented security to him when he felt he had none."

"It's an emotional journey for them, then? As well as the physical challenge?" I nod in understanding.

"Exactly. Thank you, Dai—" He clears his throat. "Thank you, Dee." His green eyes meet mine for a second and I look away quickly.

"And you guys have been married a few years now?" I turn my attention back to Kayla and Travis. Anything to prolong the inevitable info dig, which will come my way at some point.

"Yep." Kayla grins and wraps her arm around Travis' shoulders, planting a kiss on his cheek. "He's been the luckiest man alive since one game of truth or dare started it all."

Blake tips his head toward me, and the feel of his breath on my neck sends a shiver through my body. "See what you're responsible for?"

See what you're responsible for, Daisy?

I flinch at his words and let out a gasp. My movement knocks my soda over and sends liquid cascading all over the table.

"I'm sorry! I'm so sorry!" I cry, grabbing napkins and catching the spillage before it runs off the edge of the table.

"Relax, babe. It's only soda." Kayla looks at me with a strange expression on her face as I feel my cheeks heat and hurry to wipe up the mess.

"I know, it's just... I'm so clumsy." I leave the wet napkins in a ball and place my hands in my lap, my appetite gone, even though I've barely touched my burger.

The conversation moves on and I smile as I listen to Kayla talk about her and Travis' wedding, and how Blake gave a great best man's speech and arranged a brilliant bachelor party. I tell them about coming back to sort my aunt's house out, and Blake tells the story about the day he got Betsy as a puppy. All the while I fight to push away the dark images that seep in when he tells me how excited Betsy was the day he took her home.

How much she *trusted* him.

No matter what I do, those images claw at me.

After dinner we say goodbye and Blake drives me home. I don't talk much on the journey, and he seems happy to be in companionable silence until we pull up outside the house.

"Here you are, madam." He grins as he climbs out of the truck and comes round to open my door before I can say anything.

"You don't have to do that, you know?" I say as I slide out and he closes the door behind me.

His eyes light up and he flashes his perfect teeth. "I know. But I always walk you to the door."

I suck in a breath as I stare up at him. Heat radiates from his body, like he's the sun and I'm a plant, feeding off his energy.

Suddenly, I'm seventeen again. Seventeen and tipsy from home-made elderflower gin. But not tipsy enough to forget the way my stomach twisted in humiliation when he pushed me away from trying to kiss him.

I've done some stupid things in my life.

"Thanks," I mumble, pulling my keys out of my bag and walking away from him up the porch steps.

"Dee?" he calls out.

I turn back around and look into his intense gaze. "Yes?"

"It's good to have you back." He winks at me and then heads back to his truck and climbs in.

I open the door and make my way inside, knowing that he won't leave until he sees me get in.

He would never leave until the door was closed.
Some doors should stay shut forever.

"Please... No!"
My eyes widen in horror as I take in the sight in front of me.
"Stop!"
Terrified eyes look back at me.
"I didn't know... I'm so sorry, I'm so sorry," I whisper.

I come to with a scream; the sheets tangled around my legs as I bolt upright and scan the room.

Thank God.

I fall back against the pillows and swipe a hand over my brow, slick with sweat. My heart's hammering in my chest as the nightmare fades. It's always the same one. The same helplessness, the same fear.

The same smell.

I sit up again and swing my legs out of bed. It's still early, but the sun is up. The perfect time for a swim to help clear my head.

I pull off my vest and shorts and throw them in the laundry basket. I'm so glad I packed extra sleepwear. At the rate I go through it, I could open my own store.

I grab my bikini and slip it on before heading downstairs and out onto the back porch. I double check I've locked the door and take the keys and my towel down to the jetty. It's a beautiful morning. The last orange hues of the sunrise are just leaving the sky, and it's already warm.

I place my things down onto the wooden boards and then take a deep breath as I dive into the water. I slip under the surface smoothly; the water welcoming me, muffling the sounds from above, and with it, quietening the storm in my head.

I love it here. Just me and the water. It's tranquil. A haven below the real world where I can just exist. I don't have to do anything other than swim and hold my breath.

It's just me.

Me and the water.

I break the surface and gulp in a lungful of morning air, last night already like a distance memory. Maybe Mum and Dad were right. This might be good for me. I reach my arms out and cut through the water, feeling my muscles loosen with each stroke I take.

I don't know how long I swim before I realize I'm being watched; that feeling where you just know there are eyes on you.

Goosebumps form on my skin as I glance around, my breath catching in my throat.

"Betsy!" I cry in relief as I lock eyes with Blake's gorgeous chocolate lab sitting on the jetty by his house. She's sitting there pretty as a picture, watching me swim.

I look past her. If she's out here, it probably means Blake isn't far behind.

Then I see him, walking past his open back door in just a pair of sweatpants, his upper torso bare. It's only a fraction of a second, but it's long enough to make out the rippling muscles in his broad shoulders, the way his dark brown hair is ruffled from sleep, and the tattoo running down his side, all the way from his ribs, then disappearing below his waistband.

Yes... Blake Anderson definitely grew up.

I turn and swim away quietly before he sees me, grabbing my towel and keys from the jetty and heading inside.

Nothing good will come from me staring at my past.

Even if it does look great in sweatpants.

Chapter Five

Blake

I CAN'T GET THE sight of Daisy swimming away this morning out of my head. She probably thinks I didn't see her. Or *hopes* I didn't. But I've lived on the lake for years. I know every sound that comes with the dawn. The ones that are always there, and the ones that aren't—like the splash of my childhood friend diving into the water.

My childhood friend who grew up into a woman—with incredible breasts.

"Fuck this, Betsy. You want to go for a run, girl?"

Her ears prick up at the word 'run' and she leaps down from the sofa on the back porch and gives me an excited bark.

"That's a yes, then?" I laugh as her tail hits me in the calf as she runs down the steps and looks back at me expectantly.

"Okay, girl. Let me grab my sneakers."

We run for an hour. Through the woods behind the lake and up to one of my favorite viewpoints, set high on a rock edge. You can see all of Hope Cove from up there—its sandy white beach curling around the small-town center with its family-run businesses lining the street. It's quaint; I guess. At least that's what the tourists seem to think when they stay on their way to and from LA. The hotel set on the outskirts of town seems to attract the wealthier guests. Ones who aren't opposed to paying inflated prices for a spa massage with hot stones.

I smirk. I spend days in the outdoors, covered in mud, and my skin is just fine. They should bottle that and sell it at fifty bucks a jar.

When we get back to the house, I check my phone. I leave it behind when me and Betsy go out. What's the point in getting out in nature if you're going to be answering calls and reading tweets and shit like that?

Trav: Hey, want to meet at Herbies later for a drink?
I smile as I reply.
Me: Kayla got no plans for you?
Trav: Nah, she's off out somewhere.
Me: Sounds good. See you later.

"What do you reckon the deal is, then?" I ask Trav as I grab up a handful of peanuts from the bowl on the bar and drop them in my mouth.

"You know they find traces of urine in those, don't you?" He raises an eyebrow and then shakes his head as I grab a larger fistful and shove them in, holding his gaze as I chew.

"You're pure filth sometimes, you know that?"

"That's what the ladies say." I smirk, which earns me a chuckle.

"Whatever, man. That'll be why you're still single. You know married people get more sex than single people?" Trav lifts his beer bottle to his lips and takes a swig.

I turn to gape at him. "Who the fuck says?"

He shrugs. "I don't know. Some study in one of those magazines that Kayla reads."

"They obviously asked the wrong people."

My gaze wanders over to Cindy, who's serving another customer further down the bar. She tips her head back and laughs as the guy says something to her and slips her a fat tip.

I turn back to Travis. "I mean, you're here, drinking in the one bar in town with me. Hardly having wild sex right now, are you?"

"Back at you." Travis grins and then frowns as he looks past me at Cindy. "You two still hooking up?"

"Hey, I don't kiss and tell, man," I say, my eyes glancing back over to where Cindy's twirling her light brown hair around her finger as she talks to the guy she just served.

"This is Hope Cove, Blake. There are no secrets." He gives me a pointed look as I let out a sigh.

"It was one time. That's it. We spoke about it, and I thought she agreed it was a one-off. But then she texted me yesterday. I was meeting you guys for dinner. And then Daisy showed up, and I went straight home after dropping her off. I didn't even think much of it."

Truth be told, me and Cindy were never anything other than a mistake. A momentary lapse. Two people looking for something else but finding each other for one night instead. Judging by the giggle that's floating up from the other end of the bar, I'd say she's over it too.

"Blake Anderson turning down a no-strings fuck. What did you do with my best friend, dude?"

"Jackass." I shake my head and smile at him as I take a drink.

"So, what were you saying? Before we were side-tracked by piss-covered nuts and non-marital sex." Trav looks at me as I place my beer bottle down on the bar and trace my fingers up and down its spout.

"Daisy, man. What's her deal, do you think?"

"Don't you mean Dee?"

"Exactly!" I blow out a breath as I look at him. "Don't you think it's weird? She goes AWOL online three years ago and then shows up here out of the blue, looking all different."

"People change, Blake," Trav says, looking over at me.

"Yeah, but like that? You remember her. She was... Daisy." I blow out another breath as I rub a hand along my jaw, over my beard.

Trav shakes his head. "Fuck. I knew it. You never got over her leaving, did you?"

"It's not that!" I fire back before grabbing my beer and downing half of it.

"Sure looks like it." Travis raises his eyebrows as he watches me.

"She was our friend, Trav. She *still* is our friend. I just don't like the feeling that something's up with her. People don't change that much, do they?" I turn to look at him and he shrugs his shoulders.

"Maybe some do."

I turn back to my beer, my jaw tense as Cindy approaches.

"You staying for another?" she asks, cocking her head to one side, her heavily mascaraed eyes dropping over my chest and back up again.

Travis stands up and slaps a hand on my shoulder. "I'll leave you to decide if you want a night-cap. Speak to you soon, man."

"Yeah, catch you later," I reply, avoiding Cindy's gaze.

I tip my head back and drain the last remnants of my beer as she watches me.

"Not tonight."

"Maybe next time?" She raises an eyebrow at me as I stand, dropping her eyes down to my crotch and back, a small smile tugging at her lips.

"Your friend down the end there is missing you," I say, jerking my thumb in the guy's direction she was just giggling with.

She purses her lips. "He's just another tourist, Blake. Here today, gone tomorrow."

When I say nothing, she looks back into my eyes.

"I know you don't mean it, Blake. We're good together, you and me."

I was wrong. She's not over it.

Fuck.

I run my hand back through my hair and glance to the ceiling as though the magical solution to re-iterating our recent chat about our lack of future will appear before my eyes. She said she agreed with me. That she wanted more and knew I wasn't willing to give it.

"Things change, Cindy. We've spoken about this," I say softly, not wanting to hurt her.

She's a nice girl. She's just not *my* girl. She never has been.

"You say that. But *people* don't change, Blake. Not really." She looks at me with what seems like pity before turning and heading back down to the other end of the bar.

I leave Herbies and take the twenty-minute walk back to my house. Betsy jumps up from her place on the back porch and runs to greet me, panting in excitement.

"Hey, girl." I bend down to ruffle her ears and kiss her head.

There's a light shining behind her, across the other side of the lake, coming from Daisy's kitchen window.

I stand and look over at it for a long time as Cindy's words play over in my mind.

People don't change, Blake.

Chapter Six

Daisy

I DON'T SEE BLAKE again for a couple of days. I get out and have a swim early enough that he's probably still asleep. It's for the best. Ever since the diner a couple of nights ago, I've not been able to shake off the feeling that I need to keep away. He and Betsy are better off far, far away from me. He thinks I'm the girl he said goodbye to on the porch steps all those years ago. But I barely remember her anymore. Not since...

"Stop, just stop," I mutter as I spray the hose over the herb beds, willing my mind to think of something else.

It's early evening and the day has finally cooled down enough to do it without the risk of scorching the delicate leaves if I were to do it in the blazing sunshine.

I survey the garden. It's thriving. It really is magnificent. I'm so glad I pushed Mum and Dad to keep on a gardener. I feel closer to my aunt here, out in the place she loved most.

I sigh as I look back at the peeling paint on the house. The inside is all done. There wasn't much for me to do, really; just clean. Most of the furniture had already gone, except for the essentials. And we will probably sell the rest with the house. All that's left for me to do is to employ a painter for the outside. Something I'm putting off for as long as possible. Because once that's done, what other reason will there be for me to stay?

I turn the hose off, satisfied that the plants have had a decent drink, and turn to head back into the house.

"Hey! Dee!"

I look over to the driveway and see Kayla pulling up, her head leaning out of the open car window.

"Hi," I call back as I head over to meet her.

She cuts the engine and bounces out wearing exercise gear, her light brown hair pulled into a high ponytail.

"I was passing and thought I'd say hi!" She grins at me.

"You were passing?" My gaze goes behind her to the long drive-way, which leads up from the road

A road which has town in one direction and just forest in the other.

I raise my eyebrows at her with a knowing smirk.

"Okay." She rolls her eyes. "I drove here specially. I wanted to see how you were doing."

"Me?"

"Yes, you! Unless you're hiding some fit guy inside I don't know about?" She peers around me toward the house.

I snort. "Hardly."

"A girl can dream." She sighs theatrically.

"I thought you were happily married?" I smile at her, folding my arms.

"Exactly. That's why I need to hear about it from my unmarried friends. I will never have that first-time, lust-fueled passion again!"

I tip my head back and laugh. It may have been years, but Kayla still makes every conversation a lot more fun.

Her eyes light up. "It's good to hear that sound."

"What are you talking about?"

"You. Laughing." She smiles at me. "I've missed hearing it. We used to have fun, didn't we?"

I look back into her deep brown eyes. "Yeah, we did," I whisper.

"So, why don't we have some more tonight?" She claps her hands together. "I need to make the most of you while you're here."

I glance back at the house. Back to the peace of being alone.

I shake my head at her with reluctance. "I wasn't planning on going out tonight."

"You don't know where I'm suggesting yet." Her eyes shine with mischief. "Besides, what else are you going to do? Go to bed early with your knitting?"

I shift uncomfortably on the spot. Going to bed means one thing to me now—nightmares.

Remembering something I wish I didn't.

I chew on my bottom lip before answering. "What did you have in mind?"

Forty minutes later, my face feels like it might explode from all the blood that's being pumped into my cheeks.

"I wish I was at home knitting," I hiss to Kayla from the plank position I'm holding. My abs are on fire and my arms are shaking as I struggle not to collapse into a heap on the grass.

She winks back at me as Blake's voice calls out, "Okay, change!"

I flop down onto the floor and roll onto my back, puffing.

"Trust me. You'll feel amazing after! He may be a big-headed douche sometimes, but he sure knows what he's doing." Kayla grins at me as she swaps from doing ab crunches and rises onto her elbows and into a plank.

I sneak a glance over at Blake, further up the field, as he moves fluidly between all the bodies on the ground, dishing out words of encouragement and positive mantras. He's wearing a pair of black gym shorts and matching muscle vest. He looks like he's just about to take part in an Iron Man contest with his ripped muscles glistening with sweat.

I don't know why I let Kayla talk me into coming to one of these outdoor bootcamp style classes he runs.

"I swear the women here would not be batting their eyelashes half as much if they knew him like we do," Kayla says, holding her plank effortlessly.

I tilt my head to look around. Most of the class consists of women with beaming smiles and perfect makeup. Their eyes seem to follow Blake as he moves around, crouching down now and again, causing his shorts to ride up around his muscular thighs.

"He loves it. Attention whore," she mutters.

My stomach twists as a woman in a pink workout bra who looks like she lives off lettuce says something to him and he lets out a deep, throaty laugh.

I drag my eyes away, my cheeks burning from how ridiculous I'm being. I'm not jealous. Blake is—*was*—just a friend. Now he's just the guy who lives across the lake, who I won't see ever again once I return to England.

I screw my eyes shut and swallow down the bile in my throat at the thought of going home.

"Hey, ladies."

I open my eyes, straight into the mesmerising green gaze of Blake, who's towering over me. A little to the left and I would be able to see straight up his shorts. I frown and dart my eyes away.

"Came to check out my class, eh, Dee?" He squats down next to me.

I have no chance of escape now.

"It was Kayla's idea," I murmur, shooting her a look that says I'm never going to trust her again when she says she knows something 'fun' we can do.

"Well, seeing as you're here, I better make sure I give your body the full experience." He winks at me, a cheeky grin plastered over his face.

I want to get up and tell him I'm done, but before I can, I feel his large, warm hand rest over my belly button, his long fingers pressing lightly against my skin.

"Right, now breathe out as you lift." He brings his other hand behind my head and encourages me up into an ab crunch. My muscles fire up underneath his fingertips as I reach the top.

"Great." He beams. "And back down." He supports my head as I rest it back on the floor. "Okay, again."

I look up at his profile as I crunch. His dark brown hair is just the right length to give him a sexy, just-fucked look—unless he has just fucked before teaching the class—and his firm jaw has the perfect amount of beard stubble on it to make him look rugged. Not groomed and designer like some guys aim for, but rough and real. Like a guy who can take charge effortlessly.

I blow out a breath as I reach the top again, and my body shakes under his touch.

"Great job."

He grins at me and then his hands are gone, leaving my skin cold as he goes to assist the woman next to me, whose eyes sparkle at him as he crouches down next to her.

"Shameless flirt." Kayla tuts. "He knows exactly what he's doing."

I watch as he dishes out praise to the woman next to us, my stomach twisting again. But I notice he doesn't touch her.

I collapse back after another crunch and take a deep breath. Maybe he could tell I needed all the help I could get.

<hr/>

"Well, that was interesting," I say to Kayla as I climb out of her car and lean on the doorframe of the open window.

"You'll ache tomorrow, believe me."

I shake my head at her as I smile. "I ache now! I didn't come back here to be tortured; you know?"

She smiles back at me. "Why did you come back?" she asks gently.

The smile drops from my face as I look back into her eyes. They're curious, but not in an unkind way.

"My mum and dad want to sell the house. I just wanted to come back one more time." I shrug my shoulders as I repeat my unconvincing story. There's an element of truth to it, but I can tell from the way Kayla's studying me, her lips pursed, that she isn't buying it. Not one hundred per cent.

"I thought you said your aunt left half the house to you when we last spoke online?"

My shoulders sag. "She did. Half to me and half to my dad, her baby brother." A sad smile crosses my lips. "But he had a poor investment and needs the money for his retirement. I thought about buying him out. I dreamed about it. About coming back here permanently. But I don't have the money. Things don't always work out the way you hope they will."

Kayla gives me a lopsided smile. "You never know what's around the corner. I remember you were always so positive when we were kids. Maybe something good is on its way, and everything will change?"

I tip my head at her as I stand. "Maybe."

"I'll see you soon, yeah?" she calls through the open window.

"Yeah. See you soon," I call back as she turns her car around and heads back down the driveway.

My gaze wanders over to the far side of the lake. The rear porch light is on at Blake's house, and I can just about make out a dark shape on the sofa—Betsy.

Warmth spreads in my chest as I picture her and Blake together. They adore one another. It's so obvious by the way he talks about her and the way she sticks to his side like his shadow when they're together. I don't think I've seen anything sweeter.

That's why I have to keep away. These stupid reactions my body is having whenever he's near need to stop.

They must.

He thinks he still knows me, but he doesn't.

I don't even know myself.

Chapter Seven

Blake

DAISY SWIMS IN THE lake every morning at the break of dawn. Just as Betsy and I are return from our run. She doesn't see us, and I never call out. She seems to want the space. I get the feeling she needs it somehow. I'm not sure what it is, but I suspect she's working through something. You don't come back to a house in another country you've not seen in ten years just to clean it before it sells.

Maybe I can recognise it because when I need to think, Betsy and I take off camping in the woods for a couple of days. Whatever it is that Daisy needs, I hope she finds it here. I hope she finds her way back to herself.

"Let's go, girl."

I whistle at Betsy, and she hops down from the seat of the truck onto the sidewalk. We walk down Hope Cove's main street, saying good morning to people we pass. Betsy gets lots of fuss, which she laps up. It goes with the territory when you live in a small community.

We head inside the general store, run by Ralph. I swear the guy never ages. He ran this store when I used to come in as a kid with my brother and granddad to get a packet of sweets at a weekend, and he still runs it now. That's Hope Cove all over—family-run businesses looking out for one another.

"Hey, Ralph." I raise my hand in greeting as he nods at me from behind the counter. His dog, Duke, peers around the edge of the wood, his ears pricking up when he sees Betsy by my side. I've never quite figured out what breed Duke has in him. He's a wiry beast, who bounces around as though he believes he's half his size.

Ralph watches the pair of them, sniffing one another, tails wagging, and shuffles over to a large glass jar on the counter full of dog biscuits and pulls one out, handing it to Betsy.

"Don't you go trying to make my girl sweet on you, Ralph," I joke as Betsy crunches the biscuit down and then drops her nose to the floor to sniff out the crumbs.

Ralph shakes his head with a chuckle. It's the same routine every time we come in here.

"I don't think it's me you need to worry about." Ralph tips his head, and I follow his gaze back down to where Duke is busy licking Betsy's jaw.

I smirk. He's certainly got balls; I'll give him that.

"How's he settling in?"

"He's doing good. Settled right in. I was worried, you know, adopting and all. Can never tell what kind of past they've had. But he's a good boy." A smile settles over Ralph's face as he watches the two of them crouch down on their front legs, trying to entice the other into a game of chase. "He's been good company." Ralph's eyes mist momentarily, and I pat him on the arm.

He lost his wife six months ago. Getting Duke was Travis' suggestion, so he'd have a companion and a reason to get up each morning. Nothing like someone depending on you to force you to keep yourself going.

Ralph tuts and pats his hand over mine on his arm. "Keeps running off mind. Always comes back. But I've no idea what he's up to. I fix one spot in the fence where he's getting out, and the next day, another appears."

I chuckle. "He's running the show, Ralph."

Ralph takes his hand away from mine and bats it in the air, dismissing my comment, but not before I see the smile pulling at his lips. He loves that scruffy hound. Anyone can see that.

"You after more film then, Blake?" He lifts his chin.

"How d'you guess?"

He clicks his tongue and then lets out a deep, throaty chuckle, turning away and rummaging about on a shelf behind the counter.

"I can always tell, son. You come in here with that determined gleam in your eye, you do. The same one you have every time you've seen something you want to capture. What is it this time? Another mountain lion?"

"Nope." I grin as Ralph stands and places what I came for down on the counter.

"Spit it out, then. I ain't getting any younger here."

"Cubs, Ralph. Three, I reckon, from the tracks I've seen. Me and Betsy have been out early every morning looking for them. I was thinking we'd missed this season's; they'll have grown now."

Ralph lifts his wiry gray brows, the corners of his mouth turning down as he nods.

"I haven't seen a black bear cub in years. Mind you, I don't get up and out into the forest as much as you do. I take Duke to the beach for his run. Your pop's camera still doing you well?"

I nod at Ralph as I lean down and rub Duke and then Betsy, around the neck.

"Sure is. Never let me down in all these years."

I grin as I stand and plant some money down on the counter and grab the roll of film.

"Thanks, Ralph," I say as I throw it up in the air, catching it and shoving it into the pocket of my cargo pants.

"Come, show me what you get, won't you, Blake?" he calls after me as Betsy and I head out the door.

"I always do." I flash him a smile.

"Where to now, girl?" I ask Betsy as we go back out onto the street again.

She lets out a whisper of a bark, her tail wagging as she fixes her gaze on something across the street.

I follow her eyes and feel myself breaking into a huge grin as I clock the tiny pair of denim shorts, hugging long, slender legs.

Betsy jogs over to the opposite sidewalk with me, until we're standing right next to their owner.

"Reminding yourself of all the delights Hope Cove has to offer?" I say, my eyes tracing down the side of Daisy's face to where she's chewing on her bottom lip as she stands in front of the town noticeboard.

She turns to me, and her eyes widen, as though she's shocked someone is speaking to her.

"Blake?"

"Last time I checked." I smile at her and my hands go to my hips as she stares at me. She drops to fuss over Betsy, her face lighting up. "So, what you looking for?" I tilt my head toward the board.

Her forehead wrinkles as she stands and returns her gaze to the board, her eyes scanning over the advertisements and local news bulletins tacked up.

"Well, I was looking for a painter to help with the outside of the house."

I look at her full pink lips as she speaks, my eyes flicking back up to hers as she turns to face me.

"Also, I..." She tips her head to the side and narrows her eyes at me as though she's not sure about what she's going to say next.

"You what?" I study her as her face relaxes, and she blows out a breath.

"I was thinking about looking for some work while I'm here. Just something short-term to pay for groceries and things."

"Well, Dee"—*I swear I will never get used to calling her that*—"it's your lucky day."

"Why's that?" She tips her head back and gazes up at me, her bright blue eyes waiting.

"Because you bumped into me." I beam at her.

She snorts before it turns into a giggle. "Oh, right, must be my lucky day."

"Calm down." I smirk. "I'm being serious."

Her gaze returns to my face and I detect a flash of curiosity in her eyes.

"Enlighten me then, Blake." She folds her arms across her chest, and it takes every ounce of energy not to drop my eyes to her incredible tits, which are pushed up. "Why exactly is seeing you lucky for me?"

"Your doubt cuts me." I pull my best hurt face at her and the corners of her mouth lift.

Pride swells in my chest that I can still make her smile.

"Carry on, then." She laughs.

"Well." I puff my chest out. "For starters, did you forget my dad has his own home maintenance business?" Her mouth gapes open as though she's about to speak, so I reach my hand up and place a finger over her lips. "He'll do a significantly better job than anyone else you can find, and it'll cost you less. And second, if you're looking for a job, ask Kayla. Her and Trav know just about everyone in this town who runs their own business. They go to all these town meetings and shit. If anyone's got anything going, she'll know."

I take my finger away from Daisy's lips. Her cheeks flush the tiniest bit pink, and she looks down at Betsy.

"That's kind of you, Blake. But I'm sure your dad's busy with clients."

I arch an eyebrow at her as I lean forward into her eyeline, so she has to look at me.

"You're kidding, right? He'd love to help you out. He'll shuffle some stuff around."

Her brow wrinkles as she looks into my eyes.

"Honestly, I can sort it out myself. The same with the job."

I blow out a breath. "Sure, you can, Dee. But that's the beauty of having friends. You don't have to do it alone." I reach out and squeeze her arm.

She bristles under my touch and averts her eyes again.

"Fine," I mutter, dropping my arm from hers and pulling out my cell phone.

"What are you doing?" She glances up at me.

I tap out a message on my phone and hit send.

"That's a text to Dad. Now... Kayla." I type out another message and send it. "Right, sorted. They'll be in touch."

"Blake!" Her mouth drops open. "You didn't have to do that. I could—"

"I know you could. But you wouldn't have. So, I did." I wink at her and then pat my leg, signalling to Betsy it's time to go.

"See you around... swimming in that little bikini," I call over my shoulder as I head back across the street.

I hear her let out a frustrated sigh before she answers. "I wouldn't count on it!"

I raise a hand in a wave, chuckling all the way back to my truck.

Chapter Eight

Daisy

Two days later and I'm standing in front of a building that looks like something out of an upmarket travel magazine. It's a beautiful long white stone structure, set back from the beach. Large Grecian-style pillars stand to attention on either side of the giant double doors, which are wide open, allowing entry into the foyer.

I walk in and my hands fly to my shirt to smooth it down. When Kayla called round following Blake's text and said she knew someone who may give me a short-term job, I expected a small business in town, not the exclusive hotel on the outskirts with its own award-winning spa.

I glance around the foyer. It's got a country club feel about it. It's light and airy, but on closer inspection, the furniture looks comfy, and the people dotted about underneath the central glass domed roof are a mixed bunch. Most of them look like tourists, excitedly discussing the next stop on their list, or business professionals passing through on their way to LA. Overall, I'm pleasantly surprised at the relaxed and welcoming atmosphere.

"Good morning, how can I help?" A young man at the reception desk flashes me a bright smile as I approach.

"Hello. My name's Dee Matthews. I have a meeting with Maria?" My words come out more like a question, highlighting my nerves.

The young man picks up his desk phone and says, "Miss Matthews is here," to whomever it is that answers.

He hangs up and I smile politely, standing to one side as he assists the guest behind me. I don't have to wait long until a woman—not much older than me—wearing an immaculate white pant suit approaches, holding out her arms.

"Dee?"

"Yes. Maria?" I say, holding my hand out to shake hers. Instead, she wraps me into a gentle hug and air kisses both cheeks.

"That's me." She smiles as she draws back to look at me. "You've no idea how happy I was to get your call! Come, walk with me."

I fall into step beside her as she leads us away from the main reception area and down a hallway, where one wall is entirely glass and has views stretching out over the beach and ocean.

"It's spectacular, isn't it?" She inclines her head toward the windows, her long dark hair shining in the light.

"It's beautiful," I answer truthfully. I've always thought Hope Cove was like a paradise.

"I think you forget when you see something every day. Sometimes we need to remind ourselves of the beauty right in front of us." She beams as her heels click against the tile floor. "I'll show you the spa first, obviously. Seeing as that's where you'll be working. And then we can have a drink on the terrace, and we can talk about any questions you might have. Does that sound good?"

I nod gratefully at her. "Yes, that sounds fantastic. Thank you."

"Honestly," she rolls her eyes, "I should thank you. Summer is one of our busiest times of the year in the spa. The worst possible time to be a staff member down. And you know Kayla. So you come highly recommended."

"Yes, I do. We've been friends... we were friends, I mean, we've known each other since we were teenagers."

"Kayla's a lifesaver—*her and Travis.* You wouldn't believe the amount of people who travel with their pets and then need veterinarian help. The two of them have come to the hotel's rescue more than once, let me tell you."

I smile back as Maria opens a door at the end of the corridor and motions for me to step inside. My breath catches in my throat as the scent of lavender and eucalyptus greets me.

"Wow," I say as I look around, warmth spreading in my chest at the delicious familiarity of the scents and sights around me.

Maria grins as she looks around. "Pretty special, isn't it? We like to think so, anyway. Come on, I'll show you around."

I follow her with my mouth open and my eyes wide as I take in the beauty surrounding us. The entire spa has a magical temple feel to it. Cool stone walls, a waterfall trickling down one area and into a long sunken stream, running underneath a Perspex walkway beneath our feet. There is calming, meditative music playing softly in the background, and a gentle whisper of voices from the therapists coming out to greet clients in the waiting area. The entire space is dimly lit, with overhead fairy lights and lanterns providing a soft, atmospheric glow.

"I was impressed when I saw your resume you sent over," Maria says as we walk down a curved walkway, and she shows me inside each private treatment room. They're all beautiful. Orangey glows from natural salt lamps, private showers, massage tables piled high with sumptuous-looking towels. Some rooms even have private sunken bathtubs inside. For the oil baths I saw on their treatment menu; I imagine.

"You were?" I ask as I peer inside yet another incredible room.

"Yes. You're far more qualified than the role requires. Working as a sports massage therapist for one of London's top rugby clubs? That must have been rewarding."

"It was." I force a smile at her as my chest tightens at the mention of my old job. A job I loved.

"I saw you left without giving them the full notice period?" Maria stops and turns to look at me.

I swallow and take a deep breath. "That's true. But I asked for their permission, and I wouldn't have done it if it would have left them in a difficult position."

She nods as she looks at me. "What's his name?"

"Excuse me?"

"I can see from the way your face lit up when we walked in here, Dee. And the way it just did again at the mention of your previous job. You belong here, using your skills, feeding your passion." She smiles kindly at me. "No woman would easily give that up and move across the Atlantic. Not unless she had something she needed to leave behind."

My mouth goes dry as I look back at her.

"Mickey," I whisper.

She narrows her eyes at me and then gives me a kind smile. "Good. Well, it's our gain. When can you start?"

We spend the next hour having a look around the pool area and gardens before Maria takes me to the terrace and we have some incredible non-alcoholic fruit cocktails and matcha tea cake.

I leave feeling on top of the world. Finally, something good is happening again. I can get back to work, doing something I love. Something I wasn't sure I would ever do again just a few months ago.

I start the walk back to the house. My high mood doesn't last long when I see the familiar black, shiny truck pass me and then pull over up ahead.

"Hey, stranger!" Blake calls, opening the door and jumping out.

My heart skips a beat when I see him, and I force the ridiculous fluttering in my stomach back down.

"Hey yourself."

He's wearing old, faded jeans and a light gray t-shirt. He looks like he's spent the morning shovelling soil by the looks of the dirt smeared across them.

He drops his eyes, following my gaze.

"Been helping my dad to get this garden job finished early so he can start on your house."

My heart squeezes as he calls it my house. It feels more like home than anywhere to me. But it will never be mine, no matter how much I wish it could be.

"You want a lift?" He tips his head to his truck, and I can't help but smile at the sight of Betsy sticking her head out the window at me, her pink tongue hanging from her mouth.

"It's okay, thanks. I can walk," I say, brushing off his offer.

"I know you can walk. You've got legs." Blake's eyes roam leisurely down my pencil skirt and calves, down to the sneakers I changed into for the walk home.

His lips curl into a smile.

"I couldn't walk in my heels," I explain as his eyes slowly make their way back up and come to rest on my face. I shiver at the intensity with which he's looking at me and clamp my thighs together as an unfamiliar heat spreads in my core. "I had an interview with Maria," I add, averting my gaze from his.

"How'd it go?"

I chance a look back at his face, and he's waiting patiently for my answer.

"I start tomorrow."

He breaks into a broad grin, his green eyes sparkling.

"That's great! You'll be sticking around, then?"

"For now."

He purses his lips and then pulls them into a straight line, something flashing behind his eyes. "Hop in," he says, turning back to the truck.

"No, really, I'm fine."

"What's the matter, Dee? Worried you'll not be able to keep your hands off me?" He looks at me from behind the passenger door he's holding open.

"Don't flatter yourself, Blake Anderson," I bite back as I climb in.

He closes the door, and chuckles to himself all the way round the truck until he slides into the driver's seat next to me.

I fuss over Betsy, rubbing her ears and patting her on the back. She seems overjoyed to see me, licking at my face and whining.

"I'm only accepting your offer because you have a beautiful dog." Blake's laugh grows louder as I glare at him.

"That's what all the girls say, Dee. They're attracted to my hairy hound." His eyes crinkle at the corners as he pulls back out onto the road and drives.

Later that afternoon, I'm out in the garden, collecting some ingredients to take back into the kitchen, when I see Blake's truck pulling up the driveway.

I stand and watch him come to a stop, wiping the sweat off my brow with the back of my hand. It's a scorcher of an afternoon. Too hot to be out doing this really, but now that I'm starting work at the salon tomorrow, I don't have any other time to work on what I have in mind.

"I've been thinking," Blake announces as he jumps out the truck, followed by Betsy.

"Did it hurt?" I ask, cocking an eyebrow at him.

I swallow as I realize he's wearing a pair of loose shorts, low on his hips, and nothing else. His broad chest is tanned from the sun, and I can see his tattoos. Abstract black ink snaking around his bicep, and more running down his side from his ribs, to below his shorts.

Oh, fuck, he has a V.

I snap my eyes away from the perfect V-shaped channel running down his lower abs, but I'm not fast enough. The smug bastard is grinning at me as I look back up at his face.

"She made a joke!" He cups his hands around his mouth and calls out across the lake. "She made a joke, everyone!"

"Who are you talking to?" I snort, leaning down to pick up my basket of supplies from the grass.

"Anyone who'll hear me." His eyes light up as he looks at me. "Knew you were hiding in there somewhere."

I swallow the lump in my throat as I go to walk past him.

"Excuse me, I've got things I need to be doing."

"Hey, D... Dee." He corrects himself before he calls me Daisy.

I know he's finding it hard not to call me that. After all, it's all he's ever known me as. But I'm not the same girl I was when he knew me. The sooner he accepts that, the better.

"I'm sorry, okay." He gives me his best pathetic look, poking his bottom lip out, and I feel my body relax.

Maybe I'm being too hard on him. We were such good friends once. It must be weird for him—me coming back like this. It sure as hell is weird for me.

"Apology accepted."

"What's in the basket?" He peers down at the chamomile flowers and lemon myrtle I've gathered.

"Ingredients." I pull the basket a little closer to me, aware of how close he's now standing. How close his naked chest is.

"I can see that. What are you doing with them?" He looks up at me.

"You ask a lot of questions, don't you?"

He grins like I've paid him a compliment. "Yep."

I can't help the small smile that creeps across my face. "Fine." I sigh. "Come inside and have a drink, and I'll show you."

"Why, thank you." He gestures at me to lead the way and whistles Betsy to follow.

"Oh, and put a shirt on," I call over my shoulder as I make my way up the steps.

"Why? Are the pecs offending you?" He chuckles.

I shake my head as I go through the back door and into the kitchen. Blake follows a moment later, with a white t-shirt on, Betsy at his side.

"Here you go, beautiful," I say as I place a bowl of fresh water down for Betsy. She pads over and drinks it happily, before finding a cool spot on the tile floor and lying down.

Blake looks around the room, his green eyes scanning over the shelves of the oak dresser where I've placed glass jars containing the few ingredients I've picked from the garden since I arrived. He wanders over to the kitchen table and picks up the one book I brought with me from home.

"You making homebrew, then?" He raises a brow at me.

"Not exactly." I walk over to him and take the book from him, turning to a page I marked. My aunt's handwriting stares back at me from the paper, bringing with it a bittersweet smile.

"I didn't realize you made other things together," Blake says as he watches me carefully.

"We'd only just started, really. Most of the recipes in this book, she wrote to prepare for us to try together. She gave it to me as a gift on my last visit." My voice drops as I run my fingertip over the page.

"I'm sorry." Blake gazes at me intently, his green eyes vibrant.

I stare back into them, a tiny part of me wishing I could dive into them, like the lake outside.

Dive in and never come back up.

"Anyway," I say as I breeze over to the cooker. "You wanted to see what those were for." I point to the basket. "Now I'm going to show you."

His eyes dance in amusement as he watches me tie an apron around myself, emblazoned with 'you kill 'em, we grill 'em' in large black lettering.

"The previous tenants left it," I mutter.

"Hey, did I say anything?" He holds his hands up as his shoulders shake with a suppressed laugh.

"You didn't have to." I give him a small smile.

"It's just ironic, don't you think? You're a vegan, and you're wearing that." He points at the apron and loses the battle, a low chuckle escaping his lips.

"Ha, bloody ha." I narrow my eyes at him.

"So why did you turn vegan?" He studies my face.

My back tenses, and my stomach pulls into a tight knot. "I just did."

"You just did?" He folds his arms, arching an eyebrow at me.

I look across at him, and his eyes soften.

"What is it, Dee?"

I look over at Betsy, dozing on the floor.

"I just saw too much suffering, Blake," I whisper, my throat burning.

Two lines appear between his eyebrows and he drops his arms to his sides, taking a step toward me.

I turn away quickly and grab a pan from the counter, forcing my voice to sound bright. "Let's get started."

An hour later, the house smells amazing. A mix of chamomile and lemon myrtle, from the new body butter we've just made. We melted mango butter and coconut oil in a pan, and then when it had cooled in the refrigerator, we whipped it by hand to make it smooth and fluffy. I think I'm wearing half of it, as is Blake, who now understands why I'd told him to put a shirt on.

"That was strangely satisfying," Blake says, casting his eyes around and surveying the few small jars we've filled.

"Wasn't it?" I unfasten the apron, taking it off and throwing it down on the counter.

I know I'm grinning. Something about doing this, making my own products, just feels so right.

"This is like body butter porn to you, isn't it?" Blake's amused eyes rake over my face.

"Blake!" My hands fly to my cheeks, but my grin remains. "Yes... I love it," I confess quietly as he keeps studying me, his lips pulled into a smile. "They're all vegan friendly, and cruelty free. Much better for the environment too."

"It's great to see you so passionate," he says, his voice low and deliciously deep.

Did he always sound like that?

I shrug my shoulders, suddenly embarrassed.

He takes a step forward, and I freeze as he raises a hand to my face. His long, warm fingers dust across my cheek and his eyes drop to my lips. I'm rooted to the spot, my heart hammering in my chest. No one has been this close to me in a long time.

Not since Mick.

Blake's eyes soften and he smiles as he removes his hand and holds it up in front of my face, a smudge of pale-yellow body butter on it.

"I think I got cream on your face when I was whipping it." He arches an eyebrow at me and smirks.

"Does everything out of your mouth have to sound like a dirty innuendo?" I tut, pretending to sound disgusted, when really my heart's still threatening to gallop right out of my chest.

He grins, his green eyes darkening. "I don't know what you mean. It must be all that swimming. You've got water in your ears."

I roll my eyes and throw the screwed-up apron at him. "Here, you keep it. Call it a souvenir."

He catches it effortlessly before it hits him in the chest and then tips his head back and laughs.

I fight back my own laugh as I look at him through narrowed eyes and feel something stir inside me.

A flicker.

A seed of a memory of what it felt like to be free.

To be Daisy.

Chapter Nine

Blake

"YOU READY FOR YOUR first day?" I call, wrapping my knuckles against the open door.

"God, Blake!" Daisy shrieks from inside the hallway where she's crouching down, putting her sneakers on.

"That's what they all cry out." I chuckle as Daisy composes herself and stands, facing me head-on.

"Seriously? How the hell you have all these women chasing after you is a mystery." She tuts, her hands on her hips.

"Women are chasing after me?" I grin as she rolls her eyes and grabs her bag from the floor.

"You know what I mean. Your fan group, or whatever it's called."

I stand back as Daisy steps out onto the porch and locks the front door, double checking it before she turns to head down the steps.

"Blake's Babes."

"What?" She turns to me, her blue eyes wide.

I shrug a shoulder and lean back against the doorframe. "It's called Blake's Babes."

She stares at me before her eyes light up and she laughs, doubling over to rest her hands on her knees. "Oh," she gasps, trying to catch her breath. "That's... that's..." Her face creases up with laughter again.

I stand and watch her, my lips curled in amusement.

"Thank you, Blake," she says finally, straightening up to look at me. "I'd forgotten how good it felt to laugh. You know, really laugh." She wipes at her eyes.

I push off the doorframe and jog down the steps to her. "Glad to be of service."

She looks up at me, catching her breath, her eyes bright.

"I always loved your laugh." I pause in front of her and watch the shutters come back up over her face.

Her smile drops and her eyes lose their shine.

You idiot.

I pushed her too far.

Whatever brought her back here, she's determined to keep it buried.

"I take it you're planning on walking again?" I look down over her body, hugged by her fitted white dress and down to her sneakers.

"I don't have a car. Besides, I like the exercise, and it's not far."

"Let me give you a lift. Me and Betsy are headed that way." I motion to my truck and to Betsy, her chocolate brown head watching us from the open window.

"Really, I'm fine." She walks off, stopping to give Betsy a fuss before continuing down the driveway.

"C'mon, Dee," I say.

I swear I'm going to screw up and call her Daisy any day now.

"I'm good, Blake," she calls over her shoulder.

"Fucking stubborn..." I mutter under my breath before opening the truck door to let Betsy jump out.

"What are you doing?" Daisy scowls at me as the two of us catch up with her.

"We fancied a walk," I say, striding past her, Betsy by my side.

"You fancied a walk?"

"That's what I said." I flash her a wide grin.

"And I suppose this walk takes you down by the hotel near the beach?" She draws level with me and matches my pace.

"You're really something, Dee. Your powers of deduction are incredible. Do you have a crystal ball or something?"

She snorts, and I sneak a sideways glance at her. Her lips are twitching at the corners, fighting off a smile.

A smile that I put there.

We walk halfway there in silence, just listening to the sounds of the forest on our right, and the ocean in the distance on our left. Betsy runs off ahead, darting from tree to tree along the side of the track, sniffing at anything that grabs her attention.

"You know, I've always loved the sound of the ocean. It makes me think of all the times I came here to visit. It calms me somehow."

I look over at Daisy and her brows are pulled together, as though she's lost in a memory.

"I listen to it on an app on my phone every night before I go to bed. Is that silly?" She turns to look up at me, her crystal blue eyes searching mine.

I swallow. "That's not silly at all. Why would you think it is?"

She sighs and I watch as her eyes cloud over with something before she looks away.

"I don't sleep well, Blake. The sound helps me."

"You used to sleep just fine. I remember many nights you and Kayla woke me and Trav up snoring your heads off in the tent."

Daisy smiles at the mention of the nights we all camped out together during those long, hot summers.

"So, what happened?"

She shakes her head and keeps her gaze focussed straight ahead.

"Bad choices, Blake. That's what happened. Ones I can never take back."

I stop walking and take hold of her arm gently, turning her so she has to look at me.

"We all make mistakes. You can't let them dictate your future."

Her eyes flick back and forth between mine, two creases appearing between her brows as I stroke the bare skin of her upper arm with my thumb.

"I don't know how not to," she whispers, her eyes filling with unshed tears.

"Hey, hey." I pull her to me and wrap my arms around her tiny frame, pressing my nose into her hair and inhaling as I hold her. She smells of fresh flowers, and all things sweet.

She stiffens and presses the flats of her hands against my chest, pushing me back.

"I'm sorry, I totally ruined what should have been an enjoyable walk."

I try to pull her back into my arms, but she takes a step back. "There's no need to apo—"

"There is. I'm sorry, Blake." She turns and walks off. "Thank you for the company. I'm going to walk the rest alone," she calls over her shoulder.

I stand glued to the spot as I watch her disappear up the road and around the corner. Betsy trots over and sits next to me, her dark brown eyes looking up.

"Come on, girl. Let's go." I turn, and we walk back home.

"Great job, son. Thanks for your help." My dad wipes his brow with the back of his hand as he loads up his van.

"Thanks, Dad. I know you had to shuffle a lot to squeeze this job in."

"Ah, don't be silly, Blake. It's no bother at all." Dad shuts the back of the van up. "Besides, Iris's niece could do with someone helping her out."

"What do you mean?" I grab a bottle of water out of the cooler in my truck and hand it to him.

He twists the lid off and takes a long drink.

"Iris used to worry about her a lot. There wasn't a nice crowd where she lived. That's why she used to come here every vacation. Her parents were so worried about her falling in with the wrong people. I thought about her a lot after Iris passed. Wondered how she was getting on."

I look up at the house as I lean back against my truck, the metal hot against my back from the day's sun. The fresh, bright white paint is brilliant under the clear blue sky.

"She was getting on fine, Dad. She trained in sports therapy and massage and got a job at one of the big rugby clubs. That's before she stopped using social media. After that, I don't know."

I blow out a breath as I think about how, although she's back, she's different. She's less open, less free.

Just... less *Daisy*.

"Well, things can happen that mold you, Blake. But you'll never be changed completely. She'll find her way through whatever she's dealing with. I'm sure you'll help her." He looks over at me and smiles. "You were good friends once, Blake. She just needs help to remember."

I open my mouth to ask what he means, but he stands, his eyes lighting up.

"Ah, speak of the devil!" Dad grins and walks down to meet Daisy as she comes back up the driveway. "How was your first week?"

She grins at him and then looks over at me, our eyes meeting for a fleeting moment, before she turns her attention back to Dad.

"It was fantastic, Bill. Thank you for asking. And thank you for all your hard work!" Her eyes widen as she looks past him and up at the house. "It's incredible! It looks just like it did when..." Her voice trails off.

"I know." My dad pats her hand. "Your aunt would be so proud of you."

She dips her head down and runs her fingers along her forehead. "Thanks, Bill."

Dad turns and raises a hand. "See you, Blake. Betsy." He nods to Betsy, who's laid down in the shade underneath my truck.

"Take care of yourself." He lowers his voice to Daisy, and then he climbs in his van and drives off.

"So, good first week, then?" I ask as Daisy walks toward me.

"Yeah, it was." Her cheeks are sun-kissed and her eyes bright. "It feels good to be doing something I enjoy again. Kayla insisted we go out tonight for a drink to celebrate."

"Yeah, she told me."

She cocks her head to the side. "Does everyone know everyone's business around here?"

I grin. "You better get used to it."

She bites her lip and I lift my hand and pull it from between her teeth, watching her eyes widen as my fingers brush the soft skin on her neck as I draw my hand back.

"Have fun tonight. You deserve it." I give her a wink as Betsy and I get into the truck.

She stands and watches us leave, never moving.

When I look back at her in the rear-view mirror, she's still watching us, her fingertips pressed to her lips.

Chapter Ten

Daisy

"Do you have to wax old guys' hairy ball sacks?"

I almost spit out my drink as I cough. "Kayla! What? No! I do the massage therapy."

"Thank fuck for that." She tips her head back and downs her drink. "Another, please." She signals to the bartender.

A young woman comes and takes our glasses and replaces them with two full, fresh ones, her eyes lingering on my face.

"Thanks, Cindy." Kayla grins.

I watch her head back down to the other end of the bar. I forgot what it was like being in a small town like Hope Cove. She's probably wondering who the newcomer with the terrible DIY dyed hair is.

"You're enjoying it, then?" Kayla clinks her glass against mine, taking a sip and screwing her nose up. "God, can you please dig out one of your aunt's homebrew recipes? Then we won't have to drink this stuff... Jesus." She winces.

Despite being at the other end of the bar, Cindy throws Kayla a look, which has her mouthing, *Sorry*.

"Seriously, though," she whispers. "This stuff is like drain cleaner in comparison."

I stare into my glass at the clear liquid. She's right. My aunt's homebrewed gin would wipe the floor with this mass-produced version. But it's all we've got right now, so I take another large gulp, sucking in a breath as the burn courses down my throat.

I'm glad she talked me into coming out with her tonight. This entire week has been good for me. Being at the spa with Maria and the other therapists, and sitting here now, the heat from the liquor loosening up the coil I've been wound into for months. It feels great. For the first time in months, I'm remembering what it's like to not feel as though I'm teetering on a knife's edge. One that's ready to slash me whichever way I move.

"What? We're supposed to be celebrating, aren't we?" I laugh as Kayla grins at the sight of me knocking back another mouthful.

"Yes, we are! Come on then, tell me." Her eager eyes study my face, waiting for me to speak.

"It's great, Kayla. Really great." I can't help the warmth spreading in my chest as I talk about the spa. "It's really beautiful and so tranquil. Maria has created something so amazing there. I'm not surprised she's won all those awards. It's like stepping into an en-chanted temple where time stops, and your troubles don't exist."

"It's great, isn't it? Travis took me there for our last wedding anniversary."

My chest tightens, and I look down at the dark wood of the bar as I blink.

"I'm so sorry I never wished you a happy anniversary. Or for the others I missed before. I never even saw you on your wedding day." I lift my eyes to meet Kayla's, expecting her to be mad. I deserve it. What kind of friend keeps in touch for years and then disappears one day without a word?

Her brows lift and she reaches over, pulling me into her.

"Don't be silly. You were back in England and we were young and broke. I never expected you to make it to the wedding."

"It's not the point." I sniff as she lets me go and I sink back onto the bar stool, the room spinning slightly. "I've been such a shit friend."

I stare up at the framed photograph behind the bar to steady myself. It's a picture of Hope Cove, taken from up high in the forest somewhere. You can see the coast stretching round. The hotel at the farthest point of the beach. The town's main street. The lake. I swallow down the lump in my throat as I look at the small gray roof next to the lake. I wonder when this photo was taken. Was my aunt still alive then? Was she out in her garden? Sitting on the porch? Was I there with her, mixing up another experiment in the kitchen? Was I still the girl who believed in all things good, and pure, and sweet?

Kayla's eyes follow my gaze, and she opens her mouth as if to comment on the picture, but instead, she frowns before turning toward me.

"Why *did* you disappear from social media? We could at least talk before. None of us knew what happened to you."

I stare back into her eyes. They're kind, waiting, but not forcing anything out of me. I should at least explain something, even if I can't bring myself to say all the words out loud. I knock back another gulp of liquid courage and take a deep breath.

"I met a guy. His name was Mick. Ironic really." My voice slurs slightly. "Mickey and Daisy. We sound like two cartoon characters. But nothing about him was fun. Not in the end." I let out a humorless laugh as my eyes wander around the bar.

Herbies is a nice place. I can see why the locals like it. It's all dark wood, a long bar, deep booth seating, a TV playing in the corner. It's not trying to be anything fancy. It just is what it is, and it's proud of it. It's a warm, welcoming hug after being caught in a thunderstorm without a coat. There are a few other people in here, catching up with one another, their conversations quiet.

I refocus on Kayla, blinking as the gin gives me another head rush.

"Mick didn't like me being online. He was... he'd get jealous. In the beginning, I thought it was romantic. I thought it must be because he loved me so much."

Kayla nods, resting her elbow on the bar and cradling her chin in her hand.

"But it got to the point where he didn't like what I wore, or if I went out without him. I had an amazing job I loved, working for a rugby club as the team sports therapist. I helped them look after themselves, deal with injuries, that sort of thing."

"Sounds like a hard job. All those fit guys in shorts." Kayla raises her brows at me with a small smile.

I smile back. "Yeah. It had its perks. But I loved helping the team. It wasn't about anything else to me. But Mick... he didn't like it. He thought I was going to leave him and start a relationship with one of them."

"He sounds like an insecure jerk." Kayla takes another mouthful of her drink. "Is that why you came over here? To nurse a broken heart?"

"No. I came to sort my aunt's house out before it's put on the market," I say unconvincingly, dropping my gaze back to my glass. It's empty again. I don't even remember finishing it.

Kayla signals to Cindy, who comes to refill it.

What is this? Number four now? Five? I've lost count.

Cindy looks me up and down as she pours. I smile back. But she just purses her lips before heading off to serve someone else. For a bartender, she isn't too friendly.

"No offence, but you always were a shit liar." Kayla grins before I can ask her what Cindy's problem is.

Despite myself, I laugh. "Yeah?"

"Yep. Like that time you put shaving foam under Travis' car door handles, so it squirted out everywhere when he went to open it. You swore it was Blake."

"It was!" I laugh again, my eyes lighting up. "I swear, it was him. It was his foam."

"That just happened to make its way into your hands?" Kayla smirks at me.

I shake my head. Blake and I were as much to blame as each other. That was such a great day. We all spent the day on my aunt's jetty, swimming in the lake.

I let out a deep sigh, swirling the liquid in my glass. It looks out of focus. I should have stopped with the last one.

"So, you're here to mend your broken heart after breaking up with a jerk. We should drink to that!" Kayla grins at me, and I shake my head as I frown at my drink.

Fuck it.

What harm is one more going to do? It'll only get poured down the sink otherwise. Although, from Kayla's earlier words, that's where it belongs.

I raise my glass and tip my head back. A strange, breathy growl escapes my lips as my throat stings.

"Hell, Dee. Trav said he'll give us a lift home, but you're going to need carrying at this rate." Kayla's mouth drops open as I slam my glass back down on the counter.

"I can sling her in the back of my truck," a deep voice says.

I spin on my stool, a sudden wave of heat rushing to my head as the alcohol takes a firm hold over my senses.

"Hey, Blake." I don't know why, but I lean forward and place my palm against his solid chest. "What are you doing here?"

His green eyes dance in amusement as he watches me.

"Coming to have a drink with you, now that I've finished teaching my class. Looks like you've had a good head start, eh?"

I ignore him as my eyes drop over his khaki t-shirt and faded jeans to the boots on his feet. My hand is still glued firmly to his chest, relishing the heat radiating into my palm from his body.

"Where are the teeny, tiny shorts that have all the women staring at your thighs?" I slur.

Kayla snorts back a giggle behind me.

Blake's dark brows rise as he smiles, a flash of his perfect white teeth showing.

"Don't go smiling at me like that. I've seen them. They're huge. What do you eat for breakfast? Rocks?" I giggle suddenly, thinking I'm hilarious.

"I think the lift home might be a good idea," Kayla says as she gets up and pats Blake on the shoulder. She leans down and gives me a hug. "See you, Dee."

I watch as she heads toward the exit where Travis has just appeared. She says something to him and they both look over in our direction before giving us a wave and heading out the door.

"Travis didn't even get a drink." I sigh in exaggerated sympathy. "You want another one with me, though, don't you, Blake?" I turn my attention back to him.

He leans close, placing one hand over mine on his chest, and the other on my lower back.

"I think it's time we drive back home. With the windows down. You look like you could do with some air." His warm breath tickles my neck and I sigh as he guides me off the stool and to my feet.

"You smell good, Blake Anderson. What is that?" I turn to face him and wrap my arms up around his neck, burying my face into his neck below his chin and inhaling deeply.

A mix of wood and sea salt.

"I just showered," he says, his voice making his neck vibrate against my cheek.

"So, it's just clean, then?" I draw back to look at him, swaying a little. "Mr. Clean." I snort as I erupt into giggles. "I thought you were Mr. 'let's get dirty' Wild?"

"Okay, Daisy," he says, a smile spreading over his face as he turns me and wraps a muscular arm around my waist so he can help me walk.

I'm really not that drunk. I'm just at that nice stage of tipsy where everything feels warm and wonderful. But I don't want to tell Blake that. His arm feels too good wrapped around my body.

"Who's Daisy?" I blow out a breath, catching the eye of a man drinking at the bar as we approach the exit. "Excuse me. Do you know who Daisy is?"

He looks back at me in confusion before his eyes meet Blake's.

"It's okay, Greg. She's my friend. Who seems to have had one too many celebratory drinks. Wait until I talk to Kayla." He looks down at me, his brows raised as he smirks.

I shake my head and throw my arms wide. Blake tightens his grip around me.

"Has anyone seen Daisy?" I call out to the bar in delight. "We've lost an English girl!"

I catch sight of the bartender, Cindy, with her arms crossed, her eyes fixed on Blake.

"Thank you for the drinks!" I grin at her. "Gin for the win!" I punch up in the air as Blake ushers me out.

The night air hits me in the face, sobering me a little, and I take deep, greedy breaths as Blake walks us over to his truck and lifts me into the passenger seat. He leans over me and fastens my seatbelt, his face inches from mine.

"There. Can't have you falling out, can we?" He grins at me and then heads round, jumping into the driver's side and starting the engine.

"Okay, little Miss Gin. I think we'll take the scenic route home. It'll give you time to sober up. Here." He passes me a bottle of water he's screwed the top off. "Drink this."

"Are you always this bossy?" I turn my head to look at him.

He smirks and shakes his head as he starts the engine.

"Why? Do you like it?"

"I haven't decided yet. Is it Mr. Clean or Mr. Dirty I'm talking to?" I snort as a whole fresh wave of giggles rise and I let my head fall back against the headrest as I drink the water.

Blake doesn't say anything. He just winds down the windows like he said he would. I lean my head on my arms on the door-frame, gazing at the stars in the clear night sky as we drive.

"Can't believe you have your own fan club," I mutter as we drive along the road, through town and along the beachfront. He wasn't lying. He is taking us the long way home. I let out a sigh and finish the water.

My head is still warm, but only a little fuzzy as we pull up outside my aunt's house. I'm feeling more awake and a lot less giggly.

A lot more in control.

"Stay right there," Blake says, hopping out and coming around to open my door.

He leans over me to unfasten my seatbelt, and I hold my breath, studying the side of his face. His eyes look dark in the moonlight, faint creases at their corners from where he smiles so much.

Before I can stop myself, I lift my hand and dust my fingertips over the lines, tracing them. Blake stills as my seatbelt unlocks. The click and noise of it retracting are the only sounds echoing around the truck. He turns his face toward me, and I remember to breathe again, my chest rising and falling in the small space between us as I look back into his eyes and wet my lips with my tongue.

It's probably only a couple of seconds, but I swear my heart skips a beat as his eyes drop to follow my tongue.

"C'mon, let's get you inside." He moves back and takes my hand, helping me down from the truck.

I'm much steadier on my feet since leaving the bar, so he doesn't put his arm around me, just keeps his hand wrapped firmly around mine as he leads me up the steps and stops in front of the door.

"Will you be okay from here?" His eyes drop from my eyes to my lips and back up again.

Something stirs in my core, and suddenly I don't want this night to end.

I don't want him to go anywhere.

"Will you help me into bed if I say no?" I bite my lip and look up at him from under my lashes.

Despite the earlier gin haze, my body and mouth seem very insistent on what they want.

They want him.

Blake grits his teeth together and lets out a sound between a growl and a sigh as he runs his free hand through his hair and looks away.

My cheeks heat and my throat burns.

"I'm sorry. I shouldn't have said that. I know how... I've never forgotten."

His eyes come back to mine. "Never forgotten what?"

I stare back at him as I force myself to whisper the words. "That you don't want that. You didn't want to kiss me ten years ago on my last night here, so why would you want it now?"

I can't help feeling that I sound like a sulky teenager with my confession.

His eyes widen and his mouth drops open as if my words have shocked him.

I can't believe I just said that out loud. All these years I've kept my pass at Blake that night a closely guarded secret. Admittingly, it's not news to him. But now that I've opened my mouth, the knowledge that I remember it is no longer a secret. And not only that, but now he knows I still think about it.

I pull my hand from his, turning to the door and searching in my pockets for the key. I just want to open it and get inside. Forget this entire conversation ever happened. Maybe I can even pretend I don't remember it? He knows I've had a few drinks. Maybe Blake will buy that if I just play dumb next time I see him.

"Turn around." His voice is gruff as he lowers his lips to my ear.

I hesitate as goosebumps scatter up my spine and over my arms.

"I said. Turn. Around." His breath vibrates over the back of my neck as I swallow and turn back to face him slowly.

He rests both of his hands against the door, leaning forward and trapping me between his arms.

"You think I didn't kiss you that night because I didn't *want* to?" His brow creases as his eyes burn into mine with an intensity I've never seen before.

Not in him. Not in anyone.

I gulp and nod as I lift my chin to look up at him. He's so close; our foreheads are almost touching. My body feels like it's about to be lit on fire with the heat radiating from him. One final spark and I'll be engulfed.

His next words appear to be planned carefully before they leave his lips.

"I didn't kiss you that night because you'd been drinking. And you were my friend. What kind of creep would that have made me if you'd regretted it the next day?" His jaw tenses as he watches me, waiting for me to speak.

I open my mouth and stare at him.

"And now?" I ask, my voice barely audible.

He flexes his arms and his biceps bulge, the movement causing the tattoo on his arm to ripple, catching my attention from the corner of my eye.

"And now you've been drinking. And you're still my friend."

He stares down at me, not moving any closer, but not moving away, either. The wood of the door is hard against my back as my body tingles in anticipation under his gaze.

If I die now by spontaneous human combustion, then at least I will die knowing what being this close to him feels like.

"What if I won't regret it in the morning?" I whisper.

He sucks in a breath and takes a long pause before hissing out. "You don't know that."

I stand up straighter, so my breasts press against his. "We're not seventeen anymore, Blake. We're both adults."

"What are you saying?" he forces out, his eyes burning into mine like green fire.

Magical. Wild.

I gaze up at him and am overwhelmed with emotion. I don't want to think about the past few years. I don't want to think about what's waiting for me back in England. I don't want to think about what I wish I could forget.

I don't want to think at all.

All I want is to be here.

In this moment.

With him.

My breath hitches in my throat as I look into his eyes.

"I'm saying I want you, Blake. I want you to make me *feel.*"

My words are like the last hit, pushing through his restraint. That final strike of a match that erupts into fire. A low growl sounds in his throat as he pushes forward and crashes his lips onto mine. They're soft and warm.

And urgent.

Blake Anderson kisses me like I'm the last lungful of oxygen the world has to give.

My hands wrap around the back of his neck as I pull him closer. He bends his elbows, his hands still firmly against the door as he leans into me, pressing his giant, solid body against mine. I gasp as his unmistakable erection presses against my lower stomach.

"Open the door," he bites out, his mouth dropping to my neck and trailing scorching hot kisses from my ear to my collarbone.

I pull my hands from his neck and fish out my key from my jean pocket, turning in the tiny space between his arms to slide it into the lock. His arms finally move, giving me room to open the door. He presses against my back, one hand coming up to hold my throat, the other grasping my hip.

"Are you sure you want this?" His voice is rough, sending a shiver down my spine.

God, if one kiss and him talking to me has this effect, what the hell is sex with him going to be like?

"Yes," I murmur as the throbbing between my legs wracks up a notch.

"You don't sound sure." His grip on my neck tightens as he strokes the underside of my jaw with his thumb.

Fuck.

"Yes!" I cry as a wave of arousal rushes to me, making my core shudder.

He spins me quickly, lifting me up into his arms and striding into the hallway, kicking the door shut behind us. I wrap my legs up around his waist and hook my ankles at his back as I snake my arms around his neck and sink my hands into his hair.

He stops at the bottom of the stairs, his eyes searching mine.

"You can change your mind. It's okay."

I look at his eyes, dark with desire, and his rock-hard cock is pressing into the underside of my ass. He wants this as much as I do.

"Stop fucking stalling, Blake. I've said yes."

I drag my hands through his hair as I lower my lips to his and try to demonstrate with my kiss just how much I meant that word.

Yes.

He draws back, and his eyes have taken on a dangerous glint. He carries me up the stairs and into the bedroom while I fight to control the urge to tear my clothes off and tell him to do whatever the hell he wants with me. I've never ached for someone to touch me so badly. Every nerve ending in my body seems to be screaming out for him.

Blake Anderson. Blake Anderson.

We stop in front of the bed, and Blake releases his grip on me. I slide slowly down his body and place my feet back on the floor.

His eyes drop to the waistband of my jeans as he brushes a finger up under my t-shirt and exposes my stomach.

"You're fucking perfect," he whispers in awe as he balls the fabric up in his fist and pulls me to him.

His mouth finds mine again in the perfect mix of heat and pressure. I moan against his lips as his tongue takes control of me, making my breath stall.

Blake Anderson was made for kissing.

He lets out a low groan as his hands run up the sides of my body, taking my t-shirt off over my head with them.

I'm already short of breath as I pull back to look at him. His eyes are on my breasts and my nipples harden beneath the fabric of my bra in response to the hunger in them. I keep my eyes on his face as I push his t-shirt up over his hard stomach. He reaches one hand behind his neck and yanks it off.

I should have been ready for the sight of him after seeing him that morning in his sweatpants. But nothing could have prepared me for Blake Anderson here, in front of me, in the flesh.

"Blake..." My mouth drops open as my eyes roam over every curve of his torso. Every muscle, every line of dark ink, which only looks darker in the moonlit room.

He's a work of art.

His lips pull into a smile as he leans down to kiss me, one hand reaching around and unsnapping my bra with ease. It falls to the floor, freeing my nipples, which are tight, pleading to be touched.

I let out a strangled gasp as his hands move over my breasts, rolling my nipples between his thumb and finger.

"Fucking hell," he groans before dipping his head and wrapping his hot mouth and tongue around them. He sucks and I arch my back, crying out as a wave of pleasure floods my body.

"Blake, just you doing that... God, you're making me so wet," I pant, tilting my head back and allowing myself to become lost in the sensation.

He pauses. "Fuck, you're killing me here. You can't say things like that to a man. Not unless you want to be fucked hard." His voice sounds strained as he continues his exploration of my tits.

I let out a moan. God, yes, I want that. I want him to fuck me and not hold back. I want him to take control of me with so much force that I can't even think straight.

I *need* it.

"I do," I moan, grabbing handfuls of his hair and dragging his face back up to mine. "I do want that."

His eyes darken, and his brows knit together as he looks at me. He's so restrained. So in control. Whereas I feel like I could fall apart at any second if he doesn't touch me.

I push myself against him, so my nipples press into his chest. I hear him suck in a breath.

"Blake," I whisper, "I want *everything* you can possibly give me."

He groans. It starts deep inside his chest as he unbuttons my jeans and I grab at his. By the time he has me in just my panties, and him in his boxers, his groan has turned into a hiss caught between gritted teeth.

"It won't be gentle," he says as he pushes his boxers down and grabs his thick cock in his hand, pumping it slowly.

I can't help staring at it. It's like the rest of his body.

Big. Broad. Powerful.

"Perfect," I answer as I wriggle out of my panties and stand naked in front of him.

He looks at me one last time, as though fighting the ultimate battle in his head about what we're about to do. Then his jaw clenches, and he pushes me back on the bed, climbing over me.

"Fuck," I cry out as he pushes two thick fingers inside me, stretching me wide. My body gives in like a submissive animal that's met their alpha, and wetness rushes to him, coating his fingers and making them slick. The sound of it carries around the room as he finger-fucks me slowly, his thumb tracing circles over my clit.

"God, Blake, I can't... I can't." I throw my head back and grab fistfuls of the bedsheet by my sides as pressure builds inside me.

"You can't what?" he murmurs, his breath hot against my nipples where his mouth is.

"I can't stop... it's so... God," I groan as my body stiffens and I push off the bed, lifting my hips to meet his fingers. "It's too much... Blake," I plead with him, but I'm not sure what it is I'm pleading for.

A release? Mercy? More?

He slides down my body and gives me a wicked grin as he buries his head between my legs. He replaces his thumb with the flat of his tongue, pressing it up against my swollen clit as I writhe underneath him.

"You taste so damn sweet," he groans, placing open-mouthed kisses all over me and then sucking my clit.

"Blake!" I scream as I shudder underneath him, the pressure finally reaching its peak as I come hard on his face. He uses his free hand to push my leg down so he can swirl his tongue over me and push his fingers deeper. The muscles in my core spasm around them as sweat breaks out on my hairline.

I pant, fighting to control the waves of pleasure taking control of my body. As they slow, my fists loosen their grip on the sheets. Blake slides his fingers out and moves back up, so his face is almost touching mine, a wide grin taking over his face.

"You taste so fucking good when you come." He leans down and swipes his tongue through my lips so I can share my taste with him. "I could drink up your pussy's orgasms all night," he growls as he nips my bottom lip between his teeth.

My clit throbs at his words, and I let go of the sheets and wrap one hand around his neck, deepening our kiss as I wrap my other hand around his thick cock.

God, he's big.

My body is aching deep in my core with the need to have him inside me. I run my hand up and down, dragging his tip against me, covering it in my wetness. I circle my hips, moaning as I slip just the head of him inside me and back out again.

"You feel so good." I smile against his lips.

"I'm not going to be able to stop myself if you keep doing that," Blake hisses as I circle myself back down over the head of his cock again.

I want to feel him. Every inch of him. Inside me. Connecting with me. If he stops now, I swear I will implode.

There will be nothing left of me.

"There's never been anyone else like that, Blake." I inch down onto him a little further before pulling him back out again.

I mean it. The thought of having bare sex has never entered my mind before.

Before Blake. The Blake I have known almost my entire life.

"Fuck," he hisses, his arms shaking.

"Is that the same for you?" I whisper in his ear, breathing in his fresh, woody scent as I rub the head of his cock against me again.

"Yes," he forces out through gritted teeth. "But I don't want you to feel—"

Before he can say anything more, I hold the base of him and lift my hips, so he slides further inside me.

He lets out a deep groan and pushes all the way forward, knocking the air from my lungs as he buries himself deep.

I throw my head back, savoring the fullness his thick cock is providing. I thought I'd struggle to take him so easily, but my body knows what it wants and sends a new rush of wet arousal all around him.

"God, you feel incredible!"

"You've no idea how many times I've thought about you, beneath me like this," he says as he lifts his chin and slams into me.

My eyes meet his, but I don't have time to consider his words. All I can do is drop my mouth open and watch as he fucks me.

And I mean *fucks* me.

Blake Anderson fucking is like watching a dark, intense god command an entire existence.

Created specially to do it.

Every muscle in his body ripples and tenses as he rises onto his fists and pumps into me, slamming me down into the mattress, his dark, hungry eyes never leaving mine. My body craves him, sucking him in greedily, hungry for him—*starved.*

I put my hands over his fists and grip on, my knuckles turning white as he drives his cock deeper with each hit. It's almost more than I can stand, as my body trembles from head to toe.

"Blake, I'm going to..." The familiar tightening winds inside me, before it snaps, and I buck underneath him, coming with a force that makes me scream out his name again.

He screws his face up. "Oh, God, I can feel you clamping down on my cock when you come. It's fucking incredible!"

He thrusts into me harder, deeper, forcing his cock in as far as it will reach. I'm thrown up the bed underneath him as his heavy balls hit my skin. Sweat glistens on his chest as he pulls one hand out from underneath mine and slams his palm against the wall above the headboard with a loud thud.

"Daisy! Oh, fuck, Daisy!"

He drives into me as his orgasm explodes, ripping through him as he groans and every muscle in his body tenses. At that moment, he snaps his eyes open, and they burn into mine, stealing the breath straight from my lungs.

Then searing heat spreads inside me, filling every fiber of my soul.

Branding me forever.

I thought Blake Anderson was made for kissing.

But after this sight, I know he was made for fucking... and every filthy thing in between.

All I can do is lie in wonder, staring into his deep green eyes.

My body exhausted.

My mind in awe.

For the first time in months, I'm not in the past. I'm not anything other than right here, right now.

In the present moment.

With him.

Chapter Eleven

Blake

"HEY, DAISY?" I MURMUR, pulling her back against my chest and pressing a kiss to the soft, silky skin on her shoulder.

She stirs in my arms but doesn't wake.

I gently slide my arm from underneath her and roll onto my back on the bed, blowing out a breath.

Did that really happen?

I look over at her, sleeping soundly.

I just had sex with my childhood friend.

Correction. I just had sex with my childhood friend who's come back after a decade.

And I loved it.

I fucking *loved* it.

Every. Fucking. Second.

I prop myself up on an elbow and watch her chest rise and fall as she breathes. She looks so peaceful when she's asleep. The constant anxiety and apprehension I've seen on her face—smiles that don't meet her eyes, chewing on her lip—are gone. She looks so much more like the Daisy I know.

I lean over and brush a strand of dark hair from her face. I wonder why she cut it and dyed it. She always loved her long, blonde hair—braiding it and weaving daisy flowers through it. It would catch the sunlight and shine like a halo around her.

Her brows pull together and her eyes screw up as my fingers linger in her hair.

"Stop, Mickey." Her voice is tiny, quiet as the breeze, as it breaks through from her dream.

I pull my hand back, unease clawing at my chest from the way she sounds.

Scared.

"It's just me, Daisy," I whisper.

"Blake... Blake Anderson." A small giggle dances from her lips before she falls quiet again, returning to a deep sleep.

I shake my head with a silent chuckle. I'm glad I amuse her. Even if she must be semi-conscious to do so.

The clock on the bedside table reads 00:50. I need to get back to Betsy. She's a wonderful dog, and she's happy to sleep outside on the back porch sometimes, especially on hot summer nights. But I know she'll be waiting for me, wondering where I am. I never leave her all night.

I take one last look at Daisy, relieved that she seems to be sleeping soundly now, her face calm once again. Then I get up and move around the room as quietly as possible, retrieving my clothes and going out onto the landing to get dressed.

The keys are on the floor by the front door, dropped by Daisy when I lifted her up and carried her in. I let myself out and lock it behind me, posting the keys back through the mail slot. One last glance up at her bedroom window, and I climb into my truck and head home.

Betsy and I do our usual run the next morning and beat our personal best by two minutes forty.

"Way to go, girl. We smashed it!" I beam at her as I do some stretches.

My eyes wander over to Daisy's house. There's no way of knowing if she's even up yet. I glance at my watch. It's still early by most people's standards. I've got time to take a shower before I head over and see her.

I can't wipe the grin off my face. What a fucking amazing night. Unexpected. But amazing.

I lean down and ruffle Betsy's ears.

"You, my little champ, can have steak for breakfast today."

Despite being worn out from our run, the mention of the word 'steak' has Betsy springing to her feet and bounding behind me into the house. She only usually gets it on special occasions, but even so, she's learned the word perfectly. I laugh as she looks up at me, her tail going crazy.

"All right, all right. I'll get your breakfast first and then have a shower."

Twenty minutes later, the two of us are standing on Daisy's doorstep, waiting.

Nothing.

I take a couple of steps back and shield my eyes from the sun as I look up at her bedroom window. The curtains are open, which would indicate she's up. But were they open last night?

Fuck, I can't remember.

All I can remember is her.

Her smell. Her touch. Her taste.

I reach forward and knock on the door again. We're only met with silence from inside the house.

"C'mon, Betsy. She's not home."

Betsy gets up and pads behind me to the truck, her head down, looking as disappointed as I feel.

Maybe she's in there, ignoring us. Would she do that? She said she wouldn't regret it in the morning. But she'd had a few drinks. What if she was more drunk than I realized? But she sure didn't seem like it. In fact, she was insistent about what she wanted.

I look over at the house one more time and rub my hand across my jaw as we climb into the truck and leave.

"Hey, man." I slap an arm around Trav's shoulders as we greet each other before sliding into the booth seat at the diner.

"Hey. You got Dee home okay last night?"

"Yeah." I smile and pick up the menu, pretending to read it, even though we've been coming here our whole lives and I know it better than the back of my hand.

Trav's palm slaps down over it, pushing it onto the tabletop as he studies my face.

"What aren't you telling me?" His eyes widen. "Blake!" he hisses, lowering his voice and leaning forward. He glances around the diner, tipping his head in greeting to one local we both know, before honing his gaze back on to me. "Tell me you didn't."

I shrug. "I didn't."

He drops back in his seat and blows out a breath. "Thank fuck, man. I mean. She's our friend."

I don't take this opportunity to remind him that Kayla was also our friend—before he married her.

"I know that." I look at him, and he narrows his eyes at me, leaning forward again.

"So why do you have that smug-as-shit look on your face that you get whenever you get laid? Did you hook up with Cindy again?"

"What? No! I told you that was finished." I frown at him.

He clasps his hands together in front of his chin and runs his index fingers over his lips as he thinks.

"Okay. I believe that. Because you never looked like this afterward. You're like extra smug as shit today. With an extra lump of shit thrown on top."

"Thanks for the detailed comparison." I smirk at him.

He's still studying me. I know he will not let this drop.

"You said you didn't?" he says again slowly so it sounds more like a question.

I shrug my shoulders at him again. "You said tell me you didn't, so I did."

"But did you tell me you didn't because you actually didn't? Or did you tell me you didn't because I told you to tell me you didn't?" Travis says.

"What the fuck, man? You've lost me." I chuckle as I throw my hands up in the air.

He fixes me with his serious look, brows pulled down, eyes slanted. "Blake. Did you have sex with Dee last night?"

I run a hand over my jaw as I consider his question.

"Well, that's a tough one to answer. Because I'm still getting to know this Dee who's come back into town... but Daisy... Now, I know Daisy." I grin at Travis as he drops his head to the table and lets it bang against the hard surface.

"God, kill me now," he mutters.

"I don't think it works like that, Trav." I smirk as he lifts his head and scowls at me. "Okay, fine." I lower my voice. "Yes, okay. I had sex with Daisy last night."

"Blake!" He raises his voice, which gathers the attention of some of the other diners.

I lift a hand in apology as Trav decides now is a good time to give me shit for something I do not—and will not—ever regret.

"Doesn't your dick get enough action with all the tourists that pass through, and until recently, with Cindy?" he hisses.

"Hey. It wasn't about giving my dick action!" I fire back, glaring at him.

"Then what the hell was it, Blake? I've known you for years. You've done some stupid shit, but this tops it." He shakes his head.

"It was..." I blow out a breath, dropping my head to stare at the table. "It felt right, man. I don't know how else to describe it."

When I raise my eyes to meet his, Travis stares at me like I've grown an extra head.

"What does she think about it all? I mean..." He lifts his brows as he studies my face. "How was she this morning? Is this something she wants to make a thing? I mean, she's going back to England soon, isn't she?"

I let out a deep sigh and stare out the window. The server, Helen, who's one of the duo who runs the diner, comes over and takes our order. Despite my appetite suddenly waning, I order a turkey sandwich and smile at her as she heads back to the kitchen.

"I don't know how Daisy is," I say to Travis as I look back at him. "She wasn't there when me and Betsy stopped by this morning."

Travis slants his eyes at me again, the serious expression firmly back. "Called around this morning? Didn't you stay all night?"

I shake my head. "I couldn't. I stayed until she fell asleep, but I'd left Betsy at home. I had to get back to her."

"You left a note though, right?" Travis looks like he's about to bang his head against the table again when one look at the frown on my face tells him all he needs to know.

"How did you not leave a note? God, do you know nothing?" Travis fixes me with a stare as he tuts.

"I've never...?" I furrow my brow in confusion.

Travis snorts and shakes his head at me again. He's going to have neck ache later if he keeps it up.

"I forgot. You never stay, do you? And you leave when they're still getting their breath back."

"Hey!" I growl.

He raises an eyebrow at me, and I glare at him. He just stares back, waiting. Travis has been my friend since we were kids. He's

94

the only one, along with my brother, who calls me out on my shit and gets away with it.

"Fine. That's a fair point," I mutter, my shoulders dropping as Helen comes back with our food and drinks.

"You all right, Blake?" she asks in her usual cheery manner. It's what keeps the customers coming back in again and again. She's always pleased to see you. Even if you've got a face on you like you've had a reeking shit thrown at you—which is what mine probably looks like right about now.

"Yeah, all good, Helen." I plaster a smile back on my face as she nods at us both and tells us to enjoy our lunch.

"You think Daisy's pissed that I left without saying anything?" I pick up my sandwich and force myself to take a bite and chew. Helen's sandwiches are legendary, yet I can barely taste a thing right now.

"I think she'll be even more pissed off if you keep calling her Daisy," Trav says as he digs into his lunch.

I run a hand through my hair and drop my sandwich back onto the plate. "I'm trying, man. It's just hard not to. That's who she is."

"Not according to her," Travis says with a shake of his head.

"Hey... What do you know? Did Kayla say something?" I tilt my chin, waiting for him to swallow.

"Only that she thinks Daisy had a jerk of an ex who didn't like her going out without him. And gave her shit about her job."

"Daisy told her that?" Travis lifts an eyebrow at me, and I blow out a breath. "Fine. *Dee* told her that?"

"Apparently." He nods.

My jaw clenches as I consider his words. Daisy has an ex, who, by the sounds of it, was a controlling bully. It makes sense now why she almost legged it out of my truck to get changed that first night when I commented on her dress.

"You reckon he did something to her?" My eyes bore into Travis' as all kinds of sickening possibilities run through my mind.

"If he did, she didn't tell Kayla. Kayla would have mentioned it. If she thought Dee was in trouble, she would tell me."

"Married life, eh? No secrets," I murmur as I pick up my sandwich and take another bite.

Travis snorts. "You make it sound like a chore. Getting married is the best thing I ever did."

"I'll take your word for it." I throw him a wink, so he knows I'm joking.

"So, what are you going to do?" Travis asks carefully.

My shoulders sag as I consider the option that last night might have screwed up our friendship. I wasn't thinking straight. Maybe I shouldn't mention anything? See if she brings it up first. That way, if she wants to make like it didn't happen, I will know before saying anything that may fuck things up more.

"I dunno, Trav." I drop my head into my hands with a sigh. "I dunno."

I came into the diner pumped up by the incredible night we had. But now?

Now I'm feeling like a prize asshole.

Chapter Twelve

Daisy

"Oh, my goodness! You are a lifesaver!" Maria kisses me on both cheeks as I arrive at the salon.

"It's fine, honestly. I told you on the phone. I don't mind picking up the extra shifts if it helps you out," I reply, changing my sneakers for a pair of the silk ballet slippers Maria provides for us to wear at work. They're so soft and comfortable. We can walk around quietly, maintaining the peace of the spa.

"I know, but I called you so early! I hope I didn't interrupt anything?" She gives me a hopeful look, and I smile.

"You didn't. I was in bed. Alone. And already awake," I reassure her.

Blake had already fucked off by then. And my mind forgot how to sleep for a decent length of time months ago.

Maria smiles at me, her red lipstick making her teeth appear even whiter.

"Honestly, Dee. I appreciate it so much! I would have covered Grace's sick day today myself, but I have family staying with me, and I've felt like a terrible host neglecting them. Then there's this visit from the New York hotel guy coming up. I just can't..." She looks up at the ceiling, shaking her head. "You ever feel like you've bitten off more than you can chew?" Her deep brown eyes come back to meet my gaze.

"Yes." I sigh as I give her a small smile. "But you'll be fine. This guy is coming all the way from New York of his own accord because he's heard about this place!" I open my arms and gesture at the stone walls and waterfall in the spa reception area. "And because he heard about *you*. You've done something beautiful here, Maria. No wonder he wants to recreate it in his hotel."

Her eyes widen as she tucks a long silky strand of hair behind her ear.

"I never imagined I would be here, like this. Doing something I love and actually succeeding at it."

"Well, believe it." I laugh. "You're smashing it! Hell, your reputation has got hot hotel owners flying across the country to come and have a meeting with you."

Maria looks at me, her brows furrowed.

"The girls googled him," I explain. "Griffin Parker is certainly handsome."

Maria rolls her eyes with a smirk. "Great. My grandmother will ask me when the wedding is if she gets hold of that nugget of information."

I giggle as I hand Maria her handbag and practically usher her out the door of her own spa.

"Go! Have some time off. You've earned it."

"Thank you, Dee." She squeezes my arm, her eyes bright as she turns and heads off, leaving me to prepare for the long list of clients we have coming in today.

I'm grateful she called me this morning. It helped to avert my attention away from the sting I felt in my chest when I awoke and found Blake gone. It was just one night, that's all. One gin-fueled night, for which I am paying for now. I wince as the dull ache at the back of my head reminds me to grab my water bottle and take a long drink.

Now is not the time to think about Blake.

I glance back down at today's bookings. It's going to be a long day.

The spa doors don't stop opening and before I know it, a few hours have already passed, and I've missed lunch. I'm rummaging around in my bag, looking for my purse to grab something from the hotel restaurant, when a brown paper bag drops onto the spa reception desk in front of me.

"I come bearing gifts." Kayla grins at me.

"How did you know I was working today?" My stomach rumbles as I open the top of the bag, peeking inside.

"I bumped into Maria in town. It's all vegan, don't worry," she says as I inhale the mouth-watering scent of the falafel wrap.

I beam at her, warmth spreading in my chest. "I could kiss you! I'm so hungry!"

"I thought you might be. I'm always hungry after drinking—and sex," she adds, smirking at me.

"What?" I whisper, my eyes widening.

"Travis has the worst poker face ever." She rolls her eyes. "I knew something was up when he came back from his early lunch break. He went to meet Blake. It didn't take a genius to figure out what had ruffled his feathers. Not after I saw the way your eyes lit up when he walked into the bar last night."

"They did not!" My forehead creases as I roll the top of the paper bag down again.

Maybe they did. A little. A tiny smidge?

Oh, God. I don't know!

I thought I had it all straight in my head. I came back here to put some distance between myself and Mickey. Not to get into a whole new complicated mess. But seeing Blake again... remembering what it was like to feel something other than numb... I don't know what to make of it all.

Blake Anderson has thrown the small part of control I thought I had over my life up into the air.

Kayla takes one look at the sheer bewilderment on my face and giggles.

"Come on. It's a gorgeous day. Let's sit outside while you eat."

I let the other two therapists know I'm taking a late lunch break and walk with Kayla out into the hotel gardens, finding a bench overlooking the beach to sit on.

"Come on then, spill!" She nudges me with her elbow.

I take my time opening the bag and taking a bite of the wrap she's brought me.

"Mmm, this is good," I moan, savoring the first thing I've eaten all day.

"Is that what you said to Blake too?"

I swallow suddenly and cough. Kayla laughs as she pats me on the back.

"I can't believe you had sex with dork face."

I glance up at her when I've stopped coughing, but can see from the glint in her eye she's teasing.

"Fine. He's smoking hot. *Apparently.*" She raises her eyebrows at me. "But really? All these years you've known him, and you still wanted to go there?"

"I can't say I planned to."

I take another bite of the wrap, hoping it will buy me time to think about my answers to the barrage of questions she's probably about to fire at me. But I don't know what to tell her. Not when I don't even know how I feel about it myself.

"So... how was it?" Kayla presses her lips together, her eyes glittering as she fights to hold in her smile.

"Um, it was..."

Mind-blowing? Panty-melting? Better than I thought sex could ever be?

"You know what?" Kayla turns her head away and waves her hand in front of her cheek that's closest to me. "Do *not* tell me. I just... I just can't. I've known you both for too long. It's weird."

100

I smile in relief, letting out the breath I didn't realize I was holding. I don't need to explain it. Label it. *Understand* it. Whatever *it* was.

"I mean, I'll be picturing it if you tell me too much," Kayla rabbits on, barely breaking for air. "And I do not want that in the flick bank popping up uninvited. I mean, what if me and Travis are getting down to it and you and Blake appear in my head? I mean..." She wrinkles up her nose. "No. Just no. You're hot and everything, but..."

Her eyes widen as she looks at me, probably worried that she's offended me.

"Relax!" I laugh. "I'm more than happy for you not to picture it. *Ever.*" I take another bite of my wrap.

"Thank God." She sighs. "I get it now, though. No wonder Cindy was giving you the stink eye all night at the bar. Knowing you and Blake are childhood friends, and you've been hanging out with him since you came back..." Kayla leans back onto the bench and stretches her legs out in front of her.

"The bartender?" I frown.

"Yeah. She's had a thing about Blake for like forever! Thought she'd finally got her claws into him when they got it on one night. He broke it off before it even started as he didn't want the whole relationship and babies thing. It was right before you arrived back in town. Divine intervention—Hey?" She turns to me and her smile freezes on her face. "You knew, didn't you? We rib him about it all the time. She's been throwing herself at him since his TV series aired."

My mouth goes dry, and I force myself to swallow my mouthful of food. It moves in slow motion, scratching my throat on the way down.

"I must have missed those conversations," I mutter, feeling like I might throw it back up any second.

"Oh, shit! I'm sorry, Dee." Kayla's hand flies to her mouth. "I mean, it was weeks ago. Before you even got here. And it was just the one time, I'm sure of it."

I shrug. "It doesn't matter to me. Blake and I were just one night, too. One gin-fueled night, for which I'm sure he will not give much thought to again, anyway." I wrap my arms around myself as I stare out at the ocean.

"A gin-fueled night where you had sex with a friend you've known for decades." Kayla turns toward me, studying the side of my face.

"You did it," I say, refusing to meet her gaze.

"Yeah. And then I married him." She blows out a breath as she turns back to the ocean, staring out with me, watching as the waves break along the shore. "So, that's it? It was just one night you want to forget?"

I chew my lip before I answer. Blake said nothing to give me the impression he saw it happening again. He also said nothing about recently breaking up with a girlfriend, or whatever you'd call Cindy. Can I really believe it was just one time with her, and there wasn't more going on? Even if there was more, what's it got to do with me? So what if she was his girlfriend? I don't know why that bothers me so much.

But it does.

Maybe because I feel like the rebound fuck?

I should never have complicated things by having sex with him. He's my friend. That's all. I should have left it at that. God knows I have enough complicated stuff to work through without adding to it. It's not like I can stay here forever either, even if I wanted to. My aunt's house is ready to go on the market. As soon as I update Mum and Dad with that information, they could tell me to come home. Although, I don't see that happening straight away. Not until things calm down more there.

But the fact remains—one day I will go home.

I know it. Blake knows it. Then again, maybe he doesn't care. It's not like he stuck around. He's probably regretting last night already.

I pick at my wrap, knowing I should eat as much as I can, otherwise I will end up feeling dizzy. I've still got a few hours left of my shift. Kayla stays with me while I eat, changing the conversation on to some of the stranger cases they've seen in the vet clinic. I listen and join in as much as I can, but my mind is elsewhere.

It's on Blake, and how stupid I feel.

Chapter Thirteen

Blake

I REST AN ARM up against the doorframe, blowing out a deep breath.

"Déjà vu, eh, girl?"

Betsy's big, brown eyes look up at me before she drops her nose to the floor and sniffs at the front door. Her tail stays motionless. Even she knows.

Daisy still isn't home.

"Come on." I sigh, patting my thigh.

She turns and follows me down the steps, back toward the truck.

What Trav said has got me thinking. Maybe Daisy *is* avoiding me. Hope Cove isn't that big. And she doesn't have a car. I know Kayla was at work this morning with Trav at the clinic and is back there now, so she can't be with her. And Daisy said she didn't have work today. There aren't many other places she can be.

My thoughts are interrupted by Betsy letting out an excited bark and her tail whacking me around the knee. I look up to see what's got her attention and can't help the smile growing on my face as I spot Daisy walking up the long driveway toward us. She's wearing her white spa uniform. Her dark hair is tied up off her face in a messy pile, strands falling over her cheeks. I watch her tuck one behind her ear, only for it to fall straight back out again.

"Betsy. Go." I tilt my head in Daisy's direction and Betsy's eyes light up before she races off to greet her.

The sound of laughter breaks out in the warm evening air as Daisy drops to the floor and holds her arms out, wrapping them around Betsy, who's whining and wiggling her butt while trying to land as many slobbery licks on Daisy as she can.

"I'm beginning to think she likes you better than me." I arch a brow as I make it over to them.

Daisy's laugh dies down, and I swear she avoids looking directly at me, instead choosing to fuss over Betsy, rubbing her ears, and telling her what a beautiful girl she is.

"We stopped by this morning," I say, holding out a hand.

Daisy eyes it, chewing on her lip before she wraps her delicate hand inside mine and lets me help her to her feet. Her skin is soft in mine, and the scent of fresh flowers hits me as she stands.

"Did you? Maria called me into work to cover a shift." Her eyes still don't meet my face as she slides her hand out of mine.

"Ah." I nod as I study her, looking for a clue. Something to give away how she's feeling about what happened.

"Listen, Dai—"

"Blake—" she says at the same time, before stopping.

I shut my mouth and wait for her to continue as she glances down at Betsy again. Now I know she's avoiding looking at me. She couldn't make it any more obvious. Judging by the two deep frown lines running between her eyebrows, I'd say she can't even stomach it.

Fuck.

She stands there in awkward silence, wringing her hands together in front of her. Regret written all over her face. I can't stand it.

Time for damage control.

"Daisy..."

"Dee," she breathes out quietly.

I clear my throat. "Will you look at me, please... Dee?" My earlier smile has long since vanished, along with her carefree laugh when Betsy greeted her. Her shutters are firmly back in place.

She folds her arms over her chest and lifts her chin; her clear blue eyes finally meeting mine. Waiting.

I swallow. "Look, I just wanted to clear things up." I run a hand through my hair.

I've had similar conversations with girls before, so why does this feel like I'm slowly drowning in tar? I need to let her off the hook. Let her know that it's okay not to mention it again if she doesn't want to. We can carry on like nothing happened. If that's what she wants. I'm not an asshole. I will not push it or keep bringing it up if she wants to write it off as a momentary lapse of judgment.

"Last night was—"

"Yeah," she snaps. "Last night was... last night. Let's leave it at that, shall we?" She glares at me.

Her sudden change in tone has my full attention. My eyes bore into hers as I take a deep breath in through my nose and straighten my shoulders.

She does want to pretend it never happened.

Daisy stares back at me, unflinching, as I roll my lips and nod.

"Sure." I shrug. "If that's what you want."

Her eyes narrow and she tuts, shaking her head in disgust as she looks away again.

This is not going how I planned. I knew she may want to forget all about last night. But I didn't expect her to be so pissed about it.

I look at her, chewing on her lip, her forehead wrinkled as she stares out across the lake.

"I had to get back for Betsy, if that's what you're pissed about?" It comes out sounding less than apologetic, and more like I don't give a shit.

She snorts, letting out a humorless laugh.

"What?" I growl.

"Are you sure you didn't have to get back for Cindy?" She turns to me, her blue eyes piercing me with an icy stare.

I screw my face up as I stare at her, my mouth dropping open. "What the fuck are you talking about?"

"Like you don't know, Blake. You only think with your dick." She drops her eyes down my body and back up again with a scowl.

I stare at her, at a complete loss over how this conversation suddenly turned so ugly.

She rolls her eyes. "C'mon, Blake. You and I both know it was nothing more than a rebound fuck for you."

I tense, every muscle in my body coiling tight.

"Oh, that's what it was? A rebound fuck? I'm glad you've got that sorted out in your head. So, what was it for you, then?" I ask through clenched teeth.

I can't believe she thinks last night was a rebound fuck. There's no way in hell sex like that can happen if your mind is on anyone other than the person who's naked and tangled up with you.

A flash of something fires in her eyes before she pulls her mouth into a grim line.

"It was a mistake. Fueled by one too many drinks."

I clench and unclench my fists by my side as my blood pressure hits the fucking roof.

Fueled by one too many drinks.

"Don't you fucking dare!" I lift a hand to point at her, then throw both arms up and rake my hands through my hair instead, pulling at strands of it until my scalp screams under protest. "I would never have touched you if you hadn't said it was okay! I would never have laid a *fucking* finger on you if you hadn't seemed in control of your decision!"

Her eyes widen, and I hear her suck in a breath. She stares at me for a moment.

"I should have known better."

"What the fuck's that supposed to mean?" I can hear the way my voice sounds.

Low, gravelly, with an edge of—about to blow my fucking top.

It surprises me. I've always been great at keeping a clear head. Thinking rationally. Staying calm. It's what I do. It's my job. My life. You can't afford to have a hot head out in the wild. It could cost you your life if you lose control.

Only, standing here with Daisy staring at me like I'm something she stepped in, has my blood boiling. I can feel my control slipping. Like a frayed old rope. Its thin strands snapping.

One. By. One.

"I think you know what it means, Blake." Her cold eyes meet mine again. "You and me... last night... it was nothing. It should never have happened. We were friends. We should have left it at that."

She's riled up and I should do what I can to diffuse the situation. Except seeing her here, all pouty, pink lips, fire burning in her eyes, has me teetering on the edge of losing it.

"Yeah. Maybe we should have. Too bad we can't change the past, eh?" I glare at her, my blood rushing in my ears.

"Yeah. Too fucking bad," she hisses. Her eyes are glassy as she stares up at me.

I force myself to take a couple of deep breaths. Something isn't right. I can feel my resolve about to break and say something I can never take back. But this... this reaction from her.

This anger...

It's not the Daisy I know.

"Daisy..." It takes all my self-control to soften my voice and slow my pounding heart, grasp on to those final rope threads that are barely holding together.

"It's Dee! How many fucking times, Blake?! It's Dee!" she shouts.

Snap.

Blood rushes in my ears.

"That's funny! I don't recall you complaining about me calling you Daisy when I was inside you last night and you were digging your nails into my skin!" I shout back.

Daisy's eyes go round, and she takes a step back.

Betsy lets out a howl at our raised voices. But my eyes remain glued to Daisy's, my chest rising and falling as I suck in lungfuls of air.

"Get off my property, Blake," she says finally, her voice losing some strength.

"Daisy..." I reach for her as shame seeps into my core. "That came out wrong... I—"

"Save it. I don't care. Why don't you go find someone who does?" She turns and stomps off up the steps toward the front door. "Better still. Go find Cindy!" she yells again before slamming the front door behind her.

My anger skyrockets again. I'm like a fucking rollercoaster at Universal Studios.

"You're nuts!" I yell back at the closed door. "You're fucking nuts!"

It flies back open again and Daisy's standing behind it, her eyes wild.

"Just so you know. I couldn't care less who you stick your dick in!" she cries before slamming it shut once again, so hard that the paneling around the front door shakes.

I stand there, waiting for my anger to subside. Forcing my feet to stay rooted to the spot so I don't go and hammer on the door and make things worse.

Not that they could get much worse.

I couldn't care less who you stick your dick in.

As my breathing slows, my mind clears, and two things hits me.

One. The sight of Daisy all wound up and ready to bust my balls would have my dick ridiculously hard if I weren't so confused by what just happened.

Two. Cindy bothers her. Which means one thing.
She cares who I *stick my dick in.*
In fact, I'd say she cares a whole lot.

Chapter Fourteen

Daisy

THE TWO DAYS FOLLOWING my argument with Blake crawl along at an agonizing pace. Grace is back at work in the salon after being sick, so Maria doesn't need me to cover any shifts. I wish she needed me. I've drifted around the house and garden, not being able to concentrate on anything. I tried to make a lavender soap from a recipe in the book my aunt gave me, but it just went all sticky and never set. Plus, after giving Blake my apron, I got it all over my old favorite t-shirt with a daisy on the front, and despite washing it twice, there's still a big oily stain right over the white petals. Maybe it's for the best. Why would I want to wear a t-shirt with a daisy on it now, anyway?

I've swum in the lake as usual. I can't give that sanctuary up. Even if it runs the risk of seeing Blake. I've managed to go when his truck isn't there. Although I'm ashamed to admit I've swum closer to his house each day, trying to see inside. Some sick fascination that I need to knock on its head. I know how he feels. He was pretty clear about it. And I was too.

I place my mug of chamomile tea down on the porch step as I rub my temples with my fingertips. I was harsh. I should never have said those things to him. Made out like he just thinks with his dick with no regard for anyone else. Like he would take advantage of someone after they'd been drinking. Bile rises in my throat as I recall the hurt in his eyes when I said that. I know firsthand he would never do that. He didn't do it that night when we were seventeen. And he didn't do it two nights ago either.

I wanted it.

I wanted *him.*

And some twisted part of me still does. Even though I know I have nothing to offer him. I have *nothing*. And he has everything. The Blake Anderson I know has an enormous heart and can make you laugh on the days you feel you're barely surviving.

I was so cruel to speak to him like that. All because of what? That when I think of him with Cindy, it makes me want to retch? Like I'd rather gouge my eyes out than risk bumping into them in town together one day? Kayla says it's over between them. But who knows? He'd be better off with her, anyway. I doubt she's as screwed up as I feel most days. And she's not leaving one day, either.

I look around at my aunt's garden, trying to sear the image into my memory so I can draw on it when I'm back in England. When being here will be just a distant memory. I'm not stupid. I know I must go home one day. But the thought of what's waiting for me there just fills me with dread.

"Are you sure you're happy closing up by yourself tonight?" Maria asks, grabbing her bag, her concerned eyes on my face.

"Yes, for the tenth time." I smile.

"I'm sorry, it was a last-minute booking. We rarely have one this late." She glances at her watch and I know she's thinking about getting back in time for the dinner table she's booked to take her visiting family out.

"It's fine, honestly. I don't have anywhere else to be." I smile at her again, but I know it doesn't reach my eyes. Ever since my fight with Blake, I've been unable to shake off the low mood that's crept over me. It's all I can think of. I went around and knocked on his door this morning to apologize, but he wasn't there. I almost think he's avoiding me. It serves me right if I've lost him as a friend now, after what I said to him.

"If you're sure?" She looks at me again. "I know we've run through the lone working protocol before, but you'll be fine. If you need anyone to help with anything, Sam is on reception tonight."

"I'll be okay," I reassure her with a wave as she leaves, mouthing, *Thanks,* to me again from the door.

I let out a deep sigh. It's been a busy day in the spa, as usual, and I'm worn out. Especially knowing I still have to walk back once I finish my shift. But the other girls had plans tonight and I don't see why they should miss out, just because someone booked a late slot for a full-body massage.

I glance down at the name on the computer booking screen.

Mr. Richard Head.

I suppress my chuckle. Back home in England, he would get ribbed for a name like that.

"Has Dick Head arrived yet?"

My eyes snap up at the sudden deep voice. The lights in the spa are low, with just lanterns providing a soft glow. But even from here, I can see the incredible green eyes looking back at me.

"You're Mr. Dick Head?" My mouth goes dry as he walks over to the desk.

He rests his forearms on the marble counter and leans toward me, the muscles in his arms flexing underneath his black t-shirt. I'm hit with a woody, sea salt smell, which has me licking my lips as I stare back at him.

"Yeah," Blake whispers, his eyes dropping to my lips and back up. "I am. A *huge* dick."

Despite myself, I can't help the corners of my mouth twitching in amusement.

He isn't wrong.

My eyes scan over his face, searching for any remnants of the hurt and anger that were there the last time I saw him. They've completely vanished, and in their place are warm eyes studying me—eyes that I sometimes think see me better than anyone else does.

His gaze never leaves my face. "Have you finished hating on me?"

His brows knit together, and I drop my eyes, studying the veins running up his tanned forearms, my gaze drawn down to the long, strong fingers that were inside my body only days ago.

Surely I misheard him? He's here asking me if I'm done being mad at him? It should be the other way around. I had no right to speak to him the way I did. My stupid pride hurt at finding out about Cindy, combined with the mess my life is in right now, almost ruined years of friendship.

And God knows I could use some friends right now.

"That depends," I mumble, unable to meet his gaze.

"On what?" He lifts a hand and places the fingers I was studying underneath my chin and tilts it up, so my eyes meet his. They burn into mine with an intensity I remember only too well from that night.

Blake inside me as deep as he could get. One hand on the wall—THUD! Searing heat.

Me ruined forever.

My breath catches in my throat. "Whether you can forgive me for the hurtful things I said to you."

He gives me a small smile, which has no joy in it. "You were right. I have been known to think with my dick. A lot," he adds.

I wrinkle my nose up and he takes his hand back, my mind threatening to flood with images of Blake and other women, which I really don't want to imagine.

I take a breath. "I meant the other thing... about the drinking."

116

He must hear this. It's been eating me up knowing that I said such a thing to him.

He shrugs like it's nothing. "I forgive you." He flashes his white teeth as if to prove it.

"No." My voice is forceful. "It was a low blow, Blake. I know you would never do such a thing. I've known you for a long time. I know that's not who you are."

My eyes dart between the two of his, pleading with him to believe me.

He rolls his lips together as he nods, his eyes never leaving mine. "I said some pretty stupid shit too."

I realize I'm chewing on my lip when Blake's eyes drop to it and he frowns.

"I can overlook it if you can?" I say, tilting my head while I wait for him to say something.

His eyes roam over my face in a way that sends goosebumps scattering over my arms and up my spine.

Finally, he gives me one of his famous easy smiles.

"So? We friends again?"

My stomach drops at his choice of words, but I force myself to return his smile.

"Yeah. We're friends again. Always friends."

His eyes glitter as he grins at me. "Good. Because my back is fucking killing me. And word in town is that there's a great new therapist at the spa who can unknot a pretzel using just her mind."

I can't help but giggle as all trace of seriousness leaves Blake's face, and he's back to his usual jokey self.

"Oh, word around town, huh?"

He winks at me. "You'd better believe it. And I think my appointment has begun." He leans his head around to glance at the time on the bottom corner of the computer screen, tapping it with a finger. "I hope you aren't going to finish me off early. I've paid for the full hour. I want the complete experience."

I smirk at him and shake my head as I lead him down the lantern lit walkway to the treatment room and open the door for him so he can enter.

"Take everything off and then lie facedown on the bed, covering yourself with the towel."

I close the door again, leaving Blake inside as I stand with my hands clasped and wait on the other side of the door.

He's just another client.

I'm chanting this to myself as he calls out from inside the room.

I walk in, closing the door quietly behind me. The spa music is already playing a soothing melody, which helps to calm the racing in my chest. I'm being ridiculous. For the next hour, Blake is my client. I know what I'm doing and I'm good at it. There's no reason I should feel nervous.

I look over at the massage table.

Fuck.

Blake is laid out, facedown, like I told him, a towel folded down at his waist, barely covering his ass. Every muscle in his body is on full display. Especially the ones on his back, which I realize I've never seen naked before. I've only had the pleasure of seeing Blake Anderson—full frontal.

But this... this is back porn.

I walk over to the table of aromatherapy oils lit by the warm glow of a salt lamp. I mix a couple into a carrier oil base in a glass bowl. Ones that I've been experimenting with—a mixture of ylang ylang and ginseng. The aromas disperse around the room, and I take a deep breath, feeling myself relax.

Walking back over to Blake on the massage table, I can't help a grin from stretching over my face. If he didn't look so sexy, it would be comical. He literally only just fits on the table. His feet are right at the end, and his broad shoulders are practically spilling over the sides.

"Are you comfortable?"

"It beats sleeping in damp undergrowth with rocks in your back." He chuckles and then sucks in a breath as I place the palms of my oiled hands against the hot skin of his back. "Oh, fuck. You are good," he groans as I run my hands across him, working my way around each muscle, teasing it, stretching it out, caressing it.

Once I start, I get lost in myself. I love doing this. Working the muscles into relaxation. Giving them a release. Feeling them uncoil beneath my fingers. Knowing that I am doing something worthwhile that benefits someone else.

Blake's breathing has slowed, but his periodic groans tell me he's still awake. Clients regularly fall asleep if I'm performing a gentler massage. I take it as an enormous compliment that they're relaxed and trusting enough in my company to let themselves truly de-stress and let go.

I roll the towel up Blake's thick thighs and add more oil to my hands before I work on his legs.

"God..." He lets out a deep sigh as I stroke up, my thumb running along the inside of his upper thigh. "I can see what all those rugby dudes back in England are missing. I bet they fucking wept when you left." He chuckles as my hand freezes.

"I loved that job," I whisper, finding the strength to get my brain to communicate with my hand again so I can continue with Blake's massage.

"Why'd you leave?" he asks, groaning as my hand runs up his thigh again. If it weren't for the topic of conversation, then I think I would be in real trouble of overheating from the sounds he's making.

They're so deep. So sexual. So... *arousing*.

"I ask myself the same thing," I murmur, watching the way the oil glistens on his dark hair, slicking it down against his tanned skin.

"Did he touch you? Did he..." Blake's voice sounds strained and the muscles in his back go rigid.

I'm about to ask how he knows about Mick, my ex. But then it dawns on me.

Kayla.

I shake my head to myself. I know she means well. She probably thinks she's helping, asking for advice from her guy friends. But nothing anyone says can make any of it better. It's too late for that.

"No. Mick never... forced me. Not like you're thinking, Blake."

I continue the course my hands are taking up and down his thighs as I realize just saying both of their names in the same sentence makes me feel physically sick. They couldn't be any more different. Blake is all muscle, capable of tearing a man apart. I would bet on it. But he's gentle. He doesn't use his power as a weapon. He doesn't bully or belittle others. He isn't cruel.

Not like Mickey.

Blake relaxes for a tiny moment, but his body is still mostly tightly wound tense muscles as I move up to stand by his head and work on his neck and shoulders from that angle.

"What did he do?" His voice is careful, controlled.

"Blake... I—"

"It's okay. You don't have to tell me if you're not ready. I would hate to make you feel uncomfortable, Dee."

My heart plummets into my stomach as he calls me Dee. It's what I've been telling him I want. It's what I screamed at him about only days ago. But hearing him say it has me blinking furiously as my eyes sting. I would give anything to hear him call me Daisy again. And to really feel it. To be the girl I was when I used to come here—the girl he thinks I still am.

Before Mick.

I hate talking about him, preferring to fool myself into thinking if I don't say his name that it never really happened. He doesn't exist, and I didn't know the things I do now. I didn't see the things I wish I hadn't.

There really is bliss in ignorance sometimes.

Yet, here with Blake, in the low light, the scents of essential oils surrounding us, I feel safe. Safe enough to share some of what I left behind in England. Some of what I'm running from.

I run my hands over Blake's broad shoulders as I part my lips and draw in a breath, wetting my lips with my tongue so I can get the words out of my dry throat.

"He was a bully. Not at the start, though. To start with, he was wonderful. He would bring me flowers. Take me out on dates all the time. Watch movies he hated, because he knew I loved them."

Blake falls silent, listening. I pour more oil in my hands and run them down either side of his spine. He's much taller than me and I have to rise onto my tiptoes, the fabric of my white uniform grazing over his hair so I can reach down toward his waist. Two dimples are on either side of his spine, just visible above the white towel. I could easily let my mind wander toward much nicer thoughts from looking at him, touching him. But it's like a damn has burst, and the words keep spilling out of me of their own accord. Call it therapy or something. But as I talk to Blake, I feel the weight lift from my shoulders ever so subtly.

"Then he started to get weird. He made some new friends at the local pub we used to go to on the weekends. I suspected he was using drugs at one point. I'm still not sure that isn't the case. He would come home late, reeking of perfume, and he'd..." I swallow. "He would throw things, smash them up. The first time, I tried to stop him and he grabbed me by my hair and spat in my face. I would pretend to be asleep after that. But sometimes that didn't work... I learned to be good at hiding bruises."

"Fuck," Blake hisses as I continue.

"He was so jealous. He would comment on what I wore, how I had my hair. He thought the players at the rugby club where I worked would try to chat me up if they thought I was making an effort for them. I started tying my hair up all the time, and then one day we had such a big fight. He got right up in my face. It's the first time I really feared for my life. His eyes, they were... it's like he was possessed by something evil. I knew he was capable of hurting me, *really* hurting me. I told him I would cut it short and dye it if it meant that much to him."

Blake tenses under my palms, and I hear him suck in a breath. I swear the heat in his body ratches up a notch. I can almost see the fiery blood pumping around his veins beneath his skin as my hands glide over it.

"I didn't mean it. I wanted him to leave me alone, so I just said it, you know? The way you say things without thinking when you're arguing." I lift the last word as I try to make light of mine and Blake's recent argument.

He doesn't laugh, though. He doesn't even move.

A frown comes back to my face and I force myself to concentrate on my hands tracing low, powerful strokes over Blake's back, instead of the words leaving my lips.

"The next day, Mick drove me to a salon. He told me he'd booked me in as a treat and it was all paid for. I swear I've never seen him look as happy as the way he did sitting in that chair and watching every strand fall to the floor."

"Fucking asshole," Blake hisses as his back ripples with tension underneath my hands again.

I keep massaging up and down, holding back the tears that are threatening to fall. My cheeks are hot. Burning with shame at what I did to please Mick.

I lost a part of myself to him. And he still has it.

Blake seems to sense my sudden silence isn't a good thing, and he reaches his hands up from his sides, wrapping them around my waist. He keeps his head in the hole the table has cut out so you can lie comfortably on your front.

"You deserve so much better than him." His fingers squeeze my waist gently as he speaks. "If I ever meet him, I'll fucking kill him."

"Blake..." I don't know what I want to say. I just know that his name is the last one I want on my lips.

He rises from the bed and before I know what's happening, he's sitting up and I'm being pulled into his arms. He steadies me on my feet as I sink into the space between his parted thighs and let him hold me. His huge, warm arms wrap around my back and he presses his nose into my hair, taking a deep breath as though to calm himself.

"You are so much better than how he treated you. Don't ever forget it," he whispers, his fingertips tracing up and down my back gently.

It feels so good to be in his arms. My shoulders relax, and I let out a small, involuntary sigh of pleasure.

I could stay here forever.

Pretend that nothing else exists outside of this room. Stay here and feel safe and warm.

Blake's hands stop moving, and he draws back to look at my face. His eyes study mine as if he's seeing me again for the first time.

Understanding me.

"You are beautiful." His lips part as his gaze goes to my hair, and he tenderly tucks a dark strand behind my ear. Since coming back, it's faded from all the swimming and the sun. But it's still unrecognizable from the natural baby blonde it once was.

He keeps his hand on my cheek, cupping it as his other arm pulls me against him. My breath hitches in my throat and I get the faintest glimmer like something is about to happen before he leans forward and presses his soft lips to mine.

I freeze for the tiniest fragment of a second before I allow myself to fall into him, parting my lips and reaching my palms up to rest on his chest.

He brings his other hand to my face, cradling my head as he tilts it, angling it so he can give me a kiss so powerful, it makes me worry my legs might buckle underneath me.

"Blake," I pant. "We shouldn't."

"Just say the word and I'll stop. You know I will." His lips move to my jaw as he tilts my face to the side, kissing all the way along it, to the sensitive skin below my ear.

I let out a small moan as heat spreads through me.

Just say the word.

"Blake..."

He pauses mid-kiss to draw back and face me.

"Look at the fight we had after the last time."

My reasoning is weak, and I know it.

"Are you telling me to stop?" His lips hover millimetres above mine. I can feel the warmth of them radiating against my own.

"No," I whisper.

"Are you going to try telling me you're just a rebound fuck again?" His voice is gentle, but there's an underlying edge of something there.

A flicker...

Hurt?

"No," I moan, and his hands drop to my ass, pulling me closer.

He emits a deep growl from his throat. "Good. Because you were never that. Feel what you do to me."

The towel he had draped over him is long gone. He takes my hand and guides it to where his cock is standing—proud, hard as a rock between his legs. I wrap my fingers around him as he lets out another low groan.

"Don't ever think this isn't all because of you. And only you." His eyes penetrate deep into me, unleashing something. The need to be held by him. The need to feel him again.

The need for everything 'Blake Anderson'.

Before I can even consider that I'm at work and someone from reception could easily walk into the spa to check everything's okay, I'm unzipping my dress and peeling it off.

Blake's eyes light up as I push my white lace thong down my legs and climb on top of him, one leg on either side of his thick thighs, straddling him.

"Please don't tell me to stop either," I whisper, rising over him and holding the base of his cock so his broad, slick tip is against my entrance.

"No fucking way," he murmurs as he grins at me. "Now put me inside."

His hands bury themselves in my hair and he kisses me with a heat that melts my insides. I sink myself down onto him, moaning into his mouth as I feel the delicious stretch through my core.

"God, Blake. I'm so sorry I said those things to you." My apologies spill from my lips as I widen my legs so I can take him in deeper. A delicious bolt of electricity runs through me as I draw him in as deep as possible, each curve of him filling me perfectly.

"I'd say you're making it up to me," he hisses as his eyes drop to where our bodies meet.

I glance down. I'm stretched obscenely around him, my body sucking him in greedily like he's the last meal I'll ever taste.

"Blake, that looks..."

"Fucking incredible?!" His eyes flash as he gives me a panty-melting smile at the same time as removing my bra and throwing it across the room.

"I think you should stop wearing these." His smile turns devilish as he swoops down onto my breasts, his tongue finding my hard nipples and flicking over them.

I drop my head back with an appreciative moan and rest my hands on his shoulders as I slide up and back down onto him. He feels incredible. Another moan leaves my body, all the while his torture continues, turning me inside out with pleasure.

"You're sweet as fucking honey," he murmurs, his hot breath sending shivers over my breasts as he brings his hands to my waist, clutching tightly and quickening our pace.

He lifts me up and down in his strong arms as if I weigh nothing.

Blake's attention returns to my lips, kissing me again and nipping my bottom lip between his teeth. It takes all my strength not to come on the spot. But I want it to last. I'm not ready to let him go again—not yet. My body holds its release at bay, but clenches around him in defiance instead. A wave of wetness rushes to him, covering his thick length.

"Fuck, Dai..." He stops short and grits his teeth instead.

I look into his eyes, and his pupils dilate as he fixes his heated gaze back on me. His eyes are dark, glittering with desire, his lids slightly hooded.

I know what he almost called me, but right now, I don't care. He could call me the fucking Easter Bunny, and I would still be clamping down on his rock-hard cock as my orgasm races toward the surface once again.

When Blake Anderson looks at you like this, you don't have a choice—you're going to come harder than you ever thought possible.

Every nerve in my body is tingling and all I can do is whimper and moan as his body claims mine and sweat runs between us, snaking a course down to where his body is deeply embedded in my own.

I know I'm losing the battle. My body wanted to surrender to him from the very beginning.

"You're fucking incredible." He juts his chin forward as he thrusts up and knocks another lungful of air from my lungs in a loud moan. If anyone were to walk past the door now, there would be no question about the animalistic fucking that's going on inside this room. I'm not even embarrassed about the loud porn-worthy moans that are rolling off my lips, one after another.

"Blake, I'm going to come. I can't stop it." I rest my forehead against his as I stare into his eyes, my mouth hanging open as I pant.

"Why would you want to?" He smirks and then his face turns serious as he clasps a hand around the back of my neck and holds it tight, dropping his voice to a low growl. "Come all over my cock. And don't take your eyes off mine. You know I love watching you, don't you?"

I nod, my breath coming out in quick gasps as I look at him.

"Say it."

"You love watching me," I whisper as he squeezes the back of my neck gently.

Everything draws into my core, pulling tight until it's more than I can stand, and I let out a cross between a cry and a groan as I shudder under his intense gaze. Then I'm bursting. My *body* exploding in pulsing waves of pleasure, ripping through me without mercy. My *mind* turning blissful as all thoughts vanish.

And my heart bursting with.... My heart bursting with...

"*Blake*... God, Blake..." I pant as I shake in his arms.

"You feel so fucking good. And you look even better." His voice is tight, and his eyes are piercing into mine as he emits a deep groan, more primal and rawer than anything I've ever heard before. The fingers around my neck flex, and the hand on my hip digs into my flesh as I feel his cock thicken and throb inside me.

"Blake." I press my lips against his and pant with him as the jerk of his body, followed by a deep growl, tells me he's coming. "Oh," I whimper as liquid fire spreads inside me.

He pulls me closer, thrusting himself deep inside me over and over, his pace slowing as he rides each pulse down. Until finally, he stills, the corners of his lips curl and he pulls his bottom lip under his perfect white teeth as his eyes flash brightly at me.

I'm rendered unable to do anything other than smile back as I catch my breath, safely cocooned in his arms, my breasts rising and falling against his muscular chest.

"How can we go from not speaking to each other to doing that in less than an hour?" I pant.

"I obviously booked the massage with the happy ending option." He grins at me as he moves his arms, encircling my waist, making no attempt to move away or depart my body.

I snort and wrap my arms around his neck as he tips my chin up and brings his lips to mine again, kissing me deeply.

"I still don't enjoy fighting with you," I murmur against his warm lips.

"Then don't. Just enjoy what we have." He slides his tongue into my mouth and kisses away the question, which was on the tip of my tongue.

What exactly do we have?

Chapter Fifteen

Blake

"You should really think about leaving."

My eyes drop to Daisy's pink lips, which are a deeper shade from all our kissing. Her cheeks are flushed too, and her eyes bright.

She's fucking stunning.

"Why?" I lean forward and tease her lips apart again, sliding my tongue in to find hers.

Fuck, this woman. She tastes like vanilla and mint. I want to devour her.

My cock twitches in its position, nestled deep inside her, preparing to go again.

"Blake?"

Her arms have left their place from around my neck, and her palms are pressing gently against my chest.

"Yeah?" I murmur, holding her tighter in my arms as she lets out a small giggle and wriggles.

"I'm already late closing up. Someone could come from reception any minute to check if everything's okay." Her eyes meet mine and there's a hint of some hidden emotion in them as she pulls her lip between her teeth.

"You telling me you don't want them to walk in and find you sitting on a client's cock?" I draw my lips into a straight line and hold a serious expression on my face.

Her eyes widen and her sweet lips drop open into the perfect 'O' before she narrows her eyes and swats me on the chest.

"Blake Anderson, you're bad." A smile creeps over her face as I wink and shrug my shoulders at her.

"If it makes you smile, then I'll be the devil himself."

She snorts out a giggle as she lifts herself off me. I catch a faint sigh on her lips as we become two separate bodies again.

I stand and walk over to the chair where I laid my clothes, dressing silently as I watch Daisy retrieve her clothes and do the same.

"Okay. You ready?" She smoothes her white dress down with her palms as she looks over at me. Her brow creases suddenly, and she purses her lips. "Turn around."

"What?"

She twirls a finger in the air. "Blake. Turn around," she huffs out.

I shake my head, puzzled, and do as she says. It's only when I hear the running water and her squeezing out a washcloth that I understand what she's doing.

"I could do that for you." I turn my chin back over my shoulder.

"Ahem."

I catch her glare before I turn back around, my shoulders shaking with a silent chuckle.

"Oh, yeah. It's so funny, isn't it? It's all right for men." She tuts, although it's clear her voice has no real malice in it. She finishes up and then walks over to me.

"You know it's kind of hot." I drop my voice as I look at her pink lips.

"What is?" Her forehead creases as she grabs the towels off the bed and places them in a laundry hamper.

"Knowing that part of me is still inside you."

Her eyes snap up to mine and her cheeks flush.

I fix her with a heated stare. "Knowing you're still feeling me afterward. I love it."

I watch as her throat constricts as she swallows, seeming to take great effort to do so.

God, I love that throat.

"Do you?" It comes out as a whisper, barely there.

"I do." My eyes search hers as we stare at one another.

"Blake..." Daisy looks like she's about to say something else, but instead heads to the door and opens it. "Come on. I'll walk you out."

I look at her, understanding that she isn't ready to talk about anything else yet. But when she is... I'll be waiting.

"It's okay. What needs doing? I can help."

Her pretty face tilts to one side as she wrinkles her nose. "What do you mean?"

"I mean"—I walk over to her at the door and take hold of her chin, running my thumb over her swollen bottom lip—"what can I do to help close up?"

She processes my words before taking a step back so she's out of reach.

"There's no need for that. I'm fine."

I tip my head down and shake it as my hands go to my hips. "You've always been stubborn."

"What's that supposed to mean?" Daisy crosses her arms over her chest as she waits for me to answer.

"It means you aren't getting your way tonight. Don't tell me you thought I was going to leave and not offer to take you home?"

She stays silent.

I chuckle. "Tough. You're not walking home alone when I'm right here, *neighbor.*" I cock a brow to go with my smirk as I watch her let out a small huff of air.

"Fine. But only because I don't have the energy to argue with you again." She eyeballs me, but I'm sure I see her lips twitch at the corners.

"I never have the energy for arguing with you," I say softly, watching as she pulls her bottom lip between her teeth and holds my gaze.

She seems to realize I'm not going anywhere and gives me a small smile. "I suppose it will be quicker..."

I clap my hands together. "Great. Now that's sorted, what do you need me to do?"

Fifteen minutes later, we are in my truck, heading back home. Daisy's been staring out of the window. I can see her reflection in the glass. Her brow is furrowed, and she's chewing on her lip. Again. I don't want to break into her thoughts, though.

My eyes drop over her long, tanned legs, which look even bronzer in contrast to her white uniform. I return my eyes to the road and clear my throat.

"Hey, Blake... you just sailed right past!" Daisy turns to me, confusion on her face as she points out the window to her driveway, which is growing smaller in the rear-view mirror.

"No, I didn't."

"You did!" Her eyes widen as she jabs the glass of the passenger window with her finger. "How many times have you driven this road in and out to your house, and you can't recognise my driveway?"

"I recognised it." I shrug, enjoying the game.

"Then why...?" Daisy's innocent blue eyes roam over my face.

"Betsy."

"Betsy?"

"I had to come home for her last time. And look how that turned out. You had me on your hit list." I chuckle as I pull the truck up outside my place and kill the engine.

"So, you're going to check on her and then drop me off at home? It would have only taken a minute, Blake. I could have gotten out at the bottom of the drive. You'd have saved yourself the extra journey. In fact, I'll walk back from here." Daisy hops down out of the truck and is already at the back of it with her bag slung over her shoulder as I grab hold of her wrist and pull her so she crashes up against my chest.

"Who said anything about you going home?"

She looks up at me from under her long lashes, her clear blue eyes searching mine.

"Stay here with me. All night." I tuck a stand of hair behind her ear and reach up to hold either side of her face as I lower my mouth to hers and kiss her tenderly.

It takes all my restraint not to push her back against the smooth metal of the truck and sink to my knees in front of her. It's been too long since I tasted her.

Too fucking long.

"Blake..." Her eyes dart around frantically.

I suck in a breath as I wait to see what excuse she's going to come up with.

"Hey..." Her eyes fill with warmth and her face breaks into an enormous smile as she bends down to greet Betsy who's run over from the porch to greet us. Betsy's whining and dancing around on her paws, her eyes bright and eager as Daisy runs her hands over her deep chocolate coat.

My dog gets a better response than me, huh.

I open my mouth, deciding to use this to my advantage.

"Betsy will be disappointed if you leave now."

Daisy glances up at me, a smirk on her face. "Is that so?"

She's not fooled.

"Yeah," I nod, "it is so."

She ruffles Betsy's ears as she gazes into her eyes. "Maybe I could come in for a bit, then. Give you a goodnight cuddle before I walk home?"

Betsy lets out another whine, her tongue darting out and attempting to land a lick right on Daisy's face. She's quick though and moves just in time.

"No tongue kisses." She giggles.

"Nope. They're just for Daddy." I grin as I pull Daisy to her feet and into my arms, pressing my lips to hers and sliding my tongue between her lips in search of hers. She doesn't resist. In fact, I'd say from that little sigh she just made, that she likes it.

She likes it a lot.

"Fine. I'll come in for a drink. Then I'm walking home," she says when I finally let her go.

I say nothing; just grin. I take her hand and lead her to the front door. Betsy races ahead excitedly, bouncing on her back legs as she waits for me to open it. As it swings open, she races inside, straight to her basket of toys, and comes back with one proudly held in her jaws.

I groan inwardly as I see a flash of brown and green.

Thanks for that, Betsy.

"Who's this?" Daisy holds out a hand and Betsy takes great care presenting her prize into Daisy's palm.

"Just an old toy." I scoop it up and toss it over the room where it lands on the sofa. Betsy's having none of it and retrieves it with more speed than an Olympic sprinter, once again bringing it back to Daisy.

"Fuck, Betsy. You're killing me here, girl," I mutter, leaning down and wrapping my hand under her jaw. I rub her chin, melting a little when her big brown eyes look back at me.

Daisy's turning the small, knitted doll over in her hands with pure delight on her face. Her brows shoot up her forehead.

"Blake, is this—?"

"Yes, it's me." I blow out a breath as I rake a hand back through my hair.

Her eyes dance as she looks up at me. "But who made it?"

I look at the doll in Daisy's hand. It's a pretty good likeness, as far as knitted dolls go. He's got dark brown strands of hair, and they even gave him lumps of muscles underneath his army green cargo pants and t-shirt.

"Blake's Babes," I murmur, heading over the polished hardwood floors of the open living and dining area toward the kitchen. I flick the kettle on and get out a couple of mugs.

"Your fan group?"

I thought I'd said it quietly. Obviously not quiet enough.

"Yep."

It goes quiet and I chance a glance up. Daisy's crouched down, one arm around Betsy, talking softly to her as she holds the toy. I strain my ears but can only make out one word.

Lucky.

I grin to myself as I watch them.

"She's taking good care of him for you." Daisy's eyes light up as she looks over at me, catching me staring.

I huff out a laugh as she stands and walks over. "He's not mine."

"I don't understand."

"They sent him for Betsy. They may be called Blake's Babes, but I swear they're Betsy's fan club. She gets way more love than me."

Daisy throws her head back and laughs. "Do you want me to get out the world's smallest violin so you can play it?"

I keep my face straight as I lift the box of herbal tea bags, waving them in front of her nose. "Just for that, you can forget getting one of these." I turn to throw them in the cupboard.

"Wait!" Daisy grabs my hand and prises the box from my grip. "Blake Anderson, what is this?" She dangles the box between her thumb and forefinger as though it's some racy little number, and not a box of herbs shoved in little individual, brewable bags.

I smirk at her. "It's the fucking Holy Grail. What do you think it is?"

She narrows her eyes at me, returning my smirk. "I know you don't drink herbal tea."

"I don't. They're not mine."

I watch her face fall before she recovers, her voice suddenly taking on a polite formality. "Whose are they, then? Cindy's? No!" She holds up a hand. "Don't answer that. I don't want to know. It's none of my business."

I take them back from her and drop one into each mug, my eyes studying her face. "They're Holly's."

"Oh." The corners of her mouth turn down and she looks over at Betsy who's laid out on her beanbag, giving knitted Blake some love—licking his hair down over and over so it looks worthy of a bad comb over joke.

"My sister-in-law." I pour boiling water over each bag and watch as Daisy's face relaxes.

"Oh, yes. Of course. Jay's wife." Her voice is lighter, and she looks back at me, her eyes meeting mine, before a flush creeps over her cheeks.

"And you're wrong." My hand grazes hers as I hand her the steaming mug of peppermint tea.

"Huh?"

"It is your business."

The flush deepens in her cheeks as I tip my head to the side door. She follows me as I unlatch it and slide the entire thing open, revealing the porch, and beyond it the lake, lit only by moonlight.

"So, this is where you two hang out." She follows me and sinks down into one of the giant sofas and it practically swallows her up. "It's like a big warm hug." She sighs and then giggles.

If I were to close my eyes and just listen, I could believe we were seventeen again. Her voice has taken on a new lightness tonight, one that I haven't heard since she came back. She almost sounds carefree—the way she used to.

"Sure is." I clink mugs with her as I sit down next to her, my thigh resting snugly against hers. Her eyes dart from our legs to the other big, empty sofa alongside us and back again. "Problem?" I ask, keeping my gaze fixed ahead on the lake.

She blows across the top of her mug. "No."

"Good." I sigh as I stretch my free arm out and wrap it around her shoulders.

I can see her look at me from the corner of my eye. Her eyes trace over my face and down to my jaw as I take a mouthful of tea.

"How's the tea?" She turns to look out at the lake.

"Thirst-quenching." I smack my lips together.

She giggles. "I never thought I'd see you drinking tea on your back porch. What the hell happened while I was gone?"

I chuckle. "I know how I'm perceived. All brawn, no depth. It's not all muddy workouts and drinking raw eggs."

"Blake, I didn't mean it like that." Daisy turns to me, her eyes fixed on mine, worry growing in them.

"Hey, I know you didn't." I smile at her. "I'm not offended. It is what it is. I know how some people see me, and that's their choice." I rub my hand up and down her arm, where I can feel goosebumps forming. "You're getting cold."

She ignores my comment. "You honestly don't care what other people think about you? About your job? What you do? Who you are?" Her blue eyes search mine, confusion, and something else hidden in their depths.

"Why would I?" I shrug as I study her. "They only know a part of who I am and what I'm about. If they choose to fill in the rest themselves and get it wrong... who cares? I know who I am. Other people's opinions of me don't define me."

I learned fast growing up that you can never please everyone. People assume because my brother is stupid rich and successful that I should be jealous. But I'm not. I'm happy for him. He's doing something he loves, and I couldn't be happier that he's settled and enjoying living his life. Just like I love mine. I get to work outside and be active, help people, and have Betsy with me.

I'd say I'm pretty fucking lucky.

Daisy's eyes haven't left mine. It's like she's searching for the answer to something in my words.

"You're strong though, Blake. You can handle it if people don't like something you do. Even if they judged you for it, you'd not care."

I frown. "You're strong too, Dee. Why am I sensing you don't think you are?"

She blows out a breath and looks back over the lake. "I'm not strong, Blake. I'm a coward. You've no idea."

The lightness from her voice earlier has vanished. Replaced by something that sounds a lot like regret.

"Hey." I take her mug and place it down with mine on the ground. "Where's all this coming from?"

She shakes her head, her shoulders tensing up. "Nowhere. Just ignore me."

"You're talking about him?" My chest tightens just at the thought of her ex, and I realize I'm clenching my teeth. "He didn't deserve you. I've told you. Getting away from him was the bravest thing you could do. Why are you questioning yourself over it?"

She turns to me and I swear, in that second, I see inside her. To what he's done to her. To how he's left her. The easy-going, upbeat girl I knew, who was like a ray of walking sunshine...

Broken.

Broken by every vile thing that bastard did to her.

"You don't understand, Blake. I—"

I cut her off with a kiss as I wrap her in my arms and pull her body against mine. She tenses, her hands on my chest as though she might push me away any second. But then she lets out a small sigh from deep in her chest and kisses me deeply, losing herself for a few precious seconds.

I could so easily fall into her all over again. But I sense that's not what she needs right now. The look in her eyes moments ago, her hands on my chest, creating a barrier between us. She doesn't need me to be the guy who thinks he might lose his mind if he doesn't touch her. She needs the guy who's been her friend for over a decade.

She needs him.

I pull my lips from hers and reach up to cup her face. "I understand perfectly. Come on, I'm taking you to bed."

I'm prepared with my counter argument. Ready for the struggle. But she merely nods at me, her body drained of energy. She takes my hand and allows me to walk her to my bedroom.

There's barely enough light to see, so I turn the torch on my cell phone on and place it on the bedside table as I pull back the covers. I strip down to my boxers, my eyes never leaving Daisy's as she follows my lead and removes her dress, so she's standing in front of me in just her white lace bra and thong.

"Here." I take out one of my t-shirts from a drawer and hand it to her, dropping my eyes as she takes off her bra and slips it over her head.

I pull her down onto the mattress with me and wrap an arm underneath her, so she's tucked into the side of my chest. She's so quiet, which only makes my blood boil more in my veins as I begin to understand what a number this guy, Mick, has done on her. She didn't deserve it. Whatever she's not told me yet—the thought there's more makes me sick to my stomach—she sure as hell didn't deserve it.

Not Daisy.

Not the sweetest girl I've ever known.

I reach for my cell phone and turn the torch off as I set the meditation app going. The room fills with the sound of waves crashing against a shore.

I hear her suck in a breath, and then she slowly slides her hand up to rest on my chest.

"Sleep, babe." I kiss her forehead. "I've got you."

Chapter Sixteen

Daisy

I CAN FEEL THE smile spread over my face as I snuggle my head down into the soft coolness and take a deep breath in. The scent of sea salt and wood fills my nostrils, and I let out a sigh as my eyes open. I blink, looking around. I'm surrounded by white waves in a sea of green. I bolt upright and swing my head around, remembering where I am.

Blake's bed.

It was dark last night, and I felt so weary suddenly—tiredness hitting me like a sledgehammer—that I hadn't taken it in properly.

I'm in the middle of a bed covered in the softest white bedding I think I've had the pleasure of sleeping on, surrounded by green walls. The furniture is minimal, some dark wooden bedside tables and drawers. There looks to be a dressing room and an en suite off to one side, but it's the walls that have my attention. Placed around the deep green in dark wood frames are different photographs of forest. Some taken from up high, looking down over morning mist, trees spreading far below. Others up close, showing intricate bark patterns and colorful leaves.

It's like being in a jungle paradise.

Blake isn't here. But I get the feeling he was until recently, like I can still sense him in the air. I glance down over my white lace bra. It's dry. I'm dry. This is the first morning I can remember that I haven't woken up drenched in sweat. That I haven't woken up

141

with my heart beating wildly in my chest as I feel like I might pass out from lack of oxygen.

It's the first time I can remember I haven't had the nightmares.

It must have been the wave sounds. I can't believe Blake remembered that I had told him I fall asleep to them. They're the only thing that soothes me enough so I can drift off. I swallow the dry lump in my throat. That's all they do. They don't stop the nightmare coming. They aren't the reason I slept so well. There's only one thing that could have been.

Blake.

I swing my legs out the side of the bed and accidentally knock the bedside table. It wobbles, and that's when I notice the glass on top of it with what looks like freshly squeezed orange juice inside. I lift it up and sniff at it, as though it might have been put there by aliens in the night. I take a sip and conclude it's just orange juice—incredibly mouth-watering, throat soothing, energy-enhancing orange juice. Just what I needed to wake up and prepare myself for coming face to face with Blake this morning.

Just what the hell do I say?

I can't believe we had sex again yesterday. Despite knowing it's a bad idea, I still did it. He thinks I'm the same girl I was ten years ago. I'm not. And I'll be leaving soon. It's all just a mess that could ruin a perfectly wonderful friendship. Yet, I can't seem to resist. It's like my body is a compass and he's true north. It radiates toward him. Aching for him, screaming out for his touch.

The best thing I can do is to keep my distance. Maybe it would have been better if we hadn't made up from our fight. It's easier to resist him when I don't see him. It's just my body doing stupid things. It's been a long time since anyone touched me in a way that made me feel safe and desired all at the same time. I'm probably just drunk with lust and hormones. That's all.

I look around the room for something to put on over Blake's tshirt, which only just covers my ass. I'm sure my work dress was here last night, but now it's vanished. My eyes fall on to a dark gray robe hanging on the back of the door. I slip it around my shoulders and tie the belt. The scent of Blake surrounds me on its soft fabric. This was probably a bad idea.

The sound of "Pony" by Ginuwine is playing from somewhere as I enter the open living area. I almost drop the now empty glass of orange juice on the hardwood floor as I take in the sight in front of me.

Blake is wearing nothing but gray sweatpants, his back to me, muscles rippling as his hips roll side to side in time to the music. I stand rooted to the spot as he gyrates, humming softly to himself as he walks around the kitchen.

It is the hottest fucking thing I have ever seen in my life.

Every muscle in his back is in high definition, the ink of his tattoos dark against his smooth skin as he moves side to side. The man has rhythm. But then I know that from the way he can play my body like it's tuned only for him.

I must make a sound—probably something akin to a stifled moan laced with sexual desire, judging by the way heat is flaring through my core—because Blake turns suddenly. When he sees me, he gives me a slow smile, before hooking a finger at me, beckoning me toward him.

I shake my head, my eyes wide as they drop down his torso and over his perfect washboard stomach. He grins at me and nods, repeating the beckoning motion. I don't even realize my feet are moving, but somehow, I end up right in front of him. He grabs the knot of the dressing gown and pulls me against him, continuing gyrating his hips as he gives me the best come-fuck-me look I've ever seen.

All I can do is stare at him as he locks eyes with me and continues moving, mere inches from me, but not touching. He rolls his body down mine with a glint in his eye before he lifts me under the arms and places me down on the kitchen counter.

As the sexy chorus starts again, he grabs each of my knees with strong, capable hands and throws my legs apart so he can stand between them and lean into me, grinding against me.

The heat coming off him is intense. Or maybe it's coming from me. I can't even tell anymore. The lines between the two of us blur when he's this close. I don't know where he ends and I begin.

And I don't care.

He leans into me further, placing his hands on either side of me on the tiled wall behind so his lips are barely grazing mine. Then he screws up his face as he sings along to the lyrics of the song in a high-pitched squeaky voice. It does exactly what I suspect he intended it to, and I throw my head back and laugh in delight.

I laugh deep from in my belly.

I laugh all the way from my toes.

I laugh as though I've never felt pain or heartache in my life.

I can't stop it and before I know it, tears are streaming down my cheeks. Nothing else exists in this moment except me and him, and the knowledge that he's always been able to make me laugh better than anyone. He's always been able to speak to my soul and make it sing.

Blake Anderson—earth's very own little slice of heaven.

He grins as the song comes to an end, wiping the tears from my cheeks with his thumbs before pressing a soft kiss to my lips, which is over far too quick.

"Good morning." He winks and then turns to fill the kettle up as the weather report plays on the radio.

"Morning." My eyes drop to his tight ass as I loosen the neck of the dressing gown to cool myself down. I wipe at my eyes again as my laugh subsides and I take a deep breath.

"How did you sleep?" He smiles at me over his shoulder, his eyes glittering as he turns the radio on the worktop down.

"Good. Great. You?" I bite my lip as I smile back at him.

"Best night's sleep I've had in ages." He turns and takes the glass I'm still clutching from my hand. His fingers graze mine and send a frisson of electric current up my arm. "Suits you." He lifts a brow as he places the glass in the sink.

"Oh. Sorry, I couldn't find my dress." I fiddle with the belt of the robe.

"Don't be sorry. I'd rather wake up to the sight of you in it. And I hung your dress up. It's in my closet."

"Oh." My brows shoot up. "Thanks."

"Don't mention it. Anything for you, Dai—" He clears his throat and turns to a drawer to pull something out. "Oatmeal good?"

"Pardon?" I frown as I realize I was looking at the V shape running down into his pants along with furrowing my brow at the fact he almost called me Daisy again.

He smirks. "For breakfast. Or would you rather eat something else?" He cocks a brow at me and my cheeks heat as I realize it's totally obvious where my gaze was seconds ago.

"Oatmeal sounds good." I turn away, taking a steadying breath as I look around the room. I need a distraction. Something to stop me from thinking about Blake.

Naked.

Naked Blake.

On top of me.

Underneath me.

Behind me.

I shake my head and glance around. I never took this room in last night, either. It's stunning. High, beamed ceilings in pale, stripped back, honey-colored wood. A great big open fireplace with a large sectional sofa in front of it. Everything is light and airy. But it feels inviting too. There are some giant potted plants providing color, and large, framed photographic prints on the walls. The ones in here are more neutral in color than the bedroom, mostly coastal shots, and sunrises.

I look back at Blake, who's got his back to me at the cooker. The kitchen area is vast, a giant wood topped breakfast bar extends out with six stools along it, and the tall cabinets are painted in a whitewash. It's got a sort of modern forest lodge feel about it.

"You did all this?" My eyes roam around again and over to the side of the room, which is all one large glass sliding door out onto the porch. I can see the lake, its surface glistening with the morning sun, and Betsy, laid out snoring in a patch of sunshine on the wooden deck.

"Yeah. My dad helped too. And my brother. Kind of a family project."

I look back at Blake as he turns around. My hand flies to my mouth as I snort out a laugh. I thought I'd just about recovered from my laughing fit, but I can feel a rumble in my chest and wetness at the corners of my eyes again.

"I didn't think you'd actually keep it."

"Why not? I didn't have one." He grins at me, but all I can do is try to stop my shoulders from shaking as I look at him.

If anyone can make a flame printed apron with *You kill 'em, We grill em'* on it look sexy, then it's Blake Anderson.

"Fine. If it's that bad." He undoes the ties and pulls it off, tossing it on the counter with a wink.

Fuck.

That's even worse. At least the apron distracted me. Now I'm face to face with the sight of Blake half naked again. The outline of his dick is glaringly obvious in his pants and, what's more, I think he knows.

And doesn't care.

"Come on. Sit." He grins at me as he turns to pour a mug of tea and places a bowl of oatmeal down on the breakfast bar. The top of it is covered in dried berries and seeds. "You're going to need your slow-burning carbs today for what I have in mind." My mouth drops open and Blake lifts two fingers to my chin, closing it. "Now who's the one with the dirty innuendo mind?" He smirks as I narrow my eyes at him.

"What exactly do you have in mind?" I slide off the counter and sit at the breakfast bar where he's placed the bowl, waiting for him to join me. He pulls another stool close to mine, so he's practically in my lap, and then relaxes down onto it.

"I want to show you something." His eyes light up as he spoons a mouthful of oatmeal past his sinful lips.

"Yeah? What kind of something?" I break my gaze away and take a mouthful of mine. It's delicious and creamy and I lick my lips letting out a small moan of appreciation.

Blake smirks as he watches me. "A black, hairy beast of a something."

"You already showed me that. Twice."

He smiles at me, cocking a brow wickedly in response to my joke. I drop my spoon into my bowl and laugh. I can't ever remember feeling so light. So free. Not since... my shoulders drop, and I let out a sigh as I smile to myself.

Not since I was seventeen.

"This one you'll really want to see. Trust me. You won't forget it."

I smile back at him as we eat.

He's right.

I won't forget.

Ever.

Chapter Seventeen

Blake

"Right. Stay real still. You see there?" I extend an arm past Daisy's face and point to a spot of shingle shore on the other side of the river.

"Where?" she whispers, her eyes scanning the area.

I lean closer so my cheek is dusting hers. One arm is around her waist, and my other is still pointing out the spot I want her to focus on. We're crouched down next to a bush up on a ledge overlooking the river a short drop below.

We've got the perfect view.

My jaw grazes at her temple as she tilts her head to get a better look. And the scent of wildflowers and vanilla hits me. My dick stirs in my pants and I draw in a breath. Now is not the time to lose my head. I have no trouble staying focused out here in the forest. It's where I'm most at ease. But then, I've never been here with Daisy before. All logical thought is rendered useless when she's near.

"There."

I motion to movement on the bank and hear a small gasp come from Daisy as she goes rigid and then holds her breath. Her hand goes to my arm around her waist, and she squeezes it. I can feel the excitement oozing out of her through her touch.

I take in her face from the corner of my vision as her eyes widen and a beaming smile spreads over her face. She's the picture of pure joy.

"Blake," she whispers. "Oh, my God."

I turn back and watch as the mother black bear leads her three cubs to the river to drink.

Me and Betsy have been coming to this spot for weeks after noticing paw prints on one of our morning runs. We've seen them a few times, but this is the first time I've seen all three cubs so clearly with the mother.

"You beauty," I murmur as I slide my arm from Daisy's waist and grab my camera from the outer pocket of my rucksack. I lift it up and get a few shots. Betsy's sat still as a statue, her eyes trained on the cubs, bright and alert.

"We got them, girl." I grin as I pat her on the back. Her ear lifts in my direction so I know she heard me, but her focus stays fixed on the bears.

The three of us sit in stunned silence as we watch. The bears stay for a few minutes, drinking, the mother always on the lookout, until they all slowly make their way back into the treeline and disappear.

"That was incredible!" Daisy's eyes are filled with energy as she turns to me. Her entire face is lit up, brighter than the sun.

"Pretty special, huh?" I'm grinning too as I put my camera away and pull out a bottle of water, handing it to her.

She takes it and tilts her head back, her throat moving as she drinks.

"Thanks." She hands it back to me, licking the wetness off her lips. My eyes linger on them as I take a swig and then screw the lid back on.

"You want to head back? I reckon we might just make it." I gaze up at the sky and the deep pewter cloud that's in the distance but moving our way.

"Sure. I can't believe we just saw that!" Daisy's practically bouncing from foot to foot as she takes my hand and I help her to her feet. "This is incredible, Blake. I told you this place is paradise." She turns and looks out over the forest and river below.

"It's about to be a wet paradise." I chuckle as I glance back at the cloud that's moving faster than I thought. Even the air is heavy with that dense pressure that comes before a good rainstorm from Mother Nature.

"It still looks far away." Daisy wrinkles up her nose as she looks at the darkening sky.

"Trust me. I'm in tune with this stuff."

Daisy smirks at me.

"See these?" I lift both biceps and flex them. "Thunder"—I tilt my head to the left—"and lightning." I tilt my head to the right. "And when they come together"—I clap my hands—"you'd better be prepared for the storm."

Betsy jumps up and wags her tail, watching Daisy as she doubles over, clutching her sides.

"Please." She holds up a hand. "No more of your jokes, Blake. They're just too..." She cracks up again, the sounds of her delight overflowing and pouring from her easily.

It's fucking music to my ears.

"Hey." I bite back my smile. "No one's ever complained about my jokes before?"

That only makes Daisy laugh harder.

"Maybe not to your face," she splutters as she straightens herself up and lets out a final sigh.

"You done?" I arch a brow at her.

She sucks in a breath and her answer comes out as a squeak. "Yep. I think so. I mean... nope." Her eyes screw shut again as she has one final laugh and then blows out a big breath. "Okay. I'm good. I'm good." She nods at me. "Come on, Mr. Wild, let's get going." She strides past me, Betsy at her side.

I shake my head with a chuckle as I swing my backpack up onto my back and follow them.

The walk back doesn't take as long as the way up, but the chill that's come over in the air and the quiet of the birds, who've returned to the treetops, tell me it still won't be quick enough. The first roll of thunder sounds in the distance, its deep rumble echoing off the rock ledges and down the valley behind us.

"I hope you don't mind getting wet," I call to Daisy who's ahead of me on the trail path.

It's perfect really; I've had a front-row seat to the show her gorgeous round ass is giving me in those tiny shorts she put on this morning after we stopped by her house to get her a change of clothes.

She didn't want to take me up on my suggestion of naked hiking.

"I think we'll make it, Blake. Think positive." She speeds up on the path ahead as her words strike a heated torch to life in my chest.

Think positive.

It sounds so much more like her than most of the things she's said since she came back here. I knew she hadn't changed. Not deep down.

"I hate to rain on your parade—literally." I grin as my eyes roam over her ass again. "But I think you're wrong. W. R O. N. G."

She shakes her head as she walks on. "And I think you're—" She doesn't get to finish whatever she was about to say as the heavens open and sheets of rain hammer down over us. The small positive snippet is that it's quite refreshing in the hot, summer air.

"Blake!" she squeals, breaking into a run to reach the more sheltered area of the nearby trees.

"Stop! We're on a slope. This path is just going to turn to mud. You'll slip!" I shout.

It's no use, though. The rain is battering us, along with the sounds of the nearing thunder vibrating the surrounding air.

She can't hear me.

"Dee!" I yell again. But she's farther down the path now, her white t-shirt see-through and sticking to her body. Betsy's got much further ahead, and I can make out her dark form in the treeline, waiting for us. "Wait up!"

The next thing I see is a flash of white followed by a startled scream as Daisy slips and slides down what is now a stream of muddy sludge flowing down the path. I do the exact thing I told her not to do and run to get to her. When I catch up, she's lying on her back, face toward the sky with a huge grin on her face.

"You okay down there?" I rest my hands on my knees, laughing as water runs off my nose and eyelashes.

"I think I bruised my butt, Blake." She laughs. "But I'm good."

"Come on." I hold my hand out to her and she wraps her wet, mud-coated fingers around mine.

I peel her off the ground and there's a squelching *pop* when she's freed from the mud pie she'd effectively landed in.

She stands in front of me, hair soaked, mud covering her, streaks over her face, her clothes ruined. But the light in her eyes makes her look more beautiful than ever as she gazes up at me, raindrops dripping down her face.

"Dee, let's get you—"

She places a finger against my lips, her eyes fixed on mine. Then she slides her arms around my neck, rising onto her toes, and crashes her lips against mine. Her kiss is frantic and urgent, and I can taste mud on her lips. But I couldn't give a shit. I kiss her back, sliding my tongue into her mouth and fisting my hands in her hair as the rain falls around us, thunder bellowing in our ears.

She presses her body against mine and despite our clothes being soaked through; the heat radiating off her seeps into my chest as I hold her against me.

"Blake," she pants, looking up at me, her eyes shining.

Bright blue and full of desire and need.

"Fuck, do you know what you do to me when you look at me like that?"

I press my erection into her torso. I'm raring to go. Blood rushes to my ears—what's left of it, anyway. I think it's almost all gone to my cock, which is throbbing out a beat in my pants.

A flash lights the sky behind us, accompanied by another clap of thunder, stinging the surrounding air.

I take my hands out of her hair and clasp her hand tightly in mine.

"We've got to go, babe. We don't want to be out when the lightning reaches here."

She wraps her fingers around mine and grips on as I lead her down the path, being careful of my footing. One wrong step and we could both end up landing in a dirty pile on top of each other. Although, there are much worse places I can think of.

I glance back. "You okay?" I raise my voice over the thunder and torrential rain.

Daisy giggles and shakes her head. My eyes drop to the swell of her breasts and hardened nipples on full display in her soaked top.

"Come on, almost there."

She follows me and we keep a steady pace behind Betsy until my house comes into view. We rush up the front steps just as another crack of lightning flashes. Betsy shakes herself and flings more mud all over the two of us.

"Thanks, girl." I laugh, opening the door and pulling Daisy's hand.

She doesn't move.

"Blake, I cannot go inside like this! I will wreck your house!" She looks down at the mud covering her boots and the rest of her body.

"Don't be silly. You're getting cold." Goosebumps are popping up all over her arms, and she lets go of my hand to wrap her arms around herself. I point through the open door. "Get in."

She shakes her head. "No way. My clothes are covered in mud. Can you bring me out a towel or something?" She bends down and starts pulling her boots and socks off.

I know I'm not going to win this argument, so I yank my boots off and head inside, returning a minute later with three towels.

"Thanks." Daisy smiles as she takes one and wipes her cheeks.

"You going to come inside now? Or do you want to stay out in that storm?" I look past her at the lightning forking in the sky above the lake as I bend down and give Betsy a vigorous rub with her own towel. Her back leg lifts off the ground and thumps by her side as I hit a sweet spot.

"You're good, girl." I pat her on the back, and she pads into the house.

Fortunately, storms don't bother her. We've been caught in a few when we've been out camping, and she's got used to the noise and flashing. I watch as she heads to her beanbag and drops onto it happily.

"You going to come in now?" I grab Daisy's hand and pull her up against my chest. "You need to get warm." My eyes drop to her lips, inches away from my own. The urge to bite down on them is overwhelming.

"I need to get *clean*." She smiles as I wipe a streak of mud off her face with my free hand. "Can I use your shower?"

I dust my knuckles back over her cheek. "You can use anything of mine you want. You know that."

Her eyes pinch slightly at the corners as she studies me, giving me a small smile.

"Come on." I pull her inside by the hand as another crack of lightning flashes at the same time as a deep rumble of thunder.

"This is crazy! It's right on top of us." Daisy beams at me as I lead her into the bathroom and turn the shower on.

"How long's it been since you saw a storm?" I grin back at the delight on her face as I peel my wet t-shirt off and drop it on the tiled floor.

"I don't know." Her voice is fast and full of excitement. "Ages... years!" She drags her t-shirt up over her head. "I love them. I find them cleansing, you know? And the way the air clears, and how everything smells afterward... the petrichor." She's grinning from ear to ear as she peels her shorts off and stands in front of me in just a white lace bra and panties.

"You getting in then?" I cock my head toward the walk-in shower I've turned on.

Daisy's eyes widen and she looks down at herself, as though just realising she's almost naked.

"Um..."

"It's okay. I'm happy to just watch if you don't want company. Although it's big enough for two." I smirk at her as I push my cargo pants and boxers down to my feet and kick them off so I'm completely naked. "And these..." I take a step toward her and slide my hands over her hips and under the fabric of her panties. "...these need to come off. They're wet."

She sucks in a breath as my fingers trail down her thighs, sliding her panties with them, until they drop to the floor. I'm waiting for her to stop me—hoping she won't.

"It wasn't the rain."

I drop my mouth to her neck and press my lips against her skin as I unclip her bra and peel it away from her breasts.

"What wasn't?" I murmur as I reach up to palm her breasts. Her nipples pebble as I rub my thumbs over them, and I bury my nose into her neck so I can inhale her scent.

"The reason my panties are wet."

A small moan vibrates in her throat as I run my nose along her jaw and kiss the other side of her neck. Her breathing quickens as I walk her backward, into the shower and underneath the hot spray of the water.

"Really?" I smile against her throat as I place another kiss there. "Why *are* they soaking, then? Tell me."

"Blake," she gasps as I sink two fingers deep inside her. Her arms go to my shoulders and she clings to me. Steam rises around us as hot water heats our skin.

"Tell me," I repeat as I fist my cock with one hand and slowly finger her with the other. She leans back against the tile wall and her eyes meet mine as I raise my head.

"Because of you," she pants and her mouth drops open as I add a third finger and pin her to the wall.

"Me?" I watch the way her cheeks flush and her eyelids flutter as I curl my fingers and stroke the sensitive spot on her front wall.

"Uh-huh." She digs her nails into my skin as I rub my thumb over her clit, keeping my fingers wedged deep inside her.

"What did I do?" I lift my chin and hold her gaze as she squirms against my hand.

"Blake, please," she pants; her chest rising and falling as her body holds me tight.

"Tell me, babe. And I'll give you what you need." My voice is deep, fighting to stay in control when all I can think about is losing myself in her.

Her eyes roll back in her head as she rides my fingers, soft moans falling from her lips one after another.

"Blake..."

"Tell me." I lean my forehead against hers and watch her lips part as she pants.

Her eyes fall closed as she tilts her head back.

"It's all for you."

I swirl my fingers inside her and she sucks in a breath and tenses.

"Keep going," I grit out, unable to tear my eyes away from her face and the pleasure on it.

Pleasure I'm giving her.

"It's all for you, Blake. Thinking about what I want to do with you makes me so wet." Her voice turns into a groan as I quicken my pace.

"Good girl," I growl.

I press my thumb harder against her clit and lower my lips to hers, catching her bottom lip between my teeth as she comes undone in my arms.

"Blake!" Her breaths are coming fast as the first tight spasm erupts around my fingers. She cries out as I draw her pleasure from deep inside her and pull it to the surface, taking it as my own—claiming it. "Blake!" She shudders around me.

"I could watch you come all day, babe... all day," I groan as she grinds herself down onto my hand.

"Blake." Daisy's voice is barely a whisper above the sounds of the shower and the storm outside. "I need... I want..." Our eyes lock and she runs her hands up into my hair. "I want you to fill every part of me so all I can see, all I can hear, all I can feel. Is *you*."

She kisses my lips and places her hand on my wrist, sliding my fingers out of her.

"Don't leave room for anything else, Blake. Only you." She turns around to face the tiled wall and looks back at me over her shoulder.

The sight of her here like this is almost more than I can take.

I fist my cock harder.

"Put your hands on the wall."

She places her palms flat against the tiles, arching back against me as my lips find the junction where her neck meets her shoulder.

"You're fucking beautiful."

My free hand palms her breast, and she cries out, her body quivering as I pinch her nipple.

"Blake, please."

The urgency in her voice has me ready to combust. She's here, ready for me. Asking for it. Begging for me to fill her.

I've died and gone to heaven.

"You want it like this? Me fucking you from behind?" I whisper in her ear as I nip it between my teeth.

She sighs, tipping her head back against my shoulder.

"Yes."

I hold the base of my cock and push it up between her folds, her body wrapping around it, sucking it in—welcoming it back to where it craves to be.

Where it belongs.

"Fuck," I hiss as I slide all the way inside her. She lets out a loud gasp as I draw back and slam back in.

"Yes, like that. Hard, Blake. Please. Do it hard."

I grasp her hip with one hand and take my other hand from her breast, snaking it up to her throat.

"You want me to fuck you hard? Is that what you're asking for, babe?" I growl in her ear.

She whimpers and clenches around me.

"Yes."

"Are you sure that's what you want?" I drive into her again, throwing her body forward.

"Yes! Do it, Blake."

I press my chest against her back, so she's flattened against the tile wall, her cheek resting against the back of her palm. I squeeze her neck gently.

"You know how hard I like to fuck you once I start. Are you sure that's what you want?" I growl in her ear.

She sucks in a breath and nods. "I know."

I bite her neck and she shudders, her pussy clamping down onto me. It's the final straw that breaks me.

I grab her hips with both hands and take a step back, taking her with me, my body staying buried deep inside hers. Daisy slides her hands down the tiles and lifts her ass, arching her spine so I can sink further into her with each punishing hit I deliver.

"Fuck, babe. You look incredible."

My eyes drop to where my cock pumps in and out of her body. She never lets me go; just sucks me back in and clamps down harder each time I push back in, taking everything I give her.

"Harder."

I look up at her tensed hands against the tiles as she pushes back onto me. Her tits are bouncing, and the room fills with the sound of slapping skin as I thrust into her.

"Fuck!" I tip my head back and bite my lip as every muscle in my body gears up for what I know is coming.

Daisy's panting and, as I drop my gaze back down, I find the most incredible sight. She's moved one hand to between her legs and is touching herself. Pleasuring herself.

"Tell me you're rubbing that swollen clit, babe. Please fucking tell me," I groan as I increase my pace.

"I'm... Blake... God. You feel so good inside me!" Her voice cracks as she cries out.

I feel good?

"It's you that feels good." My eyes drop to her arm, moving frantically as she brings herself closer to her release.

"Come on me," I hiss, driving into her harder, making her toes dance against the floor of the shower. "Come around my cock and then let me fill you up."

She tenses at my words, going silent for a few seconds, before a scream breaks from her lips and she shakes around me.

"Blake! Oh, my God!"

Her body spasms in deep, consuming waves, drowning me along with it.

"Fuck!"

I screw my eyes shut and dig my fingers into her hips as I jerk. Pulse after pulse forces its way from my body to meet hers. I growl like an animal from deep inside my chest. It's primal and rough as I sink deeper. She cries out, matching every pulse of pleasure my body feels with her own.

I lose myself in her, surrendering everything until all I hear is my heart thundering in my ears, and my lungs sucking in deep breaths.

"Blake?"

The tension leaves my body, leaving a blissful calm washing over me.

"Blake?"

I open my eyes and flex my fingers. My senses pulling back together, enabling me to focus.

Water. Heat. Steam.

Soft. Skin. *Her.*

"Blake?"

Beautiful blue eyes look back at me. Then they're moving closer as the heat around my cock is replaced with the heat of skin pressing against my chest. Hands slide up into my hair and then the eyes are right in front of me.

I stare back into them, my heart still hammering in my chest.

Warm lips graze mine and two words are whispered.

"Thank you."

Chapter Eighteen

Daisy

"WHY ARE YOU THANKING me?" Deep green eyes search mine as large, firm hands reach up and cup my face.

As I bite my lip, my gaze drops to Blake's mouth and I lift a finger, running it absentmindedly along his full lower lip.

"You make me forget." My finger keeps tracing his lip until he leans forward, pressing a kiss to my forehead.

"I wish you didn't have things you feel you need to forget." His lips rest against my skin as he keeps me close.

Leaning into him, I squeeze my eyes shut. I could stay here forever, listening to the water rain down over us. Being held in his arms. Just being in the moment. Blake is a vacation from my actual life. The one I left back in England.

My eyes burn and I pull away, grabbing a bottle of shower gel as I turn my back to him so he can't see my face.

"Will you help make sure I get all the mud off?" I glance back over my shoulder at him.

"Any excuse to get my hands over your hot little body." He winks as he takes the bottle from me and squeezes some gel into his hand. Then I feel the sweetest relief as tension leaves my shoulders.

"Hey, I hope you aren't thinking about stealing my job," I groan in pleasure as his capable hands work out the knots in my neck.

He chuckles as he moves his hands around the front and massages foamy bubbles over my breasts. I push them into his hands as he rolls my nipples between his thumb and finger.

"I'm never going to want to leave this shower." I sigh as he slides his hands down over my hips.

"That's fine by me."

His breath tickles my ear before he spins me to face him and brings his mouth down over mine. I lose myself in the warmth of his kiss. It's gentle and tender. But there's no doubt about who's in control as his tongue slides inside my mouth and I moan in response. He wraps his arms around me lazily, pulling me closer, as though me being here is the most natural thing in the world to him.

As if I belong.

"Do you think the storm's stopped?"

I break the kiss and tilt my head, listening. All I can hear is the pounding of my heart in my ears. I swallow down the queasiness threatening to rise from my stomach from thinking about going home. I don't want to think about it now. Not when I'm here with Blake, and everything feels so good. So real, and so right.

"Sounds like it. You want to make our own storm again?" He grins and drops his mouth to my neck, tracing kisses down to my shoulder.

The feel of his lips against my skin sends warmth radiating through my chest.

"Blake Anderson. Don't you need to rest?" I giggle as he presses his hard length against my side.

"With you? Never." He laughs and then begins his assault on my neck again.

I tilt my head back and close my eyes, letting the water wash away the dirt.

And letting Blake's mouth wash away my memories again.

For now.

"Hey, guys. You're looking very... energized." Kayla's eyes drop to Blake's arm wrapped around me; his hand tucked into the back pocket of my denim shorts.

"Amazing what a good storm does for the body and senses, isn't it, babe?" He grins at me, then takes his arm back and heads off toward the kitchen to seek out Travis, Betsy following him.

Babe? Kayla mouths at me, her eyebrows shooting up.

I glance behind her up the hallway to make sure Blake is out of earshot.

"Yeah." I shrug, biting my lip.

"Oh, no! No, no, no!" Her eyes go wide. "You do not get to say nothing! What the hell's been going on? You two look like you've been banging each other's brains out!" she whisper-shouts at me and I grab her arm and pull her into their downstairs study.

"Shh. I don't want Blake to think I'm talking about him."

Kayla folds her arms and fixes me with an unimpressed smirk.

"This is Blake we're talking about. He'll love knowing you're talking about him!" She shakes her head in disbelief. "So last week wasn't a one-off, then?"

I bite my lip and drop my eyes to the floor.

Kayla groans. "Just how many times have you two boned?"

"Three, wait... no, four," I admit, realising the shower counts as two. It's the reason we were late to Kayla and Travis' when they texted to invite us both to dinner at their house tonight. Two separate texts, one to each of our phones, that came through as Blake was fucking me in the shower for the second time. It was comical, really. Kayla texting me, Travis texting Blake. I'm sure they suspected we were together, but neither said a word. Not until now, anyway.

"This is a thing, then? The two of you?" Kayla watches me closely, waiting for an answer.

"I don't know. I don't..." I blow out a breath as my shoulders drop. "I don't know what it is, Kayla."

"Well, looks pretty cozy to me. Blake's hand can't even use his own pocket."

I look her in the eye, biting my cheek. "His own pocket?"

Her eyes light up as we look at each other. She's the first one to crack. Her shoulders shake as she puts her hand over her mouth and laughs.

I can't help joining in either and burst into laughter. "From all of that, you took his hand in my pocket as being the biggest factor?"

She shakes her head, trying to stop her laugh.

"It is!" She points at me, fixing her eyes on my face. "It's all familiar and cozy. It's couple shit. Anyone can fuck, Dee. But that hand in your pocket? He may as well have been asking you to move in!"

My laugh dies in my throat, and I stare at her, dumbfounded.

"What? That's not what it is. It's nothing like that. Blake and I... we are just friends. It's..."

I hope the words will come to me. The right words to explain to Kayla that what I and Blake are doing is just... well, it's helping each other. It's a distraction for me, and it's nothing for him.

Just sex.

She looks at me and sighs. "What happened to you, Dee?" Concern is suddenly etched over her face as she pulls her brows together, a line forming between them.

"What do you mean?" I shift from foot to foot, wondering if it suddenly got hotter in here, or if it's just me.

"When did you stop seeing what's going on? When did you stop noticing?" She stares at me, waiting for an answer.

Her words sting like salt on a wound.

"That's not what I'm doing."

Kayla raises an eyebrow.

"It isn't! There's nothing between us! Nothing!"

"Trav wants to know what you want to drink," a deep voice cuts in.

My eyes whip around to the doorway. Blake's leaning against the frame, his arms crossed, biceps bulging in his black t-shirt. I swallow down the lump in my throat as my eyes meet his.

"I'll give him a hand." Kayla's eyes catch mine before she brushes past Blake and disappears, leaving me feeling like a deer caught in headlights.

"I um—" I glance away at a photograph on the desk. It's of Kayla and Travis spraying a bottle of champagne in the street outside the veterinary clinic. It must be the day they started the business. My chest tightens. Another life event of theirs I missed.

"You, what?"

Blake has moved while I was staring at the photo and is standing so close to me, I can smell his woody sea salt scent. I close my eyes briefly as the aroma calms me.

"I was just talking with Kayla." I open my eyes into the intense green stare he's fixed on me. He says nothing, just watches me as I wriggle like a worm on a hook. "I was telling her about—"

He lifts his hand and grasps the back of my neck, drawing me toward him as he presses his lips down to mine and kisses me so deeply, I'm panting when he pulls back. My lips tingle and all I can do is stare up at him as his eyes search mine, his hand still holding me in place behind my neck.

"Try listening to your body and not your head." His words are gentle. Whispered. But the fire in his eyes tells me he heard every word. "Come on, they're waiting for us."

He grabs my hand, leading me to the kitchen before I can say anything. Before I can tell him I'm sorry. Before I can explain that it wasn't meant to sound harsh, but that I know what this is. It's not serious between us. I'll be leaving soon, and he'll find someone better. Someone who deserves him. He leads me away before I can say any of those things, though.

So, I don't say them.

Instead, I thread my fingers through his and even put my other hand on top of our entwined ones.

Instead, I keep my hand in his underneath the table throughout dinner with our friends, only taking it back when I really must. Returning it as soon as I can and slipping it back into his familiar grip.

Instead, I do that.

Two hours, and a load of homemade tacos later, the four of us are still sitting around the dinner table, laughing, as we bring up old stories.

"Hey, Dee. Do you remember the summer when we went cliff diving, and you lost your bikini top? You didn't even realize to start with." Kayla laughs before taking a sip of her homemade margarita.

"I do." Blake grins beside me, which earns him a playful slap from me.

"You do not! You didn't jump until after me."

"Why do you think I threw myself off the cliff behind you so fast?" His green eyes light up as I turn to him, my mouth open. He places two fingers on my chin and closes it. "You had nice tits back then, but they're fucking outstanding now." He winks as I slap him across his chest again. A deep chuckle rumbles from his chest as I laugh in shock.

I catch Kayla looking at us both, a smug smile on her face as she arches an eyebrow.

"Trav? Help me take the plates."

CAPTURED BY MR. WILD

He's busy fussing Betsy, who's sat next to the table.

"Trav. Now." Kayla knocks on the back of his chair with her hip when she stands, and I watch as he rises and picks up some plates.

"Let me help you. You guys did all the cooking."

"Sit!" Kayla barks out, her eyes darting to Blake and then back to me as she smiles sweetly. "I mean, please sit. You two look comfortable, and you're our guests."

"You've never called me a guest before," Blake pipes up, chuckling as Kayla narrows her eyes at him and sticks her tongue out.

"Shut it, dork face. Unless you want to be on clean up duty."

He throws his hands up in the air. "I didn't say anything. Did you hear anything, Betsy?" Betsy turns and looks at him when he says her name. "Nah, Betsy didn't hear anything either. And she's got super canine hearing."

"Whatever." Kayla rolls her eyes as Travis laughs and follows her across the open room to the kitchen area on the other side.

I lean back in my chair. I've missed this so much. Hanging out with these guys and just laughing together. My mum and dad sent me to a school away from where we lived. I had to get two buses every morning, but they were adamant I go to one as far away from the area we lived as possible. As a result, although I had friends, I never saw them much at weekends or after school. And then every holiday, I came over here to stay with my aunt. I used to wonder how Mum and Dad afforded all the plane tickets, but one day I overheard Dad on the phone with my aunt and realized she had been paying for them all along.

Coming here was my sanctuary. Blake, Kayla, and Travis were my best friends. They were who I told my secrets to, who I had my first illegal drink with, who I stayed up late watching movies with and eating popcorn. They took my life from gray to full-blown technicolour. The ten years not seeing them after my aunt passed were hard. The last few years, even harder.

169

ELLE NICOLL

"You look worried. You still wondering where that bikini top went?" Blake's warm gaze rests on my face as I snap out of my trip down memory lane.

"What? Oh!" I laugh. "Wherever it went, they can keep it."

"Yeah. Wouldn't fit now, anyway." Blake's eyes drop to my breasts in my low-cut vest.

"Pervert." I laugh, secretly glowing inside.

"Absolutely." He grins, wrapping an arm around me. "You make me want to be extremely pervy." He sinks his mouth into the crook of my neck and sucks, eliciting a small gasp from me. "In fact, why don't I take you home now and show you?"

"I think that's a great idea!" Kayla shouts from the kitchen. "All this sexual energy flying around has got me in the mood to be alone with my husband." She laughs as Travis' eyes widen and he grins at her.

"Yep, thanks for coming! Let yourselves out!" He raises a hand and waves at us as he grabs Kayla and kisses her.

I watch them with a giggle as Blake's arm tightens around my shoulder and he kisses my temple.

Despite their joking, it's still another forty minutes before we leave as we just keep chatting about something, which then starts off a whole new story and another round of laughter. I can't remember the last time I had such a great night.

"You good?" Blake smiles at me as we climb into his truck and he starts the engine.

"Yeah." I beam at him as I wrap an arm around Betsy, who's sat between us, and rub my nose against her silky ear.

"Give her too much love and you'll turn my dog soft." His eyes crinkle at the corners as he watches her lean into me.

"Don't give me that, Blake Anderson. I know you love Betsy more than yourself... if that's possible." I giggle as he throws his mouth open in mock outrage.

"You hear that, Betsy? Someone wants to walk home!"

I laugh as I watch a grin spread over his face.

"Someone would really like to *not* walk home, please." I reach a hand over and squeeze his thigh, giving him my best big baby doll eyes as he looks over at me.

He sucks a breath in through his teeth and looks back out the windscreen as he drives. Then the warmth of his hand covers mine as he laces his fingers through my own.

"Does your daddy make a habit of driving one-handed?" I whisper to Betsy, who looks at me and sniffs my cheek, her nose tickling my skin.

"No. He does not." Blake keeps his eyes on the road, the corners of his mouth twitching.

"I bet he does," I say to Betsy. "I bet he's held a million girls' hands in this truck."

"No. He has not." Blake's eyes are still on the road, amusement growing in them.

"A thousand, then?" I whisper.

"No." Blake keeps staring straight ahead.

"A few hundred?"

Blake's shaking his head as I look up, smiling to himself.

"Maybe just his girlfriend Cindy's, then?"

Blake's fingers tense between mine and his smile's gone when I sneak a glance at him.

"She was never my girlfriend."

"Oh."

I feel my shoulders fall as he confirms what Kayla implied. I don't know why I even started with these stupid questions. I don't want to know what Blake did before I got here. I don't want to know what he might plan to do when I leave, either.

I don't want to think about any of that, so instead I turn and stare out of my window.

Blake clears his throat.

"We were a mistake. I should never have crossed that line. I knew she liked me. But I didn't feel the same. She wanted things I didn't. I told her from the beginning that I wasn't looking for that."

"What's that?" I ask, despite knowing I should stop this conversation right now.

"Living together. Marriage. You know."

I don't.

Since Mick, my relationship expectations start and end with someone who doesn't cover up the fact they're an evil fucker with a black heart. Something I only found out about him when it was already too late.

I sigh as Blake's thumb strokes over my knuckles.

"You going to stay with us again tonight?"

I look over at him. It's hard to see his eyes now in the darkened truck. We've left the main streets and are heading up the road toward the lake. The lights of the town are behind us.

I chew my lip as I think about going to bed alone in my aunt's almost empty house, waking up drenched in sweat from another nightmare. All of that will always be waiting for me. Why can't I have one more night of blissful sleep?

"Okay," I whisper. "I'd like that."

Blake drops me at work the next morning. We didn't have sex again last night. Instead, he put the waves noise app on and just held me in his arms. I don't know if it was mentioning Cindy that did it, but he didn't even try anything or make any sexual jokes.

So unlike Blake.

Maybe he's had enough. Maybe my staying another night was the cherry on the cake. I mean, he said it himself; he doesn't want to do the living together thing. It's why he and Cindy ended things before they even started. Maybe I outstayed my welcome? But then he was the one who invited me. And the way he wrapped me in his arms, and I awoke with my head on his chest and his lips pressed to my hair? That's not what you do when you wish someone wasn't there, is it?

I smile to myself as I fold and tidy some towels behind the spa reception desk. Even if it's over and he wants to just be friends again, I don't regret a single moment. Being with Blake is the lightest I've felt in years.

"Someone looks like they enjoyed their days off?"

"Oh, hi, Maria."

I grin as I see her approach from the main door and walk over to the desk. She's wearing a fitted red dress with a white blazer over the top, and her long, sleek hair is shining as it falls over her shoulders. I've no idea how she looks so put together all the time. She's one of those people who probably wakes up looking stylish.

"Come on, then." She tilts her head to one side. "What's got you smiling so much?"

I shake my head and drop my eyes back to the stack of towels, straightening them again. "Nothing. I just had dinner with friends last night. It felt good to laugh."

When she doesn't say anything, I peek over at her and she's looking at me with narrowed eyes, a small smile on her red lips.

"I'm not buying it, Dee." She taps a red nail against her lips as she studies me. "There's something different about you. You seem brighter, more relaxed."

"I had a good night's sleep." I smile as I think about how well I slept wrapped up in Blake. Not a nightmare in sight.

"Mmm, okay." Maria arches a perfect brow, and I can't help but laugh.

"Honestly, that's all it is. Some decent sleep... finally." My shoulders relax as I sigh and stack the white towels neatly on the shelves.

"Well, I'm glad one of us is sleeping." She groans as she taps her nails on the counter. I look at her furrowed brow and the way her lips are twisting into a frown.

"Is everything okay? You look worried?" I don't think I've ever seen Maria look anything less than one hundred percent cool and collected before.

"Yes, it's just..." She huffs out a breath as she looks around the reception area. It's empty. All the clients are currently in their treatments with the other therapists, and no more are due for at least half an hour. "We may have a slight problem with our supplier."

"Oh?"

She taps her fingers on the counter again, her jaw tense as she gazes around.

"They've run out of our signature blend. Said they can't source any more banana flower. There was a problem with some fruit flies, and the entire supply was destroyed. It's going to be at least a month before they can recover and get some products for us. They didn't even tell me until this week's order never arrived and I called to chase it."

"That's awful."

The spa has its own signature blend, which it uses in most of its products. It gives them all their own unique, identifiable fragrance. Not many places make products with the same scent. We get orders for it from all over the country, from people who have either been guests at the hotel, or who have just heard of the spa.

"Yes, it's certainly causing some hiccups." Maria looks at me and sighs. "The meeting with Griffin Parker is only two days away, and I was supposed to be giving him twenty complimentary gift packs to take back to his management team to showcase the spa and its products. I don't know what I'm going to do."

I gnaw on my lip. Maria has been so excited about this opportunity in New York, and the possibility of expanding the salon. She's been so kind to me to give me a job when I needed one. I wish I could help. I wish...

"Why don't we make our own?"

Her eyes widen as she stares at me. "What do you mean?"

"I make my own soaps and hand balms. I mean, they're not the spa ones, but we could make a similar scent. I'm sure we can mix up something ourselves." I clap my hands together as another idea hits me. "Or better still, you could make a new signature scent."

Maria purses her lips in thought as she listens to me.

"Think about it. The New York spa could have its own scent, exclusive to there. Different to the Hope Cove one. Ours is tropical and beachy and... well, Californian. New York could have something heavier. Something sexy and more edgy."

Maria's eyes light up as she reaches over and grabs both of my hands.

"Dee! You're a genius!" She pulls her cell phone out of her pocket and starts tapping into it. "Okay. I can make a new signature blend, and I have enough carrier oils to do a massage one," she murmurs to herself as she makes notes on her phone.

I watch with a grin on my face at how animated she is. She told me she started making her own perfumes when she was just a little girl. She'd mix flower petals and herbs together and bottle them up for her grandma's birthday. I think her skills have come a long way since then, but it's clear by the excitement on her face that this is what she loves. Creating something new and beautiful for others to enjoy.

"Dee, if I can get the scent mix to you by tomorrow, do you think you could make twenty hand balms and twenty soaps using it?"

"Sorry, what?" I look at her, focusing back on our conversation.

"I know it's a huge ask, but I'll pay you for the materials, and your time, of course. There's just no way I can mix up all the products by myself in time and have them all ready." Her large brown eyes look at me hopefully.

"Absolutely!" I nod with enthusiasm, my mind already wondering how the hell I'm going to make forty products in time for the day after tomorrow. I need to get the ingredients, mix everything, and hope it comes out well. Cool it. Set it. My mind is already racing with the possibilities of all the things that could go wrong and ruin the entire batch.

"Oh, thank you, Dee! Thank you!" Maria comes around the desk and pulls me into a hug. "I can't believe I got so lucky to have you come and be a part of the team."

I hug her back as warmth spreads in my chest. I love it here. The other therapists are lovely, and Maria is an incredible boss. I'm the lucky one to be working here. And to hear her say I'm one of the team... I swallow the lump in my throat as a smile spreads over my face.

"It's no problem. I'm happy to help."

"Dee, you're amazing!" Maria beams at me as she pulls back. "Okay. I need to go get started on blending. I'm going to make something that smells so good that Mr. Parker is going to drool!"

I laugh and shake my head as she hurries to the door.

"I'll drop the blend around to your house first thing in the morning, okay?"

"Sure." I grin, waving to her.

When the door falls shut, my grin freezes.

Shit.

Seriously, how the hell am I going to do this? I rub my hand over my mouth as I dart my eyes around and think. I can't let Maria down, but doing this on my own is going to be almost impossible. I pull my cell out of my bag and fire off a text.

Me: Hey, Kayla. I could do with a hand doing something for work. Are you free tomorrow?

I chew my lips as I wait for her to respond.

Kayla: I wish I could say yes, but Trav has surgery booked at the clinic and I'm assisting. I can't get out of it. I can help in the evening if that'll work?

I let out a groan and rock back and forth on my heels as I respond.

Me: Thanks, but it needs to be in the day.

Kayla: Why don't you ask Blake? If you think you can stop having sex long enough to get something done, then I'm sure he'll be free?!

I snort at her words before reading them again. I *could* ask Blake. He was helpful last time, and he's got an idea of what to do already. I look down at her text again. Plus, after last night and his distinct lack of anything remotely sexual toward me, I think I can safely say we won't be a distraction to each other. As fun as it was, it looks like that ship might have sailed now. Me and my stupid big mouth asking him about Cindy, and all that.

Even though I know it was only a short-term thing, I guess I was hoping it wouldn't be this short term.

I take a deep breath and bring Blake's number up on my phone, biting my lip as it rings.

"Hey, babe," his deep voice answers, and I scold myself mentally as my stomach flutters with butterflies.

"Hey yourself," I murmur, hating that just the sound of his voice has such an effect on me.

"What's up?" His voice is warm, and I can hear him mutter something to Betsy as he waits for my answer. I smile at the thought of the two of them together.

"Are you busy tomorrow?"

"Yep," he answers without missing a beat.

"Oh." My shoulders drop. "Okay, well... sorry to have interrupted whatever it is you're doing. I better get back to work—"

"Babe." He chuckles. "I'm busy tomorrow with whatever it is you're about to suggest."

"What?" My cheeks heat as he laughs again.

"You're calling me asking what I'm doing tomorrow, so I'm assuming you're about to suggest something? Whatever it is, yes. I'll see you, then."

"Okay, then." I tuck my hair behind my ear as I smile.

"Okay, then." Blake mirrors my words.

"Thanks, Blake."

"Anytime, babe." I hear the smile in his voice as he hangs up.

I doubt it's as big as the one I can feel spreading over my face right now.

Chapter Nineteen

Blake

"I CANNOT BELIEVE YOU are wearing that again!" Daisy giggles as I tie the apron strings around my back.

"What? I can't risk having your cream spraying all over my clothes again, can I?"

Daisy's face creases up as she looks at me. "Fine." She holds up a hand. "I won't say another word."

"I find that hard to believe." I wink at her as she gasps.

"Blake Anderson! You're so rude."

I walk over to her and dip my mouth to her ear. "Only with you, babe."

She shakes her head with a smirk and turns her back to me, opening a high cupboard and reaching up to a shelf with bowls on.

"Need a hand?" I move behind her.

"No, thanks. I've got it." Her fingers wrap around a bowl and she lifts it down.

"I wasn't talking about the bowl." I grin at her as I wrap a hand around her waist and spin her, pulling her up against me. I ease my thumb under the fabric of her t-shirt and stroke her hip bone as I stare into her eyes.

She tilts her head back to look up at me, her lips parted. "I thought the other day was the last time."

My thumb freezes against her skin. "Really?"

Her eyes drop to my lips and back up, and I watch as she licks her own. "Yes."

I stroke her skin again, more gently this time.

"Did you want it to be?" I lean closer to her, placing my other hand up on her neck. Her pulse beats out a fast rhythm beneath my fingertips.

Her bright blue eyes search mine as she opens her mouth. "I..."

Betsy's sudden bark has Daisy jumping back from me and clutching her chest. Her eyes flash with something before she takes a deep, steadying breath.

"God, Betsy. You scared me." She smiles as relief washes over her face and the reason for Betsy's bark becomes apparent as there's a knock at the door.

"She must have heard someone coming up the steps. You okay?" I search Daisy's face for the earlier emotion I saw in her eyes. The same one I heard in her voice the first night I spent with her and she talked in her sleep.

Fear.

"I'm fine." She smiles at me brightly, blowing off my concern as she heads to the door and opens it.

I can hear another woman's voice carrying down the hallway toward the kitchen as Daisy walks back in. A woman with long dark hair, wearing a skirt suit comes in behind her. Betsy jumps up off the bean bag I brought around for her and pads over to say hello.

"Blake, this is Maria, my boss."

I reach out and shake the woman's hand after she's finished giving Betsy a fuss.

"Oh, Blake Anderson! I've seen your show." She smiles warmly at me. There's no hidden tone like I've noticed in a lot of women's voices when they mention the show.

"You have, huh?"

"Yes. My grandmother loves it! She's staying with me at the moment."

"I really need to see what I'm missing. I haven't watched it. But if your grandmother recommends it..." Daisy's eyes light up as I grab her around the waist and pull her into my side, widening my eyes at her in a playful warning.

"She sure does. She says she'd go camping any night of the week with you." Maria grins as Daisy lets out a snort and covers her mouth with her hand. "And your pictures! Oh, my goodness. Ralph showed me some in the store in town you'd given him. I know the hotel would be interested if you're selling any?" Maria's eyes light up as she looks at me.

I run a hand around the back of my neck. I'm sure Ralph means well. But those photos are for his eyes only.

"Nah, it's just a hobby."

"Oh. Well, if you change your mind..." She smiles at me and then places a dark glass bottle down on the counter.

Daisy gives me a puzzled look, which I return with my best comedy 'smolder', causing her to burst out in a giggle.

"I was going to suggest I stay and help for an hour before I head back to finish the products I'm working on. But I can see you've already got someone hands-on to assist." Maria arches an eyebrow at the two of us, her eyes dropping to my apron.

"Thanks, Maria. I think we'll manage." Daisy giggles again.

"I'm sure you will. Nice to meet you, Blake." She smiles at me and then turns to Daisy. "Thank you again, Dee. Honestly, you are a lifesaver! I swear, once I've met this Mr. Parker, I'm going to need a vacation to recover."

"It's no problem, honestly. I'm more than happy after everything you've done for me." Daisy grins at her and the two of them head back toward the front door as I look over at Betsy.

"Her grandmother likes the show, girl." Betsy's eyes light up as I waggle my brows at her. "Yeah, all right. I know they tune in for you, really. You don't have to rub it in." She wags her tail and pads over to me, dropping to the floor and rolling onto her back, looking up and waiting expectantly. "Seriously? You want to be the star *and* get your belly scratched."

I chuckle as I squat down and pat my hand against her stomach, giving her some love.

"And you said I would make her soft." Daisy's leaning against the doorframe, her arms crossed, pushing her perfect tits up as she watches the two of us.

"Playtime's over, girl. The boss is back," I whisper to Betsy as I stand.

Daisy shakes her head and tuts, a small smile playing on her lips as she pushes off the frame and heads to the counter, picking up the glass bottle Maria left.

She unscrews the lid and her eyelids flutter closed as she inhales. "That woman is a genius! Blake, come and smell this."

I move next to her and breathe in as she raises the bottle for me to smell.

"Wow. That smells... erotic."

It's deep and spicy... sensual. It reminds me of the massage Daisy gave me. My dick twitches at the thought.

"Incredible, isn't it? I think she must have used ginseng as one ingredient." Daisy sniffs it again. "It's an aphrodisiac."

"Really?" I smirk at her. "So that massage you gave me at the spa... you drugged me into submission?"

"What?" Daisy's eyes go wild, and she pushes me in the chest.

I laugh as I grab her hand and turn it so I can kiss her palm. Her eyes are watching my lips against her skin.

"The only thing being drugged is myself."

Her tongue comes out, wetting her lips as I step closer to her and wrap my other arm around her waist.

"What are you talking about?" I murmur as I lean down and brush my lips over her neck.

Her eyes shutter closed as she lets out a sigh. "I've been playing around."

"Oh, yeah? I like the sound of that. Can I join in?"

I chuckle as she pulls back to look at me and then rolls her eyes. "Blake."

"I'm sorry. Tell me more about what you've been playing with when you're by yourself." I grin as I look at her, keeping her firmly encircled in my arms.

"I'm not going to tell you if you can't be serious."

"I can be serious!" I relax my face and think about Travis telling a long, boring story. He takes ages to get to the point sometimes.

"You look like you're about to fall asleep." Daisy snorts. "Although, that's kind of fitting, because that's what I've been experimenting with."

"Sleep?" My arms tense around her at her confession. I know she has nightmares and can't fall asleep without her waves sound playing. But that's about all I know.

I wait for her to continue, watching as she chews on her bottom lip.

"Yeah. I've been trying out some sleep tonics. Just herbal things to add into a drink before bedtime. I'm hoping it'll help me sleep better." Her voice trails off as her eyes fix on a spot on the front of her apron I'm wearing.

"Is it helping?" I watch as a frown crosses her face, followed by a flush in her cheeks.

"I'm not sure. The last two nights, I haven't taken it."

"Ah." I nod as she meets my gaze. "I've been delaying the scientific trials."

Her eyes light up as she smiles at me. "Yeah, something like that. Maybe I should just bottle you. I sleep fine when you're there."

I smile back, but before I can say anything, she looks away and carries on talking.

"They seem to help me fall asleep. But as for the rest..."

I take one hand and hold her chin with my fingers, bringing her eyes back to mine.

"Tell me," I urge softly.

Her eyes scan between mine, and there's a long pause before she takes a deep breath.

"I have nightmares, Blake. Almost every night. I remember things. Relive them."

Her face pales, but I never take my eyes off hers as I listen intently.

"Mickey, he used to..." She gulps as her eyes turn glassy. "He used to recite that rhyme to me. You know the one—*he loves me, he loves me not.*"

My jaw tenses as her eyes return to the spot on the apron and I lower my hand to her waist.

"He'd say it while he plucked the petals out of flowers—daisies, mostly. If it ended on, *'he loves me not'*, then he'd laugh. If it ended on, *'he loves me'*, then he'd say it didn't count because a daisy isn't really a flower. It's a weed in disguise."

I suck a deep breath in through my nose, gritting my teeth as the pressure in my chest grows.

"Jesus," I hiss, tightening my arms around Daisy's waist.

"Blake?" She lays her palms flat against my chest, which is expanding with each deep breath I take as I attempt to control the livid fire that's lancing through my veins. "I'm not telling you because I want you to get mad or anything. I'm just telling you because..." She lets out a deep sigh, laced with emotion as her shoulders drop. "I'm telling you because you're my friend, and I've never really told anyone. Not all of it."

I pull her into me and place my chin on top of her head as I stare off into the distance. Thoughts about a million ways to murder a man painfully running through my head.

"So, what happened? Before you came here?"

She presses her cheek against the base of my neck, and I hear her let out a small sigh as she sinks into me. I tighten my hold on her, my nerves grating with unease over what might come from her lips next. I wait for her to speak.

"I told him it was over. That I'd had enough, and that I was fed up with the way he treated me. I said he was a bully and that he made me sick just looking at him." She takes a deep breath. "I don't know why I stayed with him for so long, Blake. I always wondered how women end up in those kinds of relationships. Why they don't just leave. But it's not until you're in that situation that you realize how hard it is. It creeps in like a poison, and by the time you know something is wrong, it's too late. They have you. They worm their way into your head and make you believe you deserve the way they speak to you, the way they use their fists. Make you think it's your fault."

She moves her palms from my chest and wraps them around my waist.

"He was charming at first. But it wasn't long before he changed. It took me a lot longer to catch up and finally see him for what he was. I should have known from his surname—Frost." She lets out a small, humorless laugh. "Frost always destroys flowers."

I blow out a long breath through gritted teeth. I'm surprised Daisy is still comfortable in my arms. The fire blazing inside me feels hotter than molten lava. I've never wanted to tear someone limb from bloody limb with my bare hands before. Break every bone in their body and make them experience pain more excruciating than the darkest nightmares born in hell could even create.

"If I ever see him—"

"Blake!" Daisy pulls back from me, her eyes wild. "No! He's caused enough pain. I..." She shakes her head. "Can we just stop talking about him now? *Please.*"

185

It takes all my strength and some deep breaths to calm myself enough to look into her eyes. I take my hands from around her waist and hold her hands in mine.

"You know what happens after frost, don't you?"

A line appears in between her brows as she looks at me.

"Spring. When the flowers push their way back out into the world. When they bloom again."

"Blake," she whispers, her eyes shining.

"Hey, I'm not trying to upset you, babe." My chest burns as I look at the water collecting on her lower lids.

"I know." She nods, giving me a small smile. "And what you just said, it's actually really beautiful, but... I can't think about him anymore today. Can we just stop?" Her eyes glance to the bottle Maria dropped around. "Maria is relying on my help, and I can't let her down."

I take another deep, steadying breath before squeezing her hands in mine. It's obvious talking about it has drained her. I can see it in her eyes. I'll do anything to take away the sadness that's hiding behind them.

"Okay. Chief Cream Whipper is here, reporting for duty." I lift a hand and salute her.

Her face relaxes, and she smiles at me. "Good. Try not to cover us both with it this time."

I open my mouth, but she presses her finger to my lips.

"And no filthy innuendos. Think you can manage that?" she asks as I stick out my bottom lip.

"I want to talk to my union rep," I mutter, watching as she turns to gather ingredients. Her shoulders shake as she laughs quietly.

"You do that. Right after you finish."

I smirk as I shake my head and move to stand next to her.

We work in companionable silence, measuring, mixing, melting, and whipping. Until finally, we are surrounded by enough product to fill forty glass jars once it's cooled.

"I think Betsy got the best deal in this." I look over to where she's laid out, dozing.

Daisy smiles as she follows my gaze. "You mean, you'd rather be napping than giving your biceps a workout, making hand cream and soap?"

"I'd rather be giving you a workout." I grin as I grab her from behind and swoop down to kiss her neck.

She giggles as she tries to fight me off. "I was thinking you were fatigued."

"What are you talking about now?" I trail kisses up her neck to her ear as I grasp her hips and pull her back against me.

"After last night, you didn't—"

I spin her around and cover her mouth with mine, pulling her into a deep kiss. Her hands go to my shoulders and she moans into my mouth as my tongue finds hers.

I pull back and rest my forehead against hers.

"You thought just because I didn't ravish you all night, that I wasn't secretly hiding how hard my dick was with you in my bed with me?"

"Blake!" Her mouth drops open.

"Come on, babe." I smirk. "You should know what you do to me by now."

I kiss her open lips. "And you should also know that I'm not going to keep you up all night riding my cock with your fantastic tits on display, when I could sense that's not what you needed."

She cocks her head to one side, her eyes roaming over my face. A low groan builds in my throat.

"Don't look at me like that."

"Like what?" She widens her eyes at me.

"Like you're picturing what I just said."

"I'm not."

My stomach drops in disappointment. "Oh."

Daisy glances over at Betsy, who's still asleep, before looking at me from under her lashes. Her pink lips part as she stands on her tiptoes and brings her lips to my ear. Her sweet breath dances against my skin as she whispers, "I'm picturing riding your face first."

I grab her face in my hands and fix my eyes on hers. "You mean that?"

She bites her lip and nods.

"Then what the fuck we still doing in here?"

She giggles as I grab her around the waist and hoist her over my shoulder, carrying her upstairs to the bedroom. I throw her down onto the bed and fall back onto it next to her.

"Get that sweet pussy on my face, babe." I grin at her as I lose the apron and yank my t-shirt up over my head.

She hesitates for a fraction of a second as she smiles at me.

My next word comes out as one low growl.

"Now!"

Chapter Twenty
Daisy

"GOOD MORNING!" I BEAM at Sam on the main reception desk as I breeze past toward the spa entrance.

"Someone woke up on the right side of the bed this morning." He waggles his eyebrows at me as I glance back over my shoulder and see Blake's truck pulling away outside.

"I sure did." I grin back, thinking about the wake-up Blake gave me this morning after he and Betsy stayed all night.

"Well, happiness suits you. Have a good day!" Sam calls after me.

"Thanks, Sam. You too!"

I'm humming to myself as I walk into the spa, a box containing the homemade products for Maria in my arms.

"Oh, my goodness, you're here!" Maria claps her hands in delight as she sees me enter, and hurries over to help me with the box.

"It's okay, it's not heavy."

We both rest it down on the counter and she opens the top, peering inside.

"Dee!" she gasps, lifting out a glass jar and unscrewing the lid to smell the smooth hand balm inside. "These are perfect! Thank you so much! Honestly, you do not know how much better I feel about this meeting now."

"You all ready, then?" I glance behind her to where twenty sleek, black, ribbon-handled gift bags are lined up, a beautiful deep teal tissue paper spilling out over the top of each one.

"I am now that you're here." She grins as she distributes the jars amongst the gift bags. I reach into the box and help her.

"These look beautiful, Maria. There's no way Mr. Parker will not want to open a branch of your spa in his hotel when he meets you and sees what you're capable of."

Maria lifts her shoulders and grins. "I hope so, Dee. It would be an incredible opportunity."

"Will you get to be involved much?" I ask as I watch her tuck her long, shiny hair behind her ear.

"I will if I have my way." She chuckles. "I want to pick the products myself, design the treatment menu... This spa is my baby, and the new one will be too. I don't want to just leave anyone running it and making the decisions."

I smile as I watch the concentration on her face as she counts off the bags and double checks each one has everything. This is her baby, all right. She's dedicated and professional. But it's her passion for what she does that sets her apart from most people I've met in my life. It's obvious how much she loves this place. She puts her heart into it.

"Okay." She rubs her hands together, bringing them into a prayer position against her red lips. "I think I'm ready. I've just got time to make myself presentable."

My eyes drop over her immaculate black suit dress and red heels.

"This is you *not* looking presentable?" I raise an eyebrow.

"Oh, no, this..." She looks down at her dress. "... this is fine. It's my hair. I should tie it up."

"What? No!" I smile as I realize how loud that came out. "Sorry, it's just... you have the most beautiful hair. Seriously, it's like a shampoo advert. I think you should keep it down."

Maria runs a hand down over it as she looks at me. "Really? You don't think he'll think it's unprofessional. It's so long."

"No. I think it's beautiful, and it looks smart all straight like that." I nod at her as she looks at me, unconvinced. "Seriously, what I'd give to have my hair back that length."

Maria tilts her head as she studies me. "How blonde are you naturally?"

I screw up my nose and shake my head. "Almost baby blonde, would you believe?"

Her eyes study my hair, which has almost grown long enough to skim my shoulders now.

"I do believe," she says slowly as she reaches up and fingers a strand between her fingers gently.

It's not as dark as when I first arrived in Hope Cove. All the sun and swimming in the lake has faded it. But it's still a far cry from what it used to be like.

Maria's still studying me, her lips pursed as she takes her hand back. "Dee, I've got to get myself ready. Mr. Parker will be here soon. But don't go home after your shift today until you've seen me, okay?"

"Sure." I watch as she heads toward the door. "Maria? Good Luck!" I call out and smile as she turns back to me.

She holds both hands up in the air with her fingers crossed and then heads out the door.

"Knock, knock!" I call from the bottom step of Blake's porch.

I'm not sure why I'm worried about just walking around to the back porch. It's probably where he and Betsy are. But it feels intrusive when I've only been at his house a couple of times before.

A scuttling of paws echoes on the wooden boards as Betsy appears around the corner and makes a beeline for me, her tail swaying around like a wind-up toy that's gone haywire.

I grin as I bend to stroke her. She fusses around me, whining and trying to lick my face.

"Hello, gorgeous girl," I coo, giggling as she almost knocks me over. "Where's that daddy of yours?"

"He's over here, picking his jaw up off the floor."

I look up and straight into Blake's glowing green eyes as they rake me in from head to foot, coming back to rest on my face.

And my hair.

"Maria did it as a thank you for helping her." I smile nervously as I run my hand through the soft strands.

"You look..." He walks over to me and I take his outstretched hand so he can pull me to my feet. His eyes roam over my face again, and he grins. "You look amazing."

"It's all Maria. I can't take any credit." I feel heat rush to the surface of my cheeks as Blake continues to take his time studying me.

"She may have done it, babe. But it's all you. There's no doubt about that."

He reaches a hand up and strokes it through my now light, golden strands. They're still not as fair as they once were, but Maria said she couldn't strip all the dark out in one go without damaging my hair. Another lift and toner, and some time, and I should be back to my natural color before long. It feels strange to be blonde again after so long being dark. I chew on my lip as Blake's eyes continue to roam over my face.

He brings both hands to cup my cheeks and gives me a look so intense that it steals the breath from my lungs in one fast rush.

"You're beautiful," he whispers before dropping his lips to mine and kissing away any self-consciousness I felt moments ago.

"You like it, then?" I murmur as I smile against his lips.

"I fucking love it. It's going to be like having sex with a whole new woman tonight!"

I laugh and push him playfully in the chest. "And who says you'll be having sex tonight at all?"

He sucks in a breath as he rounds his lips into an 'O'. "Ouch, babe. Careful with all that talk. I'll start to think you don't like me." He chuckles as I jab at him again.

"Who says I do?" I grin at him.

"They do." He arches a brow and drops his eyes.

I follow his gaze to the pale blue cotton of my sundress I changed into after work. My nipples are hard as marbles and straining beneath the fabric.

"Oh."

"Yep. Oh." He smirks as he places a palm over my breast and squeezes it, pulling my nipple between his thumb and finger just enough to make me suck in a sharp breath.

"Blake," I moan as he looks down at me.

His eyes sparkle as he lifts his other hand and runs his thumb back and forth across my lower lip.

"I like hearing you say my name." He smiles before tilting his head down to my ear. "And I *love* hearing you scream it."

I rest both hands against his chest as I dip my head and giggle when his breath against my neck sends tingles throughout my body.

How can I answer that? I have screamed his name. A lot. And it's only getting louder each time. It's not just my voice screaming it anymore. It's my entire body, and my mind.

And my heart.

The thought catches me off guard, and I stumble back a step. Blake wraps his arm around my waist, steadying me.

"You okay?"

I nod as I sneak a look up at him. He gives my waist a squeeze and then lets go.

"Wait here." He smiles, then whistles to Betsy, who follows him inside obediently.

I wrap my arms around myself and turn to gaze out over the lake. This is one of my favorite times of day. When the sun is right below the horizon, its last rays reflecting off the water's surface, glittering like diamonds.

I love this place. I love this place so much. If I could stay here forever, then I would. But my aunt's house will have to be put up for sale soon. There's no other option. I can't magic up money out of thin air to buy my dad's half. And he needs that money. I know he's playing down just how much he and Mum need it, as they don't want to worry me. But I know they're going to struggle if they don't get it soon.

But the thought of going home—if I can even call it that—makes my stomach lurch. I've never liked to think about the day I have to go back before. But now? Now, even just a second's thought about it has my chest feeling like someone's ripping it open.

"Come on then, blonde bombshell." Blake's deep, flirtatious laugh pulls me back into the moment. I turn and he's holding up a couple of bottles in one hand, and a thick padded blanket in the other. "Let's sit on the jetty."

I follow him down his porch steps, across the grass and down to the end of the small wooden jetty, which extends out over the lake. There's a matching one on the opposite side by my aunt's house. We used to have swimming races from one to the other as kids when I stayed here.

"Where's Betsy?" I ask as Blake spreads the thick blanket out and pulls me down onto it with him.

"She's got a new bone inside. It'll keep her busy for hours."

I turn to look at him. "You bribed her?"

"Now why would I do a thing like that?" The corners of his mouth curl up as I narrow my eyes at him.

"I don't know. *Why* would you?"

He lets out a deep, throaty chuckle, which makes my stomach flip as he passes me a cold bottle of fruit cider.

"Where has this mistrust come from?" He leans back on to one muscular arm as he clinks his bottle against mine. "To blondes having more fun." He winks.

"Um, try from comments like that!" I laugh as I watch him lift his bottle to his lips and take a long drink. His neck contracts as he swallows, and the short dark hair running up it and over his jaw draws my attention. I know how those dark brown rough edges feel under my fingers, in the crook of my neck, against my lips... *between my legs.*

He smirks at me as he lifts the hand holding his bottle to my chin and gently pushes my mouth closed.

I didn't realize it was open.

"How'd it go today? For Maria?"

I take a long, cool drink as I look out over the lake's calm surface. Even though it's early evening, it's still hot.

"It went well, from what she said. Mr. Parker, the guy from New York, seemed impressed with the spa. And Maria said he wanted to talk contracts with her, so that's got to be a good sign, surely?"

"Yeah. That's great news for her. Must have been our contribution that won him over." Blake's eyes crinkle at the corners as he looks at me.

"You make a few bars of soap and some pots of hand balm. *My* recipe, by the way." I tap my finger against my chest. "And suddenly you're an expert!"

Blake throws his head back and laughs. "You're putting words in my mouth now, babe."

"It's what you meant, though." I smirk at him as he reaches over and pulls me down onto my back on the blanket. He rises to hover above me on one elbow, taking my bottle and placing it down with his.

His eyes glitter. "I could have said it was all down to the way I can whip that sweet cream of yours up into little peaks, using just one hand."

"Oh, you could, could you?" I tease as he leans down, dusting his lips over mine.

"Then you wouldn't have needed to put words in my mouth. You could put something else of yours in there for me." He grins at me as he snakes a hand behind my neck and lifts my mouth to his.

His kiss is warm, deep, hypnotic. I fall into it and lose track of how long he's wrapped around me. How long I'm under his complete control. It could be minutes. It could be hours. Either way, it's not enough, and I'm reaching back for him the second he pulls away.

"Someone missed me." He sucks my bottom lip between his teeth, and I arch my back away from the blanket to get closer to him, my arms wrapped tightly around his neck.

"Suppose someone did? Don't go thinking you're special or anything." I grin at him as he shakes his head and kisses me again, his tongue finding mine and proving how weak my words are as I melt underneath him and pull him closer.

Special is a word made for Blake Anderson.

He pulls back, his face inches from mine as our breathing matches one another's.

"Tell me what you want, babe. Anything. Anything you want."

His green gaze darkens with desire as he slides one hand up my thigh and underneath my dress, hooking his thumb into the elastic at the side of my panties.

"I want..."

"Yeah?" He presses his lips to my neck as he slips his hand into my panties, stroking my skin, which is already slick with arousal.

I suck in a breath, pressing my nose against the side of his face as his mouth finds my ear. I can smell his familiar scent. One that calls to me like no other. I swear I will recognise it for the rest of my life. How can I ever forget?

"What do you want, babe?" he asks again. The warmth of his breath sends goosebumps up my arms.

"I want to stay out here, watching the sunset with you. I want..." My eyes roll back in my head as he sucks the flesh of my neck between his soft lips, grazing his teeth over my delicate skin.

"You want me to make you feel good?" he murmurs softly.

"Yes," I whisper breathily as he trails kisses down my neck to my collarbone.

"You want me to show you how I can't get enough of you?"

I wriggle underneath him, peeling my spine away from the blanket as he pulls one strap of my dress down over my shoulder and kisses my warm, bare skin.

"Yes."

"You want me to tell you what it does to me when I see you opening up for me?"

"Yes," I whimper as he twists the hand he has inside my panties, bunching up the fabric in his fist and pulling them down my legs.

"You want me to bury my head in this sweet pussy and get you so wound up, even screaming my name won't be a release enough for you?" His voice has dropped deep, and sounds strained.

I can feel blood pulsating between my legs, my body at his complete mercy. There's no question over who is in charge of it when Blake is close.

"Yes. I want all of that."

"I can never say no to you, babe." He flashes me a dark smile and then pushes my dress up over my hips and moves down my body, crashing his lips down against my wet skin.

"God!" I cry out, pulling my head up to watch as his hot mouth seals over my clit and sucks.

"Not God, babe. Blake." He chuckles as I hiss at him and drop back onto the blanket.

He returns his attention to my hot skin, which is throbbing in anticipation. Begging for him to burrow himself inside it. His warm lips kiss me all over and then part to let his tongue slide out and lick me in long, teasing strokes. I'm panting, writhing underneath him, grabbing fistfuls of his hair. But I don't care. All I care about is having Blake as close as he can get. I need him, ache for him. Each stroke of his tongue has me teetering closer and closer to the edge.

"That's so good," I moan as he slides both hands underneath my ass and lifts, stretching me open and presenting my pussy to his mouth, ravaging it as though he's addicted, and I'm his drug.

The rough stubble from his beard grazes between my ass cheeks as he slides his tongue up inside my body and circles his thumb over my clit.

"Fuck!" I throw an arm over my face as every muscle in my body tenses.

A muscular arm reaches up and grabs my chin, forcing it down so I have no choice but to move my arm and open my eyes.

His eyes blaze into mine. I thought fire was red, and the hottest flame blue. But right now, I know without a doubt, it's *green.* As his deep emerald eyes hold mine captive, I come apart. Every nerve ending in my body knits to the one next to it, forming an intricate network of electricity that explodes over my skin, pulsing in my veins, burning rivers through my flesh. I shudder and shake underneath his touch as my orgasm tears through me.

I cry out as my thighs clamp tight around Blake's head. He forces them open and rises to his knees. I barely have time to blink, my eyes trying to focus on him and the sunset sky behind as he throws his t-shirt off and slides his shorts down his legs.

Then he's over me, his hard, thick cock pushing into my body like it belongs there.

Like it owns every inch inside me.

"You're fucking everything." His eyes gaze into mine as he thrusts deep, my body being forced against the blanket so hard that I can feel each joint in the boards of the jetty underneath me scraping against my back.

"You have no idea how glad I am you came back." He juts his chin forward as I grip on to his biceps and shake below him.

My orgasm hasn't fully left my body. It's hanging on by a thread, ready to wind back up and explode all over again.

"Blake." I screw my eyes shut as my toes tingle.

"Look at me," he growls.

I open my eyes and stare back at him. Stare as he loses himself inside me, burying the past with each deep hit. Sweat is running down both of us. A bead falls from Blake's face onto my lips, and my tongue darts out to lick it before I even think about what I'm doing.

I'm panting, my breath stolen from my body each time he drives into me, the tension growing throughout each limb as he fucks me harder than anyone ever has before. His eyes never break contact with mine as his jaw tenses, and I know... I know what's coming. And that's all it takes to send me crashing over the edge, screaming out his name and burying my fingers into his skin as I clamp down around him and come with an earth-shattering force.

"Blake!"

He rests his forehead against mine, his eyes burning a hole right through my body and into my soul as his cock jerks deep inside me and he comes with a force that fires a groan from his lips.

"Fuck!" he hisses, pushing himself deeper inside me.

His eyes pinch at the corners as though he's fighting to keep them open. But he does. He keeps them fixed on mine as his breath comes in ragged gasps.

"Fuck, fuck, fuck!"

Then with a final growl all the way from in his chest, his lips part again, and I hear the words murmured on his lips before he kisses me.

"My Daisy."

Chapter Twenty-One

Blake

BLONDE HAIR SHIMMERS IN the last rays of the day's sun, pulling me back to a memory of an evening by the lake almost a decade ago. I take some deep breaths, willing myself to gain control over my body again. I'm like a loose cannon where she's concerned. Every move she makes, every word from her lips has me captured. With her, I'm weak. And that's dangerous.

I look into Daisy's eyes before I roll to the side, pulling her under my arm as I press my nose into her hair and kiss it. We stay cocooned together, listening to the sounds of the forest and lake as the light fades, neither seeming to want to move.

She rests her hand on my chest, her finger drawing tiny circles, which her eyes follow, a deep line of concentration between them.

"What's the look for?"

I feel her tense in my arms. "Nothing."

"Liar." I squeeze my arm around her. "You forget how long I've known you, babe."

"Blake." She lets out a sigh. "Why can't you call me Dee?"

I clear my throat. "I like calling you babe. You are a babe. A hot-as-fuck one." I grab her chin and smile against her lips before I kiss her. She softens in my arms and kisses me back, one hand reaching up to stroke my face.

When I pull back, her clear blue eyes search mine. "Do you think Betsy's okay?"

"With a new bone? She'll be loving life right now." I laugh before glancing back at Daisy. Her eyes are glassy as she looks at me.

"I had a dog once."

I tilt my head so I can see her face better.

"You never told me that! What kind?" I grin as I picture her walking her own dog. I can see her with a happy little terrier. Spoiling him or her, no doubt.

"Oh, he was a mongrel. A scrappy little rascal. His owner was elderly, and he needed a new home when they went into care. I promised I would look after him for them." A sad smile crosses her face as she looks back down at her hand on my chest.

"What happened to him?"

The way her face falls and her eyes squeeze shut has me pulling her close to me and kissing her forehead.

"It's hard when you lose them. They're family," I whisper softly.

She stays silent, and I rub my hand up and down her arm where goosebumps have formed.

"You're getting cold." Even though the air is still warm, there's no hiding the shiver that just ran through her body.

"I'm fine."

"Come on, Let's go inside. Maybe I can warm you up in the shower?"

She chuckles softly. "You have a one-track mind, Mr. Wild."

"Only where you're concerned." I grin as I pull us both up off the blanket and pull my shorts on, grabbing our half-drunk bottles in one hand. Daisy smoothes her dress back down over her thighs and looks at me watching her.

"What?"

"Can't a guy admire the woman who owns his cock?"

She snorts out a giggle and tucks her hair behind her ear. "How you are not married with lines like that is a total mystery!" She smirks at me. "And I'm pretty sure your cock is all your own."

I press my lips together and lean in close.

"That's not what my cock tells me every morning in my shower when all I can think about is you."

Her eyes meet mine as the slightest pink spreads over her cheeks.

"And every night too." I tip my head to the side and shrug my shoulders. "And some lunchtimes, afternoon sessions, pre-workout, post-workout..." I reel off as Daisy shakes her head and rolls her eyes.

"Come on." I tip my head toward the house and grin as I see the earlier tension finally leave her face and be replaced with a smile.

She's still smiling after we're both inside, and she's checked on Betsy and given her a load of fuss.

"If I didn't know better, I'd still say you like her more than me," I call from down the hall where I'm putting the blanket away.

"You don't know better!" Daisy calls back, and I laugh as I hear her whisper something to Betsy as I walk back into the room.

"So, you do like her more than me?" I raise a brow before swooping on to Daisy, wrapping my arms around her from behind and pressing my lips to her neck.

"Yes." Daisy laughs as I nip her neck between my teeth, making her gasp.

"I'd better up my game then, right?" I chuckle as I pull her to her feet, and she leans her head back against my shoulder. Her eyes fix on the framed photograph on the wall to the side of us.

"I don't know. You've got fierce competition. I'm not sure you'll ever succeed."

"What?" I growl in her ear, making her giggle again before she lets out a contented sigh and wraps her arms over the top of mine which are encircling her waist.

"I love this one." Her eyes are fixed on the photograph of the beach at sunrise, taken from up high so the curve of the cove reaches out across the frame.

"Me and Betsy got up at four am to get that one." I rest my chin on top of her head as she studies it.

"You took it? Did you take all of them?" Daisy spins her head to the side, looking at the other images on the walls of the living area.

"Sure did."

"Blake, I knew you used your camera a lot, but these... these are amazing! I thought they were professional prints. Now I can see what Maria was talking about."

"Hey! There's no need to sound so surprised. I can do more than push-ups, you know."

I'm grinning as she turns around, her open mouth snapping shut as she takes one look at me and tuts.

"You're so hilarious! I thought I'd really offended you."

"The only thing you could do to offend me would be to tell me you like Betsy better than me. Oh! Wait!" I laugh as Daisy's delicate hand lifts to push me in the chest. I catch it in my palm and use it to pull her close, pressing my mouth against her parted lips as my other hand cups her ass. "Feel free to think of a way to make it up to me if you like?"

"You're a doofus." She laughs before I continue my claiming of her mouth with my tongue. Each tiny moan from her speaks directly to my dick, and it takes all my strength not to lift her up and bury myself inside her against the wall.

I draw back and grin at her, before turning us both back to face the photograph. Ignoring my dick.

For now.

"It's all about the light. The right exposure. It's not about being perfect. But about capturing the beauty of what's real and right in front of you."

She turns to look at me, her eyes lighting up. "You love this, don't you?"

I run a hand around the back of my neck, blowing out a breath.

"Honestly? Yes. I remember that morning with Betsy when I took it. I'd just signed the deal on the TV series for the first season. Everything had seemed so crazy with phone calls, meetings, and contracts that I'd just wanted to get away for a bit to hear my own thoughts."

Daisy turns back to the picture.

"That's understandable. Life can get crazy. Sometimes it takes a step back to see what you're dealing with."

I look at her sideways, her lips pursed, a deep frown line growing between her eyes. I know what she's thinking about when she looks like this. I know *who* she's thinking about. My stomach knots as I open my mouth.

"Or a trip to another country?"

She turns to stare at me with wide eyes.

I hold my breath and wait.

Eventually she sighs, her shoulders slumping as though all the energy has drained from her body.

"Yes... or another country... he doesn't know I'm here. I never told him about my aunt." Daisy's gaze drops to her hands as she wrings them together in front of her stomach.

I take a deep breath, trying to clear the blood that's rushing in my ears. I hate what her ex did to her. How he bullied her, emotionally abused her, disrespected her. Calling her a weed, for fuck's sake!

And the way he laid his hands on her.

I hate him.

"I should have come and found you." I reach out and cup her chin between my fingers.

Her eyes search mine before she frowns.

"You didn't know, Blake. No one knew what he was like. Not even me, in the beginning."

"I know, but..." I grit my teeth and clench my free hand into a fist before flexing my fingers and stretching them out.

"But nothing." Daisy shakes her head. "I hadn't seen any of you in years. I know we all kept in touch online, but you were over here, and I was in England. It's not like you could have done anything. And besides, the pictures I posted of me and..." She swallows before finding the courage to continue on. "Of me and Mick were nice ones to start with. Showing a happy, normal couple who were dating and enjoying life." Her voice drops to a whisper. "Not all bastards wear it printed on their foreheads."

My jaw clenches. I remember those early photos before Daisy shut down all her social media accounts. She looked happy in them. Kayla would gush over how Daisy would be the next one of the four of us to get married. I always thought the dark-haired guy with his arms around her looked like a smug asshole. Trav said it was just me, but now... now I wish I had dug deeper.

"Kayla's told me that you all assumed I was happy and doing well, and just hadn't gotten time to keep in touch the same as before." She lets out a sigh. "I wish that's all it was. He was into some nasty stuff. Once I saw it, I thought he was just mixed up with the wrong people. But then I realized he *was* the wrong person. He was running it all, like his own dark kingdom."

A crunching from Betsy devouring her bone draws Daisy's eyes away from me, and they mist over as she watches her.

"I thought he was cheating on me again to start with. All the secret phone calls, the going out late at night. So, I followed him." She gulps, her eyes coming back to mine, full of unshed tears.

"Hey." I reach out to her, but she shakes her head, taking a deep breath.

"I wish he had been cheating again. It would have been so much better."

"Where was he going?" I grit my teeth, my eyes fixed on Daisy as I prepare for whatever shit this asshole did.

"He was going to a friend's warehouse. He ran a company that distributed cleaning supplies." Daisy reaches her hand up to her eyes and drags her fingers over her closed lids. When she talks again, her voice is shaking. "They were running illegal dog fights there at night."

"What?" I snarl as my chest expands with the giant breath I suck in.

Daisy's cheeks are shining as tears run over them. She glances to Betsy who looks back innocently, her jaws wrapped around her bone. Betsy thumps her tail against her beanbag as she gazes back at us.

"He was getting dogs to fight? And making money out of it?" I shout, snapping Daisy's focus back to me.

Her bottom lip trembles and I immediately regret the venom coursing through my body and out in my voice. I step forward and wrap my arms around her, holding her against me and dropping my face into her hair.

"I'm sorry. I'm not mad at you. I just... fucking asshole!" I hiss as she buries her face in my chest and her body heaves.

"I should have done something. I should have realized. I should have suspected something sooner."

I grab her shoulders and hold her still in front of me. "No."

She lifts her tear-stained face to look at me.

"It's not your fault. It's on him. Don't you ever blame yourself. You hear me?" My eyes bore into hers, but she doesn't acknowledge me; just drops her eyes away and shakes her head sadly.

"Is that why you have—?"

"The nightmares?" She nods. "And it's why I turned vegan. I can't..." She holds a hand over her mouth. "It's the blood. And the smell. I can't..."

"Jesus," I hiss as I pull her against my chest again. "They were having one when you followed him?"

She nods her head against my chest as a sob escapes.

"I saw it, Blake. I saw them. Their eyes. Their fear. They use the gentle ones as bait for the ones they've taught to be fierce. They set them against each other, and they... they..."

My grip on her intensifies as her shoulders shake with silent sobs.

"Oh, God. It's horrendous. I can't get it out of my head."

She lifts her face, and her haunted eyes meet mine. The pain in them pierces my heart like a dagger. I thought feeling out of control with her was dangerous. But this is worse.

Now I'm helpless.

Helpless against the agony I see in her eyes when she looks at me. Helpless against the despair in her voice. Helpless against the tears that fucker is making her shed.

I'm fucking helpless.

"I reported it all to the police." She sniffs and wipes her eyes with her fingers. "Once they'd finished questioning me and had all their statements, I came here. My mum and dad needed to sell the house, and it seemed like the perfect change. Leaving it all behind for a while. Trying to forget." She takes a deep, steadying breath. "But now I wonder if I've just been a coward. His trial is coming up. But the idea of facing him again. Being in the same room as him... I..."

"You. Are. Not. A. Coward." I enunciate each word, moving my palms up to either side of her face, my fingers threading into her hair. "Say it."

"Blake—"

"Say it!" I urge, my eyes burning into hers.

"I'm not a coward," she whispers, barely loud enough to be heard.

I drop my mouth to hers and kiss her tenderly, fighting the raging storm inside me from what she's told me. This guy—*this fucking asshole*—is a piece of shit I'd love to get my hands on. Five minutes in a room alone with him and he'd be begging someone to kill him, to put him out of his misery. Every muscle in my body tenses as I picture just what I'd do to him.

Daisy pulls back to look at me, shaking her head.

"Don't, Blake."

I brush my thumbs over her cheeks, wiping away the last tears as her eyes search mine.

"I know what you're thinking."

"You don't." I give her a tight smile. There's no way she could imagine the mental image I have. Even the horrific things she's just told me about don't even come close.

"Now you're the one forgetting how long I've known you. *Babe.*" She uses my earlier words back at me, emphasising the final one, as one side of her mouth curves into the tiniest of smiles, despite the lingering sadness still held in her eyes.

Some of the tension evaporates from my body as I smile at her properly and brush a strand of blonde hair back off her face.

"Tell me you'll stay here tonight. With us." I rest my forehead against hers and take a deep breath, willing her to choose the answer which won't cause all the tension to come hurtling back to my body.

She wraps her hands around the back of my neck, her lips parting.

"I'll stay. With both of you."

I let out the breath I'm holding and bring my lips down over hers.

Finally relaxing.

"This is some fucked up shit." Travis tilts his head back and drains the last of his beer.

"I know." My jaw tenses as I hold the top of my bottle and roll the base around in small circles on the dark wood surface of the bar.

It's late and Herbies will close in the next ten minutes. I didn't even realize that we have been sitting here for so long going over shit again and again.

My eyes rest on the photograph of mine hanging behind the bar. The one I took showing all of Hope Cove from the high viewing point me and Betsy found up in the forest. The owner, Wes, wanted it. Said he liked to look at it when he was at work and imagine he was outside in the sun. It's probably why Cindy always picked up extra shifts. Wes would rather be out somewhere than working in his own bar.

I frown as my eyes flick to Cindy at the other end of the bar, gathering up glasses. She said she was fine with the casual hanging out after her late shifts. We always went to her place. Never mine. And I never stayed long. It was mostly just fooling around. Except that one time I went too far. That one time I let her believe there was more to it for me.

I was a real asshole.

"And Dee's sure he's going to go down for it?"

I look back at Trav, who's waiting for me to zone back in.

I exhale as I let go of my bottle.

"That's what she says. Or what she hopes, at least. The police told her after their investigation and search of the warehouse that they had evidence to place him behind the bars. And enough to show he was running it all and laundering money through his friend's business. Along with her witness statement, it should mean he gets a custodial sentence."

"Makes sense." Travis nods to himself as Cindy takes his beer bottle and walks back down to the other end of the bar without making eye contact with me.

"What does?" I rest one hand on the bar and make a fist, watching my knuckles turn white as I squeeze.

"Why she hates being called Daisy now. Why she came back all jumpy and nervous. Acting like we were going to bite her head off when she knocked the drink over in the diner that first night."

My jaw tenses as I listen.

"Be careful, man. That's all I'm saying." He places his hand on my shoulder. "She's come here to get away."

"And?" I huff, giving up on clenching my fist and going back to playing with my beer bottle instead.

"And she needs the Blake that's her friend. Not the Blake who's—"

"It's not just sex, Trav!" I glare at him.

He stares back at me and gives me the look he's perfected over the years I've known him. The one that says he's not about to put up with my shit.

"I know what my past is like, okay." I frown and rub a hand over my jaw as my eyes flick to Cindy at the other end of the bar and back again. "I'm not a total idiot. This isn't like before. She's different."

"I know." Travis looks me dead in the eye. "And if you'd let me finish, you'd know that wasn't what I was going to say."

I look back at him and roll my lips as I give him a small nod.

A silent apology.

He rubs a hand over his eyes.

"She needs the Blake that's her friend." He moves his hand away and his eyes meet mine again. "And not the Blake who's madly in love with her."

"I-I'm..."

He watches me flail around like a fish on the hard, dry floor of a boat. Its mouth flapping open and closed as it tries to make sense of what's happening to it. I shake my head and blow out a breath as I drop it into my hands.

"Fuck."

"And there it is." Travis pats me on the back. "Congratulations, man. You've finally grown up."

"Fuck off." I side-eye him underneath my hand and he smirks, drawing my own smirk to my lips as I lift my head back up. "You may be a know-it-all, but you still stick thermometers up animal's asses when you go to work."

"And you still go to work in order to make money to pay me to do it when Betsy needs a check-up."

"Dick." I chuckle.

"Jerk." Travis grins.

We sit in silence for a minute until I clear my throat.

"This is why I like the forest. It's much simpler."

Travis sighs. "Someone's finally tamed Mr. Wild's heart."

The sound of glass smashing causes us both to whip our heads to the other end of the bar.

Cindy lifts a hand. "My bad, guys. It slipped. But, hey, we're closing now, anyway."

I push off the bar stool, and Travis walks with me toward the door.

Cindy's kneeling down, sweeping up the broken glass.

"Need a hand?" I ask, reaching toward another broom propped up against the wall.

"No thanks," she answers me quickly without looking up.

Travis tilts his head to the door, and I prop the broom back against the wall.

Then we both head out into the night air.

Chapter Twenty-Two

Daisy

"COME ON, IT'LL BE brilliant! Jay's been asking after you, and you'll get to meet his wife, Holly. She's British too. You probably know each other."

I laugh as we climb out of the truck and walk to Blake's parents' front door, Betsy by our side.

"I know you think England's tiny compared to the States, but we don't all know each other."

"Really?" Blake's mouth drops open as he widens his eyes. "You mean, you don't all sit around eating cucumber sandwiches and drinking tea with your pinkies out together?"

I shove him in the side. "Idiot."

He smirks. "That's not what you were calling me"—he glances at his watch and back up—"twenty minutes ago."

I narrow my eyes at him as his sparkle back at me. He leans closer and his breath on my ear sends a tingle dancing through my body.

"I seem to remember it was more like... *God! Your cock is incredible!*" His lips graze my neck as he wraps his arms around me. "Not as incredible as your ass, though," he groans, squeezing it with both hands.

I laugh and push him away. "God doesn't have a cock. She's a woman."

He throws his head back and laughs, slinging an arm around my shoulders as the front door opens.

"I thought I heard you!" Blake's dad, Bill, smiles as he stands back to let us in. He squeezes my arm, giving me a warm kiss on the cheek as he ushers me inside and out of Blake's arms.

"Hey, Dad? Where's my hello?" Blake chuckles as he follows us down the hallway to the large, bright kitchen at the back of the house.

"He sees your hairy face all the time!" Piercing blue eyes that match the deep voice—so like Blake's—meet mine.

I smile at his brother, Jay, as he lifts a hand in greeting and says hello to me. I haven't seen him in over ten years. But there's no mistaking his blue eyes and dirty blond hair, especially when he graces magazine covers every month. Even the ones in England. If I'd been paying more attention, I would have known he was married now. Maybe I would even have seen pictures of Blake at his wedding.

"At least it's not ugly!" Blake grabs his brother into a hug, and I smile as I watch the two of them slap their palms on each other's back. "Why do you think Hollywood likes you with your shirt off so much? It detracts from your face."

"I can see your jokes haven't improved since the last time I saw you," Jay says as he lets go of Blake and wraps his arm around a beautiful woman, balancing a baby on her hip, long gold hair spilling over her shoulders.

"Or your manners!" She rolls her eyes before looking at me.

"I'm Holly." She smiles at me and her entire face lights up.

I instantly feel like we could be friends. She has that warmth about her. She's barely got any make-up on, yet she's glowing. I notice her large baby bump as she shuffles the little blonde-haired baby in her arms and remember Blake saying they were expecting another. Maybe it's pregnancy. Isn't that supposed to make you glow?

"And you must be Summer?" I step forward and wave at the beautiful little one who's gazing at me with bright blue eyes from Holly's arms.

She points at Betsy by Blake's feet, and then gives me a shy smile and hides her face in Holly's chest.

Holly laughs. "She's only pretending to be shy. Wait until later, she'll be all over you."

She moves closer and Summer peeks at me, then hides her face again, giggling as I tickle under her little chubby arm.

"I'm glad we have introduced ourselves to one another, seeing as these two are too busy being big kids to remember," Holly says, looking up at Jay with a smirk.

"Who are you calling a kid?" Jay gazes down at her, his eyes crinkling at the corners as she looks up at him. For a second, it's like no one else in the room exists.

Blake catches me looking at them and he gives me a smile that makes my heart swell before he looks back at Jay.

"Yep, you're the kid part of that sentence. I'm the *big* part." He smirks before Jay reaches over and ruffles his hair. Blake jabs him in the stomach in response.

"Ooh, getting a bit soft there, bro. Those extra years you got on me finally catching up with you?"

I catch Holly's eye and the two of us shake our heads with a smile. Jay's stomach is nothing short of ab perfection, according to Hollywood's sexiest male poll I saw in a magazine at the spa last week.

I look at the two of them teasing each other, and warmth blossoms in my chest. Where Jay is all dirty-blond tousled hair and American jock handsome, Blake is dark and rugged with his short beard and tattoos. But watching them like this, smiling and joking with each other, the similarities are there. The strong jaw lines, the height, the muscles... Sheila and Bill sure made a couple of handsome sons.

"You two, honestly!" Blake's mom tuts good-naturedly as she comes over and pulls me into her arms.

"Oh, gosh. It's been far too long. It's so good to see you."

She smells of lavender and rose, just like I remember from when we were kids.

"It's good to see you too, Sheila." I beam at her, meaning every word. She always made me feel so welcome when I came here. Fueling us all up with homemade cookies and other snacks before we headed out to the lake or the beach.

"Yeah, it is good to see you back here." Jay smiles.

"It's good to be back."

I look around at them all and suddenly feel self-conscious, my gaze dropping to my hands. A warm, muscular arm snakes around my back as Blake slides his hand into the back pocket of my denim shorts. I feel my body relax as I smile at him gratefully, and he winks at me.

"Right. I'm putting the kettle and coffee machine on. Bill, you're on cookie plating duty." Sheila dishes out instructions and soon all seven of us are sitting on the back porch eating homemade salted caramel cookies with hot drinks. All except Holly, who's drinking water.

"I can't stomach my usual peppermint tea," she explains, leaning back into the double seat she's sharing with Jay.

"No, this little one has seen to that," Jay says as he strokes his hand over her bump and presses a kiss to her temple.

I realize I'm staring at the two of them again, and quickly look down at Betsy and rub her ear with one hand. They're so in love. It's plain as day for anyone who so much as glances at them. My chest constricts as I remember Blake's words in his truck after dinner at Kayla and Travis' place.

She wanted things I didn't. Living together, marriage, you know.

I know he was talking about Cindy. But he didn't say he didn't want those things with her specifically. Just that he didn't want them. And it makes sense. His training classes are packed full of people, and he's about to film the second series of his show. Plus, I know how much he relishes his alone time out in nature. Just him and Betsy out in the forest. He has his beautiful modern lake house, and everyone around town knows and likes him. Why would he want a live-in girlfriend or wife? He has the perfect bachelor lifestyle.

Me and him... what we have, it's temporary. We both know that. I always said I wasn't here to stay, and he knew that. Maybe that's why getting involved didn't worry him. He knows I will not want to move in and push him for commitment. I'm not going to ask him for anything.

I sneak a side look at Blake, but he's busy smiling down at a sleeping baby Summer in his arms as he takes another cookie off the plate on the table in front of us. He eases back into the seat next to me slowly, careful to not disturb her. She looks so cozy curled up against his chest in her little yellow duck-covered sundress. She's over a year old, but in his huge, strong arms, she looks tiny. And so sweet.

I catch his eye and grin at him as he looks up.

"My youngest fan club member, what can I say? I'm the favorite uncle."

"You're the only uncle." Jay snorts.

"But I'm still the favorite." Blake chuckles as he bends his head and places a soft kiss against Summer's head.

"Jay said you make your own aromatherapy blends?" Holly says, drawing my attention away from the ovary-melting sight in front of me.

"Oh..."

He must have been talking to his brother about me. The thought makes my stomach flip over. But then that's stupid. He could have mentioned it in passing. I know they talk often on the phone. It means nothing. And what's more, it *should* mean nothing. I'm not staying here, and he doesn't want...

Blake's hand squeezes my leg above the knee after he pushes the last of the cookie into his mouth. He's rocking Summer gently in the other arm at the same time. He rests it there so casually, leaning back into the seat cushions and emitting a moan of appreciation as he swallows. I watch his Adam's apple bob in his throat and push my thighs together as an all-too-familiar heat spreads between them.

I tear my eyes away, willing myself to stop thinking about the noises he's making and how they've got me thinking about when he had his head buried between my legs and his face covered in my orgasm earlier today. His hand slides up my leg a little higher, and he flicks his eyes to mine and winks at me.

My eyes go wide, and then I narrow them as he chuckles to himself.

The bastard knows exactly what he's doing.

I snap my eyes away from his and look at Holly's kind face.

"Oh, yes, I do. I like to experiment. It's something my aunt and I did together. I'm experimenting with making my own herbal tonics as well. Nature's medicine cabinet, that's what some people call it. They believe you can find something to help with any ailment out in nature."

"That's incredible. I think they're right." The fabric of Holly's sundress ripples as she speaks, and she breaks into a grin. "This one agrees too, judging by the roll they just did. I swear they only wake up when I'm trying to eat or sleep. It was the same with Summer at this stage."

"Pregnancy insomnia." Sheila sighs from the chair opposite. "I had it in the last trimester with these two." Her eyes look at Jay and Blake. "Pain in the backside they were, the two of them." She laughs.

I glance at Blake and then Jay and smile. It's crazy to think these two muscular giants were ever tiny babies.

"I used to give her foot rubs every night. Nothing helped," Bill pipes up.

My eyebrows raise at the thought of Bill doing that every night for Sheila. But then I shouldn't be surprised that he's such a romantic. Judging by the way Jay's fingers are stroking the back of Holly's neck, I imagine it's a trait that's been inherited.

"You could make Holly something that might help her sleep, couldn't you, babe?" Blake's hand squeezes my thigh.

My eyes snap to his and he furrows his brow as I stare at him. Why would he say that? He knows I'm experimenting with my sleep potion because of my nightmares. Why would he even bring that up?

"Don't be shy. You're great at it. Except the cream whipping part. That's all me." He breaks into a grin and my shoulders relax as I realize he's talking about the body creams and not my knock-out drug I'm trying to perfect.

"You need to be careful what you use during pregnancy, but I know which essential oils are considered safe and which aren't. I could try a few things. I mean, if you like?" I say to Holly.

She shakes her head. "I don't want to put you out. Honestly, I'm fine. It's not that bad."

"Holls, I was up for two hours with you last night," Jay murmurs into her ear.

"Snap," Blake whispers in my ear as I elbow him in the side.

In front of his family is not the appropriate time I want to be reminded of our midnight sex session. No matter how insanely hot it was, and how much I loved the burn in his eyes as he watched me welcome his release down my throat. He chuckles and squeezes my thigh again as I silently will him to shut the hell up.

"Okay, well, if you have time and it's not too much bother, then that would be great. Thank you." Holly smiles at me sweetly and I return my own back.

She's the perfect match for Jay. He's not had it easy. I remember how haunted he was before I moved away. He experienced something no one should ever have to, and his family was so worried about how he would come through it. Blake, especially. But looking at the two of them together now, I can see how someone sweet and kind like Holly is exactly what he needed. Someone to love him unconditionally and help him heal.

The rest of the afternoon passes quickly, and it's soon time for Holly, Jay, and Summer to drive back to LA. They give me hugs before they leave; Holly's obstructed by her bump. Summer presses her little rosebud lips to my cheeks in the most angelic little kiss I've ever been gifted. I swear that child will have the world eating out of her palm soon with how cute she is. I'm pretty sure she already has Blake, judging by the grin on his face at the extra squeezes and giggles she showered him with before being strapped into her car seat.

We wave them off and then climb into the truck and wave Sheila and Bill off as Blake reverses down their driveway and out to the main road.

A guy climbing into a nearby parked car with a long-lensed camera around his neck catches my attention.

"Why do you think he's taking photos here?" I peer out the window at him as we drive past.

Blake rolls his eyes. "He'll have been looking for Jay and Holly. Wherever he goes, there's at least one pap following him. Even if it's to somewhere mundane, like the gas station. He used to get away with it more. But since Summer arrived, and now the baby news is out, it's been constant. I think they're all hoping she'll go into labor on the sidewalk and they'll get a snap of Jay catching the baby as it flies out."

My hand covers my mouth as I laugh. "I'm not sure they fly out. But if they did, that would be a great shot."

Blake laughs, reaching his hand over to link his fingers through mine on the center seat. Betsy has decided to sit in the back instead and stick her head out the window, tongue out, ears flapping happily in the breeze.

I grin as I watch her in the wing mirror. Life is so simple for a dog.

Well, simple for the lucky ones.

Blake drops me off at my aunt's house. He didn't seem happy about spending the night apart, but I insisted. I know he wants to take Betsy on an evening hike, but I just don't feel up to it tonight. All I can think about is trying my sleeping tonic. I really want to get it right before it's time to go back to England. The idea of going back makes my stomach churn enough, without adding the sleeplessness back into the mix again. I've been doing so well getting sleep recently. But it's all down to Blake being there. He's not going to be there, and I need to know that I can survive on my own. I need to look after myself.

I'm heating the tonic on the stove when the house phone rings. It must be Mum or Dad. They're the only ones that ever ring the landline to have a chat, which they've been doing every few days to see how I'm getting on. They haven't mentioned getting the house on the market again yet. But I know it's only a matter of time, now that they know it's ready. I'll be honest; I didn't tell them about Bill and Blake painting it straight away. I wanted to have more time.

Just a little more.

"Hi, Mum," I answer, leaning back against the kitchen counter and turning the stove down so my drink doesn't boil over.

"Hi, sweetheart," she greets in a clear English accent. "How are you?"

I chew my lip as I stare out the window at the garden. How am I? I'm not sure how to even answer that.

I'm great when I'm with Blake because I forget about the past?

I'm swallowing down bile in my throat at the thought of coming home?

Or I have no idea who the person in the mirror is that I see each morning?

Instead, I say, "Fine," and ask Mum how she and Dad are doing.

"We're okay...." She pauses and I hold my breath, waiting for her to drop whatever bomb it is that I know is coming. This is how it works. If she doesn't go straight into a chat about what they've both been doing that day and which neighbors she's seen around, then I know something is coming.

And it's usually bad.

"We had a phone call from Detective Barnes today."

I suck in a breath and can hear blood rushing in my ears as my heart pounds against my ribs.

"Detective Barnes?" I repeat, my mind picturing the solemn-faced policeman heading up the investigation and prosecution of Mick's case. He's actually very kind and understanding. I know he wants justice and to put people like Mick away. But I guess having a job that sees what he does, doesn't give him many reasons to smile.

Mum's voice sounds far away as she continues. "Yes. He's said there's been a problem with evidence for the trial. Something about the defense getting something thrown out over a technicality."

My fingers sting where I'm gripping onto the kitchen counter like my life depends on it. "He's going to get off, isn't he?"

"Now, no... he didn't say that. He said—"

"Mum! He's going to get off! I know it!" My voice rises in panic. "He's going to get away with it. With *everything.*"

My eyes blur as hot tears pool in them. He can't get away with it. He *can't*. Where's the justice for all those dogs? All those people whose beloved pets were stolen to use as bait dogs. All those people hoping their pets are just lost and will come home again one day.

"No," I cry. "He can't, Mum. He can't!"

"There's not much else we can do, sweetheart. Detective Barnes said it weakens the case considerably. They've even relaxed his bail conditions until the hearing." Her voice is full of concern as she delivers the news that makes me feel like I'm being dangled over a vat of burning acid.

"There must be something. I can't let him get away with it."

My eyes dart around the room, and I see my passport on the kitchen table. I only left it out because Maria needed a copy for work. Thankfully, I had the foresight to apply for a short-term work visa in case I needed something while I was over here. I just haven't gotten around to putting it away again yet.

"I'm coming, Mum." The words leave my lips before I can even process what I'm saying.

"What—?"

"I'm coming home. Maybe I can give evidence in person? It might be taken more strongly if I'm there and they aren't just reading out my statement."

There's a rustling at the other end of the line and I hear mumbled voices—Mum's and then Dad's.

"We thought you wanted to stay a little longer? You said it was doing you good there?" My dad comes on the line. "We... we've been looking at options to keep the house."

I screw my eyes shut, my heart constricting at the hidden strain in his voice. He forgets I can tell when he's not being truthful a mile off. It used to be the way he pulled his left ear, but over the years, I've learned from just the tone of his voice. He needs this house to sell. His and Mum's retirement depends on it. He'll be working himself into an early grave otherwise.

"Dad, it's okay. I'm doing so much better. I was actually about to ring you and suggest I book my ticket home," I lie through my teeth.

"Oh, well... I... if that's what you want?"

I'd rather walk over hell's hot coals with bare feet.

"It is, Dad. It's what I want. I'll get a ticket booked. It may take a day or two, and I'll have to talk to Maria at work. But I will sort it. Can you call Detective Barnes and tell him I changed my mind? That I want to give evidence in person now?"

"Okay, sweetheart. We will speak to him. Let us know when you get a ticket booked and we'll pick you up when you land."

"Thanks, Dad."

I give my love to him and Mum and hang up, just as a fizz sounds from the stove. Even being careful and turning down the heat couldn't stop the pan from boiling over.

Nothing is guaranteed.

Not even justice.

Chapter Twenty-Three

Blake

THE KNOCK AT THE door cuts into my conversation with Jay.

"Hey, bro. I got to go. Someone's here. Give my love to Holls, Summer, and the baby again, won't you?" My cell phone is glued to my ear as I head over to the door, where Betsy is already sniffing underneath it and wagging her tail.

"Will do. See you again soon," Jay answers.

"Not too soon." I smirk, hanging up to the sound of his laughter.

I open the door and Betsy flies out, straight to Daisy, whining and shaking her butt about in excitement.

"Hey, girl." Daisy giggles as she bends and ruffles both of Betsy's ears, pressing a kiss to her head before Betsy tries to land a lick on her face.

"Soft, I tell you. Soft." I tut and arch an eyebrow as I place my cell phone down. Daisy takes my outstretched hand, and I pull her up and into my arms.

"Oh, shush. You and I both know that you spoil her more than anyone." Her eyes meet mine as she smiles.

My heart swells in my chest, having her here again. In my arms. She didn't want to spend last night together, and I had the shittiest night's sleep alone in bed. I even found myself up in the middle of the night and out on the back porch, looking across the lake at her place, like some weird creeper.

"I'll spoil you in a minute. Ruin you with my dick." My lips drop to her neck, and I inhale her fresh flower smell before kissing her soft skin below her ear.

"You've already done that a hell of a lot recently." She giggles as she places her palms on my chest and pushes me back gently. Her giggle stops as her eyes meet mine and she looks at me seriously. "Blake. We need to talk."

"How about I show you what I've been thinking about doing to you all day, and we talk after?" I press my lips back on her neck, claiming it.

"No. We need to talk now."

The tone in her voice makes me pull back to look at her.

"Okay. Sounds important." I raise a brow at her, and she nods, chewing on her lip as she gazes up at me. Her clear blue eyes dart between mine as two lines form between her brows.

Something isn't right.

"Are you okay? Did you have the nightmares again last night? Did you—?" The thought of her alone and waking up scared has my heart racing in my ribcage.

"It's not me, Blake. It's..." She lets out a deep breath, shaking her head, her eyes dropping to her hands, which are still resting over my chest.

Something about the way she's struggling to look at me has alarm bells—no, make that fucking sirens—blaring in my head.

I know what she is about to say. I'm not ready to hear it.

I will never be ready.

"I'm leaving, Blake. I'm going back to England."

I stare at her as the sound of blood rushing fills my ears.

"When?"

She can barely look at me. "I don't know. I need to book a ticket. A couple of days."

"But you said you wanted to stay longer? You said you'd stay forever if you could." My grip tightens on her waist, and I watch as she squeezes her eyes shut briefly, as though she's in pain. When they open again, there are tears in them.

"I know," she whispers. "But I have to go back. Mickey's trial is coming up, and they have thrown some evidence out. I have to go back and give evidence in person. It's the best chance there is of him getting found guilty."

"I'll come with you," I say quickly, my mind already running a hundred miles an hour. Filming for series two doesn't start yet. I can get someone to cover my training classes. Trav and Kayla will have Betsy for me. I know they will. It'll be fine. I nod as I come to a decision in my head. "I can come with you, and then after the trial, we can fly back."

"Blake—"

"It'll be fine. I'll make some calls and sort out our tickets?" I glance toward the hallway cupboard. I'm sure my suitcase is in the back of it somewhere.

Shit, where's my passport?

"Blake?"

Daisy looks at me with tearful eyes.

Bile rises in my throat.

"You want to go alone, don't you?"

She opens her mouth, but nothing comes out. She just continues to stare at me, more water building up along her lower lids.

"Are you coming back?" I choke out, before clearing my throat.

She shakes her head, the tears threatening to spill from her eyes.

"Blake, I—"

I snatch my arms back from her waist and turn my back to her, running both hands through my hair.

"We always knew I was leaving one day." Her voice is quiet, and it sounds like she's trying not to let it break.

"I didn't know one day was going to be so fucking soon!" I snap as I turn and glare at her.

She winces. But I can't bring myself to apologize. I can't bring myself to do anything other than stare at her, my chest rising and falling with ragged breaths as I try to control the hammering in my chest.

"You said it yourself, Blake. You don't want a relationship. You and me... this was just... it was..."

"What?" I spit. "It was just what? Fucking?"

She steps back like I've physically pushed her. I know I'm out of line. But all I can see is red.

She's fucking leaving.

"No!" Her brows knit together. "That makes it sound... that's... it..." She takes a deep breath and looks over at Betsy, who's laid in her basket, ears drooped down, watching us. "We were just being there for each other. We're friends."

Her eyes return to mine.

"We are not just fucking friends, Daisy!" I yell, clenching my hands into fists and sucking in air through my nose. "I don't have sex with my friends. Do you? Is that what you do? Have sex with all of your friends?"

Her eyes widen. "Of course not!"

"Well, then. How can you say we're just friends?" Blood courses through my veins and I stalk over to the kitchen counter and slam my fists on top of it, leaning over them. I can't believe she's just swanned in here to tell me she's leaving and not coming back.

Just like that.

Gone.

"I'm sorry. I thought..." She appears next to me, and I can feel her gaze on the side of my face where my jaw is clenched.

"You thought what?" I turn my head to look at her.

Her lips part and she looks up at the ceiling and back at me.

"I don't regret a single second of the time I spent with you. The time we spent *together*. You made me feel hopeful again. You made me remember what it feels like to laugh. *Really* laugh." She reaches out and places her hand on my bicep. "You made me forget, Blake. And I can never thank you enough for that."

"I made you forget?"

She gives me a small smile. "Yes."

"I don't want to make you fucking forget, Daisy! I want to make you remember!" My eyes burn into hers and I see the shutters she holds around her like a fucking shield, well and truly back in place.

"Stop calling me Daisy." Her voice is quiet, but the coldness in her eyes is louder than anything else in the room.

"Why? It's who you are."

The way she looks back at me has me wondering if I've imagined the past couple of months. Even her clear blue eyes don't look like hers anymore.

She looks like a stranger.

"That girl might as well have died. It's not who I am anymore. You need to accept that."

"That's a load of shit and you know it!" I push off the counter and stand facing her head-on, close enough that our bodies almost touch.

"What would you know!" She glares up at me, her pulse beating hard in her neck. The urge to wrap my hand around it and crash my lips onto hers is overwhelming. Hold her to me and never let her go.

Fuck, I'm completely screwed.

"I know who you are, Daisy. I've known you since we were kids, for fuck's sake. Don't try telling me you've changed. Because you haven't. Not really. You're still the same girl underneath."

She has to tilt her head back to look up at me, but I'll be damned if I move further away from her.

"You're not being fair."

"No, Daisy." Her eyes blaze into mine and her shoulders rise as she sucks in a breath at me calling her Daisy again. "You're the one who isn't being fair. What aren't you telling me?" I search her eyes, waiting for it.

For the extra missing piece she's keeping hidden.

She says nothing, and I know if she leaves now, I may never know the true extent of how deep her scars run.

"Your ex is a jackass. I get that. I get he did awful things to you. But what I don't get is why you keep telling me that who you are doesn't exist anymore. When I see you every day, bright as you've always been. I see your soul, Daisy. And it's the same one I've always seen."

My chest is heaving when I stop talking.

And I wait.

I wait for her to say something. Anything that will give me hope I can get through to her and make her see what I've always known—she's Daisy. She will always be Daisy. The girl with the big heart and the beautiful laugh.

Silence.

Fucking *silence* as she stares at me.

"Daisy?"

She takes a step back.

"Don't."

"Why won't you talk to me?"

"I'm not who you think I am, Blake. You can't see my soul. Because Mick... what he did... what *I* did... it destroyed a part of it. Forever."

I stare open-mouthed at her distraught face. How can she even begin to believe that? How can she not see what everyone else sees?

How can she not see what I see?

"What are you talking about?" I reach for her, but she steps back again.

"I don't deserve your kindness."

"What the hell's that supposed to mean?" I grab my hair in my fists. My eyes probably look like a madman's as I stare at her and try to make sense of something.

Of anything.

"It means you should forget about me when I leave." She drops her head and turns toward the door.

I stride past her and slam my palm against it. I can't let her leave yet. Not without knowing if it will be the last time I see her.

"You're talking like you fucking killed a person," I hiss. "Whatever it is, nothing can be that bad." I soften my voice. "Talk to me. Please."

She keeps her eyes fixed on the door, as though my hand will magically move, and it will open if only she concentrates hard enough.

"Daisy?"

She screws her eyes shut.

"Not a person."

I look at her face, her cheeks wet where her tears have finally won.

"It wasn't a person." She takes in a shaky breath. "But I am responsible for a death."

My shoulders drop, and the urge to wrap her in my arms and tell her it's okay has me lifting my hand away from the door.

"That wasn't your fault. All those dogs... the fights... You didn't know."

She takes her opportunity and yanks the door open, flying down the steps of the porch.

"Daisy!"

I run after her and see her standing in the driveway. Something in her eyes makes me freeze as she looks back at me.

"You don't understand. The dog I was supposed to re-home and look after..." Her voice breaks into a sob as she covers her mouth with her hand. "I killed him. I promised I would take care of him. And I killed him."

"I don't know what you mean." I stay rooted to the spot, afraid if I move any closer, she might take off down the driveway and I will never see her again.

Ever.

Her voice breaks as she struggles to control the racking sobs taking over her body. It's taking every ounce of strength not to run to her. Instead, I slowly inch toward the top step.

"Mickey sent me to collect him. He told me it would look better if I went on my own. That they'd be more likely to let me have him. His name was Rocket. I promised I would give him a good home. That he'd be loved." She wipes at her cheeks with the back of her hand. "We hadn't even had him two weeks when Mick said he needed a check-up. He took him when I was at work, and said they needed to keep him in overnight for some tests."

The tears stream down her face.

"That was the night I followed Mick. That was the night I saw where he was going. What he was doing."

Bile rises in my throat as I suspect what she's about to say. How can someone be so evil? I want to punch the pillar holding the porch up. Watch the wood splinter into pieces and pretend it's the fucker's face.

"The fight you saw when you got there?" I ask, knowing the answer already.

Her haunted face meets mine, confirming it, and sending my heart into overdrive at the sheer devastation in her eyes.

Now I understand.

Chapter Twenty-Four
Daisy

I HOLD BLAKE'S GAZE, swallowing the lump in my throat before I say the next words. Before I admit what I've been too ashamed to tell him.

"It was Rocket," I whisper. "He was the bait dog that night. I got there just in time to see the fear in his eyes before his throat was ripped out."

Look what you're responsible for, Daisy.

That's what Mick said to me afterward. Before he laughed. Before the smell of blood reached my nostrils, searing into my memory forever.

The last time I ever wanted to hear the name Daisy again.

Blake's standing on the top porch step, staring at me. Betsy's by his side, her tail between her legs. There's an unreadable expression on his face. He must see it now. See me for who I am. Someone who's responsible for death and suffering.

Someone weak.

"They wouldn't have given Rocket to me if Mick were there. I think he knew that. That's why he sent me on my own."

"It's not your fault, Daisy." Blake steps forward, about to come to me.

It's the last thing I want. For him to hold me in his arms and tell me it's not my fault. That it's okay.

It isn't.

It never will be.

I don't deserve his understanding. His kindness. His reassurance that I'm not to blame. That's why I must go back and give evidence in person. I'm done running. It's too little, too late, but at least I will be doing more than hiding out here in denial. I need to do this. And he needs to let me.

I need to make him let me walk out of here.

Whatever it takes.

"Stop!" I scream. "Stop calling me that! I am not that girl anymore. You still think I'm seventeen years old. But that girl, she's gone. Accept it!"

He stills, and his eyes turn dark as he stares at me, his jaw tense. I can see the anger building in his chest as he stands rigid, watching me. I'd rather he be angry at me than tell me I'm not to blame one more time.

"I'm leaving, Blake," I tell him again, ignoring my heart constricting in pain in my chest.

He throws his hands up by his side. "So, what? You think going back will magically change everything?"

"I have to try! I thought my statement would be enough with the evidence. But it's not. I have to do something."

He takes a step toward me.

"Let me come with you."

"No!"

"Why not?"

Another step closer.

"Because I said so, that's why!" I take a step backward and almost bump into his trash can.

"What's so frightening about me coming with you? We're friends, after all. Aren't we?" His lips turn down as he says *friends*, and then he takes another step.

"Yes, we're friends. Just friends." I glance into the trash can as I side-step it. There are several small plastic bags tied into knots at the top.

"*Just* friends? Jesus Christ, Daisy!" he yells as his eyes burn into mine.

"Really? Daisy again! How many times, Blake?" I feel my blood boil at him calling me Daisy again. Is he doing it to prove a point or can he just not get it into his thick skull that I don't want to be called it anymore?

"Do it, then. Go back for the trial. And then come back." He practically growls at me.

I shake my head as I look at him and my heart constricts as I realize... coming back would mean being someone else. The person he still thinks I am. The person he wishes I still was.

The thought of him finally accepting what I've been trying to tell him all along—that she doesn't exist anymore—makes me sick to my core.

He won't look at me in the same way he has been doing ever since I came back.

He'll see me for what I am—someone responsible for allowing horrific things to happen.

He won't want me.

"I can't."

His eyes are darker than I've ever seen them as he glares at me.

"Then you're still hiding. And you'll be hiding for the rest of your life. Blaming yourself for something that isn't your fault. Choosing to be the person who fits inside the warped box you've created inside your head."

Anger fires inside me and courses through my veins. Who the hell does he think he is to make out I'm hiding by leaving? Being here is hiding. Coming to Hope Cove was hiding.

I'm going home to do everything I can to put Mick away.

"You're one to talk, Mr. Wild." I sneer as the pain in my chest turns to adrenaline. "Don't tell me I'm the one hiding when you're just as bad."

"What the fuck you talking about now?"

I see the muscles in his arms ripple as he clenches his fists by his side.

"You hide behind your humor."

"Bullshit!" he fires back.

"Uh-huh." I point at him. I'm on a roll now and nothing, not even a nuclear bomb, can stop me. "You hide it so well that no one notices. You're all jokes and bravado, running your training lessons, doing your programs where you help others open up to their fears. What about yours?"

He folds his arms across his chest, his legs spread wide.

"I don't know what you're talking about."

"Oh, I think you do. Your photographs?" I raise an eyebrow. "They're incredible. And people want to buy them. But you? You're scared because they show a part of you that's more than skin deep. You can't hide behind jokes in a photo."

I watch as he bristles and juts his chin out.

"You're wrong." His mouth pulls into a grim line as he scowls at me.

"Am I?" I smile in mock sweetness. "I don't think so. I think you fear feeling exposed. What did you say? *It's not about being perfect, it's about capturing what's real and right in front of you.* Well, how real are you, huh? Or was that just some shit you made up?"

Blake's eyes are like a storm tearing into the earth of my soul. He lifts a foot, taking another step toward me.

"Don't come any closer. I'm leaving, Blake. And I don't need your permission."

A bead of sweat runs down my back. I know if he reaches me, it's game over. I will fall into his arms and cling to his belief in me. Hoping it's strong enough for the both of us.

But it isn't.

I can't do that to him.

I reach into the trash can and I grab hold of the knotted top of one of the small bags.

"I said stop."

His eyes hold mine as he purposefully takes another step toward me. Despair and anger flood my veins as I draw my arm back and hurl the bag at him. He sidesteps it easily and we both watch as it slams into the side of the house and then falls to the floor with a dull thud.

"You did not just throw a bag of my own dog's shit at me?" His face is wild as he turns back to me.

If it wasn't so horrendous fighting with him like this, then it would almost be comical.

"Looks like I did!" I glare at him before I spin on my heels and stalk off.

"You want to know what's real?" he yells after me.

"Sure, why not?" I shout back over my shoulder, trying to bring my breathing back to normal. I can't hear footsteps, so I'm pretty sure he isn't following me.

"How much I love you!"

My step falters, and I gain my balance quickly before I topple. My heartbeat pounds in my ears as I fight the desire to turn back. To turn back and look at him. Turn back and see if he means it.

If his eyes tell me that it's true.

I swallow the giant dry lump in my throat as my fingers tremble.

I don't need to turn around.

I've known Blake almost my entire life.

If he says something, he means it.

"You hear me?" His voice sounds angry, but it's drowned out by the sob that escapes my lips. I suck it in, hoping he can't hear.

"That's what's real! How fucking in love with you I am!"

Keep walking. Keep walking. Don't turn around.

"Daisy!" he yells again, desperation creeping into his voice this time.

I draw in a steadying breath.
And I keep walking.

Chapter Twenty-Five

Blake

THERE'S A SPLASH AS the stone breaks the surface on the river, sending water flying up and out in all directions. I grab another off the ground and hurl it from the ledge that I have set up camp on. It shatters the water's surface, destroying the calm. Piercing it. The way my heart felt when Daisy walked away from me after I told her I loved her.

She didn't even turn around. Couldn't even face me.

I fall back onto my ass on the dry earth. Betsy nuzzles my arm, pushing her way underneath it until she's snug against my side, her warm body pressed against my torso.

"Looks like it's just you and me again, girl."

She grumbles and looks up at me with big brown eyes.

"Hey, it would have been a squash for three in that tent, anyway." I jerk my chin to our accommodation for the night.

As soon as Daisy walked off, I grabbed our pack. I needed to be up here.

Away.

Away from the lake and her house staring at me over the water. Taunting me. It'll soon be empty. And then what? Sold? To a couple who wants to start a family together? Wants to build a life together? All on my fucking doorstep. A constant reminder of the way things turned to shit.

I drop my head into one hand, the other holding Betsy close.

"Why can't she see what we see, eh, girl?"

I squeeze my eyes shut and press my finger and thumb into the sockets. I understand that she's been emotionally manipulated and abused. I get that her ex is a piece of shit. But to tell me she thinks she's lost a piece of her soul?

Fucking hell.

I know she's still the same caring, loving person she's always been. I can see it in her eyes when she lets her guard down. Hear it in her laugh when it breaks free from deep in her chest. I can feel it on her lips when she kisses me. Sense it every time I'm in the same room as her.

She's still Daisy.

She has to be.

But then? What if I'm wrong? What if I'm seeing what I want to see? What if the girl I knew really has gone? Disappeared, never to be found again. Buried so deep that I could dig my entire life to find her again, but it wouldn't be enough.

I curl my fingers around a handful of sharp stones and squeeze. Traces of red appear, spreading as small rivulets of blood snake out between my fingers and drop to the earth.

My instincts have never let me down before. I'm not wrong.

She's in there.

I just need to show her.

Make her realize.

Before it's too late.

Trav: What the hell? Kayla just told me what happened yesterday! You okay?

I read the message as I hand Betsy a treat. We spent the night in the forest and took an early morning hike back down, just as the sun was rising. It's one of my favorite times of the day, usually.

Only this time I couldn't even be bothered to get my camera out and take a photo. I didn't even pack it. It's the first time in years I've left it at home.

Me: Good news travels fast.

My phone rings in my hand, Trav's name flashing on the screen. "Hey."

"Blake? What the hell happened? Kayla said Dee's leaving. Something about a trial for her ex-boyfriend?"

The corners of my mouth curl down in disgust at the mention of him.

"She's going back to give evidence in person. He was running an illegal dog fighting ring and laundering money to fund it."

"Fuck," Travis hisses.

"Yeah. Fuck." I rub my fingers across my eyes. "She says she doesn't know who she is anymore. That Daisy hasn't existed since. The bastard sent her to collect a dog to re-home, then used it as bait in a fight. Daisy saw the entire thing."

"What the... fucking hell! God, if—"

"I know."

I sink down onto the stool at the kitchen counter. Travis hates animal suffering. It's why he became a vet. And I know he's seen his fair share of neglect at the hands of humans. He's usually calm. The sensible one. But this? This will make him want to explode and nail that fucker. I know it will.

I hear him sucking in a breath down the phone.

"Kayla said she's booked a ticket for Friday."

That's in two days' time.

Two days and she'll be gone.

"What are you going to do?" he asks when I don't speak.

I'm too busy staring out the back window across the lake. Wondering if she's home... if she's packing.

Has she even thought about me once since yesterday?

"I don't know, Trav... You know I told her I loved her?"

"You did?" His voice raises in surprise.

"Well, kinda shouted it at her back as she left. Kayla didn't tell you?"

"No. Maybe Dee told her. But if she did, she kept it to herself."

I don't know whether it's worse that Daisy probably didn't tell Kayla or not. Don't women tell each other those sorts of things? Maybe she doesn't care? The fact that she never stopped or turned around probably means that she doesn't give a shit. I was a distraction, like she said. A way to help her forget.

"It's a load of shit. Maybe she's right. Maybe the Daisy we all knew has gone forever."

"Blake!"

The power in his voice makes me sit up straighter.

"Who've you spent the last couple of months with?"

"I'm asking myself the same thing."

I was so sure last night in the forest when my head was clear. I was convinced she's still the same girl I knew years ago. Now I'm back home, staring at her aunt's house, knowing she's inside, packing to leave with no regrets.

It has me doubting everything.

"That's a load of crap! I've seen you together, Blake. I've seen the way she lights up when you look at her. She's grown more relaxed with you the longer she's been here. And you? You're different with her."

"What are you saying?"

"I'm saying. You're good for each other. You might remember her when she was seventeen. But that's not the woman you've fallen in love with. You've fallen in love with who she is now. You've fallen in love with her. Not a memory."

I blow out a breath as I listen.

"Tell me. When you're with her, do you picture her being seventeen? Imagine that she still is?"

"What?" I screw my face up. "I'm not a creep, Trav."

"Exactly. You don't. You know why? Because you see her. You see the *real* her. The one with the pain and ugly past. That's the woman you've fallen in love with."

"You're a sweet romantic at heart, aren't you?" I sigh as his words sink in.

He's right. I've fallen in love with the woman who came back. Not the girl who left.

"Takes one to know one," Trav murmurs.

"All right, all right, don't tell anyone."

He chuckles lightly. "I've never seen you be the way you are with her before."

"A fucking mess?" I snort.

"Basically." I can hear the smile in his voice. "It takes someone special to make you think you're losing your shit."

"Kayla makes you lose your shit?"

"All the fucking time!"

"I knew it."

He laughs and I join him. It feels good to ease the weight of the boulder that's lodged itself in my chest—even if only for a second.

"Don't let her leave without telling her, Blake. And this time, try saying it instead of shouting it at her back, all caveman style."

"Jackass."

"Jerk."

I blow out a breath as Travis chuckles.

"Thanks, man."

"Anytime."

I hang up the phone with renewed purpose.

She left ten years ago without knowing what she meant to me.

I'm not making the same mistake again.

Chapter Twenty-Six

Daisy

I PUT DOWN THE watering can, my eyes wandering over the flowers and herbs. My heart squeezes, knowing this will be one of the last times I do this.

"I wish you could see how beautiful your garden is." I tip my head back and talk to the sky. I know my aunt is up there somewhere. Listening.

I turn to head inside and glimpse at Blake's house. My shoulders drop as I swallow the lump that's permanently taken up residence in my throat.

He loves me.

No.

He loves me not.

He loves Daisy. He's in love with seventeen-year-old me. I can't let myself forget that. Who I am now, who I will always be—she's not who he wants. The sooner I leave, the better. Things can go back to normal. He can find someone else. God knows he won't be short of offers.

I head back through the house, grabbing my bag and locking the door behind me. It's time I had a talk with Maria. Seeing Kayla this afternoon was hard enough. At least I got to say goodbye to her properly this time. But she wanted me to promise I would come back to visit. How can I? How can I come back and see everyone moving on with their lives when I so desperately wish I could join them? How can I ever see Blake moving on, without it feeling like an arrow to my heart? Even though the thought of never coming back here is almost enough to bring me to my knees, I know I can't.

When I leave, it will be for good.

My thoughts drift to Maria as I walk to the hotel. She's been so kind, giving me a job. Trusting me to help with the products for her business pitch to Griffin Parker. I feel like a prize bitch to be leaving her in the lurch like this. But what choice do I have? Stay here and hide while putting my parents in an even worse financial situation? Or go home and try to do everything I can to get justice for Rocket and all those other dogs? All those beautiful dogs and their owners.

My soul may not feel whole anymore. But what's left of it still wants to fight for what I believe in. Being here, with Blake; spending time with Betsy; seeing those bear cubs—it all confirms to me I'm doing the right thing. I must stand up for what I believe in. Blake may not know it, but he's made me strong enough. I know I didn't deserve the way Mick treated me. But it took Blake showing me how it felt to be loved to realize.

I am strong.

It took Blake loving me for me to realize...

Fuck.

Blake loving me.

My stomach lurches, and I suck in a deep breath as I walk. I would wish upon every leaf... every petal in my aunt's garden that he loved the real me.

The love Blake Anderson gives would be worth trading the garden of Eden itself for.

That kind of love... it's what makes every sound you hear more amplified, every colour you see brighter, every scent you inhale so much more vibrant.

When Blake Anderson loves, he loves with his body, heart, and soul.

I just wish the glimpse I had was real.

I wish I could be that girl.

His girl.

I push open the main spa door and head into the reception area. It's quiet. The other therapists are probably in appointments. Maria looks up from the desk, her long, dark hair shining as she smiles at me.

"Hi, Dee. Is everything okay? You sounded worried on the phone when we spoke?" She walks around from the back of the desk and gestures over to the soft seats in the client waiting area.

Guilt rises in a wave through my body, starting at my toes.

"I... I have something I need to talk to you about. Thank you for making time for me. I know you're busy with the New York spa negotiations and everything."

I sink into the seat and some of the tension leaves my shoulders as the scent of lavender drifts up from the fabric.

"Don't be silly." Maria waves a manicured hand in the air. "After all you've done for me? Of course I have the time! And besides, I consider you a friend, Dee."

My mouth goes dry as I look at her.

"Maybe you won't when you hear what I'm about to say."

Her forehead creases. "I don't follow?"

I wipe my hands on my thighs. I knew this would be hard. She's been so wonderful to me since I arrived. And now? Now I'm about to leave her with no notice. My voice cracks as I say the words I've been dreading since that phone call with my mum.

"I have to go back to England."

Maria's brows shoot up her forehead, before understanding fills her eyes and she looks at me with concern.

"The man you told me about?" Her voice is soft and kind. It makes me feel even worse about leaving.

I nod. "He did some terrible things. Things I thought he was going to pay for. But it turns out he may get away with it. I need to go back and help the police. Do whatever I can..." I trail off as I chew my lip and wait for Maria to say something.

"Of course. You must. You must do what you need to do." The compassion in her eyes makes my chest burn with guilt.

"But you... you've been so kind to me. Giving me a job.... being a friend. I feel awful about letting you down and—"

"Dee." She places a hand over mine and squeezes. "You've done far more for me than I've done for you."

I stare at her.

She smiles appreciatively before continuing. "You helped make another dream of mine possible. There's no way I would be negotiating a contract for a new spa at the freaking Songbird hotel in New York if it weren't for you!" Her eyes light up, and I giggle as she squeezes my hand again. "Honestly, I knew we could never keep you here forever. As much as I'd like to."

I wipe at my blurry eyes with my free hand.

"Oh. You're going to make me cry!"

"Me too!" She laughs as she releases my hand so I can root around in my bag for a tissue.

I know I've got some in here somewhere. They must be right at the bottom. I feel around with my hand and my fingers slip through a tear in the lining. Typical. *How long's that been there?*

Something scrapes against my fingers, and I wrap it inside my fingers and pull it out. As I uncurl them, a bright pink, shiny wrapper glows in my palm.

"Oh?" I study it.

"You like those too?" Maria says, looking at the pink candy.

"Huh?"

"We can't get them in the states. My grandma goes nuts for them." Maria rolls her eyes with a smile. "She brought at least four giant bags with her on her last visit."

My mind casts back to when Maria took some time off, saying she had family visiting.

"It was your grandma who came to stay with you?"

"It was. She comes as much as she can. She loves to travel, always has. When we lost my grandad, she made an even bigger point of it. She said he would want her to be happy and to live. She said she's saving up stories to tell him when it's her turn to go through the pearly gates. She's a bit of a character." Maria laughs.

I look up from the pink shiny wrapper as something slots into place in my memory.

"She certainly is. We shared a taxi from the airport when I arrived." I shake my head in disbelief as I watch Maria's face light up.

"Really? That was you?"

"That was me." I grin as I remember Vera practically forcing me into her taxi. She wouldn't take no for an answer. "I know Hope Cove's hardly the biggest town, but still... what a funny coincidence. She was really kind to me. My suitcase broke, and I was feeling all lost and emotional. I told her about my aunt's house and how I hadn't been back here since she died and was worried about selling it. Letting it go forever. She told me our memories stay in our hearts."

"You're Daisy Girl." Maria smiles.

"What?" I meet her eyes. She's always known me as Dee, I don't understand how—

She gets up and rushes over to her bag behind the counter.

"Gran called you Daisy Girl." Maria holds out a small glass jar with a daisy flower sticker on the lid.

My jar.

"I had to beg her to leave the jar with the bit that's left inside behind when she went home. This stuff is amazing!"

"She used it all?" My eyes widen.

"Put it on all the time. Handed it around to random people we met when we went out!" Maria laughs, and I shake my head, a grin spreading on my face.

"I'm so pleased she liked it. She was so kind to me. It's the only thing I had that I could thank her with. Honestly, I was such a mess that day."

"So, the flower?" Maria cocks her head and looks at me.

I puff out my cheeks as I look at the jar in her hands.

"I made those stickers a long time ago. My real name is Daisy. But I've been using Dee for a while now."

Maria smiles at me. "I see. It makes sense. You look more like a Daisy than a Dee."

"I wish I felt more like one." I pull my bottom lip in between my teeth as Maria rolls her lips together, her eyes studying me.

"You know. Who we are... it starts with what we believe in our hearts. My gran taught me that. No one else gets to tell you who you are or what you can and cannot do. If you want to feel like the person who made this incredible hand balm"—she clutches it to her chest and looks to the ceiling in glee, making me laugh—"then be her again. Believe it and make it happen."

I give her a small smile. "I wish it were that simple."

"It is simple. But it's not easy. Most things worth doing aren't. Where would be the sense of achievement if they were? What would be the point of the journey?"

I look at Maria, my mind swirling with emotions. Confusion, fear, pain, anger...

Love.

If only I could make a wish or believe it hard enough that it happens. I could be the girl that laughs again—really laughs. The girl who takes delight in nature. The girl who loves swimming at sunrise and dreams about kissing in thunderstorms.

I could be that girl again.

My breath catches in my throat, and I stare back down at the pink foil again, my heart thundering in my chest, my palms sweating.

That girl again.

A realisation hits me, like a bolt of lightning to the heart. The foil swims in front of my eyes as my vision blurs with unshed tears.

I have done all those things.

I didn't understand it at the time, when it was happening, when I was doing it. But now it's coming into focus, I can see it as clear as the sky on a cloudless day.

I have done them.

I've laughed so hard that I've cried. I've watched black bear cubs while holding my breath in awe. I've swam at sunrise and felt the calm from the water seep into my body, into my mind.

And I've kissed in a thunderstorm.

I have been that girl again.

With Blake.

My heart goes into overdrive in my chest as my fingertips tingle. I gaze down at the shiny pink gift in my hand as tears drip onto it. Vera gave me more than she could ever have realized that day. Looking at her small symbol, hearing Maria's words, I realize...

I'm *still* her.

It may be deep inside, and I may need help to remove all the weight on top of me, holding me down. But she's in there. Somewhere. And if I have to scratch away to find her—scratch until my nails break and my skin bleeds, then I will do it.

I will find myself again.

Mickey Frost thought he'd won. He thought he'd broken me.

But he didn't consider that I could re-build myself. That I could grow back from where he'd spent months cutting me down, slashing at me with his words and abuse. He may have broken me above the surface, but my roots?

He never touched those.

He didn't know I just needed that one person to help me remember. Not forget as I've so wrongly thought.

But remember.

Remember who I am and what makes my soul sing.

He didn't know about Blake Anderson.

Chapter Twenty-Seven
Blake

I PACE UP AND down the back porch, my eyes darting over the lake and across to Daisy's bedroom window. She must still be asleep. That sleep tonic she's been experimenting with obviously works because I hammered on her door like a lunatic last night, desperate to see her. To explain. To tell her I'm sorry. To say anything I can to stop her from leaving things like this between us.

I look back over the lake again. The sun is just rising. It would be a fucking stunning image to capture with my camera. The hues of pink and orange glowing against the water's still surface. The sky warm, with a promise of a new day.

Fuck, this love shit has turned me into a sap.

I run my hand over my jaw as I stride up and down. Betsy's laying on the sofa watching me with droopy eyes. She's tired too. I barely slept last night. I just kept thinking over and over in my head about what I will say to Daisy when I see her. I was up and down like a fucking Yo-Yo all night. And Betsy stayed by my side the entire time.

"What the hell we going to do, eh, girl?" She lets out a soft sigh as she stares at me. "Yeah, I know. You don't want her to leave either, do you?" I reach down and ruffle her ears.

She lies there, content as I stroke her, until something catches her attention, and her head snaps up. I follow her eyes—now fully alert and shining—to the spot she's focused on.

That's when I see her. Standing on the end of the jetty, on the other side of the lake.

Her white cotton dress makes her skin glow. And her blonde hair calls to me like a beacon.

"Daisy," I whisper, breaking into a run and flying down to the end of the jetty, stopping just in time before I slide off the end into the water.

"Blake!" she calls, rising onto her toes. "Can we talk?"

She's not even that far away. I can hear her perfectly. I can see her. See her well enough to know that she doesn't look pissed off. Something about her has changed. She's less tense, her whole body seems more relaxed. She looks... happier. At least, happier than the last time I saw her, and she'd hurled a bag of Betsy's shit at me. But although I can see and hear her, she's still not near enough.

I need to be close to her.

Whatever it is she wants to talk about, I need to look into those clear blue eyes when she says it.

I look to the right. It'll only take a few minutes to get in my truck and drive around to her side of the lake. But getting in my truck means letting her out of my sight. What if she changes her mind? What if she doesn't wait?

There's no way I'm taking that chance.

"Hold on!" I call back. "I'll come to you."

I yank my t-shirt up over my head and undo the button of my jeans, pulling them off and throwing them down on the wooden planks. Daisy's hand flies to her mouth as she watches.

"Don't move!" I shout.

My feet leave the last wooden board of the jetty behind as I dive into the cool water. It's a fresh blast to my system, waking me up, invigorating me. I push through it, swimming as far as I can before the need to break the surface and draw in two giant lungs of oxygen claws at my chest.

I suck in the morning air.

The jetty is empty.

Nausea tears through me as my pulse races. I'm not even halfway across the lake. It might as well be the fucking moon.

She's gone.

"Blake?" a breathy voice says.

I spin my head. Two bright blue eyes meet mine, wet strands of blonde hair plastered to pink cheeks underneath.

"How did...?" I glance back to the jetty and notice the pile of white fabric.

I turn back to face her, both of us treading water and staring at each other. The surface of the water distorts our bodies below. But I can tell Daisy's naked. It would usually take all my willpower not to glance down and try to make out her beautiful body. But right now, all I can do is stare deep into her eyes.

Stare and wonder if I'm about to lose her.

Forever.

"I—" We both speak at the same time.

Daisy smiles, but it falls from her face almost immediately, and she watches me with big eyes.

"You go first," I say gently.

She nods, looking up to the sky, then back at me, her bottom lip pulled between her teeth.

"Blake... I..." She blows out a breath and then swims closer. Close enough that I can see the droplets of water from the lake on her eyelashes.

I gulp down the rock that's taken residence in my throat. Whatever she's going to say can't be worse than the other day. Nothing she can say now could be worse than her telling me she's leaving again, or that her soul isn't complete.

After a long pause, she speaks. Her voice is soft, and she looks vulnerable as she fixes her focus on me. But her eyes tell a different story. They're bright, filled with a determination I haven't seen in them for a long time.

For ten years.

"I've been putting all of my energy into fighting, Blake. Fighting you. Fighting myself. When I should have been back home, fighting for what I believe in. Fighting in person. Not running away like a coward."

Her eyes turn glassy as her voice cracks, and I battle against the energy rushing to my arms, screaming at me to take her into them and hold her. I don't want to give her any reason to swim away and leave. So, I just watch her. Watch her scrunch up her face and chew her lip as she searches for the right words for whatever it is she's feeling.

"That's why I have to leave. To go home and do whatever I can to make this better. It'll never be right," she sniffs and glances away as her voice drops to a whisper. "It'll never be right. But I have to try."

The sight of her eyes filling with tears is like someone ripping open my chest and pouring salt in.

"It's okay, I understand. And coming here?... It doesn't make you a coward. It makes you strong. You got away from a situation where you could have been in danger. Guys like your ex..." I grit my teeth as my jaw ticks. "I've met guys like him. He could have killed you in a moment of rage."

Daisy nods her head. "I know. I think you're right."

We float, watching each other. There's so much to say, yet all we seem to want to do is look at each other. Is she looking at me because she knows it's the last time? Is she committing my face to memory because she knows that's all I will be soon? A distant memory. Something to think of now and then, less and less as time passes, until eventually it's faded away entirely.

Her eyes roam over my face and come back to rest on mine.

"You know, coming back here, it's been amazing." She gives me a small smile. "Seeing the house again, the lake, Kayla and Travis... You."

I force myself to swallow as I listen to her begin her goodbye speech.

"And then Maria gave me a job and became a friend. I'm so blessed. I really am. You've all been so amazing."

"But?" I can't stop myself from saying the word, leaving the question hanging in the air between us.

Daisy sighs. "But I have to do this, Blake. "

I drop my eyes from hers and look at the tree's reflection on the surface of the water. Nothing will ever look the same again. Nothing will ever feel the same again. It will all be a faded version.

Without her.

"You've given me the courage. You made me realize I am strong enough." She inches closer in the water, and I raise my eyes back to meet hers. "Spending time with you and Betsy, going up in the forest, seeing the bears." Her eyes light up. "The thunderstorm! Making all those spa products together. You found a part of me I thought was destroyed. You made me laugh, really laugh, for the first time in months."

I search her eyes as they shine back at me. The knot in my stomach tightens as the meaning of her words sink in.

"I gave you the strength to leave," I whisper.

"Yes," she says softly.

"Jesus."

I tip my head back into the water and stare up at the sky. I'm the reason she's able to leave. By helping her, I've completely screwed myself. Yet, seeing her like this—freer, more relaxed, more like the woman I know she is deep down—I can't regret a single thing. If I must lose her, then knowing she will be happier makes it worth it.

Almost.

There's still so much I need to tell her before she goes. If she's leaving, then she has to hear it.

"I'm sorry." The words come out strangled as I raise my head back up and look at her again.

"Why are you apologizing, Blake?"

She swims a little closer, and I realize we've been slowly moving toward the jetty on her side of the lake. We're only meters away from the wooden ladder that reaches into the water at the end.

"Because I made you feel uncomfortable. Because I shouted. Because I didn't listen to you."

Because I'm not enough to make you stay.

A small smile lifts the corners of her lips and I swear it's a sight more incredible than anything I've ever seen in the forest, or ever captured on film.

She is simply stunning.

If Daisy was committing my face to memory a few minutes ago, then I'm now doing the same. This is how I want to remember her. Smiling, water in her hair, the morning sun on her face.

My Daisy.

"You never listen to anyone if you don't want to. You're stubborn like that." She arches a brow. "And I've never felt more comfortable than when I'm with you. And as for shouting? We were arguing."

"That's no excuse. I lose all sense of control around you. I should have never raised my voice at you, Dai—"

Damn.

I wait for the shutters to fly up behind her eyes. But they don't.

"You said you loved me?" she whispers.

I stare back, my eyes burning into hers.

"I do."

Her mouth drops open, and she sucks in a breath.

"Even though all I've done is push you away since I came back?" Her eyes shine, tears collecting on her lower lids.

"That's not true." I inch forward in the water, so I'm close enough to touch her if I were to reach out.

"It is, Blake. You've been honest with me. And I've not given you the same. I came back here not knowing who I was. I was running away. Ashamed of what I had let happen."

She lifts her hand from the water and presses her fingers to my lips when I'm about to cut in. The softness of them makes my throat burn and I close my eyes briefly, afraid of what she'll see in them if I don't. She's healing. She's stronger. I can't jeopardize that by not having my shit together.

"I blame myself," she continues. "And I know you're going to tell me it wasn't my fault. And my head knows that's true. But my heart..." Her eyes fill with tears again. "My heart is filled with guilt. He still took a part of me that day and I never got it back."

"Have mine," I whisper beneath her fingers.

"What?"

Her brow creases as she looks at me. Her fingers slide away from my lips, and I expect her to take her hand back, but instead she rests it against my chest below the surface of the water.

Hope explodes in my chest as I stare deep into her eyes.

"I said have mine."

"Your what?" Her eyes search mine, not understanding.

"My soul."

She gasps and I place my hand over hers on my chest before she can pull it away.

"If you leave and never come back, then you'll take a part of it with you, anyway. So have it now. Before you go. And let the last time I see you be when you're complete again."

"Blake," she chokes out.

"I mean it. I don't know what the hell you've done to me since you came back here. I'm a fucking mess. But I swear, I love you. And I would give you my last breath if it meant I could see you happy again."

"I know," she whispers. "It took seeing a pink foil wrapped candy to realize it."

"What?" I smile at her, and she beams back.

"All this time I've been telling you you're helping me to forget. And you were. It's been such a relief not to think about everything that's happened at home. But what I couldn't see, or maybe didn't want to, is that you've been helping me remember this entire time. Just like you said. You've helped me remember who I am. I'm stronger because of you, Blake."

My heart is pounding in my chest beneath her palm. Her eyes drop to where our skin meets, and I know she must be able to feel it. Whenever we're together, there's this invisible charge, like electricity running between us. How can this be it? How can she have come back after all these years and turned my world upside down, only for her to leave again?

How is that fucking fair?

Life gives you chances. It's up to you whether you take them. Call it free will. Well, my free will wants to do whatever the hell it can not to lose her.

I open my mouth and force out the words, knowing that her answer will mean everything. Her answer will impact the rest of my life from this day forward.

"You say I've given you strength? Have I given you the strength to come back as well?"

Her eyes rise to meet mine and I hold my breath.

This is it.

That moment on a cliff edge where you're balancing. Straddling that thin line. One side being an exhilarating view that makes you feel alive and full of wonder and hope. And the other, a freefall down to darkness, and nothing else.

I watch as her eyelashes flutter, and she places her free hand over our entwined ones on my chest.

"You have."

I search her eyes, praying I've heard her correctly.

"I have?"

She nods, the next word from her lips coming in one gentle breath. "Yes."

Our hands stay locked on one another's over my heart, as I guide us through the water until the wooden ladder is against her back. She lifts her chin, tilting her head back. Holding the ladder with one hand, I place the other underneath her chin, gently grasping it so her eyes stay focused on mine.

"You're saying you'll come back?"

She looks at me.

"Yes. I'll come back. I'm sick of running. I want to have a life where I feel like myself again. I haven't felt like it in years. Until I saw you again."

My eyes search hers as warmth floods my body. I release the heavy breath I've been holding and drop my forehead to rest against hers.

"Thank you," I whisper.

Her eyes swim with tears, which I wipe away with my thumb as I hold her face. I tighten my grip on the ladder so our bodies are pressed together.

So she can't leave.

"Dai—Ah, fuck." I screw my eyes closed and hiss at my stupidity. Why can't I get it right?

She's telling me she will come back. But if I can't even listen to her and respect her decision not to be called Daisy, then why would she want to?

Desperation claws at my chest.

"Look, I'll call you whatever you want. Just let me love you. Because I do. I love you so fucking much! Not seventeen-year-old meat eating you. But twenty-eight-year-old you that drinks flower concoctions and has to sleep with a tidal wave blasting in her ear."

She giggles before falling silent and reaching her hands up to either side of my face. I open my eyes and crystal blue ones gaze back at me.

"Call me Daisy."

I shake my head. "But that's—?"

"It's what I want." She fixes her gaze on me and nods as she strokes my jaw with her fingertips. "Mick doesn't get to change who I am. Only I get to do that."

She looks up at me from underneath her lashes, and I feel like I might burst with pride at how strong she is. I've always known it. I've never doubted her. But to see it in her eyes, and hear it in her voice?

It's fucking incredible.

Our eyes stay locked on each other as I lower my mouth over hers. Her lids flutter closed as the heat of our lips meeting fires up something inside us both. I shut my eyes and groan into her mouth, my tongue finding hers as she runs her hands through my hair and grabs it in her fists.

She pulls back, panting. "Besides, I like it when you say it."

"Really? Do you throw bags of dog shit at everyone who says something you like?"

Her eyes glitter with regret. "I'm sorry."

I crash my mouth down over hers again. "No, you're not," I murmur between kisses.

"A little bit?"

"Nope." I kiss her again. "Don't believe you."

"Then believe me when I say this." She pulls back to look at me. "You're silly and your jokes suck."

My mouth falls open, but she places her fingers against my lips.

"And I love you, Blake Anderson. I love you so much."

Chapter Twenty-Eight

Daisy

"YOU DO?" HIS DEEP green eyes flick between mine as I run my fingers through his hair.

"I do," I whisper, biting my lip as I watch his eyes light up.

"Why didn't you fucking say so earlier?" he groans and presses his wet, naked body against mine as a giggle tumbles from my lips.

There's something about being naked in water. The way it slides over your skin, touching everywhere, heightening your senses. Making everything seem connected.

Us. Nature. *Love.*

The love two people have for one another.

The love I have for Blake.

I find the bottom rung of the ladder and use it to lift myself up higher in the water. My breasts press up against Blake's chest and raise up to his eyeline as I straighten my leg.

"Now you're talking."

He grins at me and clasps one hand around my waist as his mouth claims my nipples, sucking and teasing them until I'm moaning his name and pushing myself against him.

"Blake?"

He stops and looks up at me, reading the silent message in my eyes.

I need you.

As he brings both of his feet on to the ladder and lifts me up one rung, so our faces are level with one another, it's obvious to me—he was right. He does know me.

He's always known me.

I slide one leg up around his waist and he holds it, his other hand on the rung behind my head, holding his body against mine as he looks at me with eyes full of love.

My heart is so full in my chest it feels like it could burst.

I gasp as he slides deep inside my body, connecting us. Everything about it feels so right. We were made to fit together. Why couldn't I admit it to myself earlier? I could have saved both of us so much hurt. All those cross words said to one another. Precious hours when we could have been together the last couple of days—wasted.

"I love you," I murmur as he pushes forward and groans.

The sight of ecstasy on his face sends a wave of wetness rushing from inside me, coating him and making our bodies slick.

"Say it again."

His fingertips dig into my ass where he's holding my leg up, and his eyes burn into mine. I feel him quiver as I wrap my arms around his back and grab onto his broad shoulders.

"I love you, Blake Anderson," I say, my face inches from his, breathing in the same air.

"Daisy," he groans, his eyes burning into mine with a new level of intensity, even for him.

He pulls back and sinks into my pussy again, building up a steady pace as he drives into me. Our eyes are fixed on one another's as we pant. He pushes into me, again and again. Each time better than the last.

A low groan begins deep in his chest as he rotates his hips as our bodies meet. The friction against my swollen clit has me arching away from the ladder, pressing my tight nipples into his chest.

Everything with him feels so right.

My eyes roll back in my head as he fucks me slowly, deliberately taking his time, like he needs this.

Like he needs me.

I can feel his heavy balls kissing the skin on my ass each time he thrusts. It's sensory overload, and I squirm in his arms as tingles form in my fingers and toes.

"You feel so good," he murmurs, sinking his lips down onto mine and kissing me deeply, his tongue tracing distinct, commanding routes through my mouth and soul. I whimper, which only seems to set him off more, as he sinks even deeper inside me, stretching me deliciously around him as the tingles reach my core.

"God, Daisy," he hisses, as I dig my nails into his back.

I writhe and moan in his muscular arms, watching as his eyes close in a state of bliss. I already knew it. But each time is like a breathtaking reminder.

Blake Anderson was made for this.

"Blake," I moan when I feel the tightening balling up inside me. Drawing in everything I have. Every laugh, every touch, every kiss he's given me since I came back is turning into a fizzing energy that's pulling toward a giant mass in my core.

He opens his eyes and looks at me.

Really looks at me.

I swear he's looking at me as though he can see my soul shining back at him.

"Daisy."

He presses his forehead against mine, and I come undone at the sound of my name on his lips. The way he says it—full of awe, adoration, love—it's enough to make me lose my mind and all control over my body.

It's no longer mine. Not when Blake is here, like this.

Not when he's making love to me like never before.

His eyes never leave mine as I lose control and fall forward in his arms, using him for support. The ball in my core explodes, scattering like droplets all around us. I grip him hard, my breath leaving my body as wave after wave of intense pleasure floods through me and I come.

Hard.

My body squeezes his cock, grabbing it tight and not daring to let go.

"I love you, Daisy. I fucking love you."

His eyes sear into mine with a fiery intensity as he growls my name again. The sight of him, matched with the feel of him stretching me, my walls wrapped around him, draws out my orgasm and a second wave crashes over me, sending me convulsing in his arms again.

"That's it, babe. Come all over my cock."

He grits his teeth and then his mouth is on mine again, kissing me over and over as I whimper and moan, all control over my body gone.

All control given to him.

"God, I love you, Daisy. I love you; I love you; I love you." The words tumble from his lips as our faces press together, sweat running down our bodies, the water lapping at our thighs.

"I want to be your girl," I pant as my shuddering continues. "I don't want you to ever let me go."

There's no doubt in my mind.

No matter how many days I have on this earth.

No matter who else I meet in my lifetime.

Blake Anderson is it for me.

He bites his lip and groans, pumping a couple more times.

"You are my girl, Daisy. You'll always be my girl."

Then he holds himself balls deep as the familiar and incredible heat spreads inside me and his fingertips grip onto my ass with white knuckle force.

"Yes," I whisper, wanting everything he can give me.

Needing it all.

We stay connected, our foreheads resting on one another's as we catch our breath.

"You're amazing." His lips catch mine in a tender kiss.

"So are you." I kiss him back, pulling my arms from around his back and cupping his face.

He gives me a look that makes my heart swell, his eyes full of emotion.

"I may not be the best at showing it. Some people wear their hearts on their sleeve. But me? I wear my heart with a flower on it."

"Blake—?"

"It wears you, Daisy."

A sob bubbles in my throat, which Blake kisses away.

God, this man.

"You never gave up on me," I whisper.

Blake smiles, gently raising one hand to brush a strand of hair off my face.

"Your soul doesn't change, Daisy. It's burned in. Just like the photos I take with my camera. They're burned into the film the moment the button is pressed. Just like a memory. Forever. Like the image of you, and who you are, was burned into my heart ten years ago. I've always seen you. And nothing makes me happier than knowing you see yourself again now, too."

My mouth drops open as my eyes fill with tears.

"Yeah, I know." Blake grins. "Love's turned me into a fucking romantic, spouting off shit. I sound like Travis." His eyes crinkle at the corners as he laughs.

I pull his lips back to mine, my heart so full it could take flight, pulling us both up into the sky with it.

"I like it," I say as I kiss him.

"Oh, you do?" He raises an eyebrow with a smirk.

"Nothing makes you happier, hmm?" I kiss him again, and he flexes his cock, which is still buried deep within my body.

"Well, almost nothing." He grins as I pretend to push him away. But then I pull him back to me instead.

"You're naughty," I murmur as my lips hover over his.

"And you're perfect." He grins before kissing me again.

I allow myself to become lost in his kiss.

Right here, in the water with Blake.

There's nowhere in the world that could be better than this.

"Do you want tidal passion, or water's embrace?" Blake scrunches his nose up as he swipes through the music options on his phone.

I laugh. "Neither. I don't need them when you're here. Although, come over here and say those words again. It sounds kind of hot."

He smirks at me as he puts his phone down and pulls his t-shirt up over his head and then climbs into bed behind me.

I sink back against his chest as he pulls me against him and brings the covers up over us.

"We could have stayed at your house, you know? I'm sure Betsy settles better there."

Blake's warm arm tightens around me as he presses his nose into my hair and inhales.

"I put her bed down there in the hall. She'll be fine." He kisses my head and lets out a tired sigh. "I thought you'd want to spend the night here. Your last night before your flight tomorrow evening."

I stiffen in his arms, and I know he notices as he pulls me closer to his chest.

"I can still come with you. You can change your mind. It's not a problem."

"No. I need to do this alone. Thank you, though."

I run my fingertips up and down his forearm as I try not to think about what it will be like going home. It's only been a couple of months, but it feels like a lifetime ago in some ways. I thought what happened at home changed me. But now I see that coming back here changed me too.

Only here, I am changed for the better.

"And you'll let me book your ticket back as soon as you know what date the trial is due to finish?"

"I can get my own ticket, Blake."

We've been over this already today. I'm going back to give evidence at the trial. And then when it's over, I'm flying back. My work visa still has four months on it and Maria was ecstatic when I called her and said there's been a change of plans. She said the job will be waiting for me when I come back. Then I can apply for an extension or something more permanent. I haven't figured it out yet. All I can think about is getting through the trial.

"I know you can. But they're not cheap, babe. And you'll not be working for a bit."

"Fine. But I'll pay you back."

"Okay." He pushes his dick forward, so it fits snugly between my ass cheeks. "Just so you know, I only accept cock currency."

I snort. "Cock currency?"

"Yep. Cock riding equals fifty bucks; cock sucking—thirty."

"You know plane tickets are hundreds of dollars, right?" I giggle as I snuggle back into his arms.

"Mmm, you're right. Better make it ten dollars and five dollars... better yet, cents. Let's go with cents."

"I'll be paying you back forever."

"That's the plan!"

I laugh as he rolls us, so I'm laid on my stomach and he's on top of me, his erection pressing into my ass.

"Did I mention there's a deposit due?" He nips at my ear with his teeth, as one hand slides down and pulls my panties to the side.

I hear him hiss. "Fuck, babe, you're so wet already."

"Just counting my dimes, getting my payment ready." I giggle.

"Oh, yeah?" He nudges the entrance of my pussy with the thick head of his cock and lets out a low groan as he pushes inside me.

I gasp at how full he makes me feel in this position.

"Okay, babe. Let's count your deposit."

I laugh as he drives into me and reminds me all over again why coming back to Hope Cove was the best decision I've ever made.

It must be almost midnight by the time we finally decide to sleep. I don't need the wave noise when he's here. And I certainly don't need the sleep tonic I've been working on. I think I've got it right now. I used it last night, and it worked wonders. I seemed to sleep without waking all night and didn't feel groggy this morning. Hence why I was up with the sunrise, feeling so alert, ready to see Blake. Ready to tell him how I feel.

And God, am I glad I did.

But even the high of making things right with Blake doesn't stop me worrying about the trial. And the thought of my aunt's house being on the market by the time I return makes sickness swirl in the pit of my stomach. But it will all be okay. As long as I have Blake and Betsy waiting for me when I come back, I know it will work out. It has to. We can't have come this far and been through all this together for it not to work out.

I lay my head on Blake's chest and listen to his rhythmic breathing. In and out. In and out. It calms me like nothing else ever has, and soon I drift off with him.

The bedside clock says it's three am when we're woken by Betsy growling and barking downstairs. The sound of her claws skittering around on the floorboards in the hallway echoes up the staircase.

"I'll go." Blake rolls out of bed and pulls on a pair of sweatpants.

"What is it, girl?" I hear him call as he jogs out the room.

I pull his t-shirt on over my head and tiptoe down the stairs behind him, my heart hammering in my chest. I can make out her shape in the moonlight from the hallway window as she jumps around Blake's legs, whining and barking.

"What's she seen?"

"Not sure." Blake leans down and holds her under the chin, looking into her eyes. "Show me, girl."

She barks and runs to the front door, digging at the base until Blake unlocks it and stands back when it opens. She flies past him, jumping down all three porch steps in one giant leap and sprints off down the driveway.

I wrap my arms around myself. It's not cold, but suddenly, I'm shivering.

"It's probably just a racoon or something. She gets a whiff of them sometimes and goes crazy. I'll go check it out." He pulls on his sneakers and grabs my head in his hand, planting a kiss on my forehead. "Back in a minute, babe."

"Okay."

I watch as he disappears up the driveway into the night, only the light from his cell phone visible, until even that tiny dot disappears. That's the thing about being one of only two houses on the lake. There isn't much light. Apart from the moon reflecting off the lake, it's almost pitch black. My aunt has an outdoor security light fitted, but it stopped working last night. I intended on getting it fixed, but what with everything happening with Blake and booking the ticket to go back to England, I forgot.

I wrap myself around the edge of the door, peering out from behind it as I wait. There's only silence, except for my heart beating in my ears. And it feels like hours before Blake comes back into view, Betsy at his side, her tail wagging.

"Was it a racoon?"

They both come in and I push the door closed behind them as Blake fusses Betsy and settles her back into her bed.

"Probably. No sign of anything else, was there, girl?" He plants a kiss on Betsy's head and turns back to me.

"Come on. Let's get you back to bed. You look exhausted."

I don't argue as he leads me back up the stairs and pulls me back into bed with him. He's right. I am exhausted. As he wraps me in his arms, I forget all about racoons, and trials, and house sales. I forget about everything. And I just sleep.

···

"Morning, beautiful." Warm green eyes gaze into mine as I smile and stretch.

Blake wraps his arms around me and nuzzles into my neck, kissing his way from behind my ear and along my jaw.

"Don't you ever need a rest?" I giggle as I feel the hardness of his morning erection pushing against my inner thigh.

"I'll rest when I'm dead," he growls, making his beard vibrate against my neck. I wriggle as it tickles my skin.

"That could be soon if all your blood keeps going to this thing." I reach down and give him a squeeze. "There'll be none left in the rest of your body."

He cocks a brow and flashes his perfect white teeth at me.

"You saying I'm big?"

I laugh and shove at his chest, but it's like trying to move a tank.

"I'm saying you should go let Betsy out first, unless you want to be cleaning up a puddle."

Blake's eyes dart to the clock. We've slept much later than usual. Probably because of being woken up in the night.

"Fine." He kisses me on the lips. "But when I come back, you'd better be naked with your legs spread. I'm having breakfast in bed today."

I laugh and he grins at me at me before he heads out the bedroom door.

I hear him talking out loud to Betsy on his way down the stairs. I lie back against the pillows, a huge grin on my face. I probably look like a lunatic. But I can't help it. Even knowing I am flying back to England tonight can't spoil it. I'm in love with a man who gets me. Who makes me feel alive in ways I had lost hope of ever feeling again.

I'm in love with my best friend.

"Babe, did you let Betsy out already?" Blake shouts to me up the stairs as I slip out of bed and go out to the landing.

I look down the stairs to him, where he's standing in the open front doorway, staring out.

"No. you're the first one down there. Why?"

He turns to look up at me. "The door was open a crack. She must have gone out herself."

"She's clever, but she can't open doors. Can she?" I know I probably sound ridiculous, but there's no way that door was left open last night.

"I know I trained her, so she's pretty damn amazing." Blake grins at me. "But no, babe. She can't open doors."

"How'd she get out, then?" I walk down the stairs and into his outstretched arm. He pulls me to his side and presses a kiss into my hair.

"The latch on the door probably didn't catch on properly last night and it swung back open." He gives me a squeeze as I frown. "Don't worry, babe. She goes out by herself all the time."

I open my mouth and then close it. Could I have not shut the door properly? That's not something I would easily do. Ever since Mick, my sense of security and the need for it has been heightened. But then, it was late last night, and I was distracted. It could have happened, I guess. Maybe I didn't push it hard enough, and the latch didn't close properly, like Blake said.

"Are you going to look for her?" I ask, looking up at him.

"She'll be fine." He shakes his head with a chuckle as he catches me about to say "aww" with my bottom lip stuck out. "Fine, I'll go look for her after I have a shower. She's probably out the back somewhere following a scent. I know I said she likes you better than me. Now I'm thinking you like her better than me too."

I smile and wrap my arms around his waist, tilting my head to one side.

"Well..." I shrug my shoulders, breaking into a laugh as Blake hauls me over his shoulder and spanks me on the ass.

"Right, you asked for it! Just for that little bit of cheek, you're going to suck my cock while I shower."

"Oh, I am, am I?" I laugh upside down as he carries me up the stairs.

"Too fucking right, you are. And don't pretend it's even a punishment. I know you love me coming down your throat."

"Blake!" I shriek. "Wash your mouth out with soap!"

I giggle as he slaps me again.

"It's me washing your mouth out, babe. And you know it's not soap I've got for you."

Half an hour and a special mouthwash later, I'm kissing Blake on the doorstep.

"Call me when you find her, won't you?"

"Daisy." He fixes me with a look, bringing his lips to mine one more time. "She's fine. She does this all the time. She won't be far. She's probably been out for a runabout and then walked back home."

"Okay."

I try to sound convinced. Knowing Blake isn't worried helps calm my nerves. He says Betsy goes off around the lake by herself all the time. I guess it is like her giant backyard. I'm just not used to it as she's always been there in the mornings when I've woken up with Blake. But we were up late today, so maybe that's why.

Maybe she got fed up waiting for her lazy humans to surface and took herself off for an early morning wander.

I wave at Blake as he climbs into his truck and turns around, honking his horn as he drives off. I watch until he disappears out of sight, and then give the door a gentle push. It swings closed. At least it looks closed. But when I tap it with my finger, it pops back open a crack.

"Huh." I shake my head at it in surprise.

I can't believe how stupid I was not to check it properly last night. It must have been open the whole time. Betsy could have been out for hours. I close it and push it hard until it clicks shut.

I head upstairs and get my suitcase from the spare room. Blake said he was going to check at his house for Betsy, and then come back. It's still early. I've got hours until my flight, but I know he wants to spend today together before he takes me to the airport later, so I may as well get the small amount of packing I need doing done now. That way, when he gets back, we can just hang out until it's time to leave.

I've filled half my suitcase when my phone rings.

"Hey." I smile as I answer.

"Hey, babe. You missing me?"

"You've been gone half an hour." I grin as Blake laughs. The sound makes warmth spread in my stomach.

"Half an hour too long."

"Did you find her?" I fold a sweater to place in my case, cradling the phone between my ear and shoulder.

"Nah, she's not here." Blake blows out a breath, and I detect the first hint of concern in his voice. "I drove all around the lake and further up the road into the forest, calling her. But nothing."

I drop the sweater and take the phone into my hand.

"Where else would she be?"

"I don't know. I might just head into town quick and ask if anyone's seen her."

"That's a good idea." Hope Cove is a small community. People know Blake and Betsy. Especially since his TV show. If someone's seen her, then they will recognise her. "Shall I come with you?"

"It's okay. I won't be long. I'll pick us up something for dinner while I'm there."

"Okay, sounds good."

We say goodbye and hang up.

I'm sure she's having fun somewhere. Chasing a rabbit or something, probably. That's the most likely explanation.

I try to keep packing, but my mind keeps wandering back to the unease I felt when Mick said Rocket had to be kept in at the vets following his check-up. The non-existent check-up that Mick invented to cover up his twisted lies.

I sit back on the floor of the spare room and stare at my half-packed suitcase as that same creeping dread seeps through my veins. Instinct told me back then, and it's telling me again now.

Something is wrong.

Chapter Twenty-Nine

Blake

I DRIVE INTO TOWN and park up. I've not seen any sign of Betsy on the way here. Not that she would wander down into town by herself. She never leaves the lake without me, usually. It's unusual for her, but I'm not worried. She's a good dog, and she'll be back. Maybe I should get one of those pet cams to put on her collar. See what she really gets up to. I chuckle at the idea as I hop down out of the truck and head into the store.

"Hey, Ralph." I grin and raise a hand in greeting. "No Duke today?" My eyes drop to the empty floor next to the counter where he's usually laid.

"Nope. Left the scoundrel out in the yard. Kept me up half the night barking. Bloody mongrel." Ralph tuts, but I know he's only joking. He loves that scruffy mutt.

"Must be something in the air. Betsy did the same."

"Is that so?" Ralph eyes me with interest as he rubs the gray bristles that coat his chin.

"Yeah. You haven't seen her, have you? She took off for a run this morning and hasn't come back yet."

The corners of Ralph's mouth turn down as he shakes his head. "You try your folks?"

"Yeah. I called Dad on the way here. She hasn't turned up there, either." I dig my hand into my pocket. "Hey. Would you mind developing these for me?" I place an envelope with a couple of strips of film inside on the counter. I grabbed them from my house earlier when I went back to look for Betsy.

"These new?" Ralph's eyes light up in interest.

"Not really." I smile to myself. "But I want to show them to Daisy."

"This is Iris' niece you're talking about? The one you're sweet on?" Ralph lets out a low wheezy chuckle.

"Ah, the Hope Cove rumor mill." I laugh as he takes the cuts of negative film out of the envelope and holds them up, his eyes narrowing as he looks at the images.

"Not really a rumor if it's true, son." He gives me a wink as he chuckles again.

"Yeah, yeah. I'll swing by and collect them later, okay?"

He nods and waves a hand as I head out the door.

I try the diner next, but no one there has seen Betsy. I decide to walk to Herbies and ask there. It's lunchtime now, and I know a lot of the guys will have been out fishing and walking in the forest before heading in for lunch and a drink. One of them might have seen her if she headed up to the ledge where we like to go. I should have checked there first, thinking about it.

I push open the door and let my eyes adjust to the low light. Compared to the blazing sun outside, it's like walking into a cave. Night's okay, but coming in here at this time? What a waste of a beautiful day. Then again, some people like to be out of the sun. Can't handle the Californian summers. Especially the passing tourists.

"Hey, Gary, Alf." I call to a couple of older guys sat at a table, nursing beers.

"All right, Blake? Early for you, isn't it? Want to join us?"

"Thanks, but I'm not here for a drink. Just looking for Betsy. You seen her?"

They both shake their heads. "Nah, sorry. Sure she'll turn up, though. Best trained dog ever known, that one."

I smile as I think of Betsy. She's an obedient dog. People think it's down to my training. But a lot of it is just her nature. Just her. She wants to please, and she loves people. She'd be anyone's for a biscuit and belly rub.

"Hi, Blake. You lost Betsy?"

I turn toward the bar and find Cindy's standing behind it. She rolls her lips as she looks at me.

"Looks that way. Will you let me know if you see her?"

She nods and gives me a small smile as she crosses her arms over her chest. "Sure."

I pause for a second, wondering if she's going to say something else. Since Daisy coming back, anything I ever had with another woman before just seems so pointless. So empty. So... nothing. But I'm not an asshole. I never meant to hurt Cindy.

I turn to leave, feeling her eyes on my back.

"Blake, wait."

I turn back to face her, and her shoulders drop as she sighs.

"There's something you should know." She looks at me. "There was a reporter in here last week, asking questions."

My mind casts back to Mom and Dad's house when Jay and Holly were visiting with Summer.

"Sounds about right. My brother and sister-in-law were in town. They can't go anywhere since the new baby news broke without at least one pap following them."

Cindy shakes her head. "I think that's what brought him here originally. But he came in asking about you."

"The show?"

It's only another six weeks until we begin filming season two. I didn't expect the press to be interested yet. We haven't even aired the season trailer. I got a bit of press attention after season one, but mostly when I visited Jay in LA. It's a journey for a reporter to come all the way to Hope Cove if we aren't even filming or doing any promotional publicity yet.

"Not the show." Cindy's eyes drop to the bar towel in her hands. "I'm sorry, Blake. I would never talk to them usually. I was just angry, you know? About the way things ended between us."

"What are you talking about?" My stomach tightens as I realize she can't look me in the eye.

"I feel so stupid. I've met someone these last couple of days, and it's made me regret it even more. I was just hurt at the time. I wanted to hurt you back. Both of you."

Both?

"Cindy?" The tone in my voice makes her snap her eyes up to my face. "What did you say?"

"He had a photo he'd taken of you both outside your parents' house. Together."

My stomach twists itself into a knot as I watch her struggle to admit what she's done.

"I.... I heard you and Travis talking in the bar one night about her changing her name and having a jerk of an ex-boyfriend."

My nostrils flare as I stare at her and lean my palms on the bar. She withers under my glare. I can't fucking believe what I'm hearing.

"What the fuck did you tell him?" I hiss.

Cindy steps back, wringing the towel around her hand as she fidgets.

"I told him the girl in the photo was English and is called Daisy, and that you both were childhood friends. I said she was over here following a nasty break-up."

"Fuck!" I push my hands back through my hair. "Do you have any idea what you've done? Do you?" I snap, attracting the attention from Gary and Alf.

"I... I'm sorry." Cindy's bottom lip wobbles as she finally looks back at my face. "I didn't mean to cause any harm."

I lower my voice as the other men's attention goes back to their drinks, although I can tell their ears are still tuned in on our conversation.

"She came here to put distance between her and her ex. He's a mean piece of shit, Cindy!" She winces as I glare at her. "What did Daisy ever do to you? If you've got a problem, it's with me, not her." I clench my jaw as I push back off the bar and let out a frustrated groan.

"I'm sorry," she whispers.

Shit.

It would be easy to stay angry and blame Cindy for this. But it's not her fault. It's on me. If I'd broken things off with her better, if I'd said it differently, then she wouldn't want to hurt me by hurting Daisy. I thought we were good. I thought she knew it was a one-time thing. I thought we'd left it in the past.

"Forget it," I grit out, my mind running a million miles an hour.

What does it matter if one reporter sells a tiny story with a picture? We're in California. He's in England. It's not like he's even likely to see it over there. But it's how Daisy will react when I tell her. She's just come back to me. She's in a good place, ready to go back and face this bastard at the trial. What if something like this happening—where she thinks she's safe, where she thinks she can be herself again—is enough to bring up those shutters again? I can't stomach the idea of losing her.

Not again.

"It's fine," I say again, more gently. "It's fine. And I'm happy for you... that you've met someone. I never meant to give you the wrong idea about us before."

Cindy's shoulders drop and she looks at me with sad eyes. "I'll call you if I see Betsy, yeah?" she says in a small voice.

"Thanks." I give her a brief nod and push open the door, heading back into the blaring sunshine.

I pull out my phone and text Daisy.

Me: Going to go check up at the ridge quickly before I head back. You okay?

Daisy: Yes, I'm fine. Just find Betsy. I'm worried about her.

Me: I knew you liked her more than me!

Daisy: Us girls have to stick together.

I smile as I walk back to my truck, my earlier anger dissipating. Just picturing her face as she sent me that text is enough to make me less agitated. Girls sticking together.

My girls.

The sky has darkened and turned gray by the time I reach the ridge. The truck won't get all the way up there, it's too narrow, so I leave it further down the hill and walk the rest of the way, calling out for Betsy as I go.

I already know I'm not going to find her. For the first time, worry burns like acid in the pit of my stomach.

What if she's hurt somewhere? What if she needs me and I can't get to her?

I get to the ledge and look around. Just as I expected—no sign of her.

My cell phone rings in my pocket. I'm lucky to have reception. It's unreliable up here amongst all the trees.

"She's not here, babe."

"God, Blake. She's been gone for hours and there's a storm coming." Daisy's anxious voice has me squeezing my eyes shut.

Where the hell is she?

"She'll turn up."

If I say it enough times, then it'll come true. She must be somewhere. She can't just have disappeared.

I swallow down the bile in my throat as I peer over the ledge and down at the fast-flowing river below. I blow out a deep breath of relief when I see nothing. No dark brown fur, no bloody, lifeless body. I'm being ridiculous. Betsy wouldn't have fallen off. She knows this forest better than me. She's probably back home again. I'd bet anything that she'll be lying out on the sofa on the back porch when I get back. Covered in mud from a great day of exploring.

"I'm coming back, babe. I'll just check the house one more time. She's probably back there by now."

"It's okay. I can check. I'll walk over. I might even be able to see her from the jetty. Hang on."

I hear some rustling, and then Daisy comes back on the line.

"Sorry, was just getting my sneakers on. I'll head over now and look. You're right. She's probably there now."

"Thanks. I'll meet you there. It'll take me five minutes to drive back." A roll of thunder booms overhead as I head back down the trail toward my truck. "Ookayy, make that ten!" I shout as the sky opens and big fat rain drops come pissing down. "On second thought, wait there for me. This rain will hit you any minute. I'll come pick you up and we'll go to mine together."

"Blake, it's fine." Daisy's voice sounds miles away as another barrel of thunder vibrates through the air.

"No, stay there. I'll be there soon."

"I'm already at the front door." She giggles, knowing her stubbornness will wind me up.

"Dai—"

I'm cut off by the sound of her scream shooting down the phone.

"Daisy? What is it?" I speed up, being careful to keep a steady footing as the rain runs down the slope next to me, turning the track to mud.

I hear a sharp intake of breath, followed by heavy breathing and a muffled sob.

"Daisy!" I yell, panic creeping into my voice. Into my veins.

"I think he's got Betsy."

"What?" I strain to hear her over the rain and thunder.

"I think he has Betsy!" she cries.

What the hell?

"Who?"

"Mickey," she sobs. "I think Mickey has Betsy."

Chapter Thirty
Daisy

"WHAT DO YOU MEAN?" Blake shouts down the phone.

"Blake! He's here. Mickey's here."

My head spins as a wave of dizziness rushes through it. I stare at the pile of stalks, every petal torn off and scattered across the porch. A massacre of white, blowing around in the breeze.

He's been here.

On this doorstep.

Right where I'm standing.

My heart hammers in my chest as a cold sweat breaks on my hairline and I suck in ragged breaths.

This can't be happening. He's in England. He doesn't know I'm here. I never told him about my aunt. It's like my subconscious knew that I may need this place one day.

Away from him.

"Daisy? Daisy?" Blake's frantic voice is calling me down the phone.

"Y-yes. I'm still here," I whisper, my eyes watching the petals as a gust of wind picks them up and swirls them about. One lands on my foot, and I kick it off with a shriek.

He's touched it.

He's been here.

"Are you okay? He's there? What are you talking about?"

"He's been here, Blake." I grab hold of the doorframe to steady myself. "I know it sounds stupid. He doesn't even know I'm here, but he must have found out somehow. He must have! The petals..."

There's no other explanation for it. No logical reason why there would be a giant bouquet of long-stemmed daisy-like flowers laid on the doorstep, with every single petal torn off.

It's a warning.

My stomach heaves and I clasp my hand to my mouth.

"I believe you."

"You do?" I whisper.

"You're not crazy, Daisy. That reporter that was outside waiting for Jay and Holly... he got photos of us, too. Cindy told me when I went into Herbies to ask after Betsy."

"But that's just a photo, surely—"

"She told him who you were. That you were here from England fleeing an ex-boyfriend. I've not seen anything, but it's possible the photo got posted online somewhere."

A sudden chill hits me in the core like a shot of ice.

He always said he'd find me.

It was a joke, really. Back in the beginning. When things were good. He would tell me if I ever left, that he would track me down. I'd laughed. I thought he was being romantic, hinting that he didn't want to be without me.

Now the joke's on me.

Mick knows people. Bad people. If there was a way to find me, then he, or someone he knows, would have discovered it. I'm so stupid. I should have thought of it before. It probably wasn't even the photograph. He probably has friends who can trace my passport, or found out Maria registered me to work at the spa. Isn't that how all these organized criminal gangs operate? Favors for each other. Bribing or threatening those who can get you the information you need.

"I've been so stupid." My voice sounds like it belongs to someone else as I sob.

"It's not your fault." The sound of a truck door slamming carries down the phone.

Why would Mick come now? Has he only just found me? Or is it... I can feel my heartbeat pounding in my throat.

The trial.

He thought he had gotten away with it when some of the evidence got thrown out. The case was weak. But then I decided to go back. I decided to face him. Make him pay for what he's done. He would be told the prosecution had a new eyewitness. He must have worked out who.

Me.

My eyes dart up and across the garden, down to the jetty, and over to the lake.

Nothing.

My shoulders relax slightly, but my heart continues to pound so hard I wouldn't be surprised if it burst right out of my chest.

"It's okay, babe. I'm coming! I'll be there as soon as I can," Blake says.

"Please hurry." The earlier unease I felt when packing my case has returned. I need him here now.

"Ah, fuck!"

"What is it?" My eyes widen at his sudden outburst.

"My tire's flat. Fucking hell!" he shouts. "Daisy. Go inside, lock the door, and call the cops, okay?"

"Blake?" My hands shake as I hear the urgency in his voice.

"Do it, Daisy! Do it now!"

"Okay, okay." I step backward into the house and shut the door, pushing it hard until it clicks so I know it's closed properly. Then I put the safety chain on and give the handle a pull to double check it. "I'm inside. The door's locked."

"Okay. Good." Blake's puffing, his voice strained as though he's running.

"Now, babe. You're going to have to put the phone down and use the landline to call the cops, okay? I'll stay right here on the other end. Tell me when you've done it."

"Okay." I run to the kitchen and my fingers tremble as I place my cell phone down on the counter and pick up the handset for the landline.

Silence.

I hit the button on the cradle, jabbing it with my finger.

No, no, no.

"Blake, it's not working! There's no dial tone."

A sob breaks from my lips, and the hairs on the back of my neck stand up. I dart my eyes around the kitchen. I don't know what I'm expecting to find, but everything looks the same. Everything is exactly where it should be. A low rumble of thunder sounds outside. The sky has darkened, and the kitchen is now a gloomy gray. I know the storm is working its way down from the forest.

It must be the weather, putting the phone line out.

Unless Mick cut it.

"Shit." Blake is panting now. There's no doubt he's running. "You're going to have to use your cell."

"No!" That means hanging up on him. That means he won't be there.

That means I will be alone.

"You can do it. Then call me straight back, okay?" I picture him running down the road from the forest. He's fast, I know he is. But he still won't even be a quarter of the way back yet.

"I'm scared," I whimper, swiping at my eyes with the back of my hand.

"Daisy. You're the strongest woman I know. Now hang up the phone. Make that call. And ring me back."

"Uh-huh."

"Tell me." His voice is solid. Dependable. Grounding. Giving me what I need.

I draw in a deep breath. "I'm going to hang up. Make the call. And then ring you back."

"That's my girl," he says.

"I love you," I whisper, squeezing my eyes shut, tears spilling from them as I hang up before he can say it back.

There's silence, and for a split second, I freeze. Unable to do anything except listen to my blood rush in my ears.

Get it together.

I fumble with my cell phone, trying to dial 9-1-1. The screen lights up as I dial, but my hands are shaking so much I drop it, and it falls to the floor, skittering along the tiles and underneath the big oak dresser.

"No!"

I fall to my knees and press my cheek to the cold tile floor, stretching out a hand. But the gap's so small I can barely get my fingers underneath.

"Shit! Please!"

A strangled sob comes out as I spot a light through the small gap. I can see it. It's so close. I need something to slide underneath and scoop it out with. I pull my hand back out as an idea hits me. I can get a spatula, or a long spoon. That will fit underneath, and then I can use it to knock my phone out. They're in the kitchen drawer under the cooker. I'll grab both and see which works.

I scramble to my feet and turn.

The sight at the back door makes me stop dead, a silent scream sticking in my throat.

The blood in my veins turns to ice and the temperature in the room drops. Every nerve ending is crackling as my stomach lurches, then plummets.

I shudder as I look at his face through the glass. Dark hair, dark eyes.

Black soul.

I stand, rooted to the spot as he stares at me. His dark features and black t-shirt, coupled with the stormy sky behind him, make him look like a monster of the night. He stares me down, his eyes unblinking, burning into me like acid. He was so good at hiding himself. I never saw this side of him when we first met. Never suspected a thing. But now it's all I can see. Darkness, cruelty, *evil.* Any trace of good I once thought he had, has vanished.

It died that day with Rocket.

I hold my breath, every tiny hair on my arms and neck raised to attention.

The doorknob turns slowly, like something from a horror movie.

Please be locked. Please be locked.

I let out the tiniest whisper of a breath as the door stays shut.

Thank God.

An ear-piercing sound makes me scream, and my hands fly up to the sides of my face. A mix of giant missiles and tiny glistening splinters crash all over the tile floor, shattering and spraying across the kitchen.

He reaches his hand in through the broken glass pane and calmly flicks the lock between his thumb and finger.

Click.

I watch, paralysed, as he draws back his hand, the knuckles covered in old cuts and bruises.

Punishing someone who got in his way?

Someone like me.

The door swings open, and he stands in the doorway, his tall, dark presence sucking the air from the room. My skin tingles as though I'm being assaulted by a billion tiny needles. All wanting blood.

Just like the look in his eyes tells me he wants mine.

Mickey has come for me.

Just like he promised.

"Don't you know it's rude not to invite your guests in?"

"W-what are you doing here?" I take a step back and bump into the kitchen side.

A cruel smirk passes over his lips.

"Shouldn't I be asking you the same question?"

He steps into the room, his wet muddy boots crunching on the broken glass and leaving a smear of brown behind them. I bring my eyes back up to his face, and his eyes roam over my body and up to my face. A bitter laugh leaves his lips.

"Decided to go back to being blonde, then." His laugh stops abruptly, and he fixes his eyes on mine, narrowing them as he studies me. "It makes you look cheap." He pops the 'p' and waits for my reaction. A satisfied smile spreads over his face as I wince, his words hitting me like a fist to the face.

I know he's only saying it to hurt me.

To get a reaction.

I'm giving him exactly what he wants. But it's easy to feel strong when the creator of your torment isn't standing in front of you. Larger and colder than you remember.

He walks into the room, casting his eyes around, his lip curling up in disgust.

"So, this is where you ran away to? This is better than what I gave you in England?"

I watch, my mouth dry, as he strolls around the room, inspecting every surface. He stops when he sees a couple of jars of body butter I and Blake had left over from helping Maria. He blows a breath out of his nose as he smirks at them, tapping their lids with a long finger.

"Started playing your little beauty shop game again, have you?"

I shuffle my feet, edging my back along the counter in the direction of the hallway. If I can make it to the front door, I could get out and run.

I could get away.

Before he has the chance to kill me.

Will he really go that far? He's hit me before, and I know what little regard he has for animal lives. Surely taking a human one is just another step up the twisted, evil ladder to someone like Mick. Someone I thought I knew once, but never truly did.

How could I have *gotten it so wrong?*

I freeze as his cold eyes lock on my face. I used to think they were a warm brown. Like hot chocolate on a cold winter's night. But now I can see they're darker. Like the depths of a cave. One that once you fall in, it's almost impossible to claw your way back out of the darkness again.

But I have.

I'm back out in the light, and there's no way in hell I'm going back.

Seeing him now, roaming around like some psychotic king, makes me more determined. He may be stronger than me. I may be terrified of what he might be about to do to me. So terrified, I'm not sure whether I'm more likely to faint or be sick.

But I know one thing.

I'm not going down without a fight.

"What if I have?" I say, referring to his comment about making my own creams again.

It's something I did when we first met. He never really appreciated when I made things for him as gifts. In time, I made less and less. I always seemed to spend all my time with Mick instead, doing what he wanted.

Just how he liked it.

He turns, a light blue vein bulging in his temple as he glares at me.

"What the fuck you say, *weed*?" he hisses.

I swallow the giant lump in my throat. My confidence suddenly feeling more like gross stupidity as he strides across the room and

CAPTURED BY MR. WILD

stops, his face inches from mine. He smells like cigarettes, and I hold my breath as he lifts one hand and trails the nail of one finger slowly down the side of my face.

His dark hair falls forward over his cheekbones as he smirks at me.

"Bet I still make your cunt wet, don't I? That's one thing you got right, at least."

I gasp, turning my face to the side so I don't have to look at him. My chest heaves as I suck in a breath to stop my legs from giving away underneath me.

"Thought so." He chuckles to himself, ignoring the repulsion on my screwed-up face. Even just the thought that he once touched me has bile rising in my throat.

He keeps his face close to mine, rolling his lips.

"If you like it here so much, with your hair and your jars of shit, then tell me, Daisy. Why are you coming back to little old England?"

I swallow down the nausea. Hearing my name coming out of his mouth sounds so wrong. He could take the happiest word in existence and make it sound like a curse on your soul.

"I'm coming back for the trial." My voice betrays me. And despite my earlier surge in confidence, I know I sound scared.

I *am* scared.

He smirks, and I cower back against the counter, the edge of it digging into my spine as I try to put some distance between us.

"Oh, right? The trial." He nods, smacking his lips together. "You know I'll get off, don't you? Not enough evidence." He laughs. "I've got a lot of friends in high places, Daisy. More than you'll ever know."

I look at him sideways. "You don't deserve to be free. Not after what you did."

"What I *still* do." He grabs my chin, an evil glint in his eye. His fingers squeeze hard until pain lances up through my jaw, making my entire skull throb and my vision blur. "You can't stop it. It's business. We'll just move to another place. Pay some other cops to turn a blind eye. Find some other Rockets."

A gargled sob escapes from my squashed, distorted lips.

He laughs again. "You liked that little runt, didn't you? Too bad you started getting whiny and annoying. I might have let you keep him otherwise."

He lets go of my jaw and I grab my throbbing face with my hand, pain coursing through it as the blood returns to my flesh.

"I thought you were seeing someone else. That's why I followed you." As I rub my face, my vision returns to normal.

He cups the side of my face in his palm. The gesture is almost tender; it makes my skin crawl.

"Aww, you were jealous? Little Daisy thought I was filling another cunt instead of hers." He tips his head to the side and gives me a condescending smile.

I close my eyes so I can't look back into his dead ones. That's the only way to describe them. When you do what Mick does and don't even feel a drop of remorse, you must be dead inside.

My mind drifts to Betsy and my body tenses.

"Hit a nerve, did I?" Mick grins, then takes a step back.

The extra space means I can finally draw in a proper breath without taking in his own expelled air, or his scent.

"What did you do to her?" I whisper.

He frowns as I turn my face toward him. If he thinks he can say nothing. Say nothing while she's somewhere suffering, or God knows what... then I'll... I'll...

"Who?"

"You know who." I grit my teeth as my eyes meet his. "Where is she? Where's Betsy?"

He purses his lips, his brow creasing as he looks at me. He seems to consider something. Then he tips back his head slowly and smiles to himself.

"The guy with the black truck. His dog, you mean?"

"Her name's Betsy." I stare at him, hatred oozing from every pore. He won't care what her name is. She's just another tool to him. Something to use for his own gain, and then to discard when he's had enough.

Please don't let it be too late.

"Ah, yes. Lovely shiny coat. I considered skinning the bitch and keeping that as a souvenir."

I clasp a hand over my throat and heave. My stomach churns, but nothing comes up. Instead, my eyes and mouth water.

Betsy.

"You bastard." I squeeze my eyes shut, hoping to God he's just making it up to torture me. After what I saw, though, anything is possible with Mickey.

He laughs then. A horrid scratching laugh that makes my body feel like someone is dragging rusty nails over my spine.

"Tell you what, Daisy." He sneers, and I feel a bead of sweat run down my chest, followed by another, then another. "You do what I want, and I'll make sure you get Betsy back. In one piece."

"One unharmed piece." I look at him.

His jaw clenches as he looks down his nose at me.

"Sure." He shrugs.

I have no idea if he'll keep his word or if that's just another lie. But what choice do I have? If he's put Betsy somewhere, I have to try.

"What do you want me to do?"

"I would have thought that was obvious. I want you to retract your statement." He steps closer again, taking a clump of my hair between his fingers and holding it in front of my face.

He reaches into his pocket with his other hand and holds something down by his side.

Click.

It's as though every muscle in my body goes weak, on the verge of collapsing, as I realize what the sound was.

The click of a flick knife blade extending.

He brings the blade up between us, looking at me with amusement in his eyes.

"Tell them you got it wrong. Tell them you made it up because you found me with another woman. I don't care what shit you make up. Just tell them you won't be giving evidence."

The whites of his eyes have a yellow tinge, and the corner of one is twitching. It's slight, so subtle it's almost invisible. But it's there.

He's worried.

My mouth drops open as I study him. He was always clean shaven. But now, the dark, wiry hair covering his chin and neck looks scruffy. That, coupled with his eyes—I bet he hasn't slept properly in weeks.

As if sensing I'm figuring him out, Mickey pulls my hair in his hand and holds the blade up to it. The glistening metal narrowly misses the tip of my nose as he jerks his wrist and cuts right through the light strands. He slams his fist down on the kitchen counter and pulls his hand back. Leaving my hair lying there.

I tear my eyes away from the cut strands and back to his face. He smiles at me. It's a cold smile that doesn't reach his eyes. The smile of a bully who thinks he's made a point. Who thinks he's shown how much better than me he is.

Bigger. Stronger. *Cleverer.*

"Fine. I'll do it," I spit, narrowing my eyes at him.

A smug smile creeps over his face. "Good. I thought you'd see sense if we had this chat in person."

He retracts the knife blade back into the casing, but instead of putting it in his pocket, he runs the case down the side of my face. Pausing at my jaw and then continuing excruciatingly slowly across my throat. I fight the urge to swallow, or blink, or do anything that may give away the suffocating vise-like crushing that's taken over my chest.

He's warning me.

Warning me he will kill me next time.

"Now, why don't you make us a drink and we can toast our new agreement."

All I can do is nod as I try to find a breath to fill my empty lungs.

Finally, he drops the knife case and laughs. Laughs because he thinks he's won. Laughs because he thinks I'm weak. Laughs because he sees the fear in my eyes.

The way he saw the fear in all those poor dogs' eyes every time he sent another to an agonizing death.

The memory lights a fire in my core.

I turn to the kitchen counter to fix us both a drink, hating that he's behind me and I can feel his eyes on my back. I get two glasses out of the cupboard and avoid looking at my clump of hair as I set them down on the counter and reach for a bottle of gin.

"Make it strong." Mick's voice makes me jump, and he laughs again.

My hand falters, hovering over the bottles on the side.

Once I've poured two large glasses, I turn around and hand one to him. His eyes hold mine as he takes it and knocks half back in one large gulp. I sip mine and watch as he finishes it.

"Another." He thrusts the glass at me, and I refill it for him. Watching as he knocks back the second one just as fast.

"Do you like it? I made part of it myself."

He eyes me coolly over the rim of the glass before lowering it down.

"It's all right. At least you can drink it. Better than this shit you make. Smells like old ladies." He lifts one of the body butter jars and opens his hand, letting it fall to the floor and smash, joining the glass from the door. "Oops."

"You said you'd tell me where Betsy is." I ignore the stinging in my calf and warm trickle making its way down to my ankle from where the glass hit me.

"Oh, yeah. I lied." Mick shrugs.

I stare at him, hatred coursing through my veins. He's vile. He's every vile thing wrong in this world.

"What did you do to her?" I stare at him.

"I didn't do anything. She was gone when I came back."

"You were here?" Another bead of sweat runs down my chest as my throat grows tight.

"Last night." He smirks as my eyes go round. "I saw you. And that guy. The one with the black truck. Where is he now, eh? Where's your Mr. Wild?"

He laughs as I grip the kitchen side to keep myself up. He knows who Blake is.

"I saw the photos of the two of you. Very cute." Mick sneers. "By the way, what do you think he's teaching people to eat out there in the forest in the name of survival for a TV show?"

"H-he teaches them how to live, shows them what to do. They don't really catch anything."

Mick chuckles. "How stupid are you, Daisy? I bet he's killed animals with his bare hands. Maybe he and I ought to go for a beer. We've got a lot in common."

His eyes drop over my body and I cross my arms over my chest self-consciously.

"He's nothing like you," I whisper.

"You keep telling yourself that if it helps you sleep at night." Mick sounds bored as he looks out the window at the lightning in the sky.

I can feel heat rising through my body as I fight to make sense of his words. Blake is nothing like him. He loves Betsy. He would never hurt an animal for pleasure like Mick does. I swear he doesn't trap animals on the show. Just shows people how they could if they needed to.

To survive.

That's all. If he needed to survive, then maybe... would he? I shake my head. I can't imagine Blake doing that. He's not evil.

Not like Mickey.

I glare at him as his eyes come back to my face. He's trying to manipulate me. Just like he always does. Trying to plant seeds of doubt in my mind. First about myself—grinding me down, so I was almost too scared to leave him—and now about Blake.

"Is that how you found me? The photo?"

"I already knew you were here, Daisy. I've known for weeks. Like I said, I know people."

My eyes dart to the window, praying to see Blake, but also knowing he will still be too far away.

"He'll be here soon. Any minute," I lie.

Mick laughs. "Will he? Pretty sure slow punctures don't mend themselves. I think seeing as you live way out of town, it'll take him awhile to get here from wherever he is."

I feel the blood drain from my face, taking the color with it. He punctured Blake's tire. He planned all this. He planned to come back here and get me alone. But Betsy? I let out a deep breath. From what he says, he doesn't have her. There's one thing to be thankful for.

Mick picks up the second jar of body butter.

"Why do you like making this shit, anyway?"

I don't even flinch as the glass explodes on the kitchen tiles. I'm expecting it.

"It's amazing what you can make with time and practice."

Mick's eyes turn glassy, and he shakes his head, swaying a little.

"What the?" He lifts one hand to his head and blinks his eyes, as though struggling to focus. "What the fuck?"

299

I seize my opportunity and spin, racing through the hallway to the front door.

"Fuck! Come here!" Mick bellows behind me as I fight to pull the chain off and turn the handle.

The door flies open, and I race through it, my eyes on the lake. My head snaps back painfully as he grabs my hair.

"You fucking bitch!"

I lift my elbow and force it back, connecting with something that causes Mick to yell out loud and let go. My heart hammers in my throat as I try to move away. This time, he grabs me around my waist and we both fall. My lip connects with the top step of the porch, and the air is knocked from my lungs as pain takes over my head and I taste warm metal, sticky on my tongue.

"What the fuck did you give me?" Mick slurs as he rolls me over and straddles me. His weight crushes my stomach as his hands wrap around my neck. "I said, what the fuck did you give me?"

He squeezes, and I claw at his hands with my nails. Scratching, drawing blood, fighting for air. I wriggle and push. I fight. And fight. And Fight.

But he's stronger than me.

I want to tell him I can't breathe. But his hands are too tight. I stare at the sky rather than at his face. I don't want the last thing I see to be the eyes of the man I despise.

A flash of lightning forks across the dark gray clouds and I feel a calmness wash over me as my hands still. I can feel the rain on my cheeks. See each drop as it falls from the sky. It's stirring up the earth and sending the scents of my aunt's garden to me in the air. My eyelids grow heavy as I think of her.

God, I miss her.

A clap of thunder makes my eyes pop open. Now I'm remembering something else. This time it's Blake. It's Blake and Betsy in the thunderstorm. It's falling on my ass and Blake pulling me up into his arms. It's Blake kissing me, even though I was covered in mud and filthy. It's Blake looking at me with his deep green eyes. Wanting me.

It's all Blake.

It takes every ounce of my strength to lift my hands and dig my fingers into Mick's face. I find something soft, and I push, not stopping, even as he lets out a gurgled cry. Just as I think I can't survive one more second, his hands leave my neck.

I grasp at my chest, pulling in deep, wracking breaths, my ears filled with the sound of my lungs wheezing—screaming out at how long they've been starved. I turn and crawl, tumbling face first down the porch steps.

I raise my face from the ground, dragging myself along the grass with my fingers, building up the strength to get to my feet. Everything is a throbbing blur. I can barely make anything out.

A hand grabs me around the ankle. Then another on the same calf. Pulling their way up my body as I see the earth underneath my fingers sliding away.

And I know if I let him pull me back to him, then that's it.

This time I won't get away.

I draw in every grain of strength in my body and turn, kicking Mick in the face with my free leg. I scream with the effort, making my lungs sting and my chest shudder.

But it works.

He lets go and grabs his face, groaning like an injured animal.

I roll back to my stomach and claw my way along the grass again.

Get up! Get up!

I ignore the pounding in my face and stagger to my feet, falling to one side as my head spins. I can't see and I'm disorientated. But I know I need to get away. I need to hide.

I stumble forward and realize where I am.

Relief washes over me.

If I'm going to live, then this place will help me.

It's my best bet.

Chapter Thirty-One
Blake

I'VE NEVER RUN SO fast in my life. I'm running as though the devil himself is chasing me, mud splattering up over me as I sprint toward home.

Toward Daisy.

Hold on, babe, hold on.

My lungs are burning. Burning in my chest. But it's nothing compared to the agony of not knowing if Daisy is safe. She never called back. Then I lost signal in the trees and when I tried her cell again, it wouldn't connect.

"Fuck!" I yell as my feet pound against the hard road.

I'm almost there.

Is he there now? Is he touching her? Hurting her?

My blood courses around my body, powered by my thundering heart. I swear if he's touched her, I will kill him.

I will fucking kill him!

This is all my fault. He found her because of that photograph. Because Cindy wanted to hurt me. I can't believe she would do such a spiteful thing. I'm a fucking idiot! Despite trying my hardest not to, she got the wrong idea about us. She wanted revenge. And now Daisy's the one paying the price.

Nothing can happen to Daisy. I wouldn't survive it. I need her.

I fucking love her.

The end of the driveway comes into sight, and I power forward, willing my legs to go faster. To get me there quicker. You hear those stories about how a split second can make all the difference. What if Daisy only has a split second? I need to get there.

I must get to her.

The storm is passing, but the sky is still dark gray. The birds have stopped flying and there is an eerie silence in the air. The only sound other than the easing rain is my deep panting and the slamming of my feet on the ground.

Please be okay. Please be okay.

I race into Daisy's driveway and see red and blue flashing lights up by the house.

The cops. An ambulance.

Relief floods my body, but is instantly replaced by numbness spreading down my fingers.

Where is she?

I swing my head around, my eyes wildly darting over the scene. There are two police cars and one ambulance up ahead. The flashing lights make it hard to see beyond them.

What the fuck happened? Where is she?

"Stop right there!" a cop calls.

I ignore him, speeding up as I race toward the cars.

"I said stop!"

"Daisy!" I yell. "Where is she? What did he do to her?"

"Sir!" he shouts again and stands in my way.

I dart around him and jump, sliding over the hood of the patrol car on my ass and landing in front of the house. I swing my head around, my heart hammering in my chest as I try to process what I can see. There are two medics tending to an unmoving body on the ground.

No!

"Sir!" The officer rounds the car and approaches me.

I run over to the body, spots appearing in my vision as I clutch a hand to my chest and suck in deep breaths.

It can't be her. Please don't let it be her.

Muddy boots, black jeans...

My arms shake, and my pulse races as a medic moves to one side.

And I see him.

His face is swollen and is covered in blood. But it's him. I'd recognize him anywhere after seeing the photos of him with his arms around Daisy on social media.

"Where is she, you piece of shit? What did you do to her?"

I reach down between the two medics and grab him around the neck. His bloodied head lolls to the side, his eyes rolled back in his head. He's totally out cold. No fucking use to me.

Hands swarm me, grabbing my arms, as three officers appear and struggle to pull me back.

"What did he do to her?" I shout, turning to one of them.

"Sir, tell me who you are."

"I'm her boyfriend! Where is she? Where's Daisy?"

The officer seems to decide I'm not a threat and lowers his arms, catching the eyes of his colleagues. They release me and I look at the house. The porch steps are covered in blood. Dread twists in my stomach, making me want to hurl.

"Where is she?" I turn to the second officer, a female.

"You said you're her boyfriend?" She looks me up and down, taking in my sweat and rain drenched clothes.

"Yes! She called me and said her ex was here. She had to hang up to call 9-1-1. But she never called back. Where is she? Please," I beg, searching the officer's eyes.

She holds my gaze. "We don't know."

They were too late. They didn't help her.

I stare at her. I want to toss their stupid cars and light up into fucking orbit!

"What the fuck do you mean, you don't know?" I stride past her, past the medics, and stare out over the lake. The surface of it looks dark and gray.

And calm.

"Daisy!" I yell, cupping my hands around my mouth. "Daisy!"

"Sir, we're doing everything we can."

My eyes dart to two more officers. One searching along the edge of the lake. One searching the garden.

"Can you tell me what happened?" she probes.

"Her ex came for her, just like she said." I don't meet the officer's eyes. Instead, I frantically hunt for any sign of Daisy.

Where are you, babe?

"That's the guy on the ground?" She motions to Mickey, laid out cold.

"Didn't she tell you this on the phone?"

I spot something orange and my heart lurches, but then I see it's just the watering can that's blown over into a bush.

"We didn't speak to her. The call connected, but all control could make out was a conversation between a man and a woman. There was glass smashing and raised voices. That's when they dispatched a unit. Me and Rogan got on scene first. Found him"—she looks at Mickey—"then called in back-up and medics."

"Fuck." I rake my hands back through my hair as an officer appears from inside the house.

"Found something!" he calls out.

A pressure so great that I think I may pass out builds in my chest as I look at what he's holding up in his hand.

It's hers. There's no doubt in my mind.

Fear seeps through me, and it feels like my chest is about to implode. I clench my fist so hard my palm stings, and fight to hold in the contents of my stomach.

I stare up toward the officer in the doorway.

My eyes glue themselves to the blonde clump of hair hanging lifelessly in his hand.

What the fuck did that bastard do?

Time seems to stand still as he walks over to the other officer, and they talk in hushed voices. I'm aware of hands touching me, one on my back, one on my arm. And something warm and familiar pressing into my palm.

"Blake? What the hell's going on?"

I turn and look into Kayla's wide eyes, her hand wrapped around my arm.

"We were bringing someone home to you," Travis says, drawing my attention to my other side, where he has one hand on my back, his face pale as he watches the medics tend to Mickey.

"Huh?" is all I can manage as I stare at him. My mind racing as it tries to process what's happening.

Where is she? What's he done to her? Why is there so much blood?

Travis looks back at me and then glances down. I follow his gaze and drop to my knees, my mouth dry and my chest tight as I wrap my arms around Betsy's warm body and lean into her. She whines and licks my face.

"Where the hell have you been, girl?" I murmur as I press my face into her soft, warm fur. "Where the hell have you been?"

"Ralph dropped her into the clinic," Kayla says. "Said he found her in his yard with Duke but couldn't get you on your cell."

"I lost signal," I mutter as I run my hands up and down over Betsy's back.

"Where's Dee?" Kayla asks. "And who's that?" She looks over at Mickey, unable to recognise him from all the blood on his face.

"That's Daisy's ex," I spit, venom lacing my voice as I turn to look at him getting medical help. He doesn't deserve a second of their time. Daisy needs them. She needs their help. Wherever she is. Whatever he's done to her.

My nostrils flare as I stand. If he's in that state, what the hell is Daisy like? I ball my hands into fists at my sides.

"Blake. What do you mean? Where is she?" Travis' eyes are round as he looks at me.

"They can't find her, Trav." My voice cracks as I rub my fist against my chest. "They can't fucking find her."

I can feel my strength unraveling like a loose thread. Soon I'll just be a fucking mess on the floor.

"God!" Kayla's hand flies to her mouth and she sobs. "Has he hurt her? Has he—?"

"No," Trav cuts in. "We can't think like that. She'll be okay." He wraps his arm around Kayla as she sobs into his chest. His eyes meet mine and he gives me a look that tells me all I need to know.

He's shitting himself almost as much as me.

Betsy grumbles next to me, nudging my hand with her nose. I stare down into her large brown eyes. She looks back at me, and I swear she knows something is wrong. She can sense it. I bend down and cup her chin with my hand.

"She's in trouble. Daisy's in trouble."

Her ears prick up and she whines, then pulls her face from my hand and springs to her feet, barking at me.

"What is it, girl?"

She spins around in a circle and then bounces on her back legs, barking at me again.

Hope blooms in my chest. "Show me," I whisper. "Show me!" I say louder and she turns, tearing off across the grass, her nose rooted to the grass as she sniffs and runs from side to side, pausing to cock her head and listen.

She's looking for Daisy.

"Come on, girl! You can do it! Find her for me! Find her!" I fire off words of encouragement as I run after her, following her over the grass.

I stop dead.

She's led me to the end of the jetty.

No! Fuck, no!

"Daisy!" I cry, diving into the water without hesitation.

Panic churns inside me, and I accidentally suck in a mouthful of lake water as I surface. My throat burns and I cough as I search the surface frantically for any sign of her. A ripple, a bubble, something.

Anything.

I gasp and dive below the surface. All I can see is darkness—murky water where the storm clouds are cutting out almost all the light. I come up for air and then dive straight back under, coming up again with nothing.

I've got nothing.

She's been down here for too long. If he put her in the lake... If he did something to her and then threw her in... then she's...

I swallow down the acid that's burning a hole in my throat.

No! I can't give up on her. I will not give up on her! She did not come back into my life after ten years, to be taken like this.

I'm not letting her go.

"Daisy!" I scream, my voice growing hoarse. "Daisy!"

Betsy barks, and I turn to her. She's standing on the edge of the jetty, scratching the wooden boards beneath her paws. She looks at me, dipping her nose over the end of the final board next to the wooden ladder, and then barks again.

The red flash of the cops' lights illuminates the briefest flash of something behind the ladder.

Blonde strands of hair.

"Daisy!"

I throw my arms out and swim to the ladder. I'm only meters away, but it feels like miles as I fight through the water to get to her.

I swim under the jetty and grab her, pulling her limp body into my arms.

"Daisy?"

Her eyes don't focus on me. One is swollen shut and her lip is split. Blood covers her face, her hair matted and sticking to it.

"It's alright, babe. I'm here. You're safe. You're safe."

She grunts, and her head rolls forward onto my shoulder as she passes out. Her arms are wrapped around the ladder, keeping her head just above the surface of the water.

Another split second and she would have let go.

I would have lost her.

"Help!" I scream. "I've found her! She needs help!"

I grab the ladder and pull us around to the front of it, climbing up it with one arm, Daisy clasped firmly to my chest with the other. Two officers run to the end of the jetty and hold out their hands, helping us up. I lay her down gently on the wooden boards, supporting her head.

The officers step back as two medics appear and take over, shining a light into Daisy's good eye. When the torch moves, I see the extent of the giant swelling on the other side, and the blood seeping from her nose and lip.

"Fuck." The word comes out as a strangled sob from my throat.

Betsy appears and leans into my side. I sink my nose into her fur as I shake with a mix of adrenaline, fear, and rage.

"Oh, my god!" Kayla shrieks.

I look up. Her and Travis standing further away, their eyes wide.

"He tried to kill her! He tried to fucking kill her, and I wasn't here!" My heart drops to my stomach.

I was almost too late.

The medics have got a line into Daisy's arm, and she's hooked up to a bag. The sound of sterile packets being ripped opened fills the air as they patch her. Plug wounds. Stem bleeding.

Fight to help her.

Fight to put my girl back together again.

"Please save her. She's everything to me."

I watch, helpless as Daisy lies still, wet, and covered in blood. It's like something out of a medical drama. She's a patient. My beautiful, strong, loving girl is a silent patient.

I search the medics' faces. The girl keeps working on Daisy, injecting her with something. The guy looks at me.

"She's pretty banged up, but her pulse is strong. I'd say you've got a fighter on your hands."

I scrub my hands back through my hair, my eyes filling with tears as I glue myself to her side, following and watching as they get her onto a stretcher and into the back of another ambulance, which has arrived.

"Sorry, no animals." The female medic looks apologetic as Betsy sits on the grass at the back of the ambulance.

"Blake, we'll take her. You go with Daisy. We'll meet you at the hospital."

I nod a silent thank-you at Travis and look at Kayla, who gives me a small smile, her cheeks stained with tears.

"You did good, girl." I sniff as I press a kiss on Betsy's smooth head. "You did good." I pat her on the shoulder and then climb into the back of the ambulance.

***

The door to the hospital room opens, and Travis walks in.

"Hey, man. How are you holding up?" He places a hand on my shoulder and squeezes.

I'm leaning forward in my chair, my elbows on my knees and my head in my hands.

"I'm fine." I turn my head to the side and look at him.

"Well, you look like shit. Why don't you go home and take a shower? I can stay with her. Kayla's just saying goodbye to your parents in the hallway. She can give you a lift."

"No way." I shake my head. "I'm not leaving her."

"Blake. You'll be an hour, tops. And I will call you if anything changes."

"I said no!" I growl.

"Fine." Travis sighs. "Just don't say I didn't warn you if she takes one look at your rough-ass face when she wakes up and changes her mind about you. I'm surprised the stench hasn't woken her up already."

"Jerk," I mutter.

"Shit funk," he fires back.

The corners of his mouth lift, and I try to smirk back at him, but it's a half-assed effort. Nothing feels right about smiling or joking right now. Not when Daisy is lying in a hospital bed.

However, Travis is right. Not that I will admit that to him. I do stink.

Bad.

He brought a change of clothes to the hospital for me. I was soaked after diving into the lake. But I still haven't washed. I smell like a swamp monster that ran a marathon, and then had a fight with a skunk.

"I'm not leaving her, Trav. She hasn't even woken up properly yet. I need to hear her voice. I need to look in her eyes and tell her I'm sorry."

"What are you sorry for, you idiot? You saved her."

I laugh a humorless laugh as my eyes fall back to her face. She looks so fragile. The doctors have cleaned her up, but her lip is still bloody, one eye is black and swollen shut, and there are bruises scattered across her face.

"Betsy saved her. I left her. I wasn't there when she needed me."

"There's no way you could have known her ex was coming, Blake."

I blow out a breath as I watch Daisy. She's sleeping now. She barely came round at all in the ambulance, or since she arrived. The doctor said it's normal. Her body is exhausted.

From fighting.

From surviving.

"I *should* have known. After seeing Cindy and her telling me about the reporter... I should have known," I hiss, gritting my teeth.

"You can't think like that. So what if there was a photo? Maybe even a minor story online somewhere? The guy was all the way back in England. You could never have known he would show up like that. Neither of you could have known."

I look over at her beaten face again, my eyes moving down to her neck. At the deep purple marks cover the delicate skin there.

His fingerprints.

His fucking hands left marks on her. On her skin. The skin I've spent hours stroking, kissing, losing myself and my heart to.

"I wish I'd killed him when I had the chance." I suck a breath in through my nose, making my nostrils flare.

"When he was out cold on the floor, you mean? When your priority was Daisy, and her needing you?" Travis raises a brow at me, crossing his arms over his chest.

"Yeah, then," I mutter, looking down at the floor.

"Blake." His voice takes on his 'this means business' tone, and I know he's about to lecture me, or 'talk some sense into me', as he would call it. "She needs you. She needs you to be there for her when she wakes up. Not on some vendetta about an ex who she gave it back to pretty good."

I try to smile again, but even finding out that Mickey has a broken nose and a fractured eye socket does nothing to ease the sickening pull in the pit of my stomach.

He almost killed her.

"I'm going to go get a coffee. You want one?" Travis heads over to the door and looks back at me.

"Sure, thanks." My eyes go back to Daisy's face, and I pull my chair closer to her bedside.

"I'll let your mom and dad know you're staying. They said they were going to wait around for a while."

"Okay." I nod, only half listening. I'm too busy watching Daisy's chest rise and fall as she breathes.

The door clicks shut as Travis leaves, and I reach out and take Daisy's hand. It seems so small and fragile in mine. Her fingernails are filthy. A mix of blood and mud embedded underneath them. One of her nails is missing entirely. Ripped from her skin. I pinch the bridge of my nose with my other hand.

That fucking bastard.

The police came and took swabs earlier. From under her nails, inside her mouth, the cuts on her face. I stayed in the room with her while they photographed the marks on her neck too. The marks where he wrapped his hands so hard around her neck and tried to squeeze the life out of her. Tried to extinguish the light in my girl's eyes.

My shoulders shake as silent sobs wrack my chest, threatening to take over my body. I draw a deep breath in through my nose and tilt my head back, blinking my eyes to force the water away.

Get it together.

I need to be strong for her. Everyone thinks I'm this brawny guy. All bravado and no depth. But with Daisy? With her, it's different. I want to bawl like a baby at almost losing her. I want her to open her eyes so I can pour my heart out to her. Tell her she owns it. Tell her it will only ever belong to her. She makes me feel out of control, impulsive, wild, *alive*.

She makes me feel everything worth living for, all at once.

"God, Daisy. I know you can hear me," I whisper. "I know you can hear me." I squeeze her hand in mine. "I'm sorry I wasn't faster. I should have been there. This wouldn't have happened. You wouldn't be here, you wouldn't be—"

"Blake?" a raspy voice murmurs.

My eyes go wide, and I jump to my feet, leaning over the bed. I stroke her forehead. Light, gentle strokes as the lids of the eye she can open slowly prise apart.

My girl's awake.

"Daisy?" Warmth erupts in my chest as I gaze at her. She murmurs something barely audible, and I lean closer so I can hear.

It sounds like she says *schink.*

"You want a drink, babe?" I reach to the cup of water on the side and hold the straw to her lips so she can have a sip.

She groans and mumbles again, "You stink."

I look into her one open eye. She tries to smile at me and then winces.

I drop my chin to my chest, relief pouring over me.

She's back. My girl's back.

"It's nice to see you again too." I chuckle as she slowly moves her hand and laces her fingers between mine. I look at them. Seeing all the blood and mud again. My smile drops, and my voice drops to a low whisper as I raise my eyes to meet hers. "I'm so sorry, babe."

A frustrated sigh comes from her throat, and she tries to lift the hand which is entwined with mine. I help her, lifting our joined hands up, so our elbows are resting on the mattress. She extends a finger and clumsily drops it against my lips.

"Okay." I smile and kiss her fingertip in understanding. "I'll stop talking."

She moans a sound of agreement and then gives me the tiniest smile. It barely moves her lips, but it reaches her open eye, which shines back at me.

"I'd better tell the doctor you're awake."

She squeezes my hand to prevent me from reaching for the call button. We stare at each other for a minute, neither making a sound. We don't have to say anything. I know from the way she's looking at me, and the way my breath has stalled, that we are just lost in a moment.

Lost in a moment of finding one another again.

"Betsy?" she whispers.

"She's fine, babe. Ralph found her."

She nods, and my heart swells as she lets out a small sigh. She's lying here, in a hospital bed, black and blue, yet her first thought is for Betsy. Not herself.

That's Daisy all over.

I smile as I look at her. When she first came back, I knew. I've always known. She is the same caring, positive, loving person she's always been. She shows it every single day.

A tear escapes her eye and slides down toward her ear. I catch it with my free thumb and stroke the side of her face.

"It's okay, babe." I struggle to keep my voice steady.

"Mick—?"

"He's alive," I growl.

Although, I wish he weren't.

Daisy's gaze searches mine, and I lean forward and kiss her fingertips before I answer.

"He can't hurt you again. The police are charging him with attempted murder. Your conversation was all taped. They found your phone underneath the dresser in the kitchen. You called them, babe. You did it."

A sob escapes Daisy's lips, and another tear rolls down the side of her face.

I tense, pushing down the rage inside me as Travis' words repeat in my head. *She needs you to be there for her. Not on some vendetta about an ex.*

"They've got him recorded, admitting to everything, trying to bribe you against giving evidence at the trial. And then the..." I look at the bruises on her neck and swallow. "They know he

wouldn't have stopped, Daisy. You must have fought him off hard."
I screw my eyes shut as the images flood my mind again.

Mick threatening her.

Mick cutting a chunk of her hair out.

Mick strangling her.

Me ripping him apart and feeding him to a pack of starved wolves.

"Sleep tonic," she croaks.

"What?" My eyes pop open and I look at her.

"I gave him my sleep tonic. Four doses. Put it in his drink."

"Daisy." My shoulders drop, and I slowly release a breath. My chest expands and I shake off a sudden feeling of being lightheaded.

My girl's a fighter.

I press my lips to the back of her hand. She's so tough, so strong. I couldn't be prouder of her.

"You're incredible." I can't hold it in any longer. My eyes water as I gaze at her, so I lean over and press my lips gently to hers. "You take my fucking breath away."

She looks at me, tears falling thick and fast from her good eye.

"I love you, Blake Anderson," she whispers.

I rest my forehead against hers.

"And God, do I love you, Daisy Matthews."

Chapter Thirty-Two

Daisy

"HURRY, BLAKE! I WANT to see her!"

I turn to the truck to see what's taking Blake so long, just as he strides up next to me, slipping his arm around me and his hand into my back jean pocket.

"God, what the hell am I going to do with you two? Women." He tuts, earning a smack on the chest from me.

I smile at him. As much as I can anyway, without my lip feeling like it's about to be torn off. I had to stay in hospital for a couple of days until the doctors were happy to discharge me. They released me after a lot of begging, and on the understanding that someone was there to help look after me. Blake stepped up without missing a beat. I'm still so sore and feel like a truck hit me.

But I'm healing.

That's the main thing. I'm healing. And soon the black eye and the split lip will be gone. The short clump of hair near my face will grow back, and then there will only be the mental scars to deal with. I know those will be the hardest to heal.

I look up at Blake. His green eyes glitter down at me, and he tucks a strand of hair behind my ear with his free hand. It won't be easy, but I know I'll get there when I've got my own Mr. Wild looking out for me.

"Blake!" I scold again. "Press the damn bell already!"

He chuckles and pushes the bell. A few moments later, the door opens and Betsy barrels out.

"We told her you were coming. She's been sitting by the door all morning." Kayla smiles as she and Travis stand in the doorway.

I drop to the floor, holding my arms out wide and grabbing Betsy into a hug.

"I've missed you! You're such a good girl, such a beautiful girl," I coo as the others watch me. Betsy laps up the attention, whining and nuzzling into me. She feels so warm in my arms. She pants, and her doggy breath tickles my ear, making me giggle.

"What is this? I barely get a hello now?" Blake chuckles as Betsy turns to him, her tail flying around wildly.

"Pfft, she saw you this morning. You're old news." Kayla laughs as she and Travis stand back so we can walk inside.

"Don't I know it." Blake grins and ruffles Betsy's ears, before leaning down to kiss her on the head.

"She'll always be a daddy's girl, don't you worry. You're the only man for her." I roll my eyes as we follow Kayla and Travis into the kitchen.

Kayla snorts, slapping a hand across her mouth. Travis catches her eye and gives her a warning look. "Kayla..."

"Okay, okay. You tell them." She looks from Travis to us, her eyes bright.

"Tell us what?" Blake wraps his arm around me again as he looks between the two of them.

Travis clears his throat, his face serious. "After Ralph found Betsy in his yard with Duke, I gave her a check over. You know, just to make sure everything was okay."

"Yeah?" Blake looks at Travis, who is rolling his lips together, a look of deep concentration on his face. "Spit it out, man? Is she sick?"

I look down at Betsy, who's watching us all with eager eyes. *She doesn't look sick.*

In fact, I'd say she looks really well since staying with Kayla and Travis, maybe even a little rounder from all the extra treats Kayla has no doubt been giving her. They offered to have her until I came out of the hospital, as Blake was there with me so much.

"Oh, she's not sick." Kayla snorts again, her shoulders shaking.

Travis shoots her another warning look, then turns his attention back to Blake.

"She's not sick. She's pregnant."

My heart jumps in my chest and I grin at Kayla, who nods at me.

"What the fuck?" Blake hollers. "No way!"

"Way!" Kayla pipes up and laughs.

"She's a good girl. She doesn't run about having... having..." He screws up his nose. "Doing that with male dogs!"

Blake grits his teeth as I lay my palm on his chest. I can feel his heart beating out a strong steady beat beneath his muscles. The sight of him getting all worked up like an over-protective parent sends warmth through my body.

"Relax, Daddy. You're going to have grandpuppies." I beam at him, and his eyes meet mine.

"You think this is funny? Wait until I talk to Ralph. That Duke is about to lose his balls!" He purses his lips and I see him clench and relax his free hand by his side, as though trying to calm himself.

Kayla erupts into a new fit of laughter as Travis slaps a hand on Blake's shoulder and squeezes.

"Too late for that, man."

Blake's eyes drop to Betsy, who's come to sit at his feet. She gazes up at him with big brown eyes.

"What the hell you been up to, girl? How long, eh? How long have you been sneaking off behind my back?" The shock has gone from his voice and is replaced by warmth as he squats next to her and rubs his hand up and down her back. She licks his face as he grumbles, "Yeah, yeah, sucking up now."

"She's about four weeks along," Travis says.

ELLE NICOLL

"They've been in doggy love for ages!" Kayla claps her hands together in delight. "Looks like you aren't the only man in her life after all."

Blake looks at Betsy, shaking his head as he stands. I wrap my arms around his waist and press myself against his side.

"I think it's wonderful. Like another new start."

He looks down at me, his eyes sparkling, making my stomach flutter.

"Yeah, you would see it like that. More bags of shit for you to throw at me when you get mad."

My mouth drops open, and he smirks. I narrow my good eye at him.

"Don't. I'm the hurt one, remember? You're meant to being nice to me."

"I'm always nice to you." He presses his lips to my forehead.

I sigh and sink into him. "I wish my lip was better already so I could kiss you properly."

"I'll kiss your lips as soon as we get home if you like, babe?" he whispers, and I giggle as he slides his palm to my ass and grabs a handful of it.

"Yuk! I heard that," Kayla groans. "You know, it makes sense why you bust that eye. Now you only see dork face with one. Must be an enormous improvement." She grins at me, and I laugh as Blake mumbles something under his breath.

"Are you sure you're okay?" Her face turns serious as she looks at me. Travis lifts his arm, and she slides underneath it.

I take a deep breath and nod, feeling Blake's arm tighten around me, supporting me.

"I am. The police have got Mickey in medical custody, and he'll be sent back to England once he's cleared to fly. He's already been told he won't be granted bail while he awaits trial."

My throat feels scratchy as I talk about him. I know what he did to me. *What he tried to do to me.* And I know it's likely to cause

322

an entire load of new nightmares, for a while at least. But I'm not scared this time. I'm ready for that trial. I'm going to stand there and look him in the eye while I give evidence. While I make justice finally happen. Not just for me, but for Rocket, and every animal he hurt, and every family who lost a loved pet when he stole them.

I'm doing it for all of us.

"What about your parents?" Kayla asks.

"They're arriving tomorrow. It's the first flight they could get."

I'm looking forward to seeing them both. It's been over two months now since I left England. They were heartbroken when I called them from the hospital. Blake already told them what was happening when I was first admitted, so at least I didn't have to make *that* phone call. But the ones since then have been bad enough, hearing both my mum and dad sob at what Mickey did when he came after me. They always worried about me. They just wanted to keep me safe. Get me away from the area I grew up. The trial will be hard for them. Hearing what their daughter went through? It must be every parents' worst nightmare. But we'll get through it.

"I think they're going to stay in my aunt's house, while I stay with Blake," I continue. "Then they can arrange the real estate agent themselves while they're here."

"They're still selling it?" Travis asks.

I shrug, my stomach twisting into the same knot it always does at the idea of my aunt's house being sold.

"I guess so. Nothings changed for them financially, so it's the only option."

Kayla gives me a sad smile before perking up. "Well, you'll have your hands full with lots of little fur babies soon! You'll be far too busy to notice!"

I smile at her gratefully. "You're right. We'll be busy, won't we, Blake?"

"Hm," he grumbles, looking down at Betsy again.

"Come on, *Grand-daddy.*" I smirk. "Let's go home. You've got two women to wait on hand and foot now."

"Fucking hell." He blows out a long breath as we all laugh.

Four weeks later

My arm stretches over the cold, unoccupied pillow next to me. "Blake?"

He must be up already. I rub my eyes as I yawn. It's so good to finally do it without my eye feeling like it may pop out of my head. My face has almost completely healed now, and the last traces of bruises are fading.

I turn and smile as I see the glass of juice on the bedside table, a white card propped up in front of it. I reach out and pick it up, bringing it closer to read Blake's handwriting.

You're still the sweetest flower, with the SWEETEST flower.

I turn it over and gasp as my breath catches in my throat.

He still has this?

I run my finger over the photograph. Down over my seventeen-year-old face, which is lit up, and beaming at the person behind the camera lens. My heart stalls as I remember the exact moment this photograph was taken.

Do you ever wish you could stay in a moment forever?

Those were the words I said to Blake that night. Before we walked around the lake for an hour beneath a sky of stars. Before he took this photo of me on my aunt's front porch.

Before I lost her.

And then him.

I smile as I let myself be lost in memories of her. I still feel her all around each time I swim in the lake. I know she's not gone. Not completely. She was there that day with me. Betsy may have led Blake to me. And he may have dragged me out of the water. But my aunt sowed a seed long before. A seed that helped me live that day. She taught me all about her garden and her herbs—nature's medicine cabinet. Without that, there would have been no sleep tonic. There would have been nothing to lace Mickey's drink with, slow him down. Give me a fighting chance.

He would have killed me for sure.

I wipe at the tears rolling down my cheeks. I may have to wait longer until I see my aunt's face again, but Blake? I'm lucky enough to see his every single day since he insisted I stay in his house with him. We both know I'm never moving back to England. I'll go back for the trial, but my life is here now.

With him and Betsy.

I swing my legs out of bed and pull on one of his t-shirts over my naked body. Then I pad into the kitchen in search of him, clutching the photograph against my chest.

The sight in the kitchen makes me freeze. Blake's tight, naked ass is on full display as he rolls his hips from side to side, whisking something in a bowl. A familiar song plays on the radio, and he leans over, turning the volume up.

"Enjoying the show, babe?" He calls over his shoulder as Ginuwine's "Pony" blares out. He rotates his ass side to side and then pumps against the kitchen side. When I don't move, he calls out again, "Get over here, Daisy."

I walk over to him, pausing as I notice the strings tied around his waist. I was too busy admiring his ass—and the nail marks I left in it from last night—to notice them before.

He turns, and I read the words on the apron:

Vegan men last longer.

"Where did you get that?" I squeal as his perfect white teeth flash at me in a wide grin.

"I found it online."

I clasp my hand over my mouth as I laugh.

"Did you know, not only do we last longer, but our cocks get even harder too?" He raises an eyebrow at me.

"Really?" I smile at him. "I'm not sure I believe you."

"I thought you may say that, so I came prepared, ready to demonstrate." He smirks as he throws the apron off and stands in front of me, his cock standing to attention, pre-cum glistening on its thick, smooth head.

I step closer and wrap my hand around it, licking my lips as I gaze up into his eyes. They darken with desire as I give him two slow pumps up and down.

"What's next in your demonstration?" I ask, biting my lip as his eyes drop to my mouth.

"Now you spread your petals for me and give me that sweet fucking pollen," Blake growls as he whips the t-shirt off over my head and lifts me onto the kitchen side.

I laugh as I part my legs so he can stand between them. "It's like that, is it?"

"Oh yes, it most certainly is like that," he groans as he pulls me closer, his eyes flashing with desire.

I suck in a breath as he sinks his into me, and I feel myself stretching around him. No matter how many times we do this, the first time he slides inside me is always pure heaven. I will never have enough of connecting with him like this.

I drop my head, leaning back on my hands, and let out a long moan.

"You feel so good."

"So do you, babe."

He pushes forward, burying himself to the hilt and letting out a deep groan. His fingers flex against my skin as he holds my ass, lifting my hips to where he wants me, so he can fuck me harder.

"Fuck," I cry out as he slams into me, building up pace.

His lips drop to my neck, and I arch up, forcing my nipples against his chest and spreading my legs wider. My wet arousal coats him, making him slick, and I clamp down on to him, looking at where our bodies meet.

His eyes follow mine, and he hisses. "That's right, babe. Squeeze my cock with your sweet little pussy. Milk it dry."

The sight of his cock getting buried deep inside my body is one of the hottest things I've ever seen. My mouth goes slack in wonder, thinking about how it even fits. He pulls almost all the way out and I see the rim around his head, shining with my arousal. Then, as he pushes back inside me, the incredible fullness has me crying out again.

"So, so good!" I pant, letting out a whimper and biting my bottom lip.

"Tell me, babe," he moans, his fingers digging harder into my ass.

I drop my head back and close my eyes, ecstasy storming through my body as he changes angle and the friction from his head rubs my G-spot.

"I love your cock."

"My cock fucking loves you," he grits out.

A high-pitched moan catches in my throat as he rolls his hips and the rim on his thick head rubs me inside again, sending a shudder through my body.

"Don't you mean your cock loves fucking me?" I grin as I look back at him, my chest rising and falling with each pant.

He smirks and bucks his hips so his balls slap against my ass. "That too."

My breasts are bouncing up and down with each thrust as he grips me and pulls me closer to him, fucking me deeper than I thought possible.

"Blake," I groan as the first tingles begin in my toes.

This is how it is with him most of the time. Hot, dirty, and wild. And I love it. He has total control over my body, and he knows it. It sings to his tune. Just like my heart does. Just like my soul does.

They all sing to Blake Anderson's sweet melody.

It's like we can't get enough of each other, and it's only getting stronger. Each time with him, I discover something new. I unearth another part of myself. A new pleasure, a new desire, a new sensation. It's like parts of me have been buried away until we found each other again.

Until he uncovered me. Set me free.

His mouth finds mine, and he kisses me in the way I love so much. Passionate. Intense, Commanding. The right mix of pressure. His tongue seeking mine, stroking, sucking, devouring. The way he first kissed me.

Like I'm the last lungful of oxygen the world has to give.

Then he rests his forehead against mine and stares deeply into my eyes, murmuring my name as he continues to thrust into me. His cock reaches places inside me that make me cry out and has my body sending wetness gushing to meet him. He dusts his lips against mine, kissing me softly as our breath mingles.

This is the other side of him that I love. The gentler, tender side. The side that makes love to me like I'm the only woman in the world.

But I know in his world, I am.

"Daisy," he groans. "I love you, babe. I fucking love you. Never leave me again."

His eyes grow dark and intense as they sear into me, fueling the fire that burns for him deep inside my core.

One that will never dim.

"Blake..." I whimper as everything pulls tight, coiling inside me.

"Come for me, Daisy. Let your pretty pussy bloom like a fucking flower and come all over my cock." He growls deep in his chest. "Do it!"

I shudder underneath him, a mess of shaking limbs and quivering muscles as I explode, convulsing around him, crying out his name and shuddering. Blake wraps his arms around my back before my own arms give way, and then pulls me against his chest as he growls out deeply, "FuuuuccckkIcanfeelyoucoming!"

I love hearing the strain in his voice when I come and knowing how much it turns him on. I swear he holds his own orgasm back most times we have sex just so he can feel mine more than once.

"Do they come harder too?" I pant, shaking again as the sensation of his hard cock pounding into me is too much to handle, and I do what I know he's waiting for, and come again, my chest jutting out and forcing me closer against his as euphoria takes command of body.

"Fuck. Yes, we do," he groans.

I look at him. "I thought so. Now fill me up. I want it all." I widen my legs further and moan loudly as he pumps me hard.

God, he's incredible.

His eyes burn into mine as he holds himself deep inside me and clenches his jaw. His abdominal muscles ripple as his cock swells inside me. I watch in awe as he comes, shooting his heat hard and fast, jerking inside me as he pumps out all that he has.

Giving me everything and more.

"Yes," I whisper, holding his gaze.

He growls from deep in his chest, and then his hands are in my hair, pulling my lips to his as he slides his tongue between them and moans into my mouth. I open to him, letting him have me. I'm his now, and he knows it. But I wouldn't want it any other way.

His lips leave mine, and he lets out a deep sigh, resting his forehead against mine again. I draw in a deep breath as my body relaxes and I revel in the calm washing over me.

The release.

The perfection.

"Good job you talked me into it, isn't it?" He grins at me as his cock twitches inside me.

"You didn't need much persuading." I sigh as he turns his attention back to my neck, kissing below my ear.

"I'd do anything for you, Daisy. You know that."

We had a long talk after I came home from hospital. Blake sat and listened to everything Mickey said and did that day when he tried to kill me. I didn't want the first time he heard every gory detail to be when he comes to the trial with me. He looked like he was struggling not to erupt into a Hulk-like rage the entire time I spoke. He sat there in stony silence, his jaw set, his eyes dark, as I told him everything.

When I repeated what Mickey said about him showing people how to trap animals for survival on his show, he reassured me he only shows people what to do if it's life or death. He said the forest has so many other food sources that you can find with less effort if you know where to look. It was enough for me, but not for Blake. He told me he was turning vegan from that moment on. Made up some story about it being easier to cook the same meal. But I know the real reason.

He did it for me.

Because I've seen too much animal suffering—it still turns my stomach to think about the fear in their eyes and the smell of blood.

And because he would do anything for me.

He always would. Even when we were seventeen and he stopped a drunken kiss in case I regretted it the next day.

Blake Anderson has always put me first.

I smile as I reach up and stroke his jaw. "I love you."

"You'd better." He grins, pressing a kiss to my lips. "Because I have something else to show you."

"You mean, this"—I reach my hands down to squeeze his delicious muscular ass—"is not my only surprise this morning?"

"Nope." He grins at me as he pulls out and grabs a clean wash-cloth from the sink to wipe me with.

I narrow my eyes at him, and he smirks. I know he put it there in preparation—confident in his ability to get me having sex with him as soon as I woke up. I shake my head and smile.

He knows me so well.

"Okay. Show me, then."

He grins as he lifts me down from the counter. He holds his t-shirt out so I can slip it over my head and then he pulls on a pair of sweatpants.

"Close your eyes."

"Blake!" I laugh.

"Do it!"

I roll my eyes and do as he says. He leads me outside, walking slowly, holding my hand in his.

"Okay, I know we're on the back porch. I can hear the birds."

He laughs. "Correct. Come on, keep going."

We walk over the grass and then smooth, warm wood is beneath my toes.

"Okay, okay, we're on the jetty." I grin. "Are we going swimming?" My voice lifts in excitement as I bounce on my toes.

"No. Guess again." He chuckles.

I chew my lip, my eyes still firmly closed. "I don't know, Blake. Can I look yet?" I whine.

"Okay. You can look."

I open my eyes and look at the jetty. My hands fly to my face as I take it in. Every edge of the jetty is lined with vases, jars, and pots. Each spilling over with bright white daisies, their white petals are yellow centers dazzling in the bright sunshine. Sitting in the middle—pretty as a picture with her growing belly—is Betsy with a daisy chain around her neck.

"Blake!" I gasp.

"You like it?"

I turn and throw my arms up around his neck. "It's so beautiful. Thank you!" I wipe my tears away as he leads me to Betsy and pulls us both down to sit.

"I want you to know you've always got a home here with us." His green eyes shine as he looks at me.

"I know," I whisper, looking at them both. "I wouldn't want to be anywhere else."

"And since Maria asked you to run the salon for her while she's in New York, we figured you'd agree to stay." He shrugs his shoulders and chuckles as I push him playfully.

"Idiot," I murmur, grinning at him. He knows full well I'm staying for him and Betsy. I've told him enough times. The new job is just a bonus.

He laughs, grabbing my left hand in his, and holding up a small black box in his other.

"I got you a new job present."

I suck in a breath as butterflies rush about in my stomach.

Is he about to...?

He takes the lid off, and I find a key inside.

My brow creases in confusion as the fluttering in my stomach stills.

"It's yours now, Daisy. It could never be anyone else's."

I look at him and he's watching me closely, gauging my reaction. Then he tips his head to the lake, and I look across the water. My aunt's house looks back at me, a giant yellow bow tied to the front door.

"Blake, you didn't!" My eyes are wide as I turn back to him.

"I fucking did!" He laughs when my mouth drops open.

"But how? Mum and Dad sold it last week. They signed the papers."

"Yeah. So did I."

"You mean, you own it?" I study his face and blow out a breath. "I know you're doing well with your show and everything. But a house, Blake? You bought my aunt's house? You own it now?"

"No. You own it." He smiles at me.

"What are you talking about? I didn't sign anything."

"Not yet. But I'm pretty sure if you agree to this, then it makes it just as much your name on that paperwork as it is mine."

"What are you talking abo—?"

My words freeze in the air as he pulls out another box from behind one of the vases. This one is a dark green velvet. My eyes fill with tears as he lifts the lid and I see the giant yellow diamond ring inside.

"Blake?"

He looks at me with such love and adoration in his eyes that I think someone is about to shout "Cut!" and I'm going to find out it's all an act. A make-believe fairy-tale being filmed, and not my life. Not my actual life. I stare back at him, my mouth wide open.

"Marry me, Daisy. Marry me and stay with me. Have fur babies with us." His eyes dart to Betsy and back to me. "Have human babies with me. Just say you'll never leave again. I love you with everything I have, and I always will. That I promise you."

"God," I sob, nodding as I hold out my hand and he slides the ring onto my finger.

"No. It's Blake." He chuckles.

I laugh and then launch myself at him, knocking him and a vase of flowers over. He falls down on his back against the jetty, with me on top of him. The water from the upturned vase runs across the jetty, washing some daisies into the lake where they float on the surface of the water.

Warmth spreads in my chest as I bring my eyes back to him and wrap my arms around him.

"Is that a yes, then?"

"It's a hell yes!" I laugh, as he pulls me down into a kiss. I sigh as his tongue finds mine.

He loves me, he loves me not.

I know for a fact Blake loves me. He's taken every broken and battered part of me and slotted it back together. Where my soul felt like it was missing a part, he planted love there, and let it grow.

He is everything.

As I get lost in our kiss, I hear Betsy jump to her feet, skittering across the boards to join in. She licks us both all over the face before we can move away.

"Stop!" Blake calls out as she lands one right on his mouth.

I wrap an arm around her, pulling her into a group hug, being careful of her swollen tummy. She only has a week or two left until the puppies are due.

My heart swells as I look at them both.

This moment, right here...

This is what paradise looks like.

Chapter Thirty-Three

Blake

Epilogue – 10 Years Later

"PREPARE TO BE ANNIHILATED!" Daisy calls as she and Savannah aim water shooters at me and the boys.

"Take cover, men! We're under fire!" I yell as we all swim toward the jetty.

Brent, our eldest, gets there first, followed by his two younger brothers, Seth and Cole. We hide underneath, our eyes wide as I hold a finger to my lips, and then point to the jetty overhead.

A wild laugh erupts as Savannah appears, being held upside down by her ankles. She points her water shooter at me and gets me square in the eye.

"Truce! Truce!" I call, holding my hands up in mock surrender. "Please! No more! We promise to behave!"

She whoops and then disappears as she's pulled up. Me and the boys take it in turns to climb the ladder onto the jetty.

"Daddy!" Savannah calls, jumping into my arms before my feet leave the last rung. "Guess what?" She grabs my cheeks and squeezes them together, laughing when my lips squish up like a fish's.

"What?" I try to say, which has her giggling even more.

"Girls float like a boat, and boys stink and sink."

"Is that so?" I widen my eyes at her as she lets go of my face. She giggles again as I bury my face in her neck underneath her blonde hair and make a mixture of growling and eating noises.

335

"Daddy!" she squeals, trying to push me away.

"Oh, yum, yum. I do love a tasty three-year-old," I say as I pretend to gobble her again.

"Come on, you two!"

I look up and catch Daisy's eye. She's shaking her head and grinning at us. She and the boys are already sitting down on the back porch, drinking juice, and wrapped in towels.

"Better go. Mommy's waiting." I haul Savannah up over my shoulder and carry her to the porch.

"Daddy, put me down." She giggles.

"What? Who said that?" I spin around, so she's facing her brothers.

"Dad." Brent rolls his eyes.

At nine years old, he's not only the eldest, but the most sensible.

"That's Wild Daddy to you!" I grin at him as he snorts.

"You're not going to make us watch your old programs again, are you?" he moans.

Daisy laughs as I put Savannah down on one seat and then drop onto the sofa next to her.

"Mommy likes it when Mr. Wild comes out. Don't you, babe?"

The kids ignore us and guzzle down their drinks, jumping back up, and grabbing a ball, running onto the grass with it.

Daisy narrows her eyes at me as I smirk.

"At least that's what she told me this morning," I whisper in her ear, "when I had her pinned into submission with my cock."

"You have certain redeeming qualities, I guess." She tilts her head to the side and runs a finger over my jaw.

"I think you'll find I have many—"

She puts a finger to my mouth and smiles as she replaces it with her lips. I cup her face in my hands and kiss her gently, pulling back to laugh and rest my forehead against hers as the kids shout out.

"Never a quiet moment, eh?"

"What did you expect with four kids and three dogs?" She smiles at me and presses another quick kiss to my lips. "You can finish that later."

"You bet I will."

I wrap my arm around her, and she leans into me as we watch the kids throw the ball for Molly and Jack. Betsy's lying on her favorite sofa, watching the action unfold.

"Keeping an eye on the kids, girl?" I call.

She lifts her head and looks over at me, her tail wagging against the cushions.

"She's a wonderful mum," Daisy says, resting her palm against my chest and letting out a sigh.

I smile at my girls. "You both are."

Betsy had eight puppies in total. Seven boys and one girl. We kept Molly, and Jack, who's the spitting image of Betsy—all silky brown hair and big eyes. Ralph had one boy to keep Duke company, and the others all went to good local homes. We see most of them out walking around town when we go in. And Betsy still meets Duke for a run at the beach most weekends. Although Travis saw to it that neither of them would provide any more surprises again.

"How are you feeling about tomorrow?" Daisy looks up at me, her blue eyes clear and bright.

I shrug. "Good. It's not my first interview about it."

"No. But it's your first big award! And you'll be accepting it on live TV. No time for re-takes."

"You saying I need lots of re-takes?" I stick out my bottom lip at her and she smiles and swats my chest.

"I'm so proud of you. You deserve the recognition. Your photos, Blake..." She sighs as she looks out across the lake toward my old house—the house which has turned into my photography studio. "They're incredible. You capture something so fragile and raw in them."

"Why, thank you." I puff out my chest, and she shoves me lightly.

"Big head."

"Big cock too."

She snorts. "Idiot." Then her voice drops low and serious again. "I mean it, Blake. The way you captured the contestants on all the series of your show. Caught them at their most intimate moments. At their most incredible, defining moments of growth. It's real and inspiring. And the world is better for seeing them."

"I'm definitely getting some later, aren't I?" I wiggle my eyebrows at her.

She shakes her head with a smile.

"I love your smile," I say, pulling her close and pressing a kiss to her hair. "I'll do whatever it takes to see it every day. You know that, right?"

"I do." She leans her head against my chest and traces her fingers in circles over my t-shirt. "And I'll do whatever it takes to always make you smile too.

We fall into a contented quiet as we watch the kids and dogs play. What a difference ten years make. In some ways, it feels like it's flown by; but in others, it feels like so much has happened that it must be longer.

The trial was hard. We were over in England for weeks. The press hounded Daisy every time we appeared at court. It was all over the papers there. The true extent of Mickey's criminal activities only came to life as the case against him was built. The jury found him guilty of attempted murder, as well as a host of other charges. It took them seventeen minutes to reach a verdict. Daisy's lawyer said it was fast. I think it should have taken seconds. He won't be due for parole for a few more years yet. Daisy's strong, but I know it will be tough when the time comes. But I'll be here to do whatever she needs. And this time, if he's stupid enough to come back, I know without a doubt he will leave in a body bag.

Daisy snuggles into me, and Betsy shuffles about with a sigh as the sounds of our family playing carries around the lake.

This right here, is perfect.

I've got my girl, my family, my career. Daisy still makes her organic products. But it's more for fun now. She struck up a deal with a large distillery to have sole rights to her Aunt's homebrew recipes. Iris' Brew is drunk in bars around the world now.

And it all started here on this lake.

"You are brilliant at capturing life with your camera, you know," Daisy says.

"Did I capture you as well?" I look down as she gazes up at me from underneath her lashes.

"Blake Anderson, you captured me a long time ago." She smiles as I rest my forehead against hers.

"And you captured me when you were seventeen, babe."

We look at each other, not needing to say anything else. We both know how fucking lucky we are to have been given a second chance. Our house is always noisy and chaotic now. But I know we wouldn't have it any other way.

It's vibrant.

Full of energy and life.

There's one word that sums up this fucking amazing ride of life I'm on with her.

Wild.

The (Almost) End

Chapter Thirty-Four

Daisy

Extended Epilogue

"WHAT DO YOU RECKON the boys are up to?" I lean over my forearms and gaze at Kayla and Maria.

"Who the hell cares!" Kayla snorts, waving her glass in the air, champagne sloshing over the side and splashing on the dark brown wood of the booth table.

Maria smiles at me. "Probably having a beer around the campfire and chatting. They'll be fine," she adds as I gnaw on my bottom lip.

"Yeah. Blake knows the forest better than his own reflection." Kayla's laugh bubbles out around the bar.

I sit back in my seat and lift my glass to my lips, knocking back the rest of the champagne and letting my eyes fall closed as the bubbles dance on my tongue.

It's kind of sappy to admit. But I miss Blake. This isn't the first night we've had apart since we got engaged. Series two of his show was filmed over the past few months, so he spent several nights away on his wild, camping adventures. But I still miss him like crazy. And Betsy, of course. She's an honorary bachelor for the night with Blake, Travis, Jay, and Stefan, whilst Ralph from the store looks after the two puppies we kept, Molly and Jack. Not that they're even small anymore.

"Wake up!" Kayla prods me, and I snap my eyes open. "It's your bachelorette! I told you we should have hired strippers," she says to Maria.

Maria laughs and then places her hand over mine and pats it reassuringly, lowering her voice. "I wouldn't have let her, don't worry."

My shoulders drop with a laugh as I take in Kayla's disgruntled face.

"Fine. We could have been feasting our eyes on six packs and giant"—she gazes around Herbies, where there are just a handful of locals having an evening drink—"you know what. But here we are." She sighs dramatically, making me laugh louder.

"It's perfect." I shake my head and look between the two of them. "We've had an amazing day at the spa." Maria grins and squeezes my hand. She spoiled us thoroughly, what with flying back in from her new job in New York and transforming the spa into our own private nirvana for the day. I wondered why the system was all booked out for a 'private party'. Now I know why.

"Yeah, it was pretty awesome." Kayla beams and rounds her eyes on Maria. "Daisy filled us in on this big meeting she has coming up with Mr. Silver about her aunt's home brew, but we didn't hear much about the elusive Mr. Parker."

My eyes bounce between the two of them as Kayla fixes her target. She's like Betsy with a new bone.

Obsessed.

She had to know every little detail about this Mr. Silver with whom I'm meeting to discuss taking my aunt's homebrew recipes and making them on a larger scale. And I barely know anything myself yet. Just that he seems interested, and his family has a long history in the spirits business.

But this is Kayla. Loyal, always in your corner, an amazing friend who wants the best for those she loves.

"Please." Maria rolls her eyes, sweeping her long, dark hair over her shoulder. "You're really not missing anything. He's the most difficult person I've ever worked with."

"Really?" Kayla's shoulders drop as she rests her chin in her hand and exhales heavily. "Shame. He's stupidly hot in his Google photos. Billionaire hotelier, cheekbones that could cut glass..." She trails off with a dreamy sigh.

Maria arches a brow and sips her drink through her scarlet lips. "Well, he's a nightmare, frankly."

Kayla's mouth drops open and I know she's about to quiz Maria more, even though she's barely been working at the prestigious world-famous Songbird hotel in New York for more than two minutes.

"More drinks?"

I catch Cindy staring at me with wide eyes, holding a bottle-filled ice bucket in both hands like a peace offering.

"It's on the house," she adds when no one answers.

"Sure. Thank you." I smile, and she visibly relaxes, placing the bucket down on the table.

"Do you want to join us?"

I ignore Kayla's foot connecting with my shin underneath the table and look at Cindy with what I hope is a friendly expression.

If these past months have taught me anything, then it's that life is too short. I know other people blame her for talking to the reporter, and for Mickey finding me. But I feel bad for her. It wasn't her fault. He knew where I was all along. He admitted as much when he came after me.

She shouldn't have to live with guilt like that. I know what guilt can do to a person if you leave it in the dark and let it breed like bacteria.

"Oh." Her brows shoot up to her forehead, and she glances at Maria and Kayla. I widen my eyes at them, inclining my head toward Cindy, and on cue, they smile and nod. "That's kind, Daisy, but I..." She chews her lip and then looks back toward the bar. "I actually have a friend visiting me tonight from out of town, so..."

I follow her gaze to a fair-haired man sitting at the bar. He raises a hand in greeting as he catches us staring.

"But, thank you. I appreciate it." She smiles at me, her eyes softening. "And congratulations to you and Blake. I've never seen him so happy."

"Thanks." She makes her way to the bar to join her friend and his face lights up as she gets closer.

"What the fuck?" Kayla hisses over the table.

"You did the right thing, Daisy," Maria says.

Kayla sticks out her bottom lip as she studies me, before dropping her shoulders. "Yeah, you did. I guess one of you has to be the adult in your relationship if you're marrying dork-face."

I throw her a look of mock outrage. She's kidding. She loves Blake.

Just not like I do.

"Oh God. She's thinking of him now. I can tell from the little hearts that appear in her eyes." Kayla rolls her eyes at Maria, her face splitting into a grin as she fills our glasses to the top with more champagne. "Come on! Let's drink! The boys will be having their asses bitten by ants about now. I know where I'd rather be."

We all raise our glasses and clink.

"To marrying your best friend," Kayla says.

"To marrying your best friend," Maria echoes.

"To marrying my best friend." I grin.

Chapter Thirty-Five

Blake

"THERE'S NO SIGNAL UP here. You can try higher on the ledge, but you'll be lucky."

Jay's best friend and manager, Stefan, heads off to the edge of the rock ledge, holding his cell phone in the air, searching for a signal, his mouth in a flattened line.

"Course, you need to watch out for the mountain lions. The light attracts them."

"What?" His eyes widen as I chuckle and shake out my sleeping bag.

"He's messing with you," Travis calls from his seat on a log in front of the campfire.

"Yeah... it's the bears you need to watch for."

Stefan curses in the distance, and Jay laughs and fist-bumps me.

"Good one, bro."

"Yeah, can't have my baby bro telling all the jokes." He grins and lifts his beer bottle to his lips.

"Ignore the Andersons," Travis calls again.

"Thank you," a distant voice cries.

"Yeah... it's the wolves you should watch out for!" He looks to me and Jay, and the three of us burst into alcohol-induced raucous laughter as Stefan comes running back into view with a face as ghostly pale as tonight's full moon.

"Matt will understand if I don't call him. He'd rather I come back in one piece than die trying to text him." Stefan pushes his black-framed glasses up his nose as he sits down next to the fire as Jay hands him a beer.

I chuckle to myself.

He has to sleep in a sleeping bag under the stars yet. Then I'm planning on a wild swim at dawn in the river, followed by a rigorous hike back down to the cove. This is baby steps compared to what I put the men and women through on my show.

"So, any tips for a happy married life?" I turn to Jay and Travis as I sit by the low campfire and wrap an arm around Betsy, who licks my cheek and lets out a small whine as I stroke her.

"Yeah. Don't do it," Travis jokes.

Jay shakes his head, his lips curling into a smile as he looks down at the floor.

"Best decision I ever made. You'll see."

"It's true," Stefan interjects. "It's like living in a Valentine's card with him and Holly as they make googly eyes at each other." He smiles, his voice full of warmth as Jay's eyes crinkle at the corners and he runs a hand around the back of his neck.

"He's right." He blows out a breath with a grin. "When you find the one... it's..."

"Pretty fucking special," Travis finishes for him, slapping me on the back. "Pretty fucking special, man."

We sit in silence for a few moments, just enjoying the peace of the darkened forest, lit only by the moonlight and the soft glow of the fire. I didn't want a mad night on the town for my bachelor party.

This.

Here in the open. Out in the wild.

It's perfect.

Betsy lies down next to me as the fire crackles and pops, and I sigh and tip my head back to look at the stars.

"Do you ever wish you could stay in a moment?"

Warmth expands in my chest as I remember that night ten years ago, lying on my back by the lake with Daisy.

The lost kiss.

The kiss I've been making up for ever since. I must have kissed her lips a billion times by now. Claimed them, made them mine.

Just like she did with my heart.

I'm a total goner for that girl.

My girl.

I would literally tear up space and time for her.

"Enough!" Travis calls suddenly. "This is a bachelor party! My wife isn't here to witness how many"—he squints at the beer label on his fourth bottle—"whatever the fuck these are that I'm drinking." He thrusts the bottle into the air. "So, I say we make this night more interesting."

"What you gonna do? Find some of the local animals to use your vet thermometer on?"

I laugh as Travis points his bottle at me, blinking. He really doesn't drink a lot anymore. Four beers and he's already rosy cheeked and halfway on his way to belting out every song from our youth that he likes to break out on the rare occasions when he has more than three beers.

"Noooo." He looks at me, the corners of his mouth twitching. "I say we play a game."

"A game?"

He nods slowly, a wicked grin spreading on his lips.

"You can go first, Mr. Wild. Truth or dare."

Chapter Thirty-Six

Daisy

"THERE'S MY BEAUTIFUL GIRL."

Warm arms wrap around me from behind and I'm pulled across the cool cotton sheets toward a hot and muscular inferno.

"I wasn't expecting you back yet." I grin sleepily as Blake's lips dust over my neck, placing kisses against the sensitive dip of delicate skin behind my ear.

It's still relatively dark in our bedroom. Although, that means nothing. Once I started sleeping better and the nightmares became less frequent, Blake installed extra blackout blinds to the windows, so I can lie in when I fancy it. He, on the other hand, still springs out of bed at the crack of dawn with as much energy as one of Betsy's puppies every morning. Off for a run or early morning hike, usually.

That man has stamina.

"I couldn't wait to get back to you." He nuzzles into me, a familiar hardness pressing against my ass cheek.

"Where's Betsy?" I murmur as his hands snake around and inside my vest, cupping my nipples and tugging them as his teeth graze my earlobe.

"Nice. Your fiancé is gone all night, and you ask after Betsy. I always said you loved her best."

I giggle as his voice rumbles in my ear.

"Girls have to stick together, I told you."

"She's out on the deck sleeping. So why don't you and I practice sticking together," he growls, his short beard dragging over my skin as his lips press hot kisses over the juncture where my neck meets my shoulder.

"Blake," I moan, thrusting my breasts into his palms.

"Fuck, babe. My dick's ready to burst here."

I laugh. He's so dramatic. But I love it. I love everything about the way he is with me. The way we are together.

Daisy and Blake.

Friends and lovers.

"We can't have that, can we?" My breath hitches as his hands leave my breasts and slide my pajama shorts and panties down my thighs.

"No, we can't have that," he murmurs, sucking in a breath as his fingers swipe through my already soaked flesh. "Always so ready for me."

I moan as he lifts one of my thighs easily in his large hand and thrusts up inside me in one steady movement.

"Blake!" My head falls back against his shoulder as he fucks me fully awake. Each pump of his thick cock sends ripples of pleasure rushing through my body, like a river racing to meet the ocean.

"That's soon-to-be husband," he groans as he picks up the pace at the same time as his other hand slides underneath my body and around to stroke my swollen clit.

"Oh, yeah? I could still change my mind, you know."

He twists his hips and I gasp as the thick head of his cock rubs against my G-spot.

"I wouldn't let you. I'd hunt you down. Betsy would make a great sniffer hound."

I laugh, because although Blake's words 'hunt you down' should evoke powerful, frightening memories for me after what Mickey did... they don't.

I've never felt safer than when I'm in Blake's strong arms.

When I have him backing me up like the world's strongest army.

Ready to fight with the power of love and the depths it can go to, even after ten years apart.

If I could tell seventeen-year-old Daisy just where she would be today... in the arms of her best friend, and the man who captured her heart all those years ago... would she have believed me?

"Argh, fuck, babe," Blake growls, his hand grasping my thigh tighter as his other one increases its assault on my throbbing clit.

"Wow, that feels..." I swallow and then let out a whimper as his cock swells inside me, stretching me around him further and setting tingles racing around my body, starting at my toes.

It's always like this with him.

Deep. Raw. Passionate.

Even when he's making love to me, and his green eyes are burning themselves into my soul with an intensity that steals my breath.

He's always vibrant, intoxicating, selfless...

"Plant your flower on my lawn, Babe, and water it with your juices."

And crazy.

Stupidly, ridiculously silly, in a way only he can be, and still make it sound oh-so-sexy.

I can't even laugh.

I'm past the point of no return.

"Blake!" I cry as the familiar tightening draws deep in my core, building alongside the searing heat that's boiling with enough pressure it feels like it could explode and take the entire house with it.

"Come, Babe. I'm barely hanging on here," he hisses out as though his teeth are clenched.

The pads of his fingers continue rubbing my soaking clit, and I let go.

CAPTURED BY MR. WILD

I let go, allowing the first wave of blinding pleasure to reach its peak and then bring me shattering and shaking down around him as he holds me tight.

"Yes, babe. Fuck, you feel incredible."

He groans and continues thrusting deep inside me as my orgasm continues on and on, sucking his own deep into my body as he growls and shakes, filling me with his heat.

Then when I think I can barely take anymore and my breath has all but left my body, he pinches my clit, his warm breath dusting over my ear as he whispers, "I love you".

And I come.

Again.

"Blake!" I cry out as he holds me tight.

He keeps his grip tight on me as I come down, my orgasm finally bottoming out and leaving me breathless and panting.

"Daisy," he murmurs with a smile, which I can just make out in the low light as he turns my chin to him so he can kiss me over my shoulder. "I'm going away more often."

"Sure," I answer, enjoying teasing him. "So long as you leave Betsy with me."

The slap of his palm connecting with my ass rings out in the room as I gasp.

"That, Miss Matthews, is for your cheek."

"And this"—I clench hard around his cock, which is still seated deeply inside my body—"is for calling your cock a lawn when I'm about to come."

His chest rumbles with a deep groan as he flexes his cock inside me.

"Where do you even come up with these things?" I reluctantly slide forward, separating us so I can turn inside his arms and face him.

"Bachelor parties."

"Figures." I snort, running my hand down the side of his face and over his jaw.

I can't even imagine the weird and wonderful things guys discuss over a crate of beer. Maybe that's where all of Blake's jokes come from. Drunken pondering.

"... And games."

"What do you mean, games?" I blink twice. His eyes are shining in the dark. Shining enough for me to recognize that look of mischief he gets.

He thinks he's a joker. Well, he is.

But he doesn't realize that I'm onto him now.

He can't catch me out like he used to.

I can read him.

The way his green eyes glitter every time he's up to something, is the dead giveaway.

He's silent as I reach for the remote for the window blinds.

"Blake...?"

"Okay. Just one game." He chuckles, his warm arms encasing me as he plants kisses over my forehead and into my hair.

"Blake? What did you do?"

His chest vibrates as his chuckle transforms into a deep laugh.

I click the button on the remote and the room fills with sunshine, pouring in through the windows, the glistening surface of the lake like a bed of shimmering crystals just outside.

"It was truth or dare, babe. Like I could turn it down."

I gasp as the sun light falls onto him, illuminating his body like a spotlight.

"Blake! You're..."

I clasp a hand over my mouth, my eyes popping open.

"I know." He bites his lip, amusement dancing in his eyes as he watches my reaction.

"It'll wash out before the wedding, babe. Don't worry."

"It better!"

My eyes roam over his hair and beard.

Both are green.

Deep, inky, forest green.

My shoulders shake as my laugh threatens to burst from my body.

Only Blake could make deep green hair and a deep green beard look good...

And kind of sexy.

Like some sort of wild, emerald god.

It matches his eyes, though.

"Who—?"

"Jay," he answers with a smirk. "I think he's getting me back for the giant cut-outs of him as a kid dressed as a shrimp I got made up for his."

I stare at him dumbfounded.

"You can help me wash in the shower if you like?" He pops a brow at me.

"Yeah." I nod slowly, still taking in the green.

"Come on. Let's go wash my lawn."

His eyes crease in the corners, lighting up as he presses his lips together.

"Your—Hang on!" I lift the covers and look down. "Blake Anderson!"

He laughs as my eyes land on his perfectly manicured 'lawn'.

"You did there, too?" I whisper-hiss, even though there's no one around to hear.

"Told you to plant your flower there and water it."

"You are such a Doofus!" I place my palms over his chest and shove him lightly as I laugh in shock.

"Best fucking watered lawn in the whole of Hope Cove." He laughs, his eyes widening as I scream out, "Blake!" and shove at him playfully again.

He places his fingers to my lips. "Shh, babe. You know who will—"

It's too late.

The bedroom door flies open, and in the next second, a warm, rough tongue and nose is in the middle of us on the bed, attacking us both.

"Betsy!" I laugh, wrapping my arms around her and pulling her down to lie between us.

She does this. If I scream or shout, she comes running, her paws skittering over the stripped wood floors. Thankfully, she seems to know the difference in my tone and only comes to my rescue on the occasions my outbursts are not caused by Blake and his delicious assaults on my body.

I've been fully welcomed into the pack.

I look between her and my now green hulk-like fiancé as he wraps us both in his giant, tattooed arms.

He might look ridiculous for a few days. Like one of those cress heads you grow as a kid.

Ridiculous, and like I said, weirdly sexy still.

But he will always be Blake Anderson.

The man who speaks to my soul and knows how to make it sing.

Only now green—the green of nature and new beginnings.

The green of all things wild.

My Mr. Wild.

The (Actual) End.

Elle's Books

Captured by Mr. Wild is book 4 in 'The Men Series', a collection of interconnected standalone stories.

They can be read in any order, however, for full enjoyment of the overlapping characters, the suggested reading order is:

Meeting Mr. Anderson – Holly and Jay

Discovering Mr. X – Rachel and Tanner

Drawn to Mr. King – Megan and Jaxon

Captured by Mr. Wild – Daisy and Blake

Pleasing Mr. Parker – Maria and Griffin

Trapped with Mr. Walker – Harley and Reed

Time with Mr. Silver – Rose and Dax

(Also available by Elle, **Forget-me-nots and Fireworks**, Shona and Trent's story, a novella length prequel to The Men Series)

Get all of Elle's books here: http://author.to/ellenicoll

About the Author

Elle Nicoll is an ex long-haul flight attendant and
mum of two from the UK.
After fourteen years of having her head in the clouds whilst working at 38,000ft, she is now usually found with her head between
the pages of a book reading or furiously typing and making notes
on another new idea for a book boyfriend who is sweet-talking
her.
Elle finds it funny that she's frequently told she looks too sweet
and innocent to write a steamy book, but she never wants to stop.
Writing stories about people, passion, and love, what better thing
is there?
Because,
Love Always Wins
xxx
To keep up to date with the latest news and releases, find Elle in
the following places, and sign up for her newsletter below;

https://www.subscribepage.com/ellenicollauthorcom
Facebook Reader Group – Love always Wins – https://www.face-
book.com/groups/686742179258218
Website – https://www.ellenicollauthor.com

Acknowledgments

My first thank you must go to the incredible TL Swan and her Cygnet Inkers Group. As with my earlier books, you gave me the courage to chase a dream. You've had a huge impact on my life, and others too. No amount of thank yous will ever be enough for the support you give so selflessly. You are an inspiration.

Thank you to the wonderful author friends I have met on this journey; many fellow cygnets. I really wouldn't have gotten this far if it wasn't for such an awesome group who are always there to support one another.

My beta readers; Christi, Hannah, Rita and Kelly. Thank you all so much for your time, wise words, support, and late night emails.

To my editor, Zee; thank you, thank you, thank you! You are amazing! Your comments have me giggling, and make editing so much more fun.

Thank you to Sherri for the beautiful cover.

Thank you to my family for putting up with all of my late nights and constant book talk.

Thank you to my amazing ARC readers and street team, to Jo and the team at Give Me Books, and to the bloggers, bookstagrammers, booktokkers, and everyone who has shared reviews and made beautiful photo edits. They make me emotional, they really do! I love seeing how you picture the story.

Finally, a huge thanks to you, the reader. Thank you for reading Daisy and Blake's story. I hope you enjoyed it.

Please consider leaving a review on Amazon. It is one of the best ways to help other readers try out a new author. I never realised just how helpful they can be until I started on this journey.

Until the next book...

Elle x

Printed in Great Britain
by Amazon

3c27e87d-6389-4177-b27c-36858057ee40R02